E R

She was alone with the man she loved, but he wasn't the man she'd married . . .

She had stayed awake many a night, thinking about Patrick. Now those memories heated her cheeks. She felt so flustered that she wasn't aware he'd followed her until she felt his hand on hers.

Before she quite knew how it happened, she was in his arms and kissing him shamelessly, reveling in the touch, the scent, the sight of him, feeling as if she'd been lost for years and had finally found her way home.

Patrick's kiss awakened a part of her she hadn't even known existed. Now she understood why her parents had hurried her off to bed no matter how she begged for just one more story. Now she understood the secret language of their sighs, their tremulous smiles, their soft touches. Now she knew the river of emotion they'd swum in— and Dear God, she wanted to bathe in it herself.

Her parents had spent twenty joyous years together.

She would only know this one moment—and she prayed it would last forever. . . .

Praise for Alexandra Thorne's *Lawless*

"Fast-paced, sexy, . . . will hold the reader to the end."
—Library Journal

"Very talented rising star Alexandra Thorne continues to deliver lush and exciting stories. . . ."
—Romantic Times

ALEXANDRA THORNE

BOUNDLESS

PINNACLE BOOKS
WINDSOR PUBLISHING CORP.

PINNACLE BOOKS are published by

Windsor Publishing Corp.
850 Third Ave
New York, NY 10022

The P logo Reg U.S. Pat & TM off. Pinnacle is a trademark
of Windsor Publishing Corp.

First Pinnacle Printing: December, 1994

Printed in the United States of America

*To Denise Little, editor and friend,
live long and prosper.*

Author's Note

When I began writing *Lawless,* I intended it to be a single title release. However, by the end of the book, I had fallen in love with the Pride family and their fabled Texas ranch, and wanted to know more about their history. This new novel, *Boundless,* is the result of that love affair.

Thanks are due to Tomasina Robinson, Anna Phegley, and Anita Bunkley for their thoughtful reading, and to my editor, Denise Little, for all her help.

In researching the book, I found *Lone Star* by T. S. Fehrenbach, *German Pioneers in Texas* by Don H. Biggs, *Pioneers in God's Hills,* compiled by the Gillespie County Historical Society, and *Indianola* by Brownson March, to be particularly helpful.

Prologue

Indianola, Texas, 1846

Elke picked her way over the nettle-strewn sand, mentally damning the Prince and the Adelsverein Society—the so-called society of nobles—for all their empty promises. For the sum of six hundred kroners they had guaranteed passage to the New World and transportation from a port on the Gulf of Mexico to a flourishing town in the interior.

But there had been no port city; only a miserable collection of tents and huts surrounded by a pestilential, mosquito-infested swamp. And no transportation inland, either. Thanks to a war with Mexico, the government had availed itself of every draft animal, drover, and wagon. The hundreds of newly arrived German settlers were stranded as surely as if they had somehow taken ship to the moon.

Elke used her fury as a shield against an emotional devastation too deep for tears. Her only comfort came from the knowledge that her parents had died hours apart and had never known of the other's passing. They had loved each other so much that life alone would have been unthinkable for them both.

Would she ever know such love? Would she ever have a husband and a home to call her own? Or would she die alone here with no one to mark or mourn her death?

At least her mother and father had been spared the grief that shook her now. She had to go on. But, dear God, how? Who would help her? She was only fourteen. The child inside her cried out even as the woman she must become fought for courage.

How could she travel alone and on foot the three hundred miles to the faraway hill town of Fredericksburg? Was there really such a town—or was it only another empty promise?

Her father, Herr Professor Von Braun, a man of unequaled warmth and charm, had expected to be a school master in the inland settlement. Her mother, the daughter of a minor nobleman, had planned to teach music. But at the rate that typhoid, dysentery, and malaria were claiming the stranded settlers, there wouldn't have been any pupils anyway.

As the cart finally creaked to a stop at the burial ground, she realized how utterly without foundation all their hopes and dreams had been. The Indianola cemetery, with its pathetic harvest of new graves, offered mute proof of the dangers all around. The promised land was a raw wilderness, and it had already exacted a cruel price from those who sought to tame it.

Approaching the shallow depression where her parents would lie, she bit her lips, fighting tears, knowing they would have expected her to say farewell with dignity.

A couple of women had accompanied her to the graveyard. Their canvas-shrouded dead would lie not far from hers. She had only been peripherally aware of them until now. In desperate need of comfort, she turned to the closest one, a woman she recalled from the voyage as the mother of nine lively children.

"Frau Knopf, would you stay with me while my parents are buried?"

Tears welled in Frau Knopf's eyes. "I'm sorry but I can't, I just can't." She gestured at the cart containing the dead, and sobbed. "My baby died last night and my husband and four other children are sick. But surely someone else . . ." Frau Knopf's voice trailed off. She didn't even attempt to staunch the tears streaming down her face.

Elke fought to control her rising hysteria, to maintain her equanimity as the women moved away. Engulfed in misery, she hunched her shoulders and lowered her head. The muffled sound of sand hitting canvas as a couple of shovel-wielding men covered her parents' remains finally captured her attention.

Surely the graves should have been deeper, she thought anxiously, her gaze drawn upward by the shrill cry of gulls wheeling overhead.

Closing her eyes, her voice quavering, she began the Lord's Prayer. " 'Our Father Who art in Heaven, hallowed be thy name . . .' " The familiar litany offered no comfort. She wasn't even sure she believed in God anymore, but she said the words for her parents' sake.

When she finished she opened her eyes and gazed

around to find herself alone. Stooping, she took the wildflowers she had picked that morning—Indian paintbrush someone had called them—and spread the wilted blood-red blossoms on the mounded graves.

"Ashes to ashes, dust to dust," she solemnly intoned, then realized she didn't know the rest of the service. Somehow it was the final blow. Her parents had died unshriven and now she couldn't even give them a proper burial. She prostrated herself on her mother's grave and wept the tears she had held in check all day, her body shaking with the force of her grief.

Not until dusk drew its silent curtain over the lonely landscape did Elke have the strength to rise. She walked the couple of hundred yards to the shore and gazed out to sea. The tide caressed the beach so tenderly, as though the lonely strand found favor in the water's fathomless depths.

How sweet it must be to be caressed like that. She missed her mother's gentle touch, her father's quiet strength. Would anyone ever care for her the way they had?

The last week she had been too busy with futile nursing to think about anything but battling for her parents' lives. Now she had to decide her what to do with her own.

They had left a small nest egg—money that would have supported the family until they were able to earn a living. However, her passage back to Germany would take every kroner of it. She couldn't return to Karlsruhe a penniless orphan. Germany's rigid society wasn't kind to those who lacked the means to support themselves.

No, she thought, she could never go back to the place

her parents had fled in search of a better life. Turning, she looked inland at the empty horizon stretching to infinity, her gaze seeking the future.

She had two choices. Either she summoned the courage to go on by herself—or she might as well lie down and die here and now.

She straightened her spine, squared her shoulders, and clenched her fists. Somehow, she vowed, she would find a way to fulfill her parents' dream.

She wouldn't let this desolate land, this place called Texas, defeat her.

Chapter One

Fredericksburg, Texas, 1860

Elke Sonnschein frowned as she studied the bakery's account books. Considering Fredericksburg's increasing population, they should be showing more of a profit. But the city's growth had resulted in diminishing returns for the business. And, she fretted, Otto was to blame.

Her husband was generous to a fault. He couldn't turn away from a human being in need. She didn't object to the fact that as many free baked goods went out the back door to impoverished settlers as out the front with paying customers. But she couldn't help longing for financial security, especially now with the specter of war looming on the horizon.

Elke shifted on her stool behind the counter, rolled her shoulders to ease the tension in her cramped muscles, then lifted her head to gaze at her surroundings. They had moved into the sturdy limestone building on Main Street three years ago. It consisted of the front room where she waited on customers, the bakery proper in the back, and an apartment upstairs where she and Otto lived.

The building boasted luxuries such as fireplaces in every room, a cavernous wood-burning stove in the kitchen, and the latest in kerosene-fueled chandeliers. It had replaced the cramped *fachwerk* log structure Otto had built when he arrived in Fredericksburg in 1845. Although Elke loved their new quarters, she wasn't at all sure they should have spent so much money on them.

The wide expanse of windows across the front room had cost a small fortune. The row of pie safes which kept the torts, cakes, and pies fresh were of the very best quality. A variety of breads protruded from baskets in front of the high-priced counter that had been shipped all the way from New Orleans, while cookies and other delicacies were displayed under its glass top. The porcelain potbelly stove, imported from Germany at great expense, sat in the center of the room, its warmth enticing patrons to linger over coffee and Otto's famous strudel.

The free coffee, savory aromas, cloth-covered tables and robust oak chairs helped make the Sonnschein Bakery the most popular gathering place in town—except, of course, for the saloons and whorehouses!

Today the room was more crowded than usual thanks to the chilly March wind blowing outside. A dozen ranchers, farmers, and German burghers—all regular customers—kept inharmonious company at the tables. The ranchers and farmers, most of them from southern states, were arguing hotly in favor of slavery as the only path to prosperity. The burghers stolidly refused to agree.

It was a quarrel Elke had heard many times before, one she had participated in herself with considerable abolitionist fervor—a disagreement that had been exacerbated by the coming national election. Loudest of all in their opinions this morning were the Detweiler twins. Why did uneducated men always try to win an argument by raising their voices while intelligent ones lowered theirs?

She had felt sorry for Eli and Jode Detweiler when they were small. Their family had been the beneficiaries of Otto's back-door handouts. Then their mother had passed on and their father had taken them off somewhere. When they came back a few years later, the twins had turned meaner than rattlers shedding their skins.

She sighed, wishing the two troublemakers didn't have such a craving for sweets. She recalled the hard time they had given her last month when they tried to force an elderly black man to leave the shop. She had ordered the Detweiler twins out at gunpoint then and told them not to return. But they had slunk back in today and, considering what the account books revealed, she had let them stay.

Smoothing an errant blond tendril back into the chignon at her nape, she returned to the books. The cost of sugar, flour, and spices had been rising. She dreaded the inflation and the shortages that a war would inevitably bring. How would she make ends meet then?

She sighed again, more heavily than before. She hadn't worked and struggled for fourteen years to wind up without a home again.

Seeking a way to increase their profit, she returned to

the numbers she had inked on the pages. Absorbed in them, she didn't even hear the tinkling bell over the front door announcing another customer's arrival.

A deep masculine voice saying, "Good afternoon, Elke" jerked her from her calculations.

She looked up to see Patrick Pride across the counter. Her heart paused in its orderly rhythm. Her face heated up. Her palms turned icy cold.

Her joy at seeing him was only equaled by her guilt. A married woman shouldn't feel the way she did about her husband's best friend.

"Good afternoon." She smiled up at Patrick. Thank heaven her voice sounded steadier than her pulse.

The first time she laid eyes on Patrick Pride she had been a seventeen-year-old bride. He had ridden down Main Street on a magnificent white stallion, sitting so tall and straight in the saddle that he instantly conjured up memories of the princes in the fairy tales her parents used to read to her.

Now, despite her resolve to treat him like nothing more than a dear friend, her gaze lingered on his face. Although his countenance was too rough-hewn to be conventionally handsome, to her it epitomized masculine beauty.

His broad forehead, fierce nose, and square jaw were framed by jet-black hair curling to his collar. A scar slashing across his left cheek—a result of his heroism in the battle of Palo Alto—enhanced his rugged appeal. A trim mustache emphasized the appealing curve of his lips. But it was his eyes, the crystalline gray of a rain-washed sky, that she loved the best. And right now they were regarding her with curiosity and concern.

"You look troubled. Is something wrong, Sunshine?" He used the nickname that was a rough translation of *Sonnschein*—a name only he called her.

She laughed feebly. "Something's always wrong when I'm going over the books."

"I'd be happy to help if you're short of funds."

He had made the offer many times before. Thanks to a land grant on the Guadalupe River that he had built into a flourishing ranch, he was by far the wealthiest man in the Texas Hill Country.

"Things aren't that bad," she said, too proud to admit the truth. A nod of her head indicated the customers at the tables. "In fact, we've never been busier. Now, what brings you to town today?"

"It's a long story," he replied. "Is Otto around? I'd like to tell the two of you together."

She had never seen him look so solemn. And why in the world was he wearing a beautifully tailored suit under his oil-cloth duster? Good heavens, where could he be going in such finery? And who did he plan to see?

With an in-drawn breath, she realized he was dressed for courting. A spasm of jealousy contracted her stomach as she silently enumerated the list of the town's single women. In her opinion, not one was good enough for Patrick Pride.

"What's this about wanting to tell the two of us something?" Otto asked, suddenly materializing at her side as if by magic. He held a tray of *Pfeffernussen* in one meaty hand. "Here, have one of these, Patrick. They're fresh from the oven and you must be hungry from your long ride." After Patrick helped himself to a couple of the spice-rich cookies, Otto added, "It's good to see you again, *mein Freund.*"

Elke couldn't help contrasting Otto's heavily accented English with Patrick's refined speech, and Otto's thick-set body with Patrick's athletic figure. Her husband's thinning hair and portly build made him look even older than his forty-two years. But there was no kinder man in the world, she reminded herself sternly.

Her mother used to caution her about judging people by their appearance. And yet her father had been a handsome man and her mother clearly adored him for it. Elke had inherited his height, his wide-set blue eyes, and his golden coloring. If only her parents were here now, she thought with a hollow ache of longing, she might be able to confess the secrets of her heart to them. Somehow she felt certain they would have understood.

The day of their burial she had stood by their graves wondering if she would ever experience the singular love they had shared. Now she knew the answer. A cruel quirk of fate had denied her that bliss. If Patrick had ridden into town one month earlier she would never have married Otto—not even if it had meant living the rest of her life alone.

The sound of voices raised in anger interrupted her unhappy reverie. Jude and Eli Detweiler were the cause. Bullies who never picked a fight with anyone capable of fighting back, they were arguing with John Keller, a small-framed elderly man.

Jude jumped to his feet so abruptly that he knocked his chair over. "You goddamn cabbage eaters are all alike. Stupider than mule piss," he shouted loud enough to rattle the windows. "How many times do you have to be told that niggers ain't even human?"

"Why don't you go back home to Germany where you belong?" Eli chimed in.

Here we go again, Elke thought, reaching for the shotgun she had kept under the counter since the days when marauding Indians were an ever-present threat.

The twins were used to people cowering when confronted by their joint menace. But they had miscalculated this time. John Keller had faced the danger of emigrating to Texas in 1846 with the Adelsverein Society. Despite his diminutive size, Elke knew he wasn't likely to be intimidated by the bark of a pair of noisy curs.

"This *is* my home," Keller replied in a surprisingly strong voice. "And the blacks are God's creatures, just like you and I."

Both Detweilers grabbed Keller by his arms and jerked him to his feet. Concentrating on the tableau, Elke brought the gun to her shoulder. The smooth wooden stock felt as comforting as the touch of an old and trusted friend.

"Unless one of you boys plans to ask Mr. Keller for a dance, you had better let him go," she said.

Eli looked her way. "Aw, shit, lady. Not the gun again. My brother and me was just having a little fun."

"Mr. Keller and I don't share your idea of fun, and I don't care for your language," she replied.

"Pardon me all to hell. I forgot you're one of them maggot-brain abolitionists, too." Jude spat out the word *abolitionist* like an epithet. His ferretlike gaze darted around the bakery as if challenging anyone to disagree with him.

Before Elke could say or do anything, Patrick crossed the floor, and in a casual display of strength, grabbed the twins by their collars and lifted them off their feet.

"If you boys are looking for a fight, head on over to a saloon where you can mix it up with your own kind instead of bothering decent folk," Patrick said.

The Detweilers let go of Keller to confront their new antagonist. Surprise quickly replaced the anger on their brutish faces when they realized Patrick was alone. For a moment Elke felt certain they were going to launch a joint attack.

However, even the Detweiler twins weren't that stupid. At six feet two inches, Patrick towered over them. He had a mature man's strength—and obviously didn't lack the will to use it. Elke could see that his eyes had gone colder than a Texas norther as he stared the two of them down.

"You're a southerner just like us," Eli whined. "Why are you turning on your own kind?"

"I'll never be *your* kind. Now get the hell out." Patrick gave them a shove that sent them flying toward the door.

When they reached it, they turned around. Their eyes lingered on Patrick a moment before zeroing in on Elke. "We ain't goin' to fergit this," they snarled in unison.

"Neither am I. Don't bother coming back," Elke replied, not lowering the gun until they stormed out, slamming the door behind them.

"Are you all right?" Patrick asked Mr. Keller.

"I'm fine," the old man replied, smoothing his jacket. "I sure don't know what got into the two of them."

"Maybe they didn't like the strudel," Elke suggested.

As she intended, her remark elicited a burst of laughter. She could almost feel the tension in the room evaporating as she put the shotgun back in its place.

When she straightened up, Patrick had returned to the counter and was glaring at her as if *she* had done something wrong rather than the Detweilers.

Otto reached out and pumped Patrick's hand. *"Vielen dank,"* he said. "Many thanks. I'm glad you were here. I'm not much good when it comes to a fight."

Elke had held her breath while Patrick confronted the twins, fearing for him and yet thrilled by his courage. Now she realized that by humiliating them, he had made himself two dangerous enemies.

"You should have let me handle those two," she declared. "I've done it before."

Otto gazed at her fondly, then turned back to Patrick. "My wife is a real firebrand."

"Your wife is playing with fire all right. She should never draw a gun unless she's prepared to use it."

"I knew what I was doing."

The strangest expression, a curious blend of anger and something else she couldn't define, flashed across Patrick's face as he gazed down at her. "I know you used to hunt with your father. However, shooting a human being is nothing like shooting a pheasant. It's something you never forget."

He reached across the counter and clapped Otto on the shoulder. "As for you, my friend, the world has all the warriors it needs."

The encounter with the Detweilers had left Otto as red as one of his cherry pies. A gentle, civilized man, he had difficulty confronting aggression. "You were about to tell us something before all the excitement. What was it?"

"I've decided to go home to Natchez before a civil war makes travel impossible."

Elke felt as if the floor had just dropped from under her feet. The realization that Patrick believed there would be a war was troubling enough. The thought that he would soon leave cut her to the bone. She had never admitted to herself how much she looked forward to his monthly visits.

She glanced outside to see if the sun had gone behind a cloud, but the sky was as blue as it had been a few minutes ago. The darkness was inside her.

"Natchez is hundreds of miles away. You'll be gone for months," she burst out.

"Six at least. But I haven't been home since I claimed my land grant, and my parents aren't getting any younger."

Otto nodded his approval. "It is good to honor one's parents. I only wish I had been able to return to Germany to see mine before they died."

"When are you leaving?" Elke asked.

"I'm taking the stage to Galveston in the morning."

"So soon!" she cried out, her heart in her throat. "What about the ranch? Isn't it calving time?"

"All my cows have calved. My foreman, Rio de Vargas, will handle things just fine while I'm gone. He's a very capable man."

Would she never learn to curb her tongue? What Patrick did or didn't do was none of her business.

"I guess I should have told you and Otto about the trip earlier. I've been thinking about it for months," Patrick said, as casually as though he were talking about a stroll down Main Street.

"Then you must stay the night with us instead of taking a room at a hotel," Otto declared. "Elke has made something of her delicious *sauerbraten* and a few friends will be stopping by afterward to discuss the election. We can turn it into a farewell party."

"I don't want to put you to any trouble."

"It's no trouble at all, is it, *Liebchen?*" Otto looked at Elke for confirmation.

"Of course it's no trouble. I won't hear of Patrick staying at a hotel his last night in town," Elke replied, almost choking on the lump in her throat.

"Then I accept your hospitality."

"Good. It's settled." Otto gave Elke an exuberant hug. "I've been saving a bottle of *schnaps* from the old country for a special occasion. We'll give you a sendoff you won't forget."

Patrick hurried out of the bake shop without looking back. He couldn't believe Elke had been foolish enough to pull a gun on the Detweilers. She had added insult to injury by joking about it. The story would be all over town by nightfall. The Detweilers were bound to hear all the talk about them—and they wouldn't appreciate being made a laughing stock by a woman.

Didn't she know how dangerous they were? Didn't

she care what happened to her? She had to be out of her mind.

And so was he for falling in love with a gun-toting abolitionist like Elke Sonnschein. So far she had no idea how much she meant to him—and he intended to see that she never did.

It felt good to be outdoors again, away from her and the forbidden pleasures that seeing her always conjured up. He drank in the cold air greedily, hoping it would cool his fevered blood. Good God, what sort of man had lewd and lascivious thoughts about his friend's wife— thoughts that even visits to Velvet Gilhooley's whorehouse couldn't assuage?

He had tried every remedy for his unseemly desire. But he'd long since learned that cold plunges in the Guadalupe and hours of back-breaking labor couldn't dispel the image of Elke in his bed, her shining golden hair spread across his pillow, her long legs open to welcome him.

He could think of only one cure for his ill-conceived passion—and he was returning home in search of it.

Disgusted with himself, Patrick retrieved the horse he had left in front of the bakery, unwrapped its reins from the hitching post, and headed down Main Street to the livery stable, trying to concentrate on the sights and sounds of the bustling community.

The German settlers had worked wonders in the fifteen years since the city's founding. The fruits of their industry had made Fredericksburg the envy of all the neighboring towns.

Wooden sidewalks flanked both sides of the street. Substantial buildings constructed from locally quarried limestone were gradually replacing log cabins. Flourishing businesses like the bakery sat side by side with comfortable houses. The Nimitz and Schmidt hotels, with their sun-shaded verandas, offered first-class lodging to weary travelers. The octagonal Vereins Kirche, built in 1845 and used as a fort as well as a church, looked strangely out of place amidst the modern buildings.

It had taken courage to create a new city from what had been wilderness, the sort of raw courage that Elke possessed in abundance.

Damn, there he went thinking about her again. Apparently he could no more control his thoughts these days than he could his emotions. How the hell had he gotten himself in such a mess?

Loving another man's wife ran contrary to the southern code of chivalry he had imbibed with his mother's milk. That high moral code had always ruled his behavior. It had motivated him to serve his country with honor and distinction during the war with Mexico. It had governed all his adult relationships. But when he looked at Elke, that code no longer mattered.

Heaven knew she wasn't the type of woman who had attracted him in the past. He'd grown up surrounded by genteel women like his mother, women who devoted their entire lives to nurturing their families, women who wouldn't dream of intruding in the all-man worlds of business and politics—genuine ladies from head to toe.

Elke possessed none of those virtues. She couldn't hold her tongue if her life depended on it. She was stubborn and willful, and the niceties of life weren't half as important to her as doing things her way. She had a better head for figures than most men, a better seat in the saddle—and more grit. In fact, she had all the characteristics that were considered virtues in a man but were damned unseemly in a member of the gentler sex.

However, she sure as hell didn't look like a man. Every inch of her curved just the way he liked. With her height, he couldn't help thinking how perfectly she would fit in his arms. Her blond hair, the white-gold shade of corn silk, hung halfway down her back. Her skin had the same golden glow. No woman had ever been more aptly named. She reminded him of sunshine.

A few minutes ago she had threatened the Detweilers without any regard for the consequences. If he hadn't been there, God knew what would have happened.

The Detweiler twins might very well be the scum of the earth, but they were handy with their pistols. The thought of Elke getting hurt, perhaps even dying because of her headstrong ways made him sick to his stomach.

Half the time he didn't know which he wanted more, to take her across his knees and give her the paddling she deserved—or to take her in his arms and give her a loving she would never forget.

Truth was, he'd like to do both—and had no right to do either one.

Thoroughly disgusted with himself, he curbed his mount so sharply when he reached the livery stable that the horse whinnied in protest. Mistreating the animal in-

creased his self-loathing. He didn't know himself anymore.

He had damn well better get out of town before he
did something he'd spend the rest of his life regret-
ting.

Chapter Two

Elke's gaze never left Patrick as he strode from the bakery, mounted up, and rode away. A feeling of impending loss rooted her in place. What if he never returned?

Patrick had told her about his family's mansion in Natchez, had regaled her with stories of a refined lifestyle the frontier could never supply—a lifestyle heady with the scent of magnolias and shimmering with candlelight at elegant parties where beautiful women were the exception rather than the rule—a lifestyle so seductive that he might be ensnared by it.

Even if he intended to come back, there was always the possibility that war would break out before he did. Patrick was a son of the South. Considering his experience in the Mexican war, he'd probably be offered a high rank in a southern army.

Where did his deepest loyalties lie? With the slave holders—or with the ranch he'd wrested from the frontier?

How little she knew him. Her soul longed for all the

intimacies a husband and wife exchanged, the little secrets, the quiet revelations she and Patrick would never
share—intimacies of the heart and mind that went far
beyond the union of two bodies.

Although God knew, she longed for that, too.

Snapping the account book shut as if to close her
mind on her scandalous thoughts, she turned her attention back to Otto. He was transferring the *Pfeffernussen*
from the cookie sheet to a tray under the counter's glass
top, and humming one of his beloved *lieder.*

"I have to check on the sauerbraten and ready the
spare room for a guest. Can you manage without me?"
she asked.

Otto straightened up and wiped his hands on his
apron. "At your service, *Liebling.* I'm finished baking
for the day. Take the rest of the afternoon off and make
yourself pretty for our guests. I'll take care of the
shop." He gave her a noisome kiss on the cheek, then
slid his ample rump onto the stool she had so recently
vacated.

Knowing it would hurt him, Elke refrained from using a handkerchief to wipe the wetness he'd left on her
face. "Why don't you close up a little early today and
enjoy a rest before supper? You must be tired."

Otto's small brown eyes filled with tenderness. "You
take such good care of me. No man ever had a better
wife."

A good wife indeed! she brooded, leaving before Otto
could see her face flush with guilt. Not a day passed
that she didn't long to be free of him. If only they'd had
children to seal their bond, things might have been different.

She hurried through the bakery, too distracted to even say good day to Otto's helpers, then went outside into the garden.

It had been her refuge in the past, the place she went to be alone. Normally the beauty of nature eased her mind. She had always taken both hope and comfort from the miraculous way a magnificent flower grew from a tiny seed.

This afternoon, though, the wintry landscape seemed to reflect the dreariness inside her. A few crocuses, brave harbingers of spring, bobbed in the wind. She cut them, then gathered them up and ever so wearily climbed the outside stairs to the apartment over the bakery.

It consisted of five rooms—a larger parlor-dining room, the bedroom she and Otto shared, the office-sewing room, the guest room where Patrick would sleep, and a kitchen. Otto had spared no expense furnishing the rooms, seeking out the finest local craftsmen, insisting they use the best materials.

Despite all the expense, her most treasured possessions were the few things that had belonged to her parents, a faded daguerrotype taken the year they died and her mother's delicately painted bride's boxes. Would she always feel their loss?

The savory scent of sauerbraten filled her nostrils as she shut the door behind her. Of all the dishes she made, it was Otto's favorite. A week ago she had put a large roast in a stoneware crock and marinated it in a mixture of vinegar, white wine, and water seasoned with bay leaves, peppercorns, and onions.

This morning she'd transferred the roast to a cast-iron

pot and left it to simmer on the wood-burning stove. Slicing the meat, making a gravy with sweet cream, and preparing the potato *latkes* that were another of Otto's favorites would take no more than an hour.

He required so little of her—a tasty meal, a kind word, a smile, and a weekly tumble in bed. It wasn't fair to expect so much of him.

No man in Fredericksburg was more admired for his kindness. So why couldn't she stop correcting his heavily accented English? Why did she still feel disappointed because he failed to cut an elegant figure in his Sunday best? How could she fault him because his kisses never quickened her pulse?

She put the crocuses in a vase, carried them into the guest room, and placed them on the table next to the kerosene lamp so they would be the first thing Patrick saw in the morning. Then she took a set of linens from the *Kleidershrank*'s bottom drawer and made the bed, tucking the corners in neatly and smoothing a gaily colored patchwork quilt over the top.

Unable to resist the temptation, she slumped onto the covers and kissed the pillow where Patrick would lay his head that night. Then she buried her face in its downy softness. What madness, to envy a bed because Patrick would sleep in its embrace!

She exhaled a long, shuddering sigh. If only she had waited a little longer before accepting Otto's proposal all those years ago. But he'd been so kind, so solicitous of her well-being, that she had naively mistaken the gratitude she felt for love.

It was Otto who had given her a job when she arrived in Fredericksburg, one of the group of bedraggled immigrants who had fled Indianola on foot. And it was Otto who had offered her a place to stay. For the next three years the tiny room at the back of the old bakery had been her home.

Fourteen years her senior, Otto had helped fill the void created by the death of her parents. Her days had been taken up with work, her nights with learning as Otto shared his precious treasure trove of books.

Her father had seen to her early education. Otto completed the work her father had begun. Under his tutelage she'd read classics by Shakespeare, Chaucer, and Homer; philosophers like Hegel and Kant; less serious works such as *Uncle Tom's Cabin* by Harriet Beecher Stowe and *Walden* by Henry Thoreau; and Otto's all-time favorite, a slim volume of poems by Heinrich Heine.

Otto had encouraged her growing skill with English and mathematics, applauding her triumphs and commiserating over her failures, treating her more like a younger sister than an employee.

But over time, his demeanor had changed. She used to catch him staring at her the way greedy children look at a particularly toothsome pastry. And then he started giving her gifts. Nothing too ostentatious, mind you, nothing that would have made her feel awkward accepting them. Just practical, thoughtful things like a few yards of cloth to sew a dress, a packet of flower seeds from Germany, a comforter for her bed.

One day without a word of warning he'd told her that he'd made arrangements for her to move in with a family who lived at the edge of town.

"People are talking about you staying here," he'd

said. "Since you have no parents it's up to me to look out for your reputation. Now that you're a grown woman, it's best you go."

But she hadn't felt like a grown woman. Only seventeen, she'd felt like a child being abandoned by her dearest friend. "I don't care what people say," she had declared, her voice thick with tears. "Besides, you need me here."

"You're right. I do need you," he had agreed in a strangely throaty tone, "more than you'll ever know, *Liebling.*"

The endearment had startled her. Her father had called her *Liebling.*

"There is another way to keep the gossips quiet."

"How?"

"We could get married."

"Married? To you?" The thought had never crossed her mind.

"I'll spend the rest of my life making you happy, *Liebling.*"

Relieved at not having to leave the only home she'd known since her parents' death, she had said yes without considering the commitment she would have to make. And so the banns had been read and three weeks later she and Otto stood up together before God, Pastor Basse, and the Vereins Kirche's congregation.

She had sworn to love him until death did them part before she even know what the words meant.

But she did now, God help her.

How cruel it was to long for one man and be tied by honor, duty, and sacred vows to another.

Getting to her feet, Elke abandoned her useless introspection. Her thoughts had been in a jumble since Patrick walked into the bakery. Perhaps her foolish fancies would fade away during his absence.

Praying it would be so, she smoothed the covers to erase all sign of her brief occupancy. She hadn't indulged in endless self-pity when her parents died. She wouldn't permit herself to do so now. She had made her marriage bed and she would have to lie in it.

And not with a sour face, either.

Patrick arrived at the bakery promptly at six, carrying a portmanteau in one hand and a bottle of Liebfraumilch in the other. He walked around the building and climbed the stairs to the Sonnscheins' apartment.

He had just spent an hour in the bar at the Nimitz Hotel fortifying himself for the evening ahead, drinking a couple of whiskies and telling himself it would be wonderful to revisit the sophisticated world he'd left in Natchez.

Seeing Elke open the door, he realized he had been fooling himself. It wouldn't be wonderful at all. Leaving her was going to be pure hell.

"I thought you might enjoy this," he said, handing her the wine.

"Thank you, Patrick. Come on in." She stood aside to let him pass.

Her scent—a blend of soap, good food, and sweet woman—filled his head and weakened his knees.

"*Gruss Gott,*" Otto called, his broad face wreathed in a smile. "You're just in time. Leave your bag by the door. I was about to pour the schnaps."

Although the last thing he needed was another drink, Patrick accepted the glass Otto held out. Following Otto's lead, he took a deep draught and gasped as the *schnaps* trailed liquid fire from his gullet to his stomach.

Patrick was no stranger to strong drink. In an effort to ensure that he could hold his liquor like a gentleman, his father had given him his first taste of bourbon and branch water on his twelfth birthday. In the twenty years since he'd sampled every conceivable brew from the finest French wines at parties in Natchez, to Mescal and tequila during the war, to rotgut whiskey on the frontier. But he had never tasted anything so potent.

"What did you say this drink is?" he asked in a strangled voice.

"It's called *Steinhager.* It comes from the southern part of Germany where I grew up."

A chuckle tickled its way up Patrick's blazing throat. "Now I know why I like you so much, Otto. You're a southerner, too." He took a more tentative sip. "What the hell's is in this?"

"The peasants make it from potatoes and bottle it in stone because it's supposed to eat its way through glass," Otto replied, refilling Patrick's glass.

"And stomachs, too," Elke said, a smile on her generous mouth.

God, she looked lovely with her golden hair floating around her shoulders like that. She'd put on a dress he'd never seen before. The watered silk matched her eyes. The way the fabric molded her breasts, waist, and hips riveted his attention.

Like many women who lived on the edge of civilization, Elke didn't wear a hoop. Seeing the outline of her long legs under her skirt sent a spiralling warmth to his groin. He'd been far too long without a woman—a lack he intended to remedy in Natchez.

"Did you take care of your business, Patrick?" she asked.

She looked utterly cool and calm, as if his leaving meant nothing to her.

She looked breathtakingly beautiful.

She looked like more trouble than he could handle.

She looked like heaven—and he felt like hell.

Yes, damn it, he was right to leave. And the sooner the better. All he had to do was get through this last night. A few more hours and he'd be free of the spell Little Miss Sunshine had cast over him. Surely he could act the gentleman for so short a time.

If he ever got lathered over a woman again she had better be single, suitable, and a good breeder—a proper wife for a man who had come to Texas to build a dynasty. He needed children to carry on after he was gone. Without them the years of endless toil establishing the P bar P Ranch wouldn't mean a damn thing.

"Here's to a safe journey," Otto said, lifting his glass high.

"To a safe journey," Elke echoed. "And now if you gentlemen will excuse me, I'll get dinner on the table."

It was all Patrick could do to tear his eyes away from her as she walked into the kitchen. Carrying his Steinhager, he followed Otto to a couple of chairs by the fireplace.

"I need a favor," Otto said after they were settled.

"All you have to do is ask."

"When you get to Natchez I'd be most grateful if you could send me a couple of books: Emerson's *The Conduct of Life* and Longfellow's *The Courtship of Miles Standish.*"

"I'd be delighted as long as you don't mind if I read them first."

Their mutual love of literature had helped forge their friendship. At first Patrick had been surprised to find a fellow bibliophile in the unlikely guise of a German baker. But he'd soon realized that Otto was as well read as any graduate of his alma mater, William and Mary.

He had been even more surprised to learn Elke was, too. They had spent many an evening talking of literature, history, and philosophy.

"If it's not too much trouble, could you include the latest copies of Godey's Lady's Book for Elke?" Otto said.

Patrick blinked in surprise. "I didn't realize Elke was interested in fashion."

Otto's booming laugh filled the room. "She's not. But she's been devoted to Godey's ever since they started a column about working women. My wife has a strong opinion about a woman's place in the greater scheme of things." Giving him a conspiratorial wink, Otto continued. "She believes a woman has a right to be more than a receptacle for a man's seed."

"And what do you think?"

"I don't know about other women. I wasn't exactly a ladies' man before I married. But I do know my Elke. She's much too smart," Otto pronounced it *schmart,* "to spend twenty-four hours a day keeping house. The bakery would have long since failed without her. She takes care of the business end of things completely."

"You've never minded her working, have you?" Patrick said, marveling at Otto's *laissez-faire* attitude. Steeped in southern tradition, Patrick couldn't imagine women toiling in the work place alongside men. That sort of propinquity could only lead to trouble.

Leaning closer, Otto lowered his voice. "I don't have to tell you my Elke has a mind of her own. I'll never forget the first time I saw her. She had walked all the way from Indianola and she looked as starved as an orphan pup. I offered her a free meal but she wouldn't accept charity. She insisted on working for her food."

Their long friendship notwithstanding, Otto had never discussed his relationship with Elke in detail before. Perhaps it was the Steinhager, or the fact that Patrick was leaving that made him do so now.

"Was it love at first sight?" Patrick asked, feeling like one of those idiots who can't resist probing a wound even though he knows it's going to hurt.

Otto chortled. "How could it be? She told me her name was Hansel. She had cut off her hair, dressed in her father's clothes, and she was already taller than I am. I didn't know she was a girl for six months. By then, although I'm not bent that way, I was having some pretty strange feelings about my helper, Hansel."

"Were you angry at her for deceiving you?"

"Angry? *Nein*. I was relieved when I learned the truth. At least I knew I wasn't—how to put it?—suffering from unusual longings."

"What did you do when she told you?"

"She didn't. I happened to pass by her room one evening when she thought I was out. She'd forgotten to shut the door and I looked in to say good night. Hansel was having a bath, and I have to tell you, I've never seen a boy built like that! I was thunderstruck."

Patrick had no trouble imagining the effect Elke had had on Otto. Fully clothed, she had the same effect on him. "Did she see you?"

"No, thank God. The next day I told her she could stop cutting her hair because I had guessed the truth. My heart went out to her when she said she'd only dressed as a man for protection. And who can blame her considering what she'd been through? I made up my mind to marry her then and there." Otto paused. "Of course I had to wait for her to ripen a little. But it was worth it. Such a *schoene madchen* as my Elke is a rare prize."

Patrick couldn't have agreed more. Although both Otto and Elke believed the bakery's success was due to Otto's fine hand with sweets, Patrick knew many a lonely ranch hand who rode for miles to get a glimpse of the lovely Elke Sonnschein—himself included. "I've always wondered how a man worked up the courage to propose to a beautiful woman."

"I just blurted it out one day. And I'm proud to say my Elke could hardly wait to marry me." Grinning, Otto puffed out his already barreled chest.

So it had been a love match rather than a marriage of convenience, Patrick mused with a sinking heart. "You're a very lucky man. I just hope I'm as lucky someday."

"You will be. It's a mystery to me that you haven't married before now. Let me tell you, it's far better to share a bed with a woman than to burn alone."

Closing his mind to the image Otto's remark conjured up, Patrick finished his drink. If Otto knew how he was burning at this very minute . . .

Otto refilled Patrick's glass. "It's high time you had a passion for something other than the land. I know you named your ranch the P Bar P. But considering the way you feel about it, folks around here have taken to calling it Pride's Passion. It's appropriate, *nicht var?*"

"I suppose so," Patrick agreed, grateful that Otto had never guessed his real passion.

"Dinner's ready." Elke's voice brought the conversation to a halt.

"Bottoms up," Otto said, drinking down his Steinhager as if it were water.

Not to be outdone, Patrick emptied his glass, too.

The meal was ambrosial, the Steinhager ever present. By the time Otto excused himself to go down to the bakery, Patrick's earlier qualms about the evening had been drowned in *schnaps*. He couldn't have felt more relaxed.

"I'll clear the table and do the dishes," Elke said. "Why don't you go sit by the fire until our other guests get here?"

"I wouldn't dream of letting you do all that work by yourself." Determined to be a perfect gentleman, Patrick got to his feet and gave Elke an extravagant bow.

"That really won't be necessary." Elke stacked their plates and carried them into the kitchen.

"Oh, but I insist." Patrick picked up a platter and followed in her wake.

She began priming the pump over the sink.

"Let me do that," he said, reaching from behind her. He swore he only wanted to help. But their fingers touched—and he felt the contact all the way to the tips of his toes.

"Please, don't do that," she cried out, whirling to face him. She stood so close that he could feel the warmth radiating from her body.

If it hadn't been for the little beauty mark to the left of her mouth, he would have nobly resisted the temptation she unwittingly presented. However, he just had to know if that beauty mark was genuine, or if she'd penciled it on the way the belles of Natchez did.

He leaned across the inches separating them and touched the spot with the tip of his tongue.

She shivered, then moaned, swaying like a woman on the brink of a swoon.

Being a gentleman, he had no choice but to take her in his arms—just to keep her from falling, he told himself.

And then, when he felt the full, lush length of her body against his—he stopped telling himself anything.

For the next few minutes he existed in a world where right and wrong ceased to matter, a world of pure sensation that held him prisoner as surely as if he'd been bound in chains.

Her breath fluttered against his cheek like the touch of a butterfly's wings. He could see her pulse beating in her throat. Her breasts pressed against his chest. The sweet swell of her stomach mated with his flat belly.

The warmth between her legs sent an answering rush of heat to his groin.

While Otto and Patrick had been enjoying the sauerbraten and Steinhager, Elke had barely tasted the food. She felt more like a prisoner eating a last meal than a hostess sharing a pleasant evening with a cherished friend.

She kept on stealing glances at Patrick, trying to memorize his face in anticipation of the long days and even longer nights before she saw him again. Lost in her own thoughts, she didn't realize the meal had drawn to a close until Otto got to his feet and said something about needing to go down to the bakery.

"Must you?" She dreaded being alone with Patrick for fear he'd somehow read in her eyes what had been in her mind.

Otto came around the table and bussed the top of her head. "Surely you can do without me for a few minutes."

Indeed she could—but not these few minutes. She watched in dismay as Otto walked out the door. Then, although it was rude to leave a guest alone, she turned to Patrick and said, "I'll clear the table and do the dishes."

She had stayed awake many a night, thinking about him. Now those memories heated her cheeks. She felt so flustered that she didn't hear his reply and wasn't aware he had followed her to the sink until she felt his hand on hers.

Before she knew quite how it had happened, she

was in his arms and kissing him shamelessly, reveling in the touch, the scent, the sight of him, feeling as if she'd been lost for years and had finally found her way home.

She strained against him as if to merge her flesh with his. His hand at the small of her back pressed her even closer. He was aroused and ready, but no more so than she. Her insides melted with a liquid warmth that dampened the tender tissues between her thighs. Her nipples hardened.

Otto had taught her all she knew of a couple's intimate relations, explaining things on their wedding night, and then following his explanation with an all too graphic example.

After her initial shock, she had come to accept that a man needed a woman that way. But she had never dreamed that she might have those same feelings. Certainly she had never had them with her husband.

When Otto kissed her, he never opened his mouth to touch her tongue. She wasn't sure she'd even let him if he tried! Experiencing the new intimacy with Patrick seemed intrinsically right.

Patrick's kiss awakened a part of her she hadn't known existed. She was behaving the way she imagined Velvet Gilhooley's whores behaved, thrusting her tongue in Patrick's mouth, lifting his hand to her breast, parting her thighs to cradle his straining manhood.

Now she understood why her parents had hurried her off to bed no matter how she begged for just one more story. Now she understood the secret language of their sighs, their tremulous smiles, their soft touches. Now she knew the river of emotion they'd swum in—and dear God, she wanted to bathe in it herself.

Her parents had spent twenty joyous years together.

She would only know this moment—and she prayed it would last forever.

As the kiss deepened she clung to Patrick, her senses running riot. She had never been more aware of her body and the pleasure it could give a man. Her skin burned, her breasts swelled. She felt completely female at a primitive level she had never known before. A wild exultation raced through her blood, an intoxication so overwhelming that she felt as if her soul had taken flight.

But she couldn't let the kiss go on. Reason finally returned, and with it—shame. Otto mustn't find her tangled in Patrick's arms, mouth to mouth, chest to chest, thigh to thigh. Tears pooling in her eyes, she finally found the strength to push Patrick away.

He reached for her again, and it took all her courage not to surrender to her heart's deepest desire. "You mustn't. *We* mustn't," she said past the choking lump in her throat.

He reeled back. "Oh my God, Elke, I'm so sorry. Please forgive me. It was the damn Steinhager. I never would have kissed you if I hadn't had too much to drink."

Elke didn't know which distressed her more. The kiss itself—or the realization that he'd only done it because he'd been under the influence of alcohol. She didn't know whether to weep—or to slap him until his ears rang.

But discretion demanded she do neither because just then, she heard Otto's heavy tread coming up the stairs.

Chapter Three

Elke's stomach spasmed, her hands shook, her nerves vibrated like violin strings. Otto mustn't find her trembling from Patrick's kiss.

She kept her back to the door and primed the pump as if her life depended on it. When water finally gushed from the faucet, she let it run on her wrists, then wet a tea towel and held it to her heated cheeks.

How could she have let Patrick kiss her like that? Even worse, how could she have kissed him back like a wanton slut?

She could hear him talking to Otto in the parlor as if nothing had happened. Perhaps it hadn't as far as he was concerned. Perhaps a kiss meant nothing to a sophisticated man like Patrick. Perhaps he had been amusing himself while she—poor fool—had felt as if they had shared their very souls.

All too soon she recognized Otto's familiar tread heading for the kitchen. "I thought you'd be finished with the dishes by now, *Liebchen*," he said, putting his arms around her waist and nuzzling her neck.

Her mouth felt so dry that she couldn't reply. Dear God, would he smell Patrick's distinctly masculine scent on her skin?

"It's my fault Elke's not done," Patrick said from the kitchen door.

Her heart bucked in her chest. For one wracking moment she thought Patrick was going to tell Otto the truth.

But then Patrick said, "I wanted the sauerbraten recipe to give my mother's cook. Once I started talking about home I couldn't stop. Elke was kind enough to listen."

"That's my Elke." Otto gave her an affectionate squeeze.

Her every instinct demanded that she recoil from his touch. Honor, however, and what remained of her shredded decency, commanded her to be still.

"Never mind the dishes," Otto said jovially. "You can do them later. Come. Sit with us and relax a while. There's still a little Steinhager left."

Elke could no more have joined Otto and Patrick at that moment than she could have grown wings and flown. If she survived the evening she vowed never to be unfaithful to her husband again—by thought, word, or deed.

"Have you forgotten we're expecting other guests? The dishes won't take me long."

"You're too conscientious, *Liebling.* But I know better than to argue with you."

Conscientious? She had no conscience at all or she would never have succumbed to Patrick's embrace. What must he think of her? Surely no worse than she thought of herself. An hour earlier she had been dreading his departure. Now she could hardly wait for the sun to rise so he'd be gone.

While Otto and Patrick returned to the parlor she washed and dried the dishes, then set cups, saucers, and plates out on the dining table, putting off the moment when she would have to join their conversation.

Reprieve came in the form of a knock at the door and she rushed to answer it. The first of their other guests had arrived.

She kept busy for the next hour greeting new arrivals, putting their coats and jackets in the bedroom, pouring coffee and serving the Black Forest cake Otto had brought up from the bakery, doing everything and anything she could to put off the moment when she would have to face Patrick again.

"For heaven's sake, Elke," Carolyn Grobe finally called out, "stop running around like a chicken without a head. We're all friends here. You don't need to wait on us. *Sitzen Sie.*" She patted the only empty chair—the one between her and Patrick.

Patrick had been surreptitiously watching Elke ever since she emerged from the kitchen. She had done a magnificent job of avoiding him, not making eye contact let alone engaging him in conversation. Not that he blamed her.

He had been the most unscrupulous cad, taking unforgivable advantage of their few minutes alone. He had presumed on their friendship, acting like a randy sailor newly arrived in a port instead of the gentleman he'd been raised to be.

He had treated Elke like a two-bit whore.

How she must hate him.

Yet, given the same opportunity, he knew he'd kiss her all over again. He had experienced a transcendent joy during their brief union that he'd never known in the most erotic coupling. Recalling the feel of her body, the sweet fragrance of her skin, the warmth of her mouth, made his blood run hot.

God, would this evening never be over? he thought, watching her cross the floor to the empty chair by his side. Her unique scent wafted in his nostrils as she settled herself. The touch of her skirt brushing his leg felt as intimate as another woman's most sensual caress.

He was well and truly hooked—and damned himself to perdition for not being immune to her charms.

Her gaze met his briefly. The disdain, disgust, and distaste he saw in her eyes cut him to the bone. Then, as if he didn't exist, she turned to Carolyn Grobe and began chatting.

He didn't pay any attention to what they were saying. He couldn't stop comparing the glacial expression he'd just seen in her eyes to the soul-searing heat of the kiss they'd exchanged.

He wasn't arrogant enough to think he'd had much to do with it. He might have been the spark, but in view of Elke's obvious devotion to her husband, he damn well knew he hadn't been the catalyst.

Who would have thought a man like Otto would have schooled his wife so well in the sensual arts? One touch and Elke had been ablaze.

No wonder Otto had been always been reluctant to speak of his and Elke's private life. No wonder he was still madly in love with his wife after a decade of marriage. Patrick repressed a shiver as he thought of the delights of their marital bed. Elke's beauty, intelligence, and passion—most especially her passion—would make ever coupling memorable.

A less discreet husband might have boasted of his wife's easy arousal and thereby made her prey to any and every rogue in town. But the only rogue who knew her secret would be gone tomorrow, Patrick mused, tugging at a collar that suddenly seemed a size too small.

By the time the last drop of coffee had been consumed and the last crumb of cake eaten, Elke had stopped wishing that the floor would open up and swallow her whole. Apparently Patrick had no more interest in her than he had in the sauerbraten recipe.

He seemed utterly undisturbed by her proximity while *she* was painfully aware that he sat not a foot away. No matter how valiantly she struggled to banish all thought of their embrace, her traitorous body remembered every second.

How dare he sit there acting as if butter wouldn't melt in his mouth while she still burned where he had touched her? She longed to shame him as he had shamed her, to take advantage of any weakness.

The evening dragged on interminably, the conversation ranging from a discussion of the weather—always a lively concern for farmers—to talk of current business conditions. Elke paid little attention to what the others were saying until Patrick became the focus of the discourse.

"So you're returning to Natchez," Herr Grobe said. "I'm surprised you're willing to leave Pride's Passion during such troubled times."

Patrick repeated what he'd told Elke and Otto earlier, about wanting to see his parents while he still could. To her ears, his excuse had a hollow ring.

"It seems to me that you're taking a risk, leaving when you may not be able to return," she said. "Isn't the real reason for the sudden trip that you're sympathetic to the southern cause?

"I've told you the real reason, Elke," he replied, enunciating each word as if she were a dull student and he a schoolmaster. "You know my father doesn't own slaves. He's a lawyer, not a planter."

Elke refused to be put off. "You haven't answered my question. Will you stay in Natchez and fight for the South if it comes to a war?"

Patrick touched the scar on his cheek as if to remind everyone—her included—of his past exploits. "War is a young man's game," he said with a self-deprecating shrug.

"You still haven't answered me," Elke insisted. "What side are you on?"

"I'm on the side of peace."

"That's not good enough. I suspect I'm not the only one who wants to know where you stand."

"I believe in state's rights," Patrick replied in the same carefully measured tone. "As far as I'm concerned, the government in Washington spends far too much time meddling in local affairs."

"Does that include the right to own slaves?"

Patrick finally turned his gaze on her, pinioning her with the fathomless depths in his eyes. "Mea culpa. You're right, Sunshine. I was born a southerner and I do think planters shouldn't be forced to free their slaves."

Murmurs of disapproval greeted his words. Slavery was abhorrent to the liberal-minded German settlers.

"But I'm a Texan now," Patrick continued, his gaze traveling around the room before it returned to Elke. "You know what my ranch means to me. Your friends are right to call it Pride's Passion. Nothing in the world will keep me from coming back to it. Does that answer your question?"

For the life of him, Otto didn't know what had gotten into Elke. She always seemed to enjoy Patrick's visits, even to look forward to them. And yet tonight she seemed determined to provoke Patrick into a fight.

"You may not like it, *Liebling,* and I may not like it, but Texas is a slave state," Otto said, hoping to placate her. "We should be grateful that most of the slave holders live east of the Brazos,"

He had always prided himself on being a moderate man whose one immoderate act had been his emigration with the Adelsverein Society. And truth to tell, he'd been scared to death once he realized what he was in for. He believed in pacification, not provocation.

"I don't know about the rest of you, but I plan to vote for Lincoln," he said. "He's the only moderate running for the presidency and I think he'll do everything in his power to hold the union together."

"I agree with you," William Arleheger, the cabinetmaker, chimed in. "This fellow, Lincoln, will be better for business, *nicht war?*"

To Otto's dismay, Elke jumped to her feet. Her eyes blazed, her breasts heaved, her chin jutted out. She looked thoroughly intimidating—and utterly adorable. "I don't understand any of you. It shouldn't be a matter of what's good for business, but what's good for humanity. Slavery is a cancer eating at the soul of this country. My parents came here because they believed all men should be equal in the eyes of God. They died for that belief. Most of you lost loved ones, too. And now you talk about what's good for business."

"We haven't forgotten the past. It's all the more reason to be concerned for the future," Herr Grobe said.

A zealot's ardor infused Elke's voice. "I don't know about the rest of you, but I couldn't live with myself if I didn't do everything in my power to see slavery abolished. I'll canvas the countryside if that's what it takes, hand out flyers—"

"You'll be asking for trouble," Patrick interrupted in harsh voice. "If it comes down to a choice, Texas will stand with the South."

"The German population won't vote for secession."

"If they don't, they will be surrounded by enemies."

"I'm not afraid. Besides, I can take care of myself."

"The way you took care of the Detweilers this afternoon?" Patrick asked scathingly.

This time, Otto thought with a mixture of exasperation and pride, his outspoken wife had gone too far. He had to diffuse the tension sparking between her and Patrick.

"You should have seen my Elke pointing a shotgun at the Detweilers," he said.

He had a gift for making an event more interesting in the retelling than it had been when it happened. Now he called on all those skills, dragging the story out, going for laughs until everyone chuckled but Elke and Patrick. By the time he finished, the angry questions Elke had hurled at Patrick seemed forgotten.

What in the world had gotten into her? Had the scene with the Detweiler twins upset her more than she'd admitted? Or was she angry with him for not playing the hero and taking it out on Patrick? Yes, he mused, that had to be it.

"I must apologize for my wife's behavior," Otto told Patrick after the other guests had gone and Elke had retired for the night.

"There's no need. She's entitled to her own opinions. I just wish she wasn't so damn vocal about them. I meant what I said earlier about trouble."

Otto returned to his seat by the fire. "How so?"

"It's one thing for Elke to express her views among friends who share them. It's quite another for her to run around the countryside waving an abolitionist banner."

"But surely no one would harm a woman?"

"People get hurt in a war—women and children as well as soldiers. And there are always men like the Detweilers who will use any excuse for violence."

Otto sighed heavily. For the first time since the Comanches had signed a peace treaty and the frontier had been tamed, he felt afraid. Terribly, shamefully afraid.

Suddenly Patrick leaned closer and gripped his shoulder. "I want you to promise me something."

Otto had never seen Patrick look so fierce, not even when he confronted the Detweilers. "What is it?"

"Promise that you'll look out for your wife, even if it means hog-tieing her to keep her out of trouble."

"I will," Otto replied. But deep down, he knew he wasn't up to the job.

When he joined the Adelsverein Society in 1845, he'd made the decision because there was no place in German society for a self-educated baker—no way to improve his status. At least that's what he told everyone.

The truth was that Germany had been in turmoil since the French Revolution—and the constant rumors of war had scared him pissless. He had been afraid to leave his house, afraid to go do work, and then afraid to return home. He had fled the civil unrest in his homeland, and now to his horror, it had come to his adopted country, too.

Suddenly he felt even wearier than the lateness of the hour warranted. Patrick's warning still tolled in his ears like a funeral bell as he walked down the short hall to the bedroom he and Elke shared.

Opening the door quietly, he slipped inside. Moonlight streamed across the bed where Elke lay, turning her golden hair into spun silver, her skin into precious ivory. The miracle of her beauty—of finding her in his bed night after night—sent such a powerful rush of desire to his loins that it literally staggered him.

He used to think he would live and die a bachelor. But then Elke came into his life and the only thing he'd thought about since had been her.

Before he met her, he'd never considered himself a

particularly lustful man. He used to feel sorry for men who spent more time thinking about the little head in their trousers than thinking with the big one above their shoulders. Now he could hardly wait to thrust his own little head between his wife's legs.

Stripping to his combination, he climbed into bed beside her, undid the buttons at his groin, and eased onto his side. Cradling her body so she'd be sure to feel his manhood, he cupped her breast.

"Ich liebe dich," he murmured in her ear.

"English, speak English," she muttered sleepily.

"I love you so much, Elke. Let me love you tonight." He pressed his throbbing organ into the cleft of her buttocks.

Elke had feigned sleep when Otto came into the room, hoping to avoid a conversation. She should have known he wouldn't have conversation on his mind after all that schnaps. Damn him, she thought as his sex stabbed her back—damn all men for being so unfeeling.

"Not tonight, Otto," she said. "I'm really tired."

"Not too tired for a little pleasure." He reached under her night gown and palmed the mound between her thighs.

Although she rarely withheld her favors, she squeezed her thighs together, refusing admittance to his probing fingers.

"For heaven's sake, Patrick will hear us."

Otto chuckled throatily. "I'm sure Patrick knows what happens between a husband and wife."

It was all Elke could do not to bolt from the bed. The thought that Patrick would hear their lovemaking churned in her stomach like spoiled food. She reached down and grasped Otto's wrist.

"*Not this husband and wife*. I won't let you shame me that way."

"But *Liebling—*"

"Don't *Liebling* me. Just this once can't you speak English?"

Otto recoiled as if she'd slapped him.

At first when he moved to the far side of the bed, all she felt was relief. As the seconds slipped by without him saying another word, regret replaced relief. She hadn't meant to hurt his feelings. But she knew the only way to soothe his injured pride would be to let him have his way. And that she couldn't do.

She lay by his side for what seemed an eternity, listening to him breathe, waiting until the even rhythm of his exhalations told her he'd fallen asleep.

With the best of intentions she had blundered from one disaster to another all night. She'd let Patrick kiss her and then as good as accused him of another sort of treachery in front of friends. And if that wasn't bad enough, she'd wounded Otto's pride.

Tomorrow she would have to find a way to set things right. However, experience had taught her that cruel words, like foul odors, had an unhappy way of lingering in the air.

While Patrick undressed for bed, he tried to ignore the intimate sounds coming from the other side of the wall—the low murmur of Otto and Elke's voices, the creaking of their bed springs. And yet his hearing had never seemed more acute.

He swore he could hear the swish of the covers as Otto pulled them aside. The springs creaked again and Patrick's imagination supplied an unwelcome vision of Elke locked in her husband's embrace. Had those particular sounds continued, Patrick wouldn't have been able to stop himself from running out into the night like a child fleeing a bad dream.

Blessedly, the noises ceased and silence reigned on the other side of the wall.

He hadn't realized he'd been holding his breath until he felt a tightness in his chest. Exhaling, he hung up his clothes, climbed into bed naked, and turned out the kerosene light.

His heart lurched as he smelled Elke's scent on the pillow. For a moment, he had the wild thought that she'd slipped into the room without him knowing it. He stared into the dark by the door, half expecting to see her there—hoping to see her there.

Consumed with painful longing, he gazed into the shadows, realizing he was alone—more alone than he'd ever been in his life.

The woman he loved slept in her husband's arms just a heartbeat away.

Chapter Four

On her way downstairs to begin the day's work, Elke paused to enjoy her garden. Primroses, zinnias, and daisies nodded in the gentle May breeze. The hum of bees promised a rich harvest of honey. She could almost feel the bounty of the earth welling up around her.

A mockingbird jumped up and down on a fence as if to challenge her right to this particular piece of land. Its antics brought a smile to her lips—an easy smile rather than a forced one. Her first genuine smile in a long time, she mused, noting it as a sort of milestone.

During the initial weeks after Patrick's departure, the northers sweeping down from Canada had reflected her mood. She'd performed her chores by rote, determined to get through the endless hours. But the ache of his absence had finally receded, taking with it the guilt she felt every time she thought about their kiss.

It had happened. She couldn't change that. However, she had made up her mind not to let it rule her life. And now at last, she could smile again.

She filled her apron with blossoms, intending to decorate the bakery with them, then opened the shop's back door and walked in.

Otto bent over the work table in the middle of the room, kneading a mound of dough, his broad hands and spatulate fingers making the job seem easy. Seeing her, he winked, then returned to his task.

One of his helpers adjusted the damper on the huge cast-iron stove while the other put a tray of rolls in its gaping interior. *"Guten Morgen, Frau Sonnschein,"* they said in unison.

"Good morning," she said back.

Without warning, a wave of nausea swept over her and she broke out in a sweat. The heat pouring from the ovens felt unbearable. "Are you sure the fire isn't too hot? It's terribly warm in here."

"It's no hotter than usual," Otto said, plopping the dough into a large bowl and covering it with a clean cloth. "Is something the matter, *Liebling?* You look a little green."

"I don't feel very well," Elke admitted. She touched her brow, testing it for fever.

Strange. She'd felt so good out in the garden. Now she was as nauseous as she had been during the terrible voyage from Germany. Swallowing a bitter rush of bile, she wrapped her arms protectively around her middle. "I think I had better go into the shop and sit down for a while."

Concern furrowed Otto's brow. "Do you want me to go with you?"

"I'll be fine." She gave him a reassuring smile, then quickly made her way into the bake shop.

The drawn curtains cast the room in soothing shadows. Her nausea receded in the cooler air. She took a couple of deep breaths, then, deciding she felt well enough to get on with her day, she filled vases with the flowers she'd just picked.

Another wave of nausea, this one even more devastating, brought her activity to a halt. She collapsed onto the nearest chair and lowered her head to the tabletop. It wasn't like her to be sick.

She ran down the list of illnesses that could cause her symptoms. It was too late in the year for influenza and too early for the flux. Nor were there any reported cases of typhoid or yellow fever in town. Besides, nausea wasn't her only symptom. She'd been having the strangest moods lately—laughing at nothing, weeping over even less as if her mind had become unhinged.

Suddenly it hit her. She'd heard other women describing the same symptoms.

Good heavens! When had she last had her monthlies?

During her first few years of marriage she'd kept careful track of her bleeding. Every month she'd hope against hope that there would be no telltale stain in her drawers, no cramping accompanied by a gush of blood.

Every month, she'd been sorely disappointed. The infants she had held so lovingly over the years had all belonged to other, more fortunate women. And so she'd stopped keeping track—stopped dreaming.

Although she had never discussed it with Otto, she knew he shared her disappointment. How sad that they felt so uncomfortable talking about the things that mattered most.

When the extra bedrooms they'd planned for children seemed to shriek with silent rebuke every time she entered them, she had put them to other uses. Before she knew it even Otto had started referring to one as her sewing room and the other as the guest room. But now, unless she missed her guess, she would have to put her sewing basket someplace else!

Her hands dropped to her still-flat stomach and she gazed down at herself in wonder. How far along was she? One month? Two? At least two if memory served her right. It must have happened right after Patrick left.

Could the day that began as one of the worst in her life have turned out to be the best?

She and Otto had accompanied Patrick to the stage stop at Otto's insistence. Patrick's farewell to her had been rigidly correct. He had shaken her hand, boarded the stagecoach, and ridden out of town without once looking back—and her heart had cracked in two. She had bitten back tears she dare not shed, hurried back to work, and avoided Otto until the dinner hour forced her into his company.

Then they had tiptoed around each other like polite strangers. On the rare occasions when their eyes met by accident, his had looked as mortally injured as a gut-shot deer. Just as she had feared, the cruel words she had said in bed the night before seemed to linger in the air.

Although Otto always had a hearty appetite, he barely touched his meal. Thinking he was still upset by her refusal to make love, she finally said, "I'm sorry about last night."

Otto turned crimson and his gaze lowered. "I am the one who should be apologizing. No woman wants to sleep with a coward."

"What in the world are you talking about?"

"It's true. I am a coward."

"Don't be ridiculous. All Fredericksburg looks up to you. You're one of the most admired men in town."

"Hush, *Liebchen*. I won't let you make excuses for me—not anymore. And I can't go on making them for myself, either. I should have sent the Detweilers packing instead of hiding behind your skirts while you and Patrick ran them off."

"Don't be silly. I know you aren't comfortable with guns."

She hoped to ease his mind. Instead he looked even more shame-faced. "It's not just a matter of being uncomfortable with guns. It's so much more than that." He covered his face with his hands and groaned out loud. "I should have told you this before we wed."

"Told me what?"

He groaned again deep in his throat. "I should have told you . . . only I knew you wouldn't have me if I did. You see, Elke, you married a man who is scared of his own shadow. All my life, I have lived with this terrible fear—of everything—even of the dark. Last night after you went to bed, Patrick warned me that there will be trouble ahead. He made me promise to take care of you. But you are the brave one in the family. Not me! I'm a poor excuse for a man. I wouldn't blame you if you never let me into your bed again."

Otto's revelation breached her heart in a way that all his professions of love had never accomplished. He had given her a rare glimpse beyond the exterior he showed the world—a glimpse at the vulnerable being inside the accomplished man.

"There's nothing wrong with being afraid," she had declared. "It doesn't make you a coward. It only makes you human." She had risen from the dinner table, hurried to his side, and cradled his head against her breasts, feeling an outpouring of sympathy that could almost have passed for love.

And then she had taken Otto into their bedroom to show him—in the most graphic way a woman has at her command—that his confession of weakness hadn't disgusted her. That, quite the contrary, it had touched her heart.

He'd been so eager, so grateful. For once there had been no discomfort when he entered her, no need to use the jar of lanolin he kept by the bed. Her body had accepted his more willingly than it ever had before.

That night their lovemaking—gentled by mutual understanding and forgiveness—had been so sweet that even now the memory of it felt like balm.

Yes, she thought, it must have happened that night. Her long-barren womb had finally welcomed his seed, even as she had finally welcomed his love.

Seven more months and she'd hold her own sweet babe in her arms.

The knowledge rocketed through her with the explosive excitement of a Roman candle. Her body was finally going to fulfill its destiny. At last, she would be a woman in every way.

Mother. She was going to be a mother. And Otto would be a *father.* How much richer and more complete those words seemed than husband and wife. They would be a real family.

Her imagination took flight with images of their fu-

ture. She saw the two of them standing side by side—
Otto rigid with pride, her melting with happiness—
while Pastor Basse christened their child. Why, she
thought, counting the months on her fingers, she might
even have the baby before Christmas. What a sweet cel-
ebration it would be—and all the Christmases to come.

Although she had never been able to love Otto as he
deserved, she knew she would adore his child. Their
baby would unite them far more than the vows they had
spoken in church ten years ago.

She touched her stomach again, wondering why she
didn't feel a telltale bulge. Could something be wrong?
Fear rose up her throat. Was twenty-seven too old to
have a baby? *Nonsense* she told herself. Many of her
friends had borne children on into their thirties.

But a cautious inner voice reminded her that those
women had all borne their first child in their teens.
Were her bones, muscles, and tendons still elastic
enough to accommodate the changes of childbearing?

Arching her back like a cat, she touched her hands to
the floor, flattening her palms. She was as limber and
lithe as she'd been at seventeen. Besides, God wouldn't
grant such a gift and then take it away.

Feeling someone pinch her bottom, she bolted upright
and whirled around to defend herself from the intruder,
to see Otto's smiling face.

"I'm sorry, *Liebling*. It was just too tempting a target
to resist. Did you lose something?"

"Only my mind."

"That's not funny."

Seeing his broad brow knit with worry, she couldn't

help laughing. "Actually, I *have* lost something. I completely lost track of time."

"I heard the church bells not long ago. It can't be much past eight."

"I don't mean this morning. I'm talking about the last couple of months."

Otto couldn't have looked more bewildered. He crossed the floor to his prize porcelain stove and laid his hand on its cool surface. "You're certainly in a peculiar mood, *Liebchen*. It's not like you to leave the stove cold and the coffeepot empty. What will our customers say?"

"Who cares what they say? Let's not open today at all."

"Now I know you're not well. How can we make a profit if we don't open?"

"For once let's forget all about making a profit. Why don't we go on a picnic?"

"Can this be my Elke speaking? You love profits and hate picnics."

"All right. Forget the picnic. But I do feel like celebrating. Let's dance." She grabbed his arms and waltzed him around the room, laughing gleefully.

Despite the puzzlement in his eyes, he tried to keep up with her flying feet. "I've never seen you like this. What's gotten into you?"

"You've gotten into me," she answered truthfully, coming to such an abrupt halt that he almost knocked her over.

"Please, Elke, stop this behavior. You're worrying me."

"I don't mean to." She turned from side to side in front of him. "Do you think I look different?"

"You're not green anymore."

"This morning wasn't the first time I felt sick. The last few weeks there have been lots of times when I thought I was going to throw up."

"*Gott in Himmel,* then you are ill. You should have said so sooner. I wouldn't have expected you to work." Taking her arms, he guided her to a chair and lowered her into it.

She longed to hug her precious secret close a little longer. However, it wasn't fair to Otto. After all, she reminded herself, but for him she wouldn't have a secret. "You really don't have any idea what's ailing me, do you?"

He shook his head.

"I'm not sick, Otto. I'm with child!"

She could see revelation dawning in his eyes. They narrowed, then widened, and finally, they sparkled with tears.

"How can it be after so many years? I thought I couldn't make a baby."

She grinned impishly, feeling closer to him than she ever had. "Why not? You have all the right equipment and it's in perfect working order."

"Are you sure?"

"We could always go upstairs right now and see."

He blushed from his collar to his hairline. "That's not what I mean. Are you sure you're in the family way?"

"As sure as I can be."

"Oh, my." He wrung his hands together, looking for all the world like a little boy who has been caught invading the cookie jar. "Are you all right? Do you want me to get the doctor?"

She burst out laughing. "It's a little early for that. The baby isn't due for seven months."

He reached down, pulled her into his arms and held her tight. For once she didn't mind that the top of her head was two inches higher than the top of his, or that her arms couldn't quite span his broad back. He wasn't anything like the Prince Charming of her girlish dreams, but he had given her a gift more precious than a fairy-tale palace.

"I love you," he said.

Her heart swelled with tenderness and gratitude. "I love you, too, Otto," she told him for the very first time.

Charlotte Devereux certainly knew how to make an entrance, Patrick thought, watching her sweep into his parents' dining room. The girl's timing had been impeccable.

The other guests were already at the table. Miss Devereux was the cynosure of all their eyes as the butler led her to the only empty chair. Fortuitously it happened to be the one next to his.

His mother must be matchmaking again, he thought with wry cynicism. Since his return to Natchez a month ago, Elizabeth Pride had made his marriage her primary goal. His older brothers already had half-grown children and his two younger sisters were happily wed. His mother wanted—no—she *expected* him to follow in their footsteps.

So far, though, none of the eligible women he'd met had managed to banish Elke from his thoughts. He still dreamed about her at night and worried about her by day, wondering it Otto kept her safe and well.

He'd just about despaired of finding a woman who could touch his inner core the way Elke did. But his mother hadn't given up. And this time she just might have succeeded, he thought, taking a second much longer look at his table companion.

Miss Devereux was petitely curvaceous. He felt quite certain he could span her waist with his hands and yet the creamy breasts swelling over the top of her gown would certainly fill his palms.

Her hair, a rich brown the color of mahogany, had been artfully arranged in curls that cascaded around her shoulders. The almond eyes staring at him with open curiosity were an unusual shade of amber. Her nose had an impudent upward tilt—her lips a decidedly kissable pout—and she had matching dimples on either side of her mouth. She looked good enough to eat, a task he wouldn't mind taking on but for her age. She couldn't be more than seventeen.

As she took her chair he saw she was that rare well-schooled Southern belle who could sit down to dinner dressed in full evening regalia, from a deep décolletage to a hoop skirt, without exposing her breasts or upsetting the wineglasses.

She settled on the damask upholstered chair as easily as a bee landing on a flower. Favoring him with a smile that deepened her dimples and revealed delicate white teeth, she snapped her fan open with the practiced ease of an experienced temptress.

If her velvet gown had been half an inch lower, he felt certain he would have been able to see her nipples. A titillating thought indeed.

He grinned at his silent *double entendre.*

"La, sir, what do you find so amusing?"

"Believe me, my dear Miss Devereux, you don't want to know."

Her eyes danced with mischief. "Oh but I do, Mr. Pride. I want to know everything about you—every last little detail, no matter how personal."

He couldn't have been more surprised if she had asked him to drop his drawers so she could inspect his private parts. Her dusky tone gave her words an unexpected eroticism. She might have only been seventeen but there could be no question that she was all woman.

"You strike me as the sort of lady who could get a man to reveal all his secrets," he teased.

"And you look like a man who has a few."

For a moment, he couldn't help wondering what she would say if he confessed to being in love with a married woman. But then, hearing Charlotte's throaty laughter, he banished Elke from his thoughts.

She leaned closer and gazed into his eyes. "You don't remember me, do you?"

"I'm afraid not. I haven't been home for twelve years. I imagine you were still in diapers when I left."

"Not exactly. I was seven." She batted her lashes, displaying the thick black fringes to their best advantage. "I certainly haven't forgotten you. You came to say goodbye to my parents before you went off to war and I was terribly smitten with your uniform. The gold braid drove me wild. I asked for your epaulets and threw a fit when you refused to part with them."

So she was *that* Charlotte Devereux—and not seventeen but almost twenty. He could hardly equate the spoiled chubby brat who had to be forcibly removed from her parents' drawing room with the desirable young woman by his side. She was living breathing proof that an ugly duckling could indeed become a swan.

He lowered his voice so only she could hear. "At the time, I thought you needed a spanking—and I would have enjoyed taking on the job. Are you still that hard to handle?"

Her cheeks colored beguilingly. "You'll just have to wait and see, Mr. Pride."

In the years that Patrick had lived and toiled in Texas, he'd all but forgotten the sybaritic pleasures of a sophisticated cuisine, fine wines, and a beautiful dinner companion. Now he indulged himself in all three.

The pompano was superb, the French Chardonnay even better. But he barely tasted them because the lovely and charming Charlotte Devereux held his attention captive.

Although custom demanded that he divide his time equally between the woman on his right and the one on his left, Patrick gave custom short shrift. Tonight the elderly Mrs. Cantewell would just have to fend for herself, he decided, abandoning himself to the delights of Charlotte's company.

She was vivacious, high-spirited, an accomplished flirt, and she didn't seem to have a serious thought in her pretty head—a definite plus from his point of view. He'd grown weary of the talk about war, the ranting about abolition, the speculation about the presidential race that had monopolized every social gathering he'd attended since the Republican convention chose Abraham Lincoln as its presidential nominee.

Every man young enough to sit a horse had boasted of whipping those damn Yankees a few weeks after war broke out. Even men old enough to know better let dreams of glory rule their minds. They seemed to think war was a gallant endeavor while he knew it was blood and horror, pain and loss.

But his delightful companion had a gift for making him forget all that. She even made him forget Elke.

By the time dessert came to the table, they were on a first-name basis. "Your parents seem very happy to have you home, Patrick," Charlotte said with a graceful nod toward the head of the table, "but no happier than I am. I hope you won't think me bold, but you're the best-looking man in Natchez—and a hero, too, so I hear."

Patrick was indisputably brave, intelligent, hard-working, and well read—but he was also a man. He responded to flattery like any other member of his sex, by deciding that the flatterer had an unusual amount of common sense. In that moment, he saw Charlotte as more than just a pretty face and a desirable body. He saw her as a woman of substance.

"I appreciate the sentiment, but most men who are regarded as heroes have had the misfortune of being in the wrong place at the right time, and have merely done everything in their power to save their own skins."

"You didn't get a wound like this trying to save your own skin." Charlotte snapped her fan shut and employed it to touch his scar. The gesture was strangely intimate, as if they had already moved beyond the roles of mere acquaintances. "You're far too modest. My father tells me you were given a huge land grant in appreciation of your exploits."

"Ten thousand acres," he replied with justifiable pride.

He'd never forgotten the scene in his father's legal offices the day before he'd gone off to war. "You're making a terrible mistake," Lamar Pride had declared, a fierce scowl molding his patrician features. "I didn't pay for your college education to see you get blown up in some damn senseless war."

"I'm sorry you feel that way, Father," Patrick had replied. "I know you hoped I'd follow in your footsteps and read law. But I just can't see myself living out my life in some office. Besides, someone has to fight our country's battles."

"That someone doesn't have to be my son. And don't try to cloak your juvenile desire for adventure in patriotism. You're looking for excitement, Patrick." Lamar had let go a sigh pregnant with disappointment. "I'm afraid you'll never amount to anything if you persist in this ill-advised venture."

Now, seated at his parents' table in their Natchez mansion, Patrick couldn't help taking satisfaction in the knowledge that he had prospered beyond his own wildest dreams, let along his father's dire predictions.

Charlotte's widening eyes at the mention of ten thousand acres enhanced his pleasure. Clearly, she was impressed.

"But that's a huge plantation," she gasped, confirming his assumption. "It must take hundreds of slaves to work the place."

"It's not a plantation, Charlotte. It's a ranch. I don't have any slaves. I employ two dozen cowboys."

"What in the world is a *cow boy?*" She enunciated it

as two separate words. "I've never heard the expression before."

"That's what Texans call the men who work with cattle. You see, I don't have slaves because I don't grow cotton. I raise longhorn cattle."

"Well, I declare! Aren't you just the smartest thing. I'm so tired of hearing about slavery and abolition and how we just can't get along without darkies to work in the cotton fields. Why, this is the first time in months that I've sat through a dinner without some tedious discourse on the subject. Now tell me all about your—what did you call it?—your ranch."

Thank heaven for a woman who wasn't interested in disputing his every opinion the way Elke did, he thought. Charlotte was the antithesis of Elke from the tips of her toes to the top of her head.

"I'd love to tell you all about the P bar P, if you're sure I won't bore you."

"Why sugar, you could never bore me." He hadn't realized how much he missed southern accents until now. Charlotte's voice oozed like melted honey as she said, "What does P bar P stand for?"

"I'm afraid I wasn't very original when I named the ranch. I just used my initials. The P bar P is the brand I used on my cattle; however, my German friends in Fredericksburg call the spread Pride's Passion."

Her eyes sparkled even brighter than the jewels at her throat and ears. "Is that because you're such a passionate man?"

"Now *you'll* just have to wait and see, Charlotte," he replied, enjoying the way his riposte made her cheeks color.

"I hope I won't have to wait too long," she murmured. Clearly, she was no novice at flirtation. "You said you were going to tell me all about your ranch."

Patrick didn't have to be asked again. Nothing pleased him more than having an opportunity to describe the place that had occupied his life for the last twelve years. He launched into a detailed account that included the terrain, the cattle operation from calving to marketing, and concluded with a verbal depiction of the house that was his pride and joy.

While he talked Charlotte seemed unaware of anyone or anything else. She kept those unusual amber eyes riveted on his face as if he were the most interesting, erudite, fascinating man she'd ever met.

"I hope you won't consider my telling you this a breach of etiquette," he concluded, "but I have the only indoor water closet west of the Brazos, complete with a sink, a zinc-lined tub for bathing, and a commode."

"It sounds perfectly marvelous—and practical, too, considering you don't have slaves to carry the—ah—the slops. I had no idea Texas was so modern."

Charlotte had listened to Patrick's long diatribe with growing boredom. His talk of branding cattle—dipping them, feeding them, ad nauseum—had practically put her to sleep.

Of course it was only natural for men to have concerns that a well-bred woman couldn't possibly share. Her mother had taught her to look interested when men talked about them. It was a simple matter of keeping your eyes fixed on a man's face while you let your mind drift.

Hers had. She'd been wondering how much longer

she could sit still considering Ella Mae had laced her corset so tightly she could barely breathe. She'd also been thinking of the new gowns she had on order at Worth's in London, and hoping they would arrive soon—especially the emerald peau de soie that promised to do so much for her coloring. But the mention of an indoor water closet quickly reawakened her interest.

Her father had never gotten around to installing one even though Windmere was one of the most prosperous plantations in the South. He said it would cost too much money, and in view of all the talk of freeing the slaves, he wasn't about to spend a penny needlessly.

Her father, bless his heart, was hopelessly old-fashioned compared to a man like Patrick Pride!

"Perhaps Mother and I could come visit you some-day. I'd love to see your ranch and meet a real cowboy." And, although she didn't say it out loud, she'd especially love to try out the water closet.

"I'd like that very much. In the meantime, though, I intend to ask your father's permission to call on you."

Now that was really exciting, Charlotte thought, feeling her pulse quicken. Patrick Pride had been the talk of Natchez for weeks. He was wealthy, handsome as all get out, and every unmarried girl in town had set her cap for him.

How should she respond to what he'd just said? she mused. With a shy flutter of her lashes, a lowering of her eyes, a surprised little gasp? Or should she boldly stare him in the eye and say what had been on her mind ever since she sat down at the table?

Suddenly she thought she knew just which response would intrigue him the most.

"I'm relieved to hear you say that, Patrick, because if you didn't call on me, I'd just have to ask your father for permission to call on you!"

Chapter Five

Elke stood naked in front of the cheval mirror in her bedroom, absorbed by the physical changes five months of pregnancy had wrought. Her breasts were larger, webbed with tiny blue veins, and her nipples had darkened. Her navel had lost its deep indentation and her formerly flat abdomen swelled below her rib cage like a miniature hillock.

Although the transformation couldn't have been more normal, she had given up hope of seeing it happen to her. How she loved being pregnant.

For the first time in her entire life, she felt grateful for her five feet eight inches. She was carrying more gracefully than the shorter women she knew. Even so, she had reached the stage where she could barely get into her own clothes.

Knowing Otto was waiting, she hurried into her camisole, drawers, stockings, and high-buttoned shoes. She retrieved a freshly laundered blouse from the *Kleidershrank* and put it on, leaving the bottom three buttons undone. Stepping into her second best gray serge skirt, she lifted the waist over her swollen belly and barely managed to close the fastening.

A corset would have helped narrow the gap, but she and Otto had agreed that she shouldn't wear one for fear of constricting the fetus. As if to affirm their wisdom, she felt the child move—and thrilled to the sensation.

She had experienced the first quickening of life a month earlier. The bigger she got, the stronger the flutters had become. Now she could almost tell if the baby was just stretching or if it had shifted position.

She could hardly wait until the child grew strong enough to assert itself with a lusty kick, even though she knew she'd be big as a house by then. Other first-time mothers might rail against losing their figures. She gloried in it. What did a waistline matter compared to the miracle of bringing a new life into the world? She had never felt better—or been happier.

From the morning she gave Otto the news, his behavior had been exemplary. Some men might be reticent about their wife's condition. Not him. He boasted of it as if he were the first man in the world to sire a child—and was so sweet doing it that no one seemed to mind.

He fussed over her like a mother hen, checking on her hourly when she worked in the bake shop. Although the doctor had told them not to worry, Otto had even insisted they give up their marital relations for fear of hurting the baby.

How many men would be so considerate? she mused, taking a shawl from a peg on the wall. Certainly not Patrick Pride! Recalling his passionate kiss, she felt certain he would still be taking her to bed, glorying in her swollen breasts, even suckling at them.

An unbidden thrill of pleasure coalesced in her loins at the thought. She shook her head in frustration, almost undoing the tightly coiled chignon at her nape. How could she forget—even for a second—that she carried Otto's child?

Heaven knew Patrick had long since put her out of *his* mind. They had only heard from him once in the five months he'd been gone. He'd sent Otto a couple of books accompanied by a brief letter saying he had arrived home safely and was completely caught up in Natchez's social life. Three issues of Godey's had been tucked into the bottom of the package, as if they'd been an afterthought.

No, she mused, Patrick certainly wasn't wasting any of his time thinking about what had happened between them. She'd be damned if she'd waste any more of hers. Wrapping her shawl around her shoulders as if to armor herself against her traitorous mind, she joined Otto in the parlor.

Pride in his impending fatherhood had brought a new straightness to his spine and an almost permanent smile to his lips. "What took you so long, *Liebchen?* I was beginning to worry."

Elke grinned. "I'm beginning to feel like a sausage and I can hardly get into my clothes."

"Then we'll just have to get you some new ones. Nothing is too good for my wife, especially when she is so beautiful that I'm the envy of every man in town."

Her pregnancy had made Otto foolish with love, she thought fondly. "The truth is, I look like a cow."

She picked up the abolitionist pamphlets that had arrived from Boston earlier that week, stuffed them into her reticule, then turned back to Otto. "You really don't need to go with me today. You work so hard all week, I hate to have you spend your Sundays driving me around the county while I hand these out."

"I wouldn't dream of letting you do it on your own. Besides, I could use the fresh air." Otto hoped he could hide his fear from Elke—a fear that gnawed at his innards, denying all his efforts to subdue it.

Since Elke learned of Abraham Lincoln's nomination for the presidency, she had insisted on passing out abolitionist tracts to all their customers when the bakery was open, and to the rest of the county when it wasn't. At first he hadn't worried about her, provided that another woman went along for company. After all, he'd told himself, Elke could handle a horse and buggy better than most men, certainly better than he!

However, as the proslavery forces gathered strength and unity, it had become painfully clear that the German population in and around Fredericksburg stood alone in its antislavery stance. The talk in the bakery had become increasingly ugly as southern-born farmers, ranchers, and German settlers clashed over the coming election.

When, one by one, Elke's friends had begged off from the Sunday excursions, he'd implored her to stop, too. *"Liebchen,"* he had said, "you can't change anyone's mind, so why go on taking risks?"

"What risks? You heard the doctor tell me there's no harm in an occasional buggy ride."

"I'm not talking about the ride. You hear how our customers argue. This politicking of yours is bound to make a few people angry."

"I keep on thinking how I would feel if I were black and pregnant. I couldn't live with myself if I didn't do what I could to ensure that every child—white and black alike—grows up free."

Although he despaired at her words, he had never loved her more. "If it means that much to you, I'll just have to go along to make sure you're safe," he had answered bravely, even though his heart knocked in his chest like a woodpecker drilling a hole.

In the weeks since, he had lived up to his word. Thank heaven Elke was oblivious to what it had cost him. Driving the buggy to outlying homesteads Sunday after Sunday had taken every ounce of courage he could muster.

He would no sooner leave town than he'd have the eerie sensation that they were being watched. He lived in the constant fear that some proslavery group would ride out from behind a rocky outcrop and . . . do God knew what.

But he hadn't confided his fears to Elke. He had already confided far too much about that particular subject.

Otto couldn't help comparing her bravery to his own trepidation—and suffering in the comparison. She faced the unknown dangers of childbirth without a qualm, while he broke into a cold sweat at taking a Sunday buggy ride in the country.

This morning in church he had prayed for courage. But God had yet to hear him. His knees felt weak as water as he followed Elke downstairs and around to the front of the bakery where he'd left the horse and buggy.

"It's a lovely day for a drive," she said, taking his

arm and climbing into the seat. She settled her skirts while he climbed up beside her, took the reins, and urged the mare forward.

"Yes, it is," he agreed, peering at the August sky, looking for any sign of the devastating storms that could appear almost without warning to flatten crops and rip roofs from buildings. How like Elke it was to appreciate the beauty of the fleecy white clouds studding the sky, while he saw them as harbingers of a killer wind that might catch them out in the open.

He repressed the shudder the thought engendered. He had damn well better act like a man even though he didn't feel like one, he chided himself, loosening his death grip on the reins. He was determined to be worthy of the brave woman by his side, and the child in her womb—if it killed him.

Patrick knotted a silk cravat at his throat, then held his arms out while Jonah, an old family retainer, helped him into his new black cutaway.

"You sho do look fine," Jonah exclaimed, his seamed black face breaking into a toothy grin. "You'all are gonna have to chase the ladies off with a stick tonight, sir."

At least one lady in particular, Patrick thought with wry amusement.

Without his quite knowing how it had happened, he and Charlotte had become a couple. It almost seemed as if the doyennes of Natchez were conspiring to get them together. After that first dinner, she had appeared at each and every event on his social calendar, from fox hunts to formal balls.

"Will you be needin' anything else before you'all go out, sir?" Jonah asked.

"No, and thank you for your help," Patrick replied, dismissing the elderly servant with a nod.

He waited until Jonah left, then took one last look at himself in the gold-framed pier glass opposite his bed. He could hardly equate the elegantly garbed man gazing back at him with the one who rode the range in heavy leather chaps and a sweat-stained shirt.

Although Pride's Passion and Natchez couldn't be more than five hundred miles distant as the crow flies, they were worlds apart in style. West of the Brazos, a man dressed for comfort, safety, and convenience. Patrick hated to think what would happen to his hide if he rode into a mesquite-filled draw in an outfit like the one he'd just put on—or how his hired hands would carry on if they saw him in it. He could just picture Rio De Vargas mincing up to him in broken-down boots and asking for the first dance.

Patrick had had to reaccustom himself to dressing for appearance' sake. His new suits had been carefully created to project an aura of unassailable dignity and prosperity. The tailor had fussed over details such as the height of a collar, the width of a lapel, and the set of the seam, as if getting them right were a matter of life and death.

Shakespeare had it all wrong when he wrote, "Vanity, thy name is woman." It was equally true for men, too— except for the hardy breed living on the frontier.

Seeing the appreciation in his mother's eyes as he

descended the stairs to the spacious entry hall, he supposed the visits to his father's tailor had been worth the effort. Elizabeth was positively beaming.

"You're as handsome as your father was at your age," she said, taking both of his hands and leading him out to the veranda to wait for the carriage that would take him to the Devereuxs'.

"Now, Mother," he demurred, feeling a vague discomfort.

Although he truly enjoyed seeing his parents again, it felt strange to be living under their roof instead of his own—and even stranger to have his mother treat him like the twenty-year-old he'd been when he left.

"Don't *now, Mother* me," Elizabeth replied, straightening his cravat. "Besides, I'm not the only one who thinks you're handsome. Charlotte's mother tells me the dear girl is in danger of swooning every time she sees you."

"Then I hope her mother keeps the smelling salts handy, because Charlotte and I sure have been seeing a lot of each other."

"If that's a complaint, I don't want to hear it. There isn't a lovelier young woman in the entire South. She could have any man she wanted—and don't you forget it."

Patrick knew better than to argue with his mother. Beneath her velvet drawl and her ladylike ways lurked a will of iron. However, he couldn't help wondering why Charlotte had set her cap for him. She must have had other more likely suitors.

His feelings toward her troubled him even more.

Common sense told him he wouldn't find a more desirable female if he searched all Mississippi. Charlotte epitomized the best of traditional southern femininity. She had been to the manor born, and she possessed an abundance of breeding, charm, and grace. He enjoyed her company, and God knew she filled a man's eyes.

So why couldn't he bring himself to ask for her hand?

Because you love Elke, the unbidden answer whispered at the back of his mind. Miss Sunshine wouldn't leave him alone no matter how hard he tried to exile her from his thoughts.

On those rare occasions when he stayed home in the evening, he'd written her a dozen different missiles— polite letters inquiring after her health and more honest ones revealing his true feelings. But he'd burned them all. If Elke had wanted even the most casual correspondence, she would have written to thank him for the magazines he'd sent.

"Did you hear me, Son?" His mother's voice distracted him.

"I'm sorry, Mother. I wasn't paying attention."

"You looked a thousand miles away."

Not a thousand, he thought. Fredericksburg was a lot closer than that.

"I asked you to give my regards to the Devereuxs."

"That goes without saying. I still don't understand why you and Father aren't attending the dinner party, too."

Elizabeth took his chin in her hand the way she used to when he was a boy, only now she had to reach up. "Your father said the same thing. Sometimes you men can be so obtuse. We aren't going because it's high time you and Charlotte were by yourselves for a while. I'm sure you two have a lot to talk about. I have it on good authority that her parents won't object if you take her for a long stroll in the garden after dinner."

"And what authority might that be?"

"Why, her mother's, silly boy. Hortense Devereux and I would just love to be related to each other." His mother grinned as shyly as a fox leaving a chicken coop. "By marriage."

Happily, the arrival of the carriage cut the conversation short. As Patrick got in, he had the feeling that events were spinning out of his control.

Hortense Devereux gazed at her daughter with a worried frown. "Are you sure you know what you're doing?"

"I'm sure." Charlotte nodded her head up and down vigorously.

Resplendent in a maribou-trimmed peignoir, she was having her hair put up by her maid, Ella Mae, while her mother watched.

It was clear where Charlotte got her looks. Perhaps it was their physical resemblance, perhaps it was a mother's instinctive closeness to her last born, but Charlotte had always been Hortense's favorite.

"Now you be still, Miss Charlotte," Ella Mae muttered. "How you 'spect me to fix yo hair when you be bouncin' around lak that?"

Mother and daughter ignored the maid as their conversation continued.

"I don't know how I let you talk me into it," Hortense said.

"Do you think Daddy will catch on?"

"Your father is a very trusting man. He'd never imagine you capable of dreaming up such a scheme. If the timing isn't just right, you could be in real trouble."

"Pish, tosh," Charlotte replied with an insouciant shrug. "The only danger is that I might lose my virginity. And frankly, I can't wait."

"If your father could hear you, he'd lock you away for the night." Hortense wrung her hands. She had never worried about her other children the way she worried about Charlotte. She'd never had to. "You've had so many marriage proposals. For the life of me, I can't see why you have your heart set on a man who doesn't seem to share your feelings."

"He *does* share my feelings. He just doesn't know it yet. And you'd have to be blind not to know why I want him."

"There's no denying he's handsome. I always did like a tall man. They look so much better in their clothes."

"And out of them, too, I hope."

Hortense bolted to her feet. "If you were younger, I'd wash your mouth out with soap."

"I prefer champagne."

Hortense bit her lip. She had spoiled Charlotte, and now the girl really had the bit between her teeth. Charlotte had no reason to think she couldn't have anything she wanted—including Patrick Pride. But it was much too late to start telling her *no* now. "You really are dreadful."

"Not dreadful, Mother. Just wildly, deliriously in love."

"*Infatuated* is more like it. And you don't seem to

care one whit for my feelings. I shall miss you terribly if you go to Texas with him."

"At least I'll be out of danger if war comes. We both agree on that."

Hortense closed her eyes and let her breath out in an audible sigh. Charlotte certainly knew how to play her trump card. The thought of exposing any of her children to a war between the states had kept Hortense up many a night. "If I didn't agree with you, I would never have entertained the thought of helping you tonight."

"I was afraid you were trying to back out."

"I want you out of harm's way. And I know Patrick will take good care of you." Hortense glanced at the or-molu clock on the mantel. "He'll be here any minute. I'll leave now so you can finish getting ready. And for heaven's sake, be careful tonight."

After her mother left, Charlotte took her own sweet time dressing for the *en famille* dinner with Patrick Pride. She firmly believed that it never hurt to keep a man waiting. It just made him all the more appreciative when you finally showed up.

Besides, hadn't he kept her waiting for weeks?

The fact that he hadn't yet proposed was becoming a public embarrassment. She could just imagine her friends saying, "This time Charlotte has set her sights too high." Or even worse, "Charlotte waited too long for the right man to come along and now she's practically an old maid."

Well, the right man *had* come along and she intended to do everything in her power to see he didn't get away. All Patrick needed was a little push, and she knew just how to give him one. However, her mother had been right about one thing. It was going to be dangerous. *Deliciously dangerous.*

She could hardly wait.

"Lace my stays tighter," she told Ella Mae.

"Now, Miss Charlotte, how you gonna eat iffen I lace them any tighter?"

"Tighter," Charlotte demanded, dropping her peignoir to the floor, presenting her bare back and clutching the bed post to steady herself. As Ella Mae did her bidding, Charlotte blew out all her breath and sucked in her stomach as hard as she could.

"I'll have to break your bones iffen you want me to do any better than that!" Ella Mae declared.

For once Charlotte agreed. Stars were swimming in front of her eyes. She blinked rapidly to clear them away.

Looking down, she could see that her waist looked a teensy-weensy bit smaller—not the impossible thirteen inches that had been declared ideal in Godey's but surely no more than seventeen.

She could barely breathe and she certainly couldn't eat. Why did looking beautiful have to be so much work—and so painful?

She was damn sure Patrick hadn't spent more than an hour getting ready to see her. All he had to do was wash, shave, put on a suit, and run a comb through his hair to look like the answer to a girl's prayers. Meanwhile, she had spent the entire day getting ready—bathing, buffing, and primping until her entire body had been cleansed and polished from the curls piled atop on her head to her toenails.

"Are you daydreamin', Miss Charlotte, or are you gonna faint?" Ella Mae asked.

"I'm fine. Just get the new silk Worth for me."

While Ella Mae went to fetch the gown from the dressing room, Charlotte reached down into her camisole and elevated her breasts above its embroidered edge.

Gazing down, she smiled. The tighter Ella Mae laced her, the more her breasts seemed to stand out. This evening, they were definitely at attention.

Ella Mae returned with the dress and lowered it over Charlotte's head, being careful not to muss her curls. Then she began the painstaking task of closing the tiny seed pearl buttons that ran down the back.

When Ella Mae finished, Charlotte flounced into her dressing room to look at herself in the mirror. She had been right to order the emerald-green peau de soie from Charles Worth, she thought, admiring the way the color enhanced her eyes and hair.

The décolletage was deeper than any she had worn before, cutting slant-wise across her breasts to reveal her creamy cleavage to its best advantage. Her skirt, supported by a hoop, measured a full ten yards at its base. It swayed when she walked, revealing her well-turned ankles and delicate feet.

"You sho be lookin' good, Miss Charlotte," Ella Mae said. "But it seems like you goin' to a lot of trouble for a family dinner. Why you wearin' your new dress?"

Charlotte gave her a cryptic smiled. "It's bait. I'm going fishing tonight."

"Your mama gonna tan your hide iffen you do something like that when you're all dressed up."

Charlotte couldn't help laughing at the consternation on the maid's face. "Don't you worry. My mother knows all about it. Now go on downstairs, see if Mr. Pride is here, and come right back up and tell me."

After Ella Mae left, Charlotte went to her dressing table and carefully applied a little rouge to her cheeks and lips. Then she put on the topaz earrings and necklace that matched her eyes. She had never looked better, she told herself.

But would the six-foot-two-inch fish take the bait?

Chapter Six

The hour-long drive to Windmere heightened Patrick's tension. He was no closer to reaching a decision about Charlotte Devereux than he had been the first night they met. How could a man who had been so decisive on the battlefield, be turned to mental mush by a beautiful woman?

One thing was crystal clear. His mother and hers had run out of patience. Undoubtedly Charlotte herself had, too. He couldn't go on seeing her unless he was prepared to ask for her hand.

His emotions had never been in more of a muddle. Would it be fair to marry a woman he didn't love? Given the propinquity of living together—having children together—would love grow? If only he could be sure.

With every passing year his longing for children increased. He had but to close his eyes to picture himself riding the P bar P with a half-grown son by his side, a youth who would appreciate the hard-won legacy of the land.

In addition to Charlotte's more obvious charms, he couldn't ignore the fact that the Devereux women were good breeders. Charlotte had five older siblings, all married, and more nieces and nephews than she could count on the fingers of both hands.

Her full breasts and hips promised the fecundity that he demanded from a prospective mate. Any man worth his salt would jump at the chance to bed her. Certainly his pulse had quickened more than once in her company and he'd felt a stirring in his loins. But damn it all, lust wasn't love. Was he a dreamer to think he could have both?

He sighed heavily as the phaeton turned onto Windmere's brick drive. A quarter of a mile away, the mansion's pillared facade gleamed ghostly white in the moonlight. He had visited Windmere several times in his youth and had half expected to find the place diminished when viewed through adult eyes. But it seemed more imposing than ever.

Seated on a bluff overlooking the Mississippi, it was surrounded by hundreds of acres of cotton fields. Patrick couldn't see the slave quarters from the driveway but knowing they were nearby oppressed him.

The Devereuxs' wealth had been built with the sweat, blood, and toil of slaves. During past visits he had seen black men, women—and even children—toiling under an overseer's whip.

He hadn't been affronted by the sight then. Now, as Windmere's opulence grew ever closer, the memory was utterly repugnant. He finally saw the injustice of what his fellow southerners referred to as "their peculiar institution."

He hadn't realized how much living among free men, men who prided themselves on doing an honest day's work for a fair wage, had changed him.

He hadn't realized how much knowing Elke had changed him.

That last night in her parlor, he'd defended the right to own slaves. Having spent the last four months in the heart of a slave state—hearing slave owners talk about the price of this buck or that wench—his feelings had changed completely. He would never defend that right again. Slavery was inherently wrong.

How Elke would enjoy saying, "I told you so."

Elke. She was never far from his thoughts.

If circumstances had been different—if Elke had been free—he wouldn't be courting a girl like Charlotte Devereux. But Elke was happily married, he reminded himself.

His silent colloquium came to a halt as the carriage stopped in front of Windmere. A black butler answered his knock and escorted him into the spacious drawing room where the Devereux clan was gathered.

He had grown up knowing Charlotte's brothers and sisters, but keeping their spouse's names straight taxed even his carefully cultivated social grace. As they greeted him one by one, he felt a bit like a prize stallion under consideration for stud—or, more truthfully, like a sheep being led to the slaughter.

Predictably, Charlotte didn't show herself until mint juleps had been served all around. He was standing by the fireplace talking to her father when she appeared in the drawing room door.

Another perfectly timed entrance, he thought. The renowned actor, Edwin Booth, couldn't have done it better.

"Patrick dear, it's so lovely to have you here at Windmere at long last," she said in her silken drawl. She moved toward him with a seductive sway that set her hoop skirt bobbing like a toy sailboat in a tub, revealing tantalizing glimpses of her exquisitely made ankles and feet.

But it wasn't her nether parts that captured his attention. And not her face, either. Her breasts shimmied above her emerald gown like the most appetizing aspic. It was all he could do to lift his eyes from their twin enticements.

"You've never looked lovelier," he said as she reached his side.

"And you, sir, are a shameless flatterer."

"Nonsense, you look absolutely splendid," Beauregard Devereux, Charlotte's father boomed in his hearty voice. "And well you should considering what that dress cost."

"Shame on you, Daddy," Charlotte pouted. "You know I'm worth every penny."

The dinner proved more pleasant than Patrick had anticipated. The Devereuxs were a lively clan, full of boisterous good spirits. And they all seemed to dote on Charlotte.

Charlotte, however, didn't seem to be herself. Although her smile never faltered, she had very little to say and seemed content to let others carry the burden of the conversation.

When the meal ended, mindful of what his mother

had suggested, Patrick asked if Charlotte might show him the gardens.

"By all means," Beauregard boomed.

A dozen pairs of surprised eyes turned toward them at Beauregard's instant acquiescence. An unchaperoned walk in the garden indicated a level of trust that was only granted to an engaged couple.

"Do be careful, dear," Hortense Devereux called out as Patrick followed Charlotte from the dining room.

The Devereux gardens were famous throughout the South. Patrick had seen them in daylight and marveled at their lush beauty. Tonight, however, the moon cast the grounds in shadow. Only the sweet scent wafting in Patrick's nostrils testified to the variety of shrubs and flowers.

"Are you warm enough?" he asked, tucking Charlotte's hand in the crook of his arm.

"I'm positively hot," she replied.

Did she realized what she'd said? he wondered, then dismissed the thought. No well-bred woman would be so bold.

She stumbled on the terrace's uneven bricks and he pulled her close to steady her. She was so tiny that the top of her head didn't reach his chin but he felt her curves right down to the tip of his toes.

"You've been unusually quiet tonight," he said as they resumed their stately progress.

Her lips pursed in a charming moue. "I have a lot on my mind."

He helped her down a short flight of stairs and around a bubbling fountain to a grassy path. "Is something troubling you?"

"Yes," she replied with unaccustomed brevity.

In the weeks he'd known her, she had never used one word when forty or fifty would do. "Is there anything I can do to help?"

"Yes," she said again, her monosyllabic answer husky with emotion.

They had reached a stand of evergreens that stretched forty feet in either direction with the martial perfection of a rank of soldiers. If memory served him, Beauregard had been planting a formal maze the last time he had seen the garden. The hedge had come up to his shoulders then. Now it towered over his head.

"Won't you tell me what's on your mind?" he asked with genuine concern.

"Oh, Patrick, it's so hard for me to talk about this," Charlotte replied as she led him into the maze.

Although he had a good sense of direction and had no difficulty navigating through foreign terrain during the Mexican war, the crowding evergreens, coupled with the sharp turns and unanticipated dead ends, gave him a sensation of being lost and far from the world.

"I thought we were friends," he said, "and friends should be able to talk about anything."

"Are you really so blind that you don't know what's wrong?" She sounded as breathless as if she'd been running. And still she guided him deeper into the maze.

"I'm not blind, but I can't see very much in here," he replied, hoping to lighten her mood.

"Don't worry, darling. I know where I'm going." The endearment startled him. But not half as much as what she said next. "You're what's wrong with me. I want you so much, it's driving me mad."

She came to a halt so abruptly that he almost ran her down. The moon highlighted her brow, nose, and breasts as she threw herself into his arms.

Damn! Surely his mother didn't have anything remotely like this in mind when she'd suggested a walk in the garden. Charlotte trembled in his embrace and he stroked her the way he would a high-strung horse. "You don't know what you're saying."

"Don't you dare talk down to me, Patrick Pride. I'm a grown woman. I know what I want."

There could be no arguing with her womanhood, he thought, feeling the pressure of her body from his chest to his thighs. He tried to disengage himself but she held fast with the tenacious strength of a limpet clinging to a rock.

"Do you remember our first dinner at your parents' house?" she asked, leaning back to gaze into his eyes. "I said I wanted to know everything about you—every intimate detail. Heaven help me, darling, it was the truth."

Her hands reached up to his face, tracing his features before lingering on his lips. Then, with stunning eroticism, she put her fingers to her own mouth and sucked them one by one. "Don't make me beg, Patrick," she murmured, throatily. "Kiss me."

He did what any gentleman would do, lowering his head to meet her waiting lips. When he tasted her for the first time, he forgot all about being a gentleman.

Patrick's kiss was all Charlotte had imagined it would be. Lord, he felt good, she thought, running her hands up and down his back. He was as lean and muscular as one of her father's coursing hounds. The feel of him sent the most delicious messages to her brain.

She loved kissing and had experimented with a dozen different beaux, learning something from each one. She knew a hard kiss wasn't half as enjoyable as a soft one. She knew that making a smacking sound with her lips had nothing to do with real kissing.

She knew how to engage in a duel of tongues that would leave a man gasping for breath and praying he'd suffocate before she stopped. And she knew what the firm shaft pressing into her belly meant.

The fish had taken the bait.

Patrick was rock hard in more ways than one, she thought with delight. And big, too. Bigger than any of the other men she had tormented and teased into arousal. Only this time she wasn't tormenting or teasing. She was playing for keeps.

She feasted on him hungrily—sucking, lapping, running her tongue over his lips and teeth, breathing into his mouth. She caressed his back the entire time, her hands moving tantalizingly lower. When they reached his buttocks and squeezed, Patrick responded with a moan and a convulsive thrust of his hips.

She had overheard slaves describing that movement as jiggedy-jig. But it sure didn't do justice to the delicious sensations flooding her body as she responded with a thrust of her own.

"For God's sake, Charlotte," Patrick muttered against her hair, "don't do that again or I won't answer for the consequences.

"I don't care. I want you. Not tomorrow or next week, either—right now." Her hoop was belling out behind her. She let him go just long enough to reach under her gown and release the single tie that held the garment in place. It dropped to the ground and she kicked it aside.

There was nothing between her and Patrick but the fragile silk of her expensive dress. But for once she gave no thought to her clothes and her appearance. She didn't care if Patrick ruined her gown and her elaborate coiffure. She had planned this encounter down to the last detail—and yet she gave no thought to her plan.

She found herself incapable of any thought as Patrick gathered her to him and lowered her décolletage with his free hand.

When he found a nipple and fondled it into a hard point, it was her turn to moan. Things were really getting interesting.

"What time is it?" Hortense asked her husband.

"Five minutes later than the last time you asked. Will you please stop pacing back and forth. You're making me nervous."

Hortense picked up the needlepoint she had put aside and sat down. She could hear the murmur of voices and the muffled sound of feet upstairs as her children put their children to bed. Although she had told them to take their time, she knew they would come trooping down soon. She couldn't wait much longer.

Had she given Charlotte enough time? Or too much?

"I'm worried about Charlotte," she said, dropping her needlepoint and getting up again.

"What's that, dear?" Beauregard looked up from his reading.

"I said, I'm worried about Charlotte."

"I don't see why. She's with Patrick."

"What if they get lost in the maze?"

"For heaven's sake, woman, don't go borrowing trouble. Charlotte knows that maze like the back of her hand."

"She could get confused in the dark. I think we should go look for them." She picked up a hurricane lamp and thrust it into his hand.

He sighed. "I suppose I won't get any peace until I do as you say."

She tugged him to his feet. "You suppose right, Mr. Devereux."

Charlotte's nipples had the taste and texture of ripe berries. The color, too, Patrick warranted, although it was too dark to be certain. The minx was giving as good as she got, rubbing her body against him with the unbridled sensuality of a cat in heat. Come to think of it, he was doing a damn good imitation of an aroused tom.

Her touch sent an erotic message from his scalp to his toes. Where in the world had she learned to pleasure a man like this? On second thought, he didn't want to know.

His brain told him it was madness. His body urged him toward completion.

"Make me a woman. Make love to me," Charlotte moaned in his ear.

"That's what I thought I was doing."

She ground her hips against him. "You know what I mean."

Indeed he did, he thought, recapturing her mouth. She was so sweet, so pliant, so filled with wanting that he never heard the footsteps coming ever nearer—never saw the wavering light, either.

Suddenly he felt a hand on his shoulder. It took a second before he realized the hand couldn't possible belong to Charlotte. Hers were busy at his crotch.

"Unhand my little girl," Beauregard Devereux boomed in Patrick's ear.

Patrick couldn't have been more off guard. He looked over his shoulder to see Charlotte's parents standing side by side like a pair of avenging angels.

Charlotte's dishabille prevented him from complying with Beauregard's demand. He continued to shield her from sight while she tucked her breasts back inside her gown.

"Don't be angry with Patrick. It's all my fault," Charlotte declared with surprising aplomb considering the circumstances.

Looking down to make sure she was decent, Patrick finally turned to confront her father. He felt like a complete cad. No matter what Charlotte had said and done to entice him, he had no right to plunder her like a pirate attacking a treasure ship.

"Are you all right?" Hortense asked moving to her daughter's side.

"Never better, Mother."

"Then he didn't—?"

"Unfortunately, no."

Beauregard took a firm grip on Patrick's arm. "It's time you and I had a serious discussions about your intentions, Son. High time!"

"Not without me, you don't!" Charlotte looked from one parent to another.

The girl has spunk, Patrick thought as Beauregard led the way out of the maze.

Thank heaven, Patrick's erection had subsided by the time they reached the well-lit house.

"We had better have our talk in the library," Hortense said. "I wouldn't want Charlotte's brothers to know what happened. They're so hot-tempered, there's no telling what they would do. And for heaven's sake, Mr. Devereux, I know you're hard of hearing, but the rest of us aren't. Please try to keep your voice down."

Patrick couldn't help thinking she should have been more upset in view of the fact that she'd practically caught him in flagrante delicto with her daughter. Apparently the Devereux women had more iron in them than he realized.

Hortense led the way to the paneled library and shut the door behind them. Patrick had last been in the room when he came to say goodbye twelve years ago. Charlotte had wanted his epaulets then. He suspected her parents would want a great deal more now.

"Your father raised you to be a gentleman, Patrick. I expected better of you," Beauregard said, wheeling about with almost military precision, his rigid posture betraying his fury far more than his words.

"I don't blame you for being angry, sir. I expected better of myself." Patrick would have given his soul for a stiff bourbon. He didn't dare ask for one, though. He'd just about worn out the Devereux's hospitality.

Beauregard had turned an unhealthy shade of crimson. "Is that all you have to say for yourself? If I were younger, I'd give you the horse-whipping you deserve."

"Calm down, dear," Hortense said. "I'm quite sure we can count on Patrick to do the right thing."

Hortense's *sang froid* would have done credit to a battlefield general. Her favorite child had come close to losing her virginity. She should have been spitting angry.

Unlike his wife, Beauregard appeared to be on the brink of apoplexy. "Damn right, he'll do the right thing."

"Now, Daddy, don't take on so. I know we can work things out to everyone's satisfaction, can't we, Patrick?" Charlotte gave Patrick a look of beguiling sweetness.

"I suppose so," he replied. The rapid progression of events—the evolution from impassioned lover to guilty knave had muddled his mind. The abrupt transition still ached through his groin. Part of him—and he knew just which part—still wanted Charlotte.

" 'Suppose so' won't do," Beauregard said angrily.

Charlotte and Hortense exchange conspiratorial winks, their behavior in stark contrast to Beauregard's righteous wrath. It didn't make sense. Or did it?

The Devereux had appeared in time to save their daughter from what old maids called a fate worse than death. And yet he and Charlotte hadn't been in the garden that long.

Was it just coincidence?

Not likely. It was just too damn convenient to be coincidence. Charlotte and her mother must have set the whole thing up between them. In view of the perfectly timed intrusion—and Charlotte did have a genius for timing—nothing else made sense. For all he knew, his mother had been in on the plan, too.

He turned his gaze from Beauregard to Charlotte— and read the truth on her face as clearly as if she'd said "I trapped you" out loud.

She stared boldly back, looking as triumphant as a duelist who has walked off the field of honor unscathed.

Instead of being angry, he felt amused. So be it. If the beauteous Charlotte wanted him that badly, who was he to deny her wishes? To the victor belong the spoils.

The thought tickled his fancy. Despite the solemnity of the occasion, he began to chuckle. To his delight, Charlotte laughed, too. Spasms of mirth shook them both while her parents gazed at the two of them as if they had lost their minds.

Perhaps he had. "Come here, bride to be," he said, opening his arms wide.

Chapter Seven

Elke had finished setting the table for supper when she heard Otto thudding up the stairs at a pace far faster than the one he ordinarily used at the end of the day.

"I have wonderful news," he declared, flinging the door wide. "Patrick will be home soon."

Elke couldn't bring herself to share his enthusiasm. Why did Patrick have to come back when her life had finally settled on an even keel?

She felt as if iron bands constricted her chest. But then, remembering that another heart beat beneath her own, she took a deep calming breath. Patrick had been gone so long that she hadn't expected him to return—had almost hoped he wouldn't for fear he would disturb her newfound tranquility.

"Are you sure?"

"The postmaster just delivered this letter. It came in on the afternoon stage. Here, let me read it to you."

With his customary solicitude, Otto took her hand, helped her to a chair, and positioned a stool under her feet. Not until she was comfortably settled did he pull a sheet of paper from his shirt pocket and sit down, too.

" 'Dear Otto'," he began. " 'My apologies for not writing sooner. I hope this letter finds you and Elke in good health.' "

Beaming, he looked up from the letter. "I can't wait to tell Patrick about the baby. I wasn't sure he'd be back in time for the christening. I was thinking about asking him to be godfather. Do you approve?"

How could she say no? She didn't dare tell Otto the truth. Besides, the truth had changed.

Seven months ago she had imagined herself madly in love with Patrick Pride. Now she knew it had only been infatuation. She knew it because she loved her unborn child with serene constancy. What she had felt for Patrick couldn't have been more different. Or more painful.

"I think you're going to be a wonderful father," she replied softly, "and I'll go along with any choice you make."

Otto reached for her hand and gave it a squeeze. "There's no one in the world like you, *Liebling*. Not a day passes when I don't thank God for giving you to me. Do you want me to continue, or would you rather read the rest of the letter yourself?"

"It's addressed to you—not me. I think you should finish it."

Otto nodded. " 'I have finally set a date for my return. I hope to be in Fredericksburg on or about the fifteenth of October, and I will be bringing someone very special with me. I can't wait for you to meet her. Please plan on joining us for dinner at the Nimitz Hotel.

" 'I do have a special favor to ask. I would be very grateful if you drove Elke out to my house to make sure it's ready. There's nothing like a woman's touch to bring a home to life.

" 'I have managed to get my hands on a bottle of Steinhager and am eager to share it with you. Until then, I remain your servant, Patrick Pride.' "

Otto folded the letter and looked back up at Elke. "I wonder who the someone special is?"

"He said he can't wait for us to meet *her* so it's obviously a woman he's bringing. Wouldn't it be wonderful if his mother finally visited Pride's Passion? Patrick worked so hard on that house, I imagine he's anxious to show it off."

"Considering his devotion to the ranch, it seems cruel that his parents never came to see him. Patrick told me he and his father quarreled before he left home. It's good that they're close again. Families should stick together."

"I promise you, ours will. I won't let anything in the world separate us," she vowed, as much for her sake as for his. "When do you want to drive to Pride's Passion?"

"I don't think we should."

"It's not like you to refuse a favor to a friend."

"I know it isn't. But I've never been a father before, either. I don't want you to do anything that will endanger the baby."

"That's ridiculous!" she burst out.

"You're seven months pregnant. You have no business gallivanting around the countryside in your condition!"

Otto had finally succeeded in convincing her not to visit outlying farms on behalf of the abolitionist movement. But she had no intention of letting him convince her to stay home this time.

She told herself any woman would be curious to see the house that was already described as the Hill Country's finest. She told herself she wanted to do a favor for Patrick's mother. She told herself everything but the truth—that she longed to see Patrick's home so she could imagine him there.

"For heaven's sake, women come west in covered wagons and stage coaches all the time, pregnant or not. I wish you would stop treating me as if I were an invalid instead of a perfectly healthy woman carrying a perfectly healthy child." As if to reinforce her words, the baby gave a lusty kick.

"Here, feel this," she said, reaching for his hand and putting it on her swollen abdomen. "Your baby is getting as tired of being cooped up inside me as I am of being cooped up in town. A ride in the country will do me a world of good."

Otto didn't seem to know whether to beam at his child's strength, or frown at its mother's insistence. The smile won out. "He is strong, isn't he?"

"*She* is doing just fine, thank you. Don't try to change the subject. The letter took so long getting here, we should go soon."

"It's a two-day trip there and back. It will mean closing the bakery. Our customers won't like it," he argued with the tenacity of a dog fighting for a bone.

"Our customers can live without us for a couple of days. When do you want to go?"

"Why do you have to be so stubborn?"

"Are you afraid of driving out there?" The moment the words left Elke's lips, she wished she could swallow them whole. She knew how sensitive Otto was about what he called his "fatal flaw." How cruel she felt, using that weapon to get her way.

Otto lowered his eyes, but not before she saw the hurt in them. "It's just that I know Patrick has a perfectly good housekeeper."

"I doubt Mrs. Alvarez is capable of keeping the place up to his mother's standards."

Otto's heavy shoulders slumped in defeat. "All right then, have it your way."

Elke jumped to her feet and threw her arms around him. "I promise, you won't be sorry. It's just that I want everything to be perfect when Patrick's mother sees Pride's Passion."

Otto still refused to meet her eyes. "Then you really think his mother is coming?"

"Of course. Who else could it be?"

The next Saturday, a reluctant Otto and an exuberant Elke climbed aboard their buggy and drove out of town at a decorous pace. Baskets stuffed with all sorts of goodies from their larder—a smoked ham, sausages, jars of jams, jellies, and pickles, a crock of cheese, and Elke's homemade sauerkraut—crowded the buggy's back. Newly baked rolls, cookies, and fried chicken completed the assortment. The chicken and rolls would be consumed along the way. The other things were intended as a welcoming gift for Mrs. Pride.

While Elke reveled in the beauty of the countryside, Otto fretted about her well-being. Every time the buggy bounced on the rough terrain, he cut a worried glance at her as if he expected her to break.

That afternoon, when the road passed through the ranching community of Kerrville, Elke gazed around with avid curiosity. She had always wondered why Patrick made the thirty-mile trip into Fredericksburg to pick up supplies, rather than shopping in the community that was closest to his ranch. Now she had her answer.

The town—reputed to be a haven for bushwhackers, rustlers, and other ne'er-do-wells—had deteriorated since the hopeful days when it had been founded by shingle cutters. It barely clung to life. No wonder the inhabitants were so envious of Fredericksburg's prosperity.

Halfway down the main street, she thought she saw the Detweiler twins lurking in front of a run-down saloon. However, they disappeared into the building before she could be sure. Knowing Otto would fret if she mentioned it, she kept her own counsel as they left Kerrville behind.

She had been right about the trip doing her a world of good, though. They followed the Guadalupe to its split and then drove along the north fork. The jade-colored river ran deep. Ducks fed on its surface, and egrets and herons foraged in its shallows. Timid white-tailed deer peered out from the oak groves that lined the banks.

Half an hour from town they passed a stout post with the P bar P branded onto its surface. "The ranch begins here," Otto said. "We'll be at the house in another hour."

No wonder Patrick loves this land so much, Elke thought, marveling at the crisp caress of the air, the indigo of the sky, the pink granite outcrops poking through the long grass, and the deep green of spreading oaks. The lowing of longhorns, the twitter of birds overhead, and the gentle play of the wind in the trees supplied the perfect counterpoint to the ranch's visual beauty.

The rutted road climbed gently upward. A couple of thick limestone pillars surmounted by an iron P bar P, defined the entrance to homestead. The buggy continued on past a series of outbuildings—the log dogtrot cabin Patrick had built his first year on the ranch, the rambling bunkhouse where the hands lived, and a massive stone barn surrounded by corrals.

The last time Elke visited the ranch a couple of years ago, the house had been under construction. Even then the limestone walls had held the promise of beauty. As she gazed to the top of the hill where the house sat, she realized how well that promise had been fulfilled.

The two stories spoke volumes about the refined taste of the man who had designed and built it. Patrick certainly had an eye for beauty. The proportions were classic in their simplicity.

Chimneys rising at all four corners gave the building a sense of strength and stability while a series of floor-to-ceiling windows on the ground floor made it seem light and airy. A wide veranda built from cedar that grew on the ranch stretched across the front of the building, beckoning travelers to rest in its shade. Cedar shingles, aged to a serene silver, covered the roof as well.

"It's beautiful," Elke said on an indrawn breath.

"*Ja*, it is." Otto cut a glance at her. "Would you like to live in a house like this, *Liebchen?*"

"Of course. What woman wouldn't?" she replied truthfully.

"Then I will build a house just like it someday, you wait and see. Nothing is too good for my wife and child."

Elke was about to say that they would never be able to afford it, and that she felt content in their own little house in Fredericksburg. Before she could get the words out, though, she became aware of the sound of hooves drumming ever closer.

Otto must have heard it, too. His hands tightened on the reins, his knuckles showing white as he cast a worried look over his shoulder. "Who can that be?"

"I suppose it's Patrick's foreman," Elke replied, although she had never met the man.

Otto wiped a slick of perspiration from his forehead with the back of his sleeve, then reined the buggy to a stop.

The stranger leapt from the saddle with the fluid grace of a man who has spent a lifetime on horseback. He tipped his sweat-stained hat in Elke's direction, then came around the buggy to Otto's side. "The name's Rio de Vargas. I'm Patrick's foreman. He wrote that you two might be coming. I've been keeping an eye out for you."

"*Gruss Gott*," Otto said, pumping Rio's hand.

"*Buenas tardes,*" Rio replied.

Otto got down from the front seat, and helped Elke

down too. "Herr de Vargas, I'm honored to present my wife, Frau Sonnschein."

Rio held out his gloved hand, lowered his gaze, and turned bright pink under his bronze tan. "Pleased to meet you, ma'am."

Patrick had told her of Rio's shyness. "The man can talk a fractious cow out of a thicket, and sing a troubled herd to sleep," Patrick had said, "but he's plain scared to death of conversing with a lady."

And yet, Rio certainly wasn't unattractive. Elke studied him from under the concealing fringe of her lashes. He looked as lean and durable as a rawhide reata. His black hair reflected his mixed Spanish and Indian blood, while his snapping blue eyes spoke of his Nordic heritage.

Rumor had it that he'd been born out of wedlock to a mountain man and a mestizo woman.

According to Patrick, Rio had shown up at Pride's Passion and asked for a job a couple of months after Patrick took possession of the land. In all the years since, he'd never volunteered any personal information about himself.

It didn't seem to bother Patrick, though. He swore he knew all he needed to know about Rio from his gentleness with animals, and his steadiness in an emergency. "If I'm ever in a real tight bind," Patrick had said, "I'll feel a hell of a lot better if Rio is at my side."

The fact that Patrick thought so highly of his foreman predisposed Elke to also like him. She wished she could tell him that she wouldn't bite.

"I'm pleased to meet you too," Elke said.

Otto took her arm and helped her up the steps to the

veranda, while Rio unloaded the baskets from the back of the buggy. "How long did you say you were fixing to stay?"

Elke couldn't help laughing at his question. Considering all they'd brought with them, it must look as though they were planning to move in. "Just overnight, Mr. de Vargas. Those things aren't for us. I brought them for Mr. Pride's guest."

Rio's brows elevated. "He told you about her?"

"Indeed he did. I can hardly wait to meet his mother."

His *mother?* Rio thought, cutting a sidelong glance at Elke. Patrick hadn't mentioned anything about his mother coming, too. But it wasn't his call to tell Mrs. Sonnschein about Patrick's business. She would learn the truth soon enough.

She sure was a pretty thing, pregnant or no, he thought. Patrick couldn't have known about her condition or he wouldn't have asked her to check on the house. But it weren't any of his never mind, Rio told himself sternly.

"Just go on in," he said. "I'm right behind you."

"Conchita!" he called out as the door swung open. Company's here."

To his relief, the sound of Conchita Alvarez's squeaky leather huaraches announced her imminent arrival. A moment later she came bustling into the hall, a dust cloth in her hand, a welcoming smile creasing her round face.

Rio stumbled through introductions all around, then beat a hasty retreat. He'd had all the socializing he could take for one day, he thought, hurrying back to the bunkhouse.

For the life of him, he didn't know how a man's man like Patrick Pride could be so at ease around women. Rio's rare contact with the gentler sex involved his monthly visits to Velvet Gilhooley's whorehouse. He could live without a lot of female jawing—but he had yet to figure out how to get by without an occasional poke.

"You're a little pale," Otto said, helping Elke into the buggy. "Are you sure you feel up to another long drive?"

"I feel fine. I slept so well last night. It's really quiet out here." She gave Otto a bright smile, determined not to tell him how tired she felt. Although she had thoroughly enjoyed their brief stay—and had reveled in a long soak in the bathtub in the water closet—seven months of pregnancy weighed heavily on her body, and yesterday's ride had sapped her energy.

Otto clucked their horse to a walk. "Promise me one thing, *Liebling*. No more trips until the baby comes."

Elke took his arm. "You were right about it being a wasted trip. Señora Alvarez couldn't be doing a better job. But I'm glad we came. I enjoyed seeing the house and meeting Rio and Mrs. Alvarez. Patrick has talked so much about the two of them."

"You really like it here, don't you?" With a flick of the reins, Otto urged the horse to a faster walk.

"What woman wouldn't? Patrick's mother is in for a real treat."

When they reached the bottom of the hill, Elke looked back over her shoulder. Patrick's mother couldn't help but *love* the place, she mused with a twinge of envy. It was a veritable palace.

Feeling her baby kick, her thoughts turned back to her own life. Although the sewing room had been transformed into a nursery, complete with a cradle and a changing table, she still had lots to do before she went into labor.

Just thinking about it increased her fatigue. Resting her head on Otto's shoulders, she closed her eyes and thought about what to name the baby. Her beloved father had been called Hansel. However, much as she would love to honor his memory, it seemed too German a name for a born-and-bred Texan. Her last conscious thought was that Melisande, her mother's name, would be truly lovely for a girl.

The next thing she knew, she was on that dreadful ship that had brought her family from Germany to Indianola. At first the boat seemed to be rocking ever so gently as it eased her to sleep in the narrow bunk in their crowded cabin.

Without any warning, the gentle rocking became a stomach-lurching heave. Terrified by the relentless motion, she looked up and saw her mother's face floating overhead, looking as ghostly pale as the moon.

"Have you kept your promise?" her mother asked.

"What promise?"

"The one you made the day we died. You swore to fulfill our dream."

"I tried, Mama, I really tried," Elke wailed.

Her mother faded away as the motion increased.

Elke came awake by degrees, clawing her way up out of the nightmare by sheer force of will. When her eyes finally opened, seeing the surrounding hills reassured her that it had only been a dream.

But then she realized the rocking motion couldn't be more real. Their horse raced along at a full gallop. Otto never drove faster than a trot. He claimed he never felt in control if he let the horse go faster.

What in the world had gotten into him?

Chapter Eight

Weather permitting, Rio de Vargas bathed in the Guadalupe River. However, once a month on a Sunday, he took a tub bath in the bunkhouse—whether he needed it or not. Afterward he'd strop his razor, shave, and get the bunkhouse cook, Pedro Alvarez, to barber his shoulder-length hair. Rio liked to be clean when he went to town. The whores he had used over the years appreciated it.

This afternoon, having finished his toilette, he took his best shirt and trousers from a hook by his bed, put them on over his newly laundered union suit, then tugged his boots over his stocking feet. A splash of bay rum completed his preparations.

He'd had the bunkhouse to himself except for a couple of young hands lazing in their beds. Even though they had the afternoon off, he hated to see them lollygagging around rather than tending to their personal needs—soaping their saddles, writing their mothers, or mending their clothes. They'd soon learn a top hand got that way from making the most of every minute.

"You sure do smell sweet, Rio," Terrell Meeks said,

looking up from his game of solitaire. "Velvet's girls will stand in line to be with you after they get a whiff."

"I hear tell you're one of their favorite customers," the other cowboy chimed in. "They like a man who smells better than they do, goes about his business, and gets done in ten minutes."

Rio settled his hat on his head, then turned to glare at the youths. He couldn't help a wry grin, though. Talk about being green. For all their smartass talk, he doubted they had much experience at getting their nuts cracked.

"Maybe you boys can take your pleasure that fast, but a man my age needs a mite longer. Besides, once isn't enough. I don't really settle in for the ride until the third or fourth juice for jelly."

That ought to shut them up, he thought, stalking from the bunkhouse with considerable dignity at his command. The two of them hadn't meant any harm. Boys like that tended to imagine they were the only ones who could salute the flag with their peckers.

The thought of a man in his midforties needing a woman undoubtedly tickled their fancy. Over the years Rio had heard every conceivable jibe about his monthly trips to town. Now they ran off his back like hot grease off a spoon. He used to be exactly like those two, talking tough around grown men and getting tongue-tied around women. At least he had grown past *one* of those traits.

In his younger days he thought no one else had the itch to get his leather stretched as bad as he did. He even dreamed of having a woman of his own someday. But bitter experience had taught him that decent females wanted nothing to do with an illegitimate half-breed cowboy.

So he'd made do with whores, schooling his desire to the size of his bank roll. He could afford the best now—and that meant Velvet Gilhooley's place.

The good Lord knew he didn't feel at ease talking to a lady. The good Lord also knew he'd had damn little practice. He fared considerably better in a woman's bed, though. He sure knew how to pleasure a female—and himself in the bargain. Again, it was a matter of practice.

Just thinking about the evening ahead heated his drawers. He looked up at the sun to calculate the time, then swung aboard the paint he'd left tied to the hitching post in front of the bunkhouse.

He liked to be with a girl before other men had a chance to wear her out. Barring any unforeseen trouble, he'd get to Velvet Gilhooley's right after she opened for business.

Now there was a real looker. Maybe one of these days he'd work up the nerve to see if she still took part in the trade.

Tugging his trousers so they wouldn't bind his private parts, he spurred his mount to an easy, ground-covering cantor. Yes sirree, he thought, smiling to himself, he intended to have one hell of a ride tonight.

But first he had to get to town.

The horse was fresh and eager. So was he.

Anticipating a good poke sure put a man in high fettle.

* * *

"For God's sake, Otto, rein the horse in!" Elke cried, coming wide-awake.

The rushing wind caught her words and blew them away. Clinging to the side of the buggy with one hand, she grabbed Otto's arm with the other. "Slow down!" she shouted even louder.

He finally glanced in her direction. The anxiety in his eyes worried her even more than their jolting speed. But he spoke bravely. "Hang on, *Liebchen*. The Detweilers are after us."

Clinging to the wildly bouncing buggy, she managed a hurried look over her shoulder. Sure enough Eli and Jude Detweiler were closing on the buggy fast—and from the hell-bent-for-leather way they rode, she doubted they were after a piece of strudel. "How long have they been following us?"

"Half an hour. Maybe more. Every time I make the horse to speed up, they also do." In his agitation, Otto had lost his fragile grip on English grammar.

"Surely they don't mean any real harm." Elke had to speak at the top of her voice to be heard above the crunch of the wagon wheels and the labored sound of their horse's breathing. "You'd better slow the horse before we have an accident."

"I'll try." Pulling the reins so tight that she could see them cutting into his palms, he yelled, "Whoa. *Halt, bitte.*"

To her dismay, the gelding didn't respond, even though the bit had to be cutting into its tender mouth.

"The damn thing is away running with us!" Otto cried out.

Elke couldn't imagine a worse time to have an inexperienced driver in command of the buggy. Otto had no feel for horses at all. Before she could tell him to pass the reins to her, she heard a sound like a firecracker.

Good God, the Detweiler twins were shooting at them. The horse heard it, too. If she had any doubt about the animal running away before, she didn't have any now.

She caught a glimpse of the Detweilers out of the corners of her eyes. They had closed the distance between them and now they rode on either side of the buggy, whooping and shouting and waving their hats like a couple of boys indulging in a wild prank. As they flew past she realized the damn fools were laughing.

"You bastards!" Otto shouted, fighting the reins in a desperate effort at regaining control. The thick leather straps jerked in his grip as if they had a mind of their own.

It felt like an eternity since he fist saw the twins trailing behind them. They had played cat-and-mouse for a while as though they could read his mind—and knew just how to increase his apprehension until it filled his chest.

His hands were raw from sawing on the reins. The muscles in his arms and shoulders ached from the strain. However, he cared nothing for his own discomfort—and even less for his fear.

He had no room in his thoughts for anything but Elke and their child. He had to save them at any cost, even if his arms tore from his shoulders in the attempt. For the first time in his life he realized that fear is bravery's handmaiden, that one goes along with the other—and he gloried in the knowledge.

"Hold on to me," he commanded.

He felt Elke's arm reach around his back, but his girth kept her from getting a real grip. He swore he'd never eat another pastry again if they survived this wild ride. He'd starve himself thin for Elke's sake. *Gott in Himmel,* just let them be all right and he'd move mountains for her sake.

Although the Detweilers had disappeared far ahead and their gunfire no longer goaded the horse, its speed never slackened. Bracing his legs against the footboard, Otto pulled back on the reins with all his might.

He saw a boulder lying across the road, and made a desperate effort to turn the horse away from it.

The frantic animal plunged straight ahead like an arrow coursing toward its target. Wordless prayers tumbled through Otto's mind as the left front wheel hit the obstruction. For a few seconds, the buggy careened half off the ground. To his horror the wheel lifted higher and higher until the buggy toppled over.

Otto felt himself leave the seat and fly through the air, the reins still clutched in his hands. The ground came up so fast, he didn't even have time to think how much hitting it was going to hurt. His head made contact first. Crimson fireworks exploded in his brain and then his world went black.

He didn't know how long he lay there before he saw the light of day again. It began as a peripheral glow at the farthest reach of his vision, growing ever brighter until it filled the horizon with mesmerizing radiance.

How he saw that light he didn't know because he couldn't seem to force his eyes open. He saw himself rise out of his body and float above the ground.

It felt strange.

It felt wonderful.

He ought be hurting like hell. Instead he experienced an overwhelming sense of joy. He tried to look for Elke only the light shone too bright. Lifting his arms toward the radiance, Otto Sonnschein flew straight to the kingdom of heaven.

Halfway to Fredericksburg, Rio de Vargas saw a dozen turkey vultures soaring in the sky a quarter of a mile ahead, their black wings outlined against the crimson sunset. Most cowboys didn't care for vultures, but he had always admired their effortless flight.

This evening their purposeful circling told him something must be dead or dying beneath them. A minute later, he made out a strange shape on the ground. As he rode closer, the shape separated into a horse and buggy. The horse seemed to be fine. The buggy was a total wreck.

His heart jolted. It looked just like the Sonnscheins' buggy. What the hell? They should have been home by now. Leaning over his horse's neck, he spurred it to a gallop, quartering the ground like a hound hunting for a coon.

He found Otto first. Rio reined the paint to a skidding stop, leapt from the saddle, and hit the ground running. The baker lay flat on his back looking for all the world like a man taking a nap—except for the place where his head had been stove in. A pool of blood spread out beneath the injury.

Rio bent to take a closer look and feel for a pulse. At

least he'd gone fast, Rio thought, crossing himself reflexively although years had passed since he last set foot in church.

"Mizz Sonnschein," he called out, grabbing his paint's reins and heading for the buggy, "can you hear me?"

Still in its traces, the Sonnscheins' horse whickered in reply.

"Mizz Sonnschein," he called again. Where the hell was she? If he didn't find her before the light failed . . .

As Rio reached the shattered buggy, he heard a low moan to his left. *Gracias a Dios,* thank God she's alive, he thought, following the sound to its source.

Make that *barely* alive, he amended after he got a good look at her. Purple bruises covered one side of her face. A gash on her forehead had streaked her golden hair with blood. Her skin looked ashen. Seeing the pale-pink stain on her skirt, he dropped to his knees and ran his hands over her body, feeling for broken bones. Suddenly her features twisted and he felt her swollen abdomen knot up.

Shit. She was in labor. That telltale stain meant her water had broke.

He'd pulled many a calf from a struggling cow, plunging his hands deep inside the cow's body to attach a rope to a slippery leg. And he'd doctored lots of cowboys, setting broken bones and stitching up cuts. The hands said he knew as much about putting a man back together as any sawbones.

The hands were dead wrong, he thought with despair. He'd have given a year's wages to have a sawbones with him now. He'd never delivered a human baby, let alone one whose mother looked half dead.

Struggling out of his sheepskin jacket, he spread it over her inert form. "You'll be just fine, Mizz Sonnschein. Old Rio's gonna take care of you. Don't you worry about a thing."

To his amazement, her eyes flew open. But it was plain she didn't see him because she said, "I knew you'd come, Patrick," before her eyes rolled back up in her head again.

The horse and buggy would keep until he could send someone back for them. And he'd have to leave poor Mr. Sonnschein to the vultures' merciless care. The trip to town might kill Mizz Sonnschein—but he damn well knew she'd die for certain if he didn't get her to a doctor.

Gathering her up in his arms, he carried her over to the paint and hoisted her across the saddle as gently as he could. Then he climbed up himself and resettled her so that his chest and arms supported most of her weight.

It was going to be a hell of a ride.

Velvet Gilhooley liked men—a good thing considering her business. Men were so predictable. No matter how big, brave, brawny, or bright they were, the poor dears couldn't get by without dipping their wicks on a regular basis.

Her considerable fortune had been based on that indisputable fact.

Orphaned at the age of thirteen, she'd earned her bread the way impoverished women from time immemorial had, by working at the world's oldest trade. She soon learned how easy it was to make men happy. All she had to do was part her legs, moan a lot, and tell each and every one she'd never seen bigger or had better.

By her twentieth birthday she had saved enough money to buy her own whorehouse in Nacodoches. But it had been a poor thing compared to the one she owned now. At the age of thirty-six, she was the sole proprietress of the finest establishment west of the Brazos. And she ran the prettiest girls, too.

She assembled them in the opulently furnished parlor every evening at seven to make sure their appearance lived up to her exacting standards. The girls came trooping in wearing outfits that ranged from the most feminine negligees to elaborate ball gowns.

Velvet knew that a virginal-looking girl in a white robe could make the most hardened gunslinger go weak in the knees—and that an elaborate gown could make an experienced whore look every inch a lady.

No matter what her girls wore, Velvet had one iron-clad rule. "Never show too much flesh," she always said. "If a man wants a look-see, he's going to have to pay for it."

Tonight, as was her habit, she walked from one girl to another adjusting a brooch here, a strap there—and giving each girl of word of encouragement. Whoring was a hard life. A lucky few married or retired rich. An unlucky few died.

She wanted all her girls to be lucky.

She had just finished her inspection when she heard a commotion at the front door. Her butler, an enormous freeman of color who also served as a bouncer—and who went by the unlikely name of Whitey—appeared in the arched entrance to the parlor.

"You'd better come out here, Miss Velvet," he said.

Velvet couldn't imagine a situation he couldn't handle. Whitey guarded her door as bravely as a lion, and as intelligently as a schoolmaster. That's why she had hired him.

"Is there a problem?"

"You can say that again. Rio de Vargas says he needs your help."

"Tell him to come on in."

The words no sooner left her mouth than Rio walked into the parlor with a woman in his arms. Velvet couldn't have been more surprised. To the best of her knowledge, the only women Rio ever talked to were her girls. And even then, he seldom said more than "Thank you, ma'am."

"Who have you got there?" she asked, hurrying to Rio's side.

"It's Elke Sonnschein, the baker's wife. She's in labor."

As a patron of the bakery, Velvet had a nodding acquaintance with Elke. Unlike some of the other ladies in town, Elke never failed to say hello if they passed each other out on the street. But Velvet barely recognized her now, except as a potential source of trouble.

"Why bring her here, for God's sake?" she asked impatiently. "The doctor is just down the street."

"I stopped there first. He weren't home. I didn't know where else to bring her. I don't know anyone else in town."

Velvet always had a soft spot for a woman in trouble—perhaps because she'd had so much trouble of her own years ago. But a lady like Elke Sonnschein had no business in a whorehouse. There'd be hell to pay when she woke up.

"I can see she's hurt, Rio, but the best place for her is in her own bed with her husband at her side."

"Her husband's at the side of the angels. He ain't going to be helping anybody anymore."

Velvet had never heard Rio string so many words together. He looked almost as pale as the woman in his arms. "All right. You win. Take her to my room. Whitey, show him the way."

To the girls, she said, "We won't be opening tonight. I want you to tear up some bandages, boil some water, and bring me clean rags and a pair of scissors. And one of you go on down to the doctor's house and stay there until he gets back."

Velvet didn't wait for a reply. She had trained all her girls well. They would do as she said.

Rio had settled Elke on Velvet's commodious bed by the time Velvet walked into her bedroom. The perfume she'd put on an hour earlier still hung in the air. Only now it mingled with the coppery odor of Elke's blood.

Taking Elke's wrist, Velvet felt for her pulse. Just then, Elke's body spasmed in a hard contraction. "Has she been having them often?" Velvet asked.

"Yep," Rio replied, keeping his eyes downcast.

"I know you're a man of few words, but you're going to have to do better than that if you want me to help your friend."

Rio swallowed so hard, she thought he would choke

on his Adam's apple. "Her pains were pretty far apart when I found her. Now they seem to be coming every few minutes."

Found her? Velvet lifted an eyebrow. The plot thickened. She could hardly wait to hear the story in its entirety. However, her questions would keep. With Elke's pains so close together, the baby could come any time now. "Help me get her out of her clothes."

Rio crimsoned. Despite the circumstances, Velvet chuckled. The man had slept with every one of her whores, and she'd heard he treated them to a hell of a good time. And yet he blushed at having to undress an unconscious woman.

"Have you ever delivered a baby, Miss Gilhooley?" Rio asked after Elke was tucked safely under the covers.

A host of unhappy memories rushed at Velvet as she recalled the last time she had held a baby in her arms. "Indeed I have. My own," she said softly.

The naked misery in her voice took Rio by surprise. Although he'd made love to so many whores that he'd lost count, he'd never thought about one of them getting pregnant—never worried how to prevent it, either. That had always seemed to be the whore's lookout.

The thought that he might have a child out there somewhere—and that Mizz Gilhooley certainly did— made him look at whoring in an entirely new light.

"How far along is she?" Velvet asked.

"I heard her tell Conchita she was due along about Christmastime."

God almighty, he'd already said more to Mizz Gilhooley than he had said to any female since his mother passed on. And he'd never ever talked about so intimate a subject. But something in Mizz Gilhooley's matter-of-fact attitude made the words come easy.

"There isn't much hope for a seven-month baby. Are you a praying man, Rio?"

Her question took him by surprise. "Not lately, Mizz Gilhooley."

"It might be a good idea if you took up the habit again. Elke and her baby are going to need all the help they can get. And by the way, please call me Velvet. We're going to know each other a hell of a lot better before this night is over."

Three hours later, Rio had said every prayer he could remember—and even made up a few new ones.

Elke had drifted in and out of consciousness during her ordeal, coming to when the pain got real bad and then passing out again when it ended. She mumbled some words from time to time. He could hardly make them out except when she said his boss's name. That came through loud and clear, and set him to wondering.

He'd never felt more inadequate. But Velvet seemed to know just what to do. She kept him busy holding Elke's hand, mopping her brow and talking to her in a low, steady voice while she kept a vigil between Elke's legs. A steady stream of whores trooped in and out of the room bringing hot water, bandages, and thick towels they had cut up into blankets and diapers for the baby.

Although they looked as pretty as ever, he forgot all about wanting them. Seeing the hell Elke endured because she'd let her husband slip his long knife between her legs, Rio didn't know if he could ever make love again.

When the birth appeared to be imminent, he helped Velvet put pillows under Elke's knees. "Is there anything else I can do before I go?"

"Go?" Velvet exploded. "Isn't it just like a man to take off when you need him the most."

"I just thought, seeing as how this is a woman thing—"

"A *woman* thing! Half the people in the world are men and they came into it the same way as the women. You can't run out on me now. Elke isn't going to be able to push. When I tell you, I want you to work your hands down her belly to help strengthen her contractions."

Rio had been holding up so far. But he didn't know if he could do as Velvet wanted. His knees felt all rubbery. "Can't one of the girls do it?"

"Your hands are stronger." Just then, another hard contraction knotted Elke's stomach. "Now!" Velvet commanded.

She took up her station between Elke's knees and applied a gentle pressure on Elke's private parts to keep the baby from coming too fast while Rio massaged Elke's heaving abdomen.

His newly laundered clothes were sweat-drenched by the time the baby finally slipped out of Elke's body, and he didn't smell any too good—but he felt as if he'd just taken part in a miracle.

Velvet caught the baby in a towel, turned it over and gave its buttocks a gentle slap to make it cry. The thin wail couldn't have sounded sweeter to Rio's ears. He'd

pulled many a calf into the world but he had never felt
the joy he experienced now.

"It's a boy," Velvet said, her voice husky with the
strain of the last few hours. Then to Rio's dismay, she
began to cry.

"What's wrong now?" Rio asked. "I thought we did
real good."

"*We* did. But the baby isn't going to. He was born
much too soon." Choking back her tears, Velvet wiped
the infant clean and wrapped him in a piece of blanket. Then she held it out to Rio.

Rio backed away as if she'd offered him a rattler.
"Aw, hell, Velvet. I don't know how to hold a baby.
Calves are more my style."

"You'd damn well better hold this one," Velvet said,
sounding as fierce as a she-wolf defending her cubs. "I
have to tend its mother." She knuckled away the tears
on her cheeks. "The baby is dying, Rio, and I don't
want it to die alone."

She thrust the tiny bundle into his arms without giving him another chance to say no, then turned back to
her patient. She had wrapped the baby so well, all he
could see was its face. The infant's complexion looked
as gray as a winter sky but its tiny features were perfectly formed.

An unexpected wave of tenderness washed over Rio
like an ocean swell. He'd never seen so small or so
pretty a human being—or one with such a frail hold on
life. Turning his back so Velvet couldn't see the tears
welling in his eyes, too, he clutched the babe to his
chest and did the only thing he could think to do.

While Velvet cleaned Elke's bloodstained thighs and

waited for the afterbirth, she was astonished to hear a
tenor voice fill the room—a voice so sweet and pure
that it might have belonged to an angel.

But there weren't any angels to be seen, just a worn-
out cowboy who had sung many a herd to sleep.

" 'I dream of Jeannie, with the light brown hair' "
came the lament to a lost love as Rio de Vargas crooned
the dying child to its eternal rest.

Chapter Nine

Elke awoke to discover that her body had been transformed into a new geography of pain—pain so all encompassing that at first she had no room in her conscious mind for anything else. The slightest motion sent white-hot spears of agony through her head. The smallest intake of breath bludgeoned her chest like a hammmberblow. Her abdomen felt achingly hollow, as if all the world's broken promises had found a way to lodge in it. And the simple act of opening her eyes sent a rivulet of nausea up her parched throat.

She could barely make out the contours of the shadowed room where she lay. Blinking, she made a futile attempt to focus on the pale blur hovering over her. Although the features remained indistinct, there could be no mistaking the rioting mass of red curls. Good heavens! What was Velvet Gilhooley doing by her bedside?

Elke tried to wet her lips to frame the question and couldn't summon any saliva. Seeming to understand her need, Velvet held a cup to her lips.

Elke drank greedily, then to her dismay retched up

every drop she had swallowed. Again Velvet anticipated her need. This time she held a basin under Elke's mouth.

When the gagging subsided, Velvet wiped Elke's face and lips with a damp cloth, then smoothed back her hair. "I know you must have a lot of questions," Velvet said, straightening the bed clothes with practiced efficiency, "but right now you mustn't try to talk. The doctor said you need all the rest you can get. You have a concussion, as well as a couple of cracked ribs."

Elke tried to process the information—and failed. *Otto,* she thought. Where was Otto? Why wasn't he there? His name still reverberated through her befuddled mind as the darkness claimed her again.

She had no idea how long she slept. Mercifully, she couldn't remember the nightmares that had plagued her slumber. When she awoke again, the pale glow of a kerosene lamp illuminated the room.

This time she had no trouble focusing. She had never seen the room before, let alone imagined one so shamelessly opulent. With its velvet-covered walls, gold brocade drapes, crystal wall sconces, and mirrors everywhere—including one over the bed—it was as alien to her experience as an ocean to a desert tribesman.

The painted female face gazing down at her with obvious concern was equally foreign. "You just lie here real still-like and I'll fetch Miss Velvet," the young woman said.

So the first woman *had* been Velvet Gilhooley, the notorious madame, Elke thought, and the girl must be one of Velvet's fallen angels. Her previous brief awakening had seemed like a bad dream. She feared this one would be even worse.

A premonition of disaster flashed through her mind like heat lightning across a summer sky. She lay absolutely still, terrified of knowing the circumstances that had brought her to this strange bed.

"Rita told me you were awake," Velvet said, appearing in Elke's limited field of vision. "How do you feel?"

"Awful," Elke croaked in a voice she barely recognized as her own. "What happened? Where's my husband?"

"Don't you remember?"

"No."

Velvet sank into the chair by the bed and took one of Elke's hands. "You were always so kind to me, Mrs. Sonnschein, I'd give anything not to have to be the one to tell you."

"Tell me what?"

"You were in an accident."

"An accident?" Elke struggled to fill the void in her memory.

"A buggy accident," Velvet prompted. "You and your husband were on your way back from Pride's Passion."

Suddenly a series of scenes flickered through Elke's brain as if she viewed them through a stereopticon.

The ground flying by.

The horse running.

Otto tugging on the reins.

Shots fired.

The Detweiler twins galloping past.

Laughing.

They were laughing.

The buggy tilting on its side.

Otto flying through the air, still holding the reins.

As suddenly as the scene appeared, it blinked out—but not before she saw Otto hit the ground.

Could he have survived such a blow? And what of her baby? Her free hand slid down the covers to her abdomen, her fingers feeling the truth before her mind could acknowledge it.

Velvet's grip tightened. "Do you remember now?"

"Only the accident. What happened afterward? Where is my husband and my baby? I want Otto," Elke wailed.

"There isn't any way to sugar coat what I have to tell you. Rio de Vargas was on his way into town when he came across the accident. He couldn't do a thing to help Mr. Sonnschein. But he got you to town as fast as he could. Doc Rothe wasn't in and Rio didn't know anyone else in Fredericksburg, so he brought you here. You were in labor. I delivered the baby myself. It was a boy—a beautiful little boy."

Elke ignored the tears streaming down Velvet's face. She refused to accept what they implied. "What do you mean, he couldn't help Otto? Is my husband all right?"

"Rio said he was hurt real bad. The truth is, your husband never knew what hit him. I know it's not much comfort, but he didn't suffer."

Elke bit her lip so hard she drew blood. Rio had it all wrong. Poor dear Otto had suffered. He'd been so frightened. He'd died with that fear. And now he'd never know he had fathered a son. Thank God a part of Otto had survived.

"I want to see my baby."

Velvet took a lacy handkerchief from an equally lacy cuff and wiped her eyes. "I'm so sorry, Mrs. Sonnschein. He didn't live but a few minutes. You see, he was born too soon. You baby boy is in heaven with his father."

"I don't believe you. Why are you trying to hurt me? What have I ever done to you?" Too weak to rise, Elke clutched the covers in her knotted fists and glared at Velvet.

"I know you don't have any call to trust me. But I would never knowingly or willingly hurt another woman. And I would never make up such a terrible story."

Elke wished she could shut her ears to the truth she heard in Velvet's voice—and her eyes to the sympathy she saw on Velvet's face. She longed to sink back into the darkness and never rise from it.

A cry rose up her throat, a terrible sound compounded of grief and rage and loss. "No!" she burst out as if she could command God to return her loved ones. "NO, NO, *NO!*"

Velvet gazed down at the woman whose sorrow had pierced her own carefully armored heart. Although the circumstances had been different, she knew all too well what it felt like to lose the man you loved—and then to lose his child, too.

In her case the no-account son of a bitch had walked out as soon as she told him she was in the family way. A few months later she had given the baby up for adoption in the hope it would have a better life than she could provide.

Yes, her circumstances had been very different. However, her devastation had been identical. She knew no way to comfort Elke because nothing anyone had said or done had comforted her all those years ago. If Velvet had learned anything from the experience, it had been that grief takes its own time. And the first taste of it was always the worst.

No one could share it. No one could ease its burden. Rising, she walked out of the room to leave Elke to shed the tears that are best shed alone.

Velvet had closed the house to business the night Rio de Vargas appeared with Elke in his arms. She had kept it closed in the two days since. The parlor with its paintings of lush unclothed women, its fainting couches where an eager man could dally with the lady of his choice, seemed more evocative of lust empty than it did on a Saturday night when her girls entertained a room full of randy men.

Velvet gazed around, wondering how soon she could open again. She sank onto one of the tufted couches, leaned back and closed her eyes, refusing to let Elke's grief reawaken her own. Water under the bridge, she told herself. Spilled milk. How she came to be in this place at this time didn't matter a damn anymore. So she didn't have a husband and a passel of children. So what? She had achieved riches beyond her wildest dreams.

"Are you all right, Miss Gilhooley?" The sound of Whitey's deep baritone rescued her from her unwanted reverie.

She opened her eyes to see the huge black man standing by her chair. He had so much dignity and presence that she couldn't help thinking he would have been a banker or a lawyer—or maybe even a congressman—but for the color of his skin. "I'm fine. Where is everyone?"

"The girls are upstairs, fussing over their clothes and their hair. Gossiping a mile a minute, too. You know how they are when they have free time."

"I guess we can all use a few days off. How about you, Whitey? Isn't there something you'd rather be doing?"

"I wouldn't think of leaving you alone, Miss Gilhooley. Some of the customers are getting anxious for you to reopen. I wouldn't want them to barge in under the circumstances."

Velvet couldn't help smiling at Whitey's turn of phrase. *Anxious,* indeed. A man who had his mind set on putting his prick inside a whore could be considerably more than anxious if he didn't get what he wanted. Cantankerous was more like it. Mean, too.

She wished she could tell Whitey when they would open for business again. But the doctor had told her Elke couldn't be moved and it didn't seem right to have a bunch of lustful studs playing at hide the sausage under the same roof as the grieving widow.

Whitey turned to leave, then turned back and said, "I forgot to tell you. Mr. de Vargas is back."

"Send him right in—and thank you, Whitey. I appreciate your loyalty. There will be a bonus for you with this month's pay." Velvet rose and walked to the mahogany bar at one end of the room. By the time the jingle of spurs announced Rio's presence, she had filled two glasses with the finest brandy to be found west of the Brazos. It came from her private stock and she only poured it for her best customers.

"You look like you could use this," she said, taking in Rio's road-weary appearance.

He hadn't changed his clothes since she last saw him. Dust and sweat grimed his formerly pristine outfit. Little more than a day had passed since he left with the baby's remains. Where had he been in the time since then, and what had he done? He looked worn out through and through, like a horse who had been ridden hard and put up wet—or a whore who had taken one man too many to her bed.

"I sure could, Miss Gilhooley," Rio replied, taking the glass she held out.

He tilted his head back and downed the contents without pausing for breath, then said, "Thank you, ma'am" as politely as a boy addressing a schoolmarm.

"For heaven's sake, Rio, considering what we've been through, won't you call me Velvet?"

He turned as deep a red as the calico cloth knotted at his throat. Suddenly, he seemed to realize he still wore his hat. He took it off, slapped it against his thigh to rid it of dust, and put it down on the bar. Shifting from foot to foot, he said, "Miss Velvet, do you think you could pour me a little more of that brandy?"

She liked the way her name fit on his lips, she realized as she refilled his glass. In fact, she found a whole lot to like about Rio from his broad shoulders to his melodious singing voice. It had been a long time since she had so good an opinion of a man.

He could have walked out on her two days ago and left her to cope with Elke's premature labor by herself. Most men would have. But not Rio. She liked him most of all for that.

"I've been thinking about the other day," she said. "I owe you for sticking around—and I pride myself on paying my debts."

"You don't owe me a thing. I was the one who brought Missus Sonnschein here in the first place."

"Just the same, the next time you come to town I want you to take your pick of the girls—on the house."

His eyes grew thoughtful. His face flushed again and he sipped at his drink. "If you really mean it about me taking my pick," he said, swallowing hard, "I ch-choose you."

Velvet couldn't have been more shocked—yet a tiny thrill raced down her spine to flutter deep in her belly. The shy foreman had surprised her again. Flattered her, too, in view of the younger, prettier girls who worked for her.

"Like I said, Rio, I believe in paying my debts," she replied throatily.

Quiet seemed suspended in the room while she considered the commitment she had just made—and thought how much she looked forward to fulfilling it. She might be an old woman of thirty-six, but by heaven, she wasn't dead yet!

"How's Mrs. Sonnschein?" Rio asked, breaking the awkward silence.

"She's in a pretty bad state."

"I suppose that's to be expected, losing her husband and all."

"Did you bring her husband's body back to town with you?"

Rio got a faraway look in his eyes, as if he were mentally trying to distance himself from something unpleasant. "What with the heat and the vultures, he weren't in no shape to bring back to town. I've seen some bad things in my day, but—"

Afraid he was about to go into the gory details, Velvet reached up and laid her fingers across his mouth to silence him. To her surprise, his drooping mustache felt soft as silk. For a moment she was so startled that she almost forgot what she intended to say.

"Ah—where is he? Mr. Sonnschein I mean."

"The boys and I buried him up to Pride's Passion under the shade of a water oak. Gave him a right proper send-off if I do say so myself. I put the baby in the grave with him. It seemed fitting somehow."

"Do you think Patrick will object to you burying strangers on his land?"

For the first time since he walked in, Rio's features relaxed in a genuine smile. "Not a chance. I don't think he'd want it any other way. He always had a soft spot for the Sonnscheins. What about Mrs. Sonnschein? How's she going to take it when she finds out her husband and baby aren't in the cemetery by the Vereins Kirche?"

Velvet let her breath go in a heavy sigh. "The poor thing is so hurt—inside and out—there's just no way to know."

"If you think it will ease her mind, I'd like to tell her myself."

* * *

Elke had experienced grief when her parents had died. But she had never known feelings as deep and devastating as the emotions that raged through her now. She pressed her hands against her newly flat belly. Thinking of the heart that had beat beneath her own, she kneaded her aching flesh as if she could magically reawaken the spark of life that had been so brutally extinguished.

Sob after sob burst from her throat with the realization that she would never see her son, never hold him in her arms, never croon a mother's songs. Why, dear God, why?

If only she hadn't insisted on going to Pride's Passion.

If only she had put her husband's wishes and her child's welfare first.

If only she had never loved Patrick Pride.

God had every reason to punish her. But why had Otto and her unborn child suffered for her sins?

Tears poured down her face as she contemplated the wreckage of her life. She had come so close to fulfilling the vow she had made all those years ago. She had sworn that Texas wouldn't defeat her. But the courage that had sustained her had been nothing more than misguided pride. At every turn in the road she had taken the wrong path, following her errant heart wherever it led.

A bitter brew of self-loathing rose up her throat as she thought of all the cruel things she had said to Otto. If only she could take them back. He had paid the ultimate price for her folly.

At least he had been spared the knowledge that their child was dead. A fresh torrent of grief raged through her at the thought. How could she have hoped to be a good mother when she was such a worthless human being? She should have died, too—deserved to die.

Her frantic gaze darted around the opulent room seeking a way to end her torment. Surely Velvet kept a weapon to defend herself. A gun. A knife.

Heedless of her pain, Elke struggled to rise from the bed, oblivious to anything but her own deadly quest. Clinging to the brass headboard, she made it to the edge of the mattress and levered herself to her feet. The room tilted and her vision narrowed to a tiny tunnel of light.

Strong arms caught her as she fell, lifted her and gently deposited her back in the bed. On the brink of a swoon, she couldn't prevent her traitorous heart from praying it was Patrick who gently settled her down on the covers.

"Good God, Missus Sonnschein, you have no business getting up so soon. Don't you know you could hurt yourself?" a male voice said.

Elke's eyes fluttered open to see Patrick's foreman, Rio de Vargas, gazing down at her, his weatherbeaten face etched with worry. Velvet had said he'd found her and brought her to town. She owed her life to him, and yet she couldn't thank him for saving it.

"Did you want something? Is that why you got up?" Velvet asked from over Rio's shoulder.

"No," Elke replied. The only thing she wanted was her husband and her baby. Nothing more and nothing less.

"I reckon you ought to know about—" Rio seemed to be searching for the right words.

"About the burial." Velvet supplied the missing phrase as if she were privy to the foreman's thoughts.

"I do. I want to know everything from the time you found us," Elke said, dreading the recounting and yet determined to hear every painful detail.

Rio retold the story slowly, like a man who is unaccustomed to stringing so many words together. When he stopped for breath, Velvet filled in the details. Together, they managed to paint a vivid picture.

"And so me and the boys buried Mr. Sonnschein with the baby in his arms," Rio finished half an hour later. "The gravesite is the prettiest I ever did see, the way it looks over the Guadalupe river. I read the Lord's Prayer over them and sang a hymn. Conchita Alvarez's husband fixed a cross and she planted a rambling rose beside it. When you're up to it, I reckon you'll want to have your pastor come out and say a few words."

When she was up to it? Elke doubted that day would ever come.

"I don't know what more I can say—except that accidents happen," Rio concluded. "I'm sure sorry this one happened to your family."

"Accident?" Elke burst out. "It wasn't any accident. It was murder."

Chapter Ten

Patrick Pride gazed out the stagecoach window, enjoying the familiar sights and sounds as the vehicle rattled down Fredericksburg's Main Street. One more night and he'd be home. He could hardly wait to reclaim his vast acres, to bring his bride to the house he'd built for the family they would create. But first, he thought with a quickening of his pulse, there would be time for old friends.

To his surprise the Sonnschein bakery seemed to be empty when the stage passed by. Strange, he thought. Was it his imagination or did the bakery have an abandoned air? The Sonnscheins would never close on a weekday. Elke must be in the back with Otto, trying out a new recipe or going over the books. Yes, that had to be it.

The guilt he'd felt over that long-ago drunken kiss had evaporated. He could hardly wait to see Otto and Elke, to introduce them to Charlotte and toast being together with the precious bottle of Steinhager he had found in Natchez.

God, it felt good to be home again. He hadn't realized how much he missed the Hill Country.

"You sho' do look happy, Mr. Patrick," Ella Mae commented from her perch on the opposite bench.

"I am," he replied, wishing Charlotte shared his pleasure. A decidedly sour expression rode his wife's lovely features. Although they sat side by side, she couldn't have been more remote if she were still in Natchez with her family.

"Lordy, Mr. Patrick, is that an honest to God Injun?" The whites of Ella Mae's eyes showed all around as she gestured at the half-naked Comanche riding by on a paint pony.

"It sure is, Ella Mae."

Patrick couldn't help smiling at the exuberant black woman. He'd bought Ella Mae's freedom because Charlotte had shed such copious tears when the moment came to leave her beloved maid behind.

At the time it had seemed like a needless expense. Now he considered it money well spent. Ella Mae had proven to be a far better traveling companion than his wife. Wide-eyed with excitement, the maid had enjoyed every minute of the long trip from Mississippi, which was a hell of a lot more than he could say for Charlotte.

"Another day and we'll be at Pride's Passion," he said, taking one of Charlotte's daintily gloved hands in his own and giving her what he hoped was a reassuring smile. He should have anticipated that a gently bred girl like Charlotte wouldn't easily withstand the rigors of their journey.

The honeymoon had started auspiciously enough with a trip from Natchez to New Orleans aboard a Mississippi paddle wheeler that boasted every conceivable luxury. However, his bride's charm, humor, and *joie de vivre* had faded away with every mile that distanced her from her home.

Little by little she had been transformed from a sensuous woman who gloried in the marital bed back into the spoiled child who had tried to snatch the gold braid from his uniform so many years ago. Her constant complaints weren't rendered any more palatable by the fact that she made them in a honeyed drawl.

She had suffered intermitten *mal de mer* from the moment their clipper ship departed New Orleans until it docked at Galveston, and had been far too ill to indulge in the nightly romps they had both enjoyed aboard the paddle wheeler.

He'd done his best to be sympathetic, holding her hand while she moaned piteously, declaring herself near death. He had even made forays to the galley at all hours of the day and night to bring her the sweets and the champagne which she swore were the only items of food and drink she could keep down.

He had promised her she would feel better when they disembarked in Galveston—and she had, physically. Her mental state was another matter. She had complained bitterly about their accommodations although he'd taken the finest suite in the Tremont Hotel, and she'd wept at the thought of having to endure the four-hundred-mile trip inland in the company of strangers.

To keep peace, he had paid for every seat in the stage so they could make the journey alone. A second wagon had been required to transport trunks full of her clothes. He still couldn't quite fathom how she and her mother had managed to amass so huge a trousseau in so short a time.

"I'm so weary of this coach, I think I'm going to be sick again," Charlotte grumbled, finally emerging from her semisomnolent state to gaze at him. "Where are we? When do we get to Fredericksburg?"

"This *is* Fredericksburg," he replied as the stage braked to a stop in front of the Nimitz Hotel. He'd described the town in detail any number of times. Good Lord, hadn't she listened to a word he'd said?

Opening the stage door, he leapt to the ground, relishing the feel of land under his feet. He breathed deeply, feasting on the crisp cool air, then turned to help his wife down. *His wife.* He still hadn't gotten used to the idea of being married. He could hardly fault Charlotte for having similar problems making the adjustment.

She had insisted on putting her hoop on every morning, saying she refused to lower her personal grooming standards even though the cumbersome hoop added to the discomfort of her journey. Now it took considerable maneuvering to extricate her from the stage's narrow door. By contrast, the hoopless Ella Mae hopped down as easily as a cricket.

Free of confinement at last, Charlotte gazed up and down the street, her nose wrinkling as if it had just been assaulted by a foul odor. "This can't be Fredericksburg!" she declared, stamping a dainty foot.

"I assure you, it is," he answered dryly, fighting his impatience. He took her elbow and gently maneuvered her toward the hotel's front doors.

"But you said Fredericksburg was a city and this,"

she cast a despairing glance over her shoulder, "would hardly qualify as a *village* back home."

Perhaps his description had been a bit too glowing, Patrick thought, trying to see the town through Charlotte's eyes. If she didn't like Fredericksburg, he hated to think how she would react when she saw Kerrville.

"Now, Miss Charlotte, don't you be takin' on so," Ella Mae chided, boldly saying what he dared not. *"This* is your home now."

So far the black woman had more than earned her freedom, he mused as the three of them walked into the lobby.

"It's good to see you again, Patrick," a deep voice boomed from the end of the room. Charles Henry Nimitz rose from his station behind the registration desk and hurried across the floor to pump Patrick's hand.

Patrick had stayed at the hotel often and had spent many hours in Nimitz's company. He was a burly man of medium height with a full beard. A former sailor who still longed for the sea despite his growing family, he'd built his hotel to resemble a ship. The prow contained the lobby.

Patrick had regarded the hotel's architecture as a delightful eccentricity on Nimitz's part—and indeed the place had become a landmark. Seeing Charlotte's frown as she gazed around, he knew she didn't share his opinion.

"And who might this lovely lady be?" Nimitz asked, looking at Charlotte.

In his pleasure at seeing a familiar face, Patrick had forgotten his manners. "Charles Henry Nimitz, I have the distinct honor of presenting my bride, Charlotte Devereux of Natchez."

"Don't you mean Charlotte Pride?" Chuckling at his own cleverness, Nimitz pumped Charlotte's hand almost as hard as he had Patrick's. "Welcome to the Nimitz, Mrs. Pride. I've saved my best rooms for you and your—ah—your friend here." A nod of his head indicated Ella Mae.

"Pleased to meet you," Charlotte replied politely, although the coldness in her eyes clearly said she wasn't impressed by her host or his establishment. "Ella Mae isn't my friend, sir. She's my slave."

"Not any more, I isn't," Patrick heard Ella Mae mutter under her breath.

While they talked, the stage driver and the wagon drover carted trunk after trunk into the lobby.

Nimitz gazed at the ever-growing pile of luggage, shook his head as if in disbelief, then headed back to his desk and said, "I guess you'll be needing another room just for your things. If you'll sign the register, I'll see about getting everything upstairs."

Patrick followed Nimitz, leaving Charlotte surrounded by her belongings.

"I reckon you haven't heard the news yet," Nimitz said as soon as they were alone.

"What news?" Patrick asked, his mind preoccupied by the oddity of writing Mr. and Mrs. Patrick Pride in the leather-bound register.

"There's been a killing—or an accident, depending on who you believe."

"Have the Comanches been acting up again?"

"Not Comanches—or Comancheros, either. It was

those no-account Detweilers. The two of them are long gone. The word is they've headed east to enlist. You know how they used to boast about fighting for the South if it came to a war. Good riddance, I say. If they did run the Sonnscheins' buggy into the ground the way Mrs. Sonnschein claims, I sure wouldn't want them hanging around these parts."

Patrick hadn't been paying close attention to Nimitz's convoluted tale. The mention of the Sonnschein name finally captured his attention. "Are the Sonnscheins all right?"

"Not hardly." Nimitz leaned across the desk and lowered his voice. "I heard Otto's brains were splattered to kingdom come when the buggy crashed."

Patrick couldn't believe his ears. Otto had been so full of life the last time he'd seen him. "Surely you're mistaken."

Nimitz pursed his lips and knit his brow. "I guess I shouldn't have blurted it out like that, seeing as how you and Otto were such good friends. But I thought you knew. It's been the talk of the town ever since it happened."

His heart thundering, Patrick reached across the desk and grabbed Henry's shoulder in an iron grip. "I want to hear the whole story from beginning to end."

Patrick had faced charging cavalry and artillery fire in the Mexican war. But those experiences hadn't terrified him half as much as listening to the hotelier recount the tragedy that had befallen the Sonnscheins. His skin iced, his heart hammered a staccato beat. The blood drained from his face to pool in his belly.

He'd come so close to losing Elke, he agonized,

never even thinking she hadn't been his to lose. And Otto, poor Otto. Gone so suddenly.

"Are you certain Elke's all right?" he asked when Nimitz's story came to a close.

"Doctor Rothe said she's lucky to be alive. But she did lose the baby."

As if he'd been dealt an unexpected body blow, Patrick expelled his breath in a harsh gasp. "What baby?"

"Elke was in the family way, and pretty far along, too. My Sophie said Elke had no business going off to Pride's Passion in her condition. But you know how Frau Sonnschein can be when she gets the bit between her teeth."

"What in the world were they doing at my ranch?"

"Nobody knows. Strange, them going there when you weren't home."

The hair on Patrick's nape rose as he suddenly realized why the Sonnscheins had gone to Pride's Passion. It had been his letter. In the hurly-burly haste of his marriage, he had forgotten about writing it.

"Damn," he cursed under his breath, "damn it to hell." He'd gladly sell his soul to the devil if, in return, he could take that letter back.

"The Sonnscheins were on their way to town when the Detweilers ran their buggy down. Your foreman found them."

"What's taking so long? I'm exhausted," Charlotte called out plaintively.

Patrick didn't hear her. In his concern for Elke, Charlotte had ceased to exist. "Where is Elke? Have you seen her? Are you sure she's all right?" The questions tumbled from his lips so quickly that the words ran into each other.

"You'll have to find that out for yourself. Like I said, your foreman took her to Velvet Gilhooley's place. She's been recuperating there ever since. We all feel mighty sorry for her troubles, but decent folk aren't about to set foot in a place like that."

"Decent folk? You prate about decency, but you and Sophie couldn't even be bothered to pay your condolences." Patrick made no effort to hide the contempt he felt.

Poor Elke. How utterly alone she must feel—how forsaken. Not only had she lost her husband and child, she had been abandoned by the very people she counted as her friends.

Well, damn it, she would never feel alone again, he silently swore—not while he had breath in his body and strength in his arms. He had but one goal in mind as he spun away from the desk and headed out of the hotel, leaving his flustered, furious bride behind.

He intended to see Elke if it meant going to hell and back to do it.

Elke sat in a plushly upholstered boudoir chair, staring out the window at a laundry line stretched across the whorehouse's backyard. The intimate garments so boldly displayed no longer made her blush—not even the crotchless pantaloons.

Recuperating in Velvet's establishment had vastly altered her opinion about a lot of things, including what was proper and what wasn't. In the three weeks she'd been there, the whores' loving care had been a godsend.

She couldn't say as much for the rest of the community. They had been scandalized by her presence in a house of ill-repute. Never mind that she'd had no choice about being there, that Dr. Rothe insisted she stay put. Never mind that she'd lost her husband and child. Pastor Basse and Carolyn Grobe had been the only ones to come and offer their condolences. And only Carolyn had visited more than once.

So no, she wasn't scandalized by lace fripperies. The whores didn't hurt people the way she'd been hurt. All they did was offer a little pleasure in a cheerless world—a world Elke had grown to hate with every fiber of her passionate being.

In the last few weeks she had plumbed the depths of man's inhumanity to his fellow man. What the Detweilers had done had been bad enough. But she'd had no reason to expect anything other than careless, mindless cruelty from them. She had expected a great deal more from the townspeople and from the sheriff—even though she had known he was a southern sympathizer.

He had come to see her three days after the accident, listened to her story, and then practically accused her of driving the Detweiler twins to attack the buggy. "I hear you threatened them with a shotgun on two occasions. You know what the Bible says. Those who live by the sword shall die by the sword."

"The Bible doesn't say anything about bullies who attack unarmed people," she said bitterly. "My husband is dead. I expect you to do your duty."

"The twins are just nineteen and they haven't had the advantages a lady like yourself has enjoyed. If their mother had lived, they might have turned out different."

Elke had been weak and in considerable pain. But hearing him attempt to justify Otto's murder had driven her to her feet. "I used to feel sorry for the Detweilers, too. But they're not the only ones to lose a parent early in life. It doesn't give them an excuse to terrorize everyone who is smaller or weaker than they are."

She had shouted so loud that Velvet had come running. But nothing she or Velvet said had changed the sheriff's mind. He had talked about the tense times, about the danger of pitting the antislavery forces against the proslavery faction if he arrested Eli and Jude Detweiler, then spoke at great length about the futility of bringing them to trial since it would only be her word against theirs. In the end, he refused to issue a warrant for the twins' arrest.

At first, Elke had been dumbfounded. Slowly, anger had replaced confusion. She had quickly learned to use anger as a shield against grief. Now that anger sustained her completely. She fed on it, never realizing that in doing so she fed on her own soul.

A knock at the door interrupted her bitter musing. "Are you up to a little company?" Velvet called out.

"Of course," Elke replied, wondering if Carolyn Grobe's curiosity had gotten the better of her again. On Carolyn's two previous visits, her eyes had practically popped from their sockets as she took in every last detail of Velvet's so-called "den of iniquity."

Pulling her borrowed negligee close, Elke gazed toward the door. It swung open to reveal a man standing in the shadowed hall, a tall man with broad shoulders and a slender body—a man she had dreamed about every night of her adult life.

With a soft cry, Elke leapt to her feet, heedless of her deshabille. Barefoot, her golden hair flowing around her, she ran across the floor. She'd had no chance to armor herself against the onslaught of emotion that trembled all through her.

For one breathless moment her eyes locked and held his, her open gaze conveying everything—all the love, the passionate need, the hours spent in hapless longing—that honor and decency had kept her from confessing.

"Dear God, I'm so glad you're back," she finally said.

He crossed the distance that still separated them and pulled her into his arms. "I'm so sorry, Elke. I should never have left you."

Standing in the doorway, Velvet watched their reunion. So that's the way it is, she thought. She had always wondered why a heartbreaker like Patrick had never married, why he came to town once a month for supplies when Kerrville was so much closer to his ranch, why he visited her establishment and left on many a night without going upstairs with one of her girls.

Now she had the answer. She knew she ought to walk away—but she couldn't tear her gaze from the riveting scene. Just once before she died, she wanted a man to hold her the way Patrick was holding Elke, to shelter her with his body and utter her name with all the love in the world expressed in just that one word.

with her dad in Phoenix, she didn't know if she'd get any—and even without a baby. "You gave up on custody and my job, since her heart had been filled with Patrick.

Chapter Eleven

Weak-kneed, her emotions rioting, Elke clung to Patrick. Her long-withheld tears soaked his shirt. She felt like a lost soul who has finally been granted a blessed vision of home.

The last time he'd held her, she had been terrified by her own passion. This afternoon she felt only joy and relief. He embodied everything she longed for and never thought to have again—happiness in the present, hope for the future, and a soul-deep sense of peace.

She had been through so much and paid such a high price for this precious moment. The guilt and loss she'd felt since awakening in Velvet's bed faded away in the ineffable rapture of being held by the only man she had ever loved.

Just last week Pastor Basse had tried to console her by saying that Otto's death and the baby's premature birth had been part of God's plan. At the time she'd had trouble imagining so cruel a deity. Now she couldn't help wondering if this joyous reunion had been what God intended.

Indeed, Patrick's presence seemed like a miracle. The image of him standing in Velvet's bedroom door, looking like all her dreams come true, would forever be engraved in her memory. She had never needed anyone more than she needed him.

"Cry it out, darling, it's all right," he murmured into her hair. "You're safe, my love. I won't let anyone hurt you again." His hands pressed her body closer, as if to meld it with his.

She reveled in the contact, not counting the passing minutes as they stood heart to beating heart. Being with him felt so right, so inevitable, that she wondered how she had endured the long years without him.

Surely he shared her emotions. Why else would he call her "my love," and vow to care for her? Six months ago, in her overweening pride, she would have resented that promise. Now she knew she couldn't always look out for herself. She needed a man whose strength would complement her determination, one who wouldn't give in to her all the time—and Patrick was such a man.

She loved him beyond her ability to describe the emotion. She loved him beyond reason, beyond any measure of right and wrong. She wanted to tilt her head back and find his lips, to kiss him long and deep as a seal of their unspoken bond. But she couldn't bring herself to break the spell that held them both fast.

She knew that the remorse she'd felt since the accident would soon return. For now, though, she grasped tightly to the succor she found in his arms. She would never forget Otto's death and the loss of the baby. However, she would not permit dark memories to cloud this golden time.

She ran her hands down Patrick's powerful torso to reassure herself he was flesh and blood and not a dream. He felt so different from Otto, so competent in his muscled strength—so utterly male.

Patrick repressed a groan of pleasure as Elke's hands roamed his back. She needed to be cherished, to be cosseted and cared for, and yet he couldn't control the feverish desire that threatened to consume him. He wanted her. Dear God, how he wanted her despite the new fragility he felt beneath her robe—a fragility that revealed how she had suffered far more succinctly than Nimitz's words.

Her body was as slender as a girl's. Didn't Velvet have the sense to see that Elke ate three meals a day? Had Dr. Rothe lost his mind, insisting she convalesce in a whorehouse? She should have been in her own home, nursed by one of the friends who had crowded her parlor the last time he saw her.

Fury swelled in his chest. He reserved his deepest anger for himself. Dear God, what had he done? he agonized, absorbing Elke's every shudder, desperately willing his strength into her body.

The enormity of the mistake he'd made thundered through his mind like martial drums, and burned in his gut like acid.

How could he have walked out of her life?

How could he have lied to himself about how much she meant to him?

Most of all, *how could he have married Charlotte?*

He knew he would carry those bitter questions to his grave.

His father had often said that timing was everything

in life. Charlotte's had been impeccable. His own had been cataclysmic. God had played a hideous joke on them all, freeing Elke while he had said his marriage vows.

He had no right to hold her, to comfort her, to caress her—no right to make love to her though his body ached for that sweet release. He belonged to another woman by virtue of the most solemn vows. And yet, God help him, he had to kiss Elke one more time.

He didn't realize he had groaned out loud until Elke lifted her head to gaze into his eyes. Her own sparkled with tears and brimmed with concern. *For him.* Despite all she had endured, she was actually worried about him.

He stilled the question he read in her gaze, brushing her mouth tenderly. Her lips quivered, then parted. He inhaled her breath, drank in her taste, then angled his head to deepen the tender contact.

The last time they kissed, he'd been filled with the importance of his own rampant masculinity—and half drunk on Steinhager. This time he had no excuse.

Only a monster would take advantage of a woman in her situation—but he was just such a monster. His hands tangled in her hair as he pressed her lips closer. His tongue pushed past her teeth into her silken inner mouth in a kiss a hundred times more intoxicating than their first one.

A shudder rippled down his spine when her tongue mated with his, tentatively at first, then with growing confidence and need. The passion he'd aroused in her seven months ago returned again, only this time he knew its true cause—knew it with his heart, mind, and soul as well, as with his yearning body.

Elke wanted him, hungered for him as much as he did her. All the kisses he'd experienced in the past—including Charlotte's—faded in the heat of Elke's ravishing response.

He lowered one hand to roam her back from her nape to her seductively curved buttocks. Lowering the other hand, he lifted her, pressing her against his arousal. Her thighs parted in acceptance of the intimacy and she moaned his name.

He saw the bed over her shoulder and imagined himself carrying her there, stripping her delicate night clothes away and feasting his greedy eyes on her femininity before plundering her body.

The fantasy seared into his brain as her pliant form told him she wouldn't object. Rather, he suspected she would glory in their union. God, how he wanted it. His manhood cried out for the joining, the merging of bodies that would forever unite their souls. His muscles ached with the strain of not fulfilling the rapturous images that danced inside his fevered brain.

He couldn't hurt Elke that way—not if he had any hope of living with himself afterward. She had already experienced far too much of men's treachery.

Unlocking his fingers one by one, he forced his hands from their seductive purchase. Reluctantly, ever so gently, he let her go.

She gazed up at him with so much trust that his heart constricted. "I didn't mean to attack you like that," she said softly. It's just that seeing you so unexpectedly . . ."

"Don't apologize."

He stepped back far enough so he couldn't feel the heat emanating from her body, as if putting a little distance between them could quell his desire.

Her mouth, all rosy and wet from his kisses, contrasted starkly with her pale face. Dark circles shadowed her matchless blue eyes. She seemed unaware that her negligee had parted to reveal a lacy nightgown—undoubtedly one of Velvet's, since he couldn't imagine practical Elke owning anything so frivolous and costly.

She didn't flinch as his gaze roamed the diaphanous material even though she surely knew how much it revealed. Her nipples pressed against the fabric, the dark areolas clearly visible and incredibly alluring. Despite her slenderness, her breasts were fuller and more womanly than he'd imagined them on all those hot hungry nights when he'd pictured himself between her legs.

Disregarding his brain's urgent command to behave like a gentleman, his gaze lowered to the sweet swell of her belly and the shadowed indentation of her navel. Heaven help him, he could imagine putting his tongue there. Finally, his glance lowered to the shadowed triangle between her thighs. He could imagine putting his tongue there, too.

He pictured himself falling to his knees, lifting her gown and drinking deep of her womanhood—and locked his knees to prevent it from happening.

"God, you're beautiful."

She gave him a smile whose fleeting mischief reminded him of the Elke he had met so many years ago. "Then you must like your women bony."

"I like you any way you are," he said huskily. What he wouldn't give to spend the rest of his life in lighthearted love play with her. A man wouldn't mind growing old with such a woman at his side.

"I've missed you so much. How did you find me?" she asked.

"I'd have gone to the ends of the earth to find you. Thank heaven you were a lot closer. Charles Nimitz told me where you were when I checked into the hotel."

"Have you been here before, then?"

"Yes."

The admission would have upset her a month ago. Now, knowing Velvet's girls, she was glad he'd found an outlet for his virility. And yet, wondering how many of them had fallen in love with him, she couldn't help a primal twinge of jealousy. How easily he aroused her emotions—the good ones and the bad.

"What exactly did Charles tell you?"

"Enough to know you've been through hell."

"Then you know about the murder?" Her voice hardened and he saw a glint of steel in her eyes. She was going to need that steel when he told her the truth.

Charlotte paced the hotel room, heedless of the way her skirt caught on the objects in her path.

"You keep that up, you gonna ruin your best travelin' suit," Ella Mae chided, rolling her eyes.

"If I do, Patrick will just have to pay for another one from Worth. It's all his fault anyway. I declare, I have never been so mortified in my life. If Daddy knew how Patrick was treating me, he'd horsewhip him for sure."

Charlotte finally came to a halt in front of a window and gazed down at the street where farm wagons mingled with mounted riders, stirring up a haze of dust. Trembling with a mixture of dismay and trepidation, she squeezed her eyes shut on the scene.

She had imagined Texas as a romantic setting for her marriage, a place where strong men—dashing heroes all—could be found on every corner. She had pictured herself indulging in the sort of idle flirtations she had mastered so well in Natchez, conjuring up images of herself presiding over local society at the dinner parties and balls she planned to give in Patrick's magnificent mansion.

From what she had already seen of the locals—men and women with no concept of fashion—there wasn't any society to preside over. She hated everything about Fredericksburg, from the dusty street with its crude populace, to the strange boat-shaped hotel, to the corner room that the odious proprietor had pronounced the best he had to offer.

Why, she mused, opening her eyes to gaze around, it wasn't half as big as her own bedroom back home, and nowhere near as luxurious. She didn't care that the accommodations were scrupulously clean. The mirror over the dresser was cracked and cloudy, the bedstead was iron rather than brass, and she shuddered to think about the creatures who dwelled in the mattress. If this was the best, heaven only knew what the other rooms looked like.

"How could Patrick abandon me like this?" she moaned piteously. "What must Mr. Nimitz think?"

"I saw the way you looked at him," Ella Mae replied, "so don't you be tellin' me you care what he thinks."

Charlotte cut a cold glance at Ella Mae that should

have left her shaking in her boots. The girl had become impossibly outspoken since Patrick bought her freedom. "I have always cared what people think. We Devereux have standards. But I don't expect you to understand."

Ella Mae had been unpacking the valise that held the necessities for an overnight stay. Closing a drawer with a thud, she turned to face Charlotte. "You'd best remember you're not a Devereux anymore. You're a Pride now—and I know how you got to be one, so don't be puttin' on any of your airs with me. Mr. Pride is the finest man I ever met. I expect he has some standards of his own for you to live up to."

Charlotte couldn't have been more appalled. She took a deep breath and drew herself up to her full height of five feet. Despite her effort to appear the soul of dignity, her lower lip quivered uncontrollably and her heart beat so frantically that she felt certain it was going to pop right out of her chest. "Are you threatening me?"

"Now why would I do a thing like that, Miss Charlotte?" Ella Mae asked in a more conciliatory tone. "I knows you're upset. But so was Mr. Patrick when he tore out of the hotel."

Upset didn't half do justice to her feelings, Charlotte thought. As for Patrick, she was far too angry to give his state of mind any consideration at all. Here she was, a new bride, far from her beloved home, forsaken by her husband and left to her own devices in a strange hotel with no one but an uppity maid for company.

Humph. Strange hotel indeed! Downright *outlandish* was more like it considering it looked just like a boat. Well, she'd had her fill of her boats on the journey here!

Just thinking about her situation brought tears to her eyes.

Ella Mae produced a handkerchief and held it out. "Now, Miss Charlotte, don't be crying on account of somethin' I said."

"I'm not crying on your account, you silly girl. I want my husband," Charlotte wailed, flinging herself onto the bed and sobbing so deeply that she knew her eyes would be red and swollen for the rest of the day. Not that Patrick would care. A man who walked out on his wife on their honeymoon wasn't likely to take it to heart because she had spent hours sobbing over his desertion.

She pummeled the pillows and drummed her feet on the covers. "How can he—*do* this to me?" she said between hiccupping sobs.

If she'd had the good sense to insist on living at Windmere like her married brothers and sisters, her mother would have learned of her sorry state and come rushing to her aid. She would have wiped away her tears with a cloth soaked in rose water, ordered a soothing camomile tea, and sat with her until she fell asleep.

Realizing her mother was hundreds of miles away made Charlotte cry even harder. She missed her family more than she had thought possible. And Windmere. What she wouldn't give to be back in her room, surrounded by her adoring family. If only she could turn the calendar back, she lamented, sinking deeper and deeper into her misery.

The harsh aroma of smelling salts made her eyes water even harder. "You gonna make yourself sick, carryin' on like that," Ella Mae declared.

Charlotte shoved the maid's hand away. "I'll be sick if you keep holding that awful stuff under my nose!" She rolled onto her back, not caring that her hoop lifted her dress high over her legs. "If you were really worried about me, you'd find my husband and tell him how much I need him."

Ella Mae hesitated a moment before she replied. She'd had about all she could take of Miss Charlotte's carryin' on, but she wasn't sure she should leave her alone. In her present state, she might accidentally hurt herself.

"Iffen you're sure you'll be all right, I'll see what I can do."

To her surprise, Charlotte popped to her feet like a marionette on a string. "He shouldn't be hard to locate in a town this size. I'm sure Mr. Nimitz can help you. I'll just undress and get into bed in the meantime."

"Do you want me to help you?"

Charlotte hastily unbuttoned her suit jacket, took it off, and presented her back. "Just unlace my stays. I can manage the rest. When you find Mr. Pride, make sure and tell him I've been crying my eyes out."

So that's her plan, Ella Mae thought, leaving the room a few minutes later. Charlotte intended to make Mr. Patrick feel guilty as sin for leavin' her alone. She'd been playin' the poor man like a banjo since they met.

Not that it was any of her business, Ella Mae reminded herself, but she couldn't help being sorry for Mr. Patrick—sorry and grateful all jumbled together.

Ella Mae had been a house slave all her life. When she learned Mr. Pride would be takin' Miss Charlotte back to Texas with him, she'd been scared that she would be sent to work in the fields—or maybe even sold away from the only home she'd ever known.

Freedom had come as the most wonderful surprise. Just thinkin' about it still took her breath away. And she owed it all to Mr. Patrick. He deserved a better bargain than he'd gotten with Miss Charlotte. He deserved a wife who would love him for who he really was rather than for who she imagined him to be.

A lifetime of habit reasserted itself as Ella Mae made her way downstairs to the lobby. What white folks did or didn't do wasn't her never mind. She'd do well to watch her business—and her runaway tongue. Freedom wouldn't mean a damn thing if she lost her job.

Charles Nimitz stood behind the registration desk where she'd last seen him. "Is something wrong with the accommodations?" he asked, looking up at her approach. "I thought I heard Mrs. Pride crying."

That would teach Charlotte to make enough noise to wake the dead, Ella Mae thought with a certain satisfaction. Miss Charlotte would be the talk of the town iffen she didn't mind her manners. One of these days she was going to pay the piper for the things she did. As far as Ella Mae was concerned, she'd just as soon not be around when it happened.

Ignoring the curiosity in Mr. Nimitz's eyes, she said, "I'm lookin' for Mr. Pride. You wouldn't happen to know where he went?"

To her surprise, Nimitz turned beet red. "I do. But it's not something I'm free to discuss."

"Unless you want Mrs. Pride askin' you herself, you'd best tell me what you know."

Ten minutes later, Ella Mae found herself walking

down a quiet side street, looking for the house Mr. Nimitz had described. Her eyes flicked from one side of the road to the other, taking in the few small buildings.

Mr. Nimitz had described her destination as a large structure well hidden by a screen of trees and shrubs. Iffen she were to run a house of ill repute, she supposed she'd want it to be out of sight, too. Out of sight and out of the minds of the customers' wives.

Who would have imagined that a fine gentleman like Mr. Pride would go dashing off to a whorehouse the minute he arrived in town. Not that he'd had any pleasure from Miss Charlotte once they set sail on the clipper ship. Despite an occasional upset stomach, Miss Charlotte could and should have gotten around to some jiggety-jig.

Ella Mae silently promised herself that iffen she ever got her hands on a handsome man like Mr. Patrick, she'd damn well make sure he didn't have to run off to some other woman. No sirree! She'd keep their mattress bouncin' every single night if that was what it took to keep her man at home.

Another block's walk brought her to the place Mr. Nimitz had described. From the looks of the spacious stone house, there was a lot of money in whorin'. Ella Mae walked up the path to the front door and knocked boldly, enjoying this new aspect of the adventure that had begun when she left Natchez.

To her surprise a black man opened the door—a tall broad-shouldered black man who was every bit as easy on the eyes as Mr. Patrick.

"My oh my!" she said on a sigh, looking him up and down, "who might you be?"

* * *

While Elke talked, filling Patrick in on everything that had transpired after he left for Natchez, he struggled to ignore the passage of time. He knew Charlotte was probably fretting over the way he'd run off, but he would worry about her later.

Elke needed him, and for the time being, nothing else mattered. He would never be able to give her the things he wanted—the love and support, the understanding, the concern, the passion he felt for her.

He owed all those things to Charlotte—and he vowed to spend the rest of his life trying to be a good husband to her. Surely a few hours wouldn't matter in the grand scheme of things, he reassured himself, holding Elke's hands tight in his own while she poured her heart out.

"I'm so very, very sorry for your loss," he said when her sad story finally came to an end. "I can't help but blame myself. If I had never written that letter . . ."

"What happened isn't your fault! I brought it all on myself."

He saw the guilt in her eyes—and would have given anything to assuage her pain. "Don't talk that way. Don't even *think* that way. So many things went wrong. We can both get all tangled up in *if onlys.*"

"What do you mean?"

"It's always easy to look back and see things you could have done differently. *If only* I hadn't written that letter. *If only* you hadn't wanted to do a favor for a friend. You know what they say about the road to hell being paved with good intentions. If you have to assign blame, don't forget the Detweilers."

"I haven't. And I never will."

"Neither will I. Someday I'll find a way to make them pay for what they did. But I don't want to waste time talking about them when we have better things to discuss. Have you made any plans for your future?"

"Doctor Rothe says I can go home in a few days. I'm going to reopen the bakery."

"I don't want you to work. Let me take care of you."

Elke gave him a smile so sweet that it left him shaken. Instead of saying he wanted to take care of her, he ought to be telling her about Charlotte. But he couldn't seem to find the words. How the hell did you tell the woman you loved that you were married to someone else?

She shook her head. "I couldn't let you do that. Besides, I wouldn't be happy without something to do. I need to work to keep my mind off— You know what I mean."

She felt so safe, so secure, so cared for with Patrick by her side. He hadn't said he loved her in so many words—he must have realized it was much too soon for her to hear such a declaration—but he'd said it in a dozen silent ways just the same. She didn't deserve such good fortune. "You haven't told me about your trip. Did everything turn out the way you hoped?"

To her surprise, Patrick paled at the question and lowered his gaze. "More or less."

She squeezed his hand in sympathy. Here she'd been going on about her own troubles without giving a thought to his. From the bleak expression in his eyes, his reunion with his father hadn't gone as well as it could have. At least his mother had come home with him. "I imagine you're anxious to get back to the ranch. When do you plan to leave town?"

"I had planned to return tomorrow. But I won't go until I'm sure you have everything you need."

She was about to say that he mustn't stay on her account, that they had all the time in the world to settle things between them. But a knock on the door interrupted their conversation.

"Patrick, there's a woman here who insists on seeing you" came the sound of Velvet's voice.

Good heavens, would Patrick's mother have followed him to a whorehouse? Elke wondered. She had so hoped to make a good impression. Now she could only pray that Mrs. Pride would understand her circumstances.

"Please, ask her to come in," Elke called out.

The door opened and to her astonishment, a handsome young black woman walked into the room. "Mr. Patrick, sir, I sho am glad I found you. Mrs. Pride is having a fit back at the hotel."

Releasing Patrick's hand, Elke said, "I really must apologize for keeping you from your mother so long."

"Mother!" the black woman burst out, a look of supreme confusion on her face. "Mrs. Pride isn't his mother. *Miss Charlotte is his wife.*"

Chapter Twelve

Wife. The word lingered in the room like an uninvited guest. Surely the black woman had misspoken, Elke thought.

Steel bands seemed to constrict her chest and the air froze in her lungs as she waited for Patrick to set the stranger straight. He didn't say a thing, though.

His skin whitened, his scar reddened. The wintry expression in his eyes and the grim tightening of his lips revealed the truth. The black woman hadn't been mistaken.

Married. Dear God, he was married. He'd asked her to ready his home for a bride. That's why Otto had died—that's why she had lost her baby. For his wife's comfort.

A new pain pierced her, more terrible in its intensity than all the suffering she had already endured. Betrayal knifed through her innards. It took all her will not to reach across the table between them and claw his eyes out.

How could she have mistaken lust for love, and self-interest for sympathy? He hadn't changed a bit from the man who had stolen a kiss in her kitchen. She had dishonored herself and her husband's memory in Patrick's arms.

She should have known better than to trust him. He had taken the cruelest advantage of her widowhood, letting her think she meant something to him, plundering her mouth, her mind, and her soul, when all the while his new wife waited for him back at the hotel. She would never forgive him for that.

And yet, she couldn't help a certain perverse curiosity about his wife. Was she young? Pretty? Well-bred? The questions ached through her.

God, why was she torturing herself? The new Mrs. Pride had nothing to do with her. If she was very lucky, they would never even meet.

Retreating into her chair until the upholstered back prevented further escape, she clutched her robe close, armoring herself for what she had to do.

"It was very thoughtful of you to stop by to offer your condolences, but I mustn't keep you from your wife."

Patrick had been glaring at Ella Mae, thinking how much he'd enjoy locking his fingers around her neck. The sound of Elke's voice brought his murderous daydream to a screeching halt.

He'd intended to tell Elke about Charlotte—to break the news as gently as possible. But Ella Mae had blurted out the truth before he'd had the chance.

"You aren't keeping me here," he said, turning from the quivering maid to lock gazes with Elke. "Damn it, I wanted to be here. I still want to be here."

"It doesn't matter now, does it? You have other obligations," Elke replied, her voice so tightly controlled that each syllable seemed to stand by itself.

"Of course it matters. *You* matter." Turning back to Ella Mae and giving her a withering look, he said, "Tell your mistress I'll return to the hotel later."

To his relief, Ella Mae fled the room without a backward glance. Then Velvet Gilhooley cut a vicious if-looks-could-kill-you'd-have-breathed-your-last glance at him.

He'd always liked her—even respected her despite her profession. Many a night he'd spent in her parlor talking because he couldn't bring himself to go upstairs with one of her girls when the only woman he wanted was Elke.

Thanks to his own misdeeds, he'd lost Velvet's friendship. But he'd be damned if he'd lose Elke, too. There had to be a way past this disaster.

"If you need me, Elke, just holler," Velvet said, shutting the bedroom with a thud that offered clear proof of the hostility she had yet to express.

However, Velvet wouldn't hold her tongue forever. What would she say about him after he'd gone?

He took a deep breath, trying to clear his mind of the chaotic thoughts tumbling through it. Perhaps he could convince Charlotte to have their marriage annulled. Perhaps he could grow wings and fly, too. He would have given all he possessed—his good name, even his ranch—not to have hurt Elke this way.

"You had better go now."

The firmness in Elke's voice took him by surprise. He could have handled her tears more easily.

"Not before I have a chance to explain."

"There's nothing to explain. You have a wife. Period. End of discussion. If you have a shred of decency inside that fancy suit you're wearing, you'll leave me alone."

Her scathing tone cut him to the bone. The steel he'd so recently admired in her character had returned full force. The grieving feminine creature who had sought comfort in his arms had metamorphosed into the stubborn, willful woman who thought nothing of pulling a gun and intimidating a man as if she were his equal. No, he silently amended. As if she were his *superior.*

Given his cowardly performance this afternoon, who could say she wasn't? Certainly not him. He had never known her to flinch from speaking the truth. Her character, as straight and true as an arrow, had embedded itself in his heart and mind so deeply that he knew he'd never get it out.

Experience told him she wouldn't listen to even the most heartfelt explanation—not in her present state of mind.

He wanted to shake her until her teeth rattled.

He wanted to shout his folly to the heavens.

He wanted to bury his head in her lap and weep for his lost dreams.

He wanted to hold her until the end of time and beyond.

But he couldn't do any of those things while she was looking at him as if he were something she wanted to scrape off her shoes. Later, he promised himself—he'd explain all about his ill-conceived marriage later.

No matter how much she despised him, duty would bring her to the ranch to visit Otto's grave. This week or the next, they'd have a chance to talk. He vowed to wait until eternity if that's what it took.

And yet, deep down, he feared Elke wouldn't let there be a later for the two of them. She had too much pride to give him another chance—and too much to lose if he failed her again. She had every right to hate him. God knew, he loathed himself.

"I'll go since that's what you think you want." He paused, waiting for—praying for—a denial. But the words he longed to hear never came.

Getting to his feet, he reached into a trouser pocket, produced a handful of gold coins and piled them on the table by Elke's chair. "I said I wanted to take care of you and I meant it. This should tide you over for a while."

"Is that the going price for a kiss? How dare you offer me money as if I were one of Velvet's whores?" Elke flung the words, then the coins, at him. Her face had gone as white and cold as winter's first snow. "Take your damn money and get out. You don't need to worry about me anymore—or Otto, either. I'll send for his . . ." her voice faltered, then firmed again, "for his body as soon as I can."

As he strode out of the house and down the street, her words reverberated in his mind like the tolling of a doomsday bell. The setting sun cast the trees in ominous shadow. The lonely howl of a distant coyote accentuated the silence. He had to force himself not to run down the road like a whipped cur.

He felt lower than any mangy dog. But if he started running, he might not be able to stop. And he couldn't run away from his mistakes.

How in the name of heaven had he gotten himself in this mess? And how could he get himself out of it without hurting his wife the way he had already hurt Elke?

If ever there was an innocent party in the whole sorry affair, it was Charlotte.

Charlotte's tears stopped the minute Ella Mae shut the hotel-room door. She had far too much to do to waste time in tears when no one was around to be affected by them. Ella Mae would soon return with Patrick, and Charlotte intended to be ready.

She searched through the dresser drawers for a virginal-looking night gown. Fortunately the one Ella Mae had just unpacked would do quite nicely. The ivory cotton batiste buttoned to the neck and yet the fabric was delicate enough to reveal her every curve.

Undressing with frantic speed, she tossed her clothes helter-skelter into the ugly chiffonier that bulked on the wall opposite the bed. Then she undid her elaborate coiffure, running her fingers through her curls until they tangled in wild disarray.

She slipped the nightgown over her head pulled the covers down, then realized getting under them would be a mistake. She wanted her errant husband to find her shivering in the frigid winter air. Thank heaven she hadn't asked Ella Mae to start a fire in the potbelly stove before she left, Charlotte thought, stretching out on top of the bed.

She'd teach Patrick Pride to leave her alone again. By the time he showed up—and it damn well better be soon or she really would catch her death—she ought to be covered with goose bumps from head to toe.

There was nothing like a chill to make her nipples pert, too. She licked her lips, imagining Patrick's widening eyes and the bulge at his crotch when he got a good look.

While she waited, she rubbed her eyes to make sure they stayed red. The sight of her tear-stained face and pouting nipples ought to bring Patrick to heel. Once he explained why he left and begged for forgiveness, she'd let him have his way with her.

He was a wonderful lover—tender, considerate, and ever mindful of her comfort. The trouble was, she had quickly wearied of his consideration.

She didn't want him to treat her like a piece of porcelain that might break if he got the least little bit rough. She wanted him to chew on her nipples until they hurt, to ram himself into her like one of her father's prize stallions.

Perhaps if he really got riled up this afternoon, he'd finally fulfill her fantasies.

Patrick's footsteps slowed as he walked down the hall to his hotel room. From what Ella Mae had told him, Charlotte was in a terrible state. By now she must be frantic with worry over his long absence.

He cracked the door open wide enough to look inside the room, half expecting a flying object—a shoe or a piece of crockery—to greet his arrival.

To his surprise, Charlotte lay stretched out on the bed in a white gown, looking for all the world like a corpse—except for the delicate snore whistling through her lips. She must be exhausted, he mused, with almost fatherly concern. He kept on forgetting she had barely left her childhood behind.

Tiptoeing across the floor so as not to wake her, he unfolded the down-filled quilt at the foot of the bed and covered her with it. The poor thing could use a good night's rest. He'd sleep in the room with their luggage.

Closing the door with infinite care, he headed down the hall to Ella Mae's room. He'd deal with her miscreant behavior first, he decided, and none too gently. Afterward he have a stiff whiskey and some supper before retiring for the night.

Ella Mae's eyes were wide with fear when she answered his knock. "I sho am sorry for what I said, Mr. Patrick," she began at once. "I would never talk out of turn in front of a fine lady like Mrs. Sonnschein. I wouldn't blame you if you sold me down the river."

She had expressed every slave's most terrible fear. Many a black had disappeared after an angry owner sold him or her down the river, never to be heard from again by their families.

It would have taken a colder man than Patrick not to respond to the quaver in Ella Mae's voice, or the genuine terror in her eyes. "Don't be silly. You're a free woman. No one can sell you anymore. But that doesn't excuse what you did this afternoon. In the future, please use a little discretion."

"I can't tell you how bad I feel. That Whitey fellow told me about Mrs. Sonnschein losing her man and all. My only excuse for talkin' out of turn is that I thought you was dallyin' with a whore." She pronounced it, "hoe." "Now I knows Miss Charlotte can be a handful, but she don't deserve no treatment like that."

"No, she certainly doesn't. I appreciate your loyalty. It's a fine quality."

"Whitey said you and Mr. Sonnschein were best friends. I'm truly sorry for your loss."

"So am I," Patrick replied wearily, thinking his loss was far greater than Ella Mae could possibly know.

Suddenly he couldn't face the thought of dining by himself. "Charlotte is sound asleep and I don't expect her to wake up until morning. Would you care to join me for supper?"

A spark of pleasure ignited in Ella Mae's doelike eyes, only to dim out just as quickly. "I don't 'spect Mr. Nimitz would appreciate a darky eatin' with the quality folk. I'll just have a bite in the kitchen."

Patrick knew she was right—and damned mankind for all the cruel customs that held so many people in needless bondage. Ella Mae would always be marked as a lesser human being by the color of her skin. And barring a miracle, he would always be married to Charlotte.

It was going to be a hell of a life.

Velvet Gilhooley waited fifteen minutes in the hall outside her own bedroom before she realized Elke wasn't going to ask for her help.

She'd left Elke alone three weeks ago because she'd known no way to soothe her grief. But Velvet felt equally certain there was nothing like a heart-to-heart with another female to help a woman deal with man trouble—and a man who looked like Patrick Pride could be trouble with a capital T.

Not bothering to knock, she opened the door wide, expecting to find Elke in tears. Elke sat where Velvet had last seen her, gazing out the window into the darkness. The expression on her face told Velvet she'd passed the tearful stage by a Hill Country mile. Her eyes had gone as cold as the night outside. Her jaws were clenched. Bright spots of color burned on her cheeks.

"Men can be such bastards—even when they're trying their best—that I wonder why any woman puts up with them," Velvet said without preamble.

Elke didn't seem to notice that Velvet had started their conversation in the middle, rather than leading up to the subject nice and easy. "Patrick has a real talent in that direction," she replied past her clamped teeth. "I feel like the world's biggest fool."

"At leave you've got company. God knows you're not the first woman to be a fool for love, and you sure as hell won't be the last. Sometimes I think it's our lot in life."

Elke jumped up and began to pace. The frilly night clothes fluttering around her slender body accentuated her rigid posture. "Is that why you never married?"

"Honey, I never married because no one ever asked me."

Velvet's confession brought Elke to a halt. "But you're so pretty."

"Pretty isn't the only thing that counts in a man's estimation. The truth is, I came close to getting hitched a long time ago. But by then I'd already taken up my trade. He swore he loved me but he couldn't seem to see his way past what I'd become, even though he knew I'd have starved otherwise. If you ask me, it's downright foolish, the stock a man puts in a woman's purity. The way they act, you'd think a woman gets all used up if she has a man or two." Velvet let go a harsh laugh. "A whore like me knows that's not true, though!"

"Don't talk about yourself that way. You're the sweetest, kindest woman I know. Your girls all love you and maybe—maybe someday a man will love you, too," Elke finished in a rush.

"And maybe pigs will fly." This time there was genuine humor in Velvet's laugh. At least she had succeeded in taking Elke's mind off her troubles. "I took a good look at Patrick when he left, and if it's any consolation, he didn't appear any too happy. I'm pretty much of an expert when it comes to the opposite sex, and unless I read him all wrong, he really does care for you."

Elke shrugged. "So what?"

"Have you considered that he might be hurting, too?"

"So what?"

"He's a man, honey, with a man's needs. No matter what he felt for you before he left for Natchez, you surely didn't expect him to spend the rest of his life alone. He couldn't have known about the accident when he got married. Imagine how it must hit him to come home and find out you were a widow."

"I don't give a good damn what he does or how he feels. He's made a fool of me for the last time."

It certainly seemed strange to hear a lady like Elke swear, Velvet mused. A man could make a woman so sour on life that she cursed like a mule skinner and vowed to keep her legs crossed for the rest of her natural life. But a truly loving man could make a woman purr like a kitten and think the nights weren't long enough for making love.

"If you don't mind, I'd just as soon not talk about Patrick anymore. I have more important things on my mind," Elke declared.

"Like what, honey?" Velvet asked, relieved to know her new friend had managed to survive yet another crisis.

"Like opening the bakery again. Christmas is just a month away and that's always been our busiest season." Elke swallowed hard, thinking how different the holiday would be from the one she'd planned.

She felt like she'd been losing bits and pieces of herself until there was hardly anything left. Thank God she still had the bakery. "There's so much to do. We always get a lot of special orders in addition to our regular business."

"Do you think you'll be able to manage by yourself?" the ever practical Velvet asked.

It was a question Elke had been asking herself. "I won't know until I try."

Chapter Thirteen

Elke sat in her accustomed place on the stool behind the bakery's glass-topped counter, going over the account books as she had so many times before and wondering if the bakery could survive its present troubles.

Although she had known it would be difficult to run the business by herself, her hopes and expectations had been so high when she came home three weeks ago. She had counted on the legacy of Otto's recipes, on his knowledgeable apprentices, and on the goodwill they had built up over the years to see her through. Most of all, she had counted on her own ability to put her grief aside.

But the things she had counted on had been as ephemeral as chimney smoke. Otto's recipes didn't taste the same without his fine hand with pastries and yeast breads. Friends and patrons had drifted away, either because the baked goods didn't live up to previously high standards—or because they didn't want to associate with a woman who counted whores as her friends.

Elke might have been able to find a way to surmount

all those difficulties. But she had yet to discover a way to manage her own emotions. The day she walked past her winter-dead garden, climbed the stairs and opened the apartment door had been one of the worst days in her life.

The nursery waited for a dead child. Otto's clothes were in the *Kleidershrank* as if he would walk into the bedroom at any moment. Every piece of furniture evoked memories—most of them painful ones. She kept on expecting to see Otto around every corner and wishing she could take back all the cruel things she had said to him.

She couldn't cope with the regret-filled past, and hardly dared to look ahead. Although the rooms looked so much the same that it tore at her heart, the landscape of her life had changed in the most fundamental ways.

She hadn't realized how much the artificial atmosphere of the whorehouse had shielded her from reality. The constant comings and goings, the giddy laughter and turbulent tears, the ever-ready companionship had been a soporific.

Her first evening at home, she had used work as a distraction, staying up all night and baking so she could reopen the shop the next morning. And that had proven to be the biggest mistake of all.

She had greeted the few customers who showed up with tears in her eyes, exposing them to her troubles when all they bargained for was a piece of pastry and a cup of coffee. No wonder so many of them hadn't bothered to come back.

If only she had waited a day or two and given herself a chance to adjust. Disaster had piled on disaster when one of Otto's helpers got burned in a freak accident and quit on the spot. She had quickly hired a replacement, but with just one experienced baker the output had been limited and the quality of the baked goods had slipped another notch.

Unable to accommodate the holiday trade, she'd been forced to tell their remaining loyal customers that she couldn't fill any special orders. Just that morning, Carolyn Grobe had stopped for a few dozen of her favorite *Kolache,* only to be told she would have to wait until tomorrow to get them.

"There's a new baker in town," Carolyn had warned, "a Herr Dietz who is planning to open his own establishment. If you can't manage on your own, perhaps you should consider selling to him while you still have a business to sell."

As Elke put the account books aside, she had to agree. Things were bad enough without the threat of competition. She found herself looking around the room, thinking about the money Otto had lavished on its furnishings and wondering what someone else would be willing to pay for them.

Another even more formidable question rose up to trouble her. If she did sell the bakery, where would she go and what would she do without a home and an income?

Whether she turned her gaze on the empty shop or looked deep inside herself, she saw failure all around. She felt every bit as bereft and lost as she had the day she buried her parents. Only this time, she didn't know if she had the strength to start over.

The tinkling of the bell over the front door interrupted her unhappy reverie. She looked up to see Velvet Gilhooley, resplendent in a fur-trimmed cloak and bonnet, waft into the shop on a zephyr of French perfume.

"Where *is* everybody?" Velvet asked, her eyes widening as she took in the empty room.

"You're my first customer today."

Velvet's discerning gaze searched Elke's face. "I gather things haven't been going too well."

Elke gave Velvet a shaky smile. "That's an understatement."

"Well, hell—why didn't you let me know? I'd have been beating your doors down to get my hands on your baked goods. I only stayed away because I wanted to give you the chance to get in full production again. The girls have been driving me crazy. They've really missed their sweets—and they've missed you, too. So have I."

Elke's eyes sheened. Would she never run out of tears? "I'm so glad you're here. I really need to talk."

"Why don't you just box up all the goodies you have on hand and help me carry them back to the house. We can talk to our heart's content over tea—or something stronger if you prefer."

"Stronger sounds better," Elke replied, although she'd never had a drink so early in the day. "But you don't need to buy everything."

Velvet let go one of her throaty chuckles. "I'm not doing you any favors. I said the girls were dying for sweets and I meant it. Making love can be damn hard work if your heart isn't in it. All that moaning and carrying on tires a girl out, and gives her an appetite."

Despite her problems, Elke couldn't help laughing. "I never thought of it that way."

"That's because you're not in my business, which, by the way, has never been better. You know how it is. The more men talk about war, the more they want to make love. It seems thinking about their own mortality is one hell of an aphrodisiac."

"Not beans again!" Charlotte declared, looking down at the greasy platter in the housekeeper's hands.

Since arriving at Pride's Passion Charlotte had endured an unrelenting diet of beans: beans and eggs for breakfast, beans and side meat for lunch, and beans and beef for dinner. She had never been more flatulent—or out of patience.

She lifted her disapproving gaze from the platter to Conchita Alvarez. The housekeeper stared right back with flat obsidian eyes. Those eyes sent a chill down Charlotte's spine. God alone knew what the woman was thinking. "I gave you this week's menus yesterday. If you'll recall, I specifically asked you to prepare pompano *en croute* for lunch," she said, determined to hold her ground. Give a servant an inch, her mother used to tell her, and they'll just naturally take a mile.

"I don't know thees *crudeza* pompano," the housekeeper replied in her heavily accented mélange of English and Spanish.

"It's a fish." In an effort to be understood, Charlotte raised her voice and enunciated every syllable. "Surely there are fish in the Guadalupe River."

Conchita clapped her hands over her ears. "I'm not deaf, señora."

The door to the kitchen burst open and Ella Mae

came running through it. "What's all the fuss? Did you say you want to go fishing, Miss Charlotte?"

"What's this about going fishing?" Patrick asked, choosing the most inopportune moment to put in his appearance for lunch.

Charlotte sank into her chair at the foot of the table. "I wasn't talking about going fishing. I told Conchita I wanted pompano for lunch. Not beans."

Patrick shook his head. "The nearest pompano is five hundred miles away. I doubt it would survive the trip. But there are some damn fine catfish in the river, and some sunnys, too. I'll have one of the boys catch us a batch."

Charlotte clutched her stomach as flatulence threatened to overcome her. She didn't know whether to be mortified—or furious at Patrick for siding with the help.

"Please leave Mr. Pride and me alone," she said, dismissing Ella Mae and Conchita with a peremptory nod toward the kitchen door.

After they had gone, she gazed down at the platter of beans and considered throwing it at her husband. Perhaps that would finally get his serious, undivided attention. The more she pouted, fussed, and fumed, the more he treated her like a child.

She glared at him, thinking how much she'd love to give him a piece of her mind. But her mother had also said that the best way to catch flies is with honey. Not that she meant to compare Patrick to a fly. He was just mean-spirited at times. She'd never felt more alone in her entire life—alone and scared, too, although she'd sooner die than admit it to him.

"I wasn't talking about a fishing expedition. I merely

asked Conchita to prepare pompano *en croute* for lunch. She should have told me she couldn't. But she took the menus I prepared as if they wouldn't be a problem."

With a jangle of spurs, Patrick took his place at the head of the table and forked a heaping serving of beans and side meat onto his plate. "Perhaps she didn't understand. English is her second language."

"She understands you, and she understands Ella Mae. The two of them spend hours in the kitchen jabbering like monkeys in a zoo."

"Ella Mae is trying to learn to speak Spanish. You know, it wouldn't hurt if you did, too."

"Why do you always take Conchita's side? Or Ella Mae's? Can't you take mine for a change?" Refusing to touch the platter of beans, she helped herself to a glass of wine.

"I'm sorry you see it that way. Believe me, Charlotte, I want you to be happy. I know you're still getting the hang of things around here. As for Conchita's culinary limitations, why don't you teach her to prepare some of your favorite recipes?"

Charlotte blinked in disbelief. It was bad enough that he'd brought her to this god forsaken place with promises of a water closet—not that it didn't work splendidly—but now he expected her to cook as well. Her. A Devereux.

"For your information, Mr. Pride, I don't know a thing about cooking. My mother taught me how to plan menus, to supervise a dinner party, to arrange flowers and choose the right wines. She didn't raise me to spend my time slaving over a hot stove."

Patrick finally looked up from his supper. "I had

hoped you would come to love the ranch as much as I do. Living here is really hard on you, isn't it?"

Seeing she had his attention—and his sympathy—she got to her feet. Swaying seductively, she walked around behind his chair and massaged his neck. "I shouldn't bother you with my little problems when you work so hard."

She had once watched her mother put an end to a disagreement in exactly the same way. For a moment she had the eerie sensation of having climbed inside her mother's skin. She pictured herself growing old and more and more like the woman who had given her life—and the thought sent an unpleasant frisson up her spine. God, she didn't want to relive her mother's dreary existence. That's why she had set her cap for Patrick in the first place.

Patrick's low groan of pleasure told her the ploy had worked. "I'm sorry," he said. "I don't mean to make light of your problems."

Now that's more like it, Charlotte thought, squeezing between the table and chair to plop in his lap. "You are the sweetest man. The trouble is, I don't see enough of you. Or any other people for that matter. I grew up in a big family and I'm used to having them around. I'm terribly lonely."

Patrick's expression hardened. "I told you the ranch was isolated before—"

"I know you did, darling," she interrupted, "but I have the most wonderful remedy for the situation. It's a pity to let this grand house of ours go to waste. Why don't we give a party? My parents always invited their friends and neighbors to celebrate Twelfth Night and I'd love for us to continue the tradition. We could ask that widow lady, the one who left all that wonderful food here, to cater it for us."

At the mention of Elke, Patrick almost dumped Charlotte on the floor. It seemed particularly offensive to discuss the woman he loved while he held his wife on his lap.

Charlotte didn't know he'd run off to see Elke that day in Fredericksburg—and he didn't want to contemplate how she'd react if she found out. Something told him her previous tantrums would pale by comparison.

"If you don't mind all the work, we can have the party. But forget Mrs. Sonnschein. She has a business to run. And now, my dear, Rio has the day off, so I really must get back to work."

He eased Charlotte to her feet, gave her a peck on the cheek, and hurriedly left the dining room—taking his heavy heart and troubled mind with him. He'd been doing his level best to forget about Elke and concentrate on his wife. But Charlotte sure didn't make it easy.

Their conversations were dominated by complaints on her part, and efforts at placation on his. Instead of getting closer, they had grown so far apart that he hardly knew what to say to her anymore.

Were all marriages a sad groping for communication? Was that why men buried themselves in work and women in child care? God, he hoped not. He'd never had a problem talking to Elke.

Otto had been wrong when he said it was better to marry than to burn alone. Patrick knew he would have been far happier if he'd spent his entire life burning for

Elke, rather than being trapped in a charade of a marriage with Charlotte.

The bitter taste of regret rose up his throat and soured in his mouth. Despite having a common birthplace and a shared heritage, he and his wife had nothing *in* common.

He loved the ranch.

Charlotte saw it as a threatening place and complained of its isolation.

She lived for luxury.

The only luxury he required was a good book and time to read it.

He enjoyed solitude.

She adored social intercourse.

She pined for her happy past in Natchez.

He dreamed of the future in the Hill Country.

The chasm between their differing hopes and expectations grew wider every day. Even their lovemaking had become perfunctory—an act that had far more to do with procreation than pleasure.

At least he hadn't lost his perspective completely, he reminded himself, mounting the gelding he'd left by the porch. He still retained enough integrity to admit he couldn't blame Charlotte for their problems.

So yes, he'd let her have her Twelfth Night party, and a dozen more if that's what it took to make her happy—as long as Elke played no part in Charlotte's plans.

Rio de Vargas had ridden halfway to Fredericksburg when he saw a rambling rose growing in the shelter of an oak tree. Its bright red blossoms put on a brave show in the wintry landscape. He reined his horse to a stop, slipped from the saddle, and took a folding knife from his trouser pocket.

His half-Comanche mother had taught him to never take more from nature than nature could spare. But nature wouldn't be hurt if he helped himself to a few flowers that would die with the first frost.

He cut the stems as long as possible and wrapped them in his handkerchief, breathing deep of their subtle fragrance. They smelled almost as sweet as the woman he planned to give them to.

He had never courted a woman before—and maybe he only fooled himself to think he was off to court one now—but he intended to make a good impression on Velvet Gilhooley. Seeing a holly bush nearby, he couldn't resist adding a few brightly berried sprigs to the thorny bouquet.

Perhaps he'd even stop in town and buy her a real present, some gewgaw that a woman would like—a bit of ribbon or a lacy handkerchief. It was almost Christmas, he told himself, feeling a blush spread from his head to his toes. Damn it all, a grown man shouldn't feel so foolish at the mere thought of giving a lady a gift. So why had his palms turned wet and his throat dry?

He'd no sooner swung back into the saddle than he heard a rider drawing near. Looking up, he was startled to see Velvet's butler, Whitey, trotting up the road on a magnificent black stallion that sure as hell didn't come from no livery stable. The ebony horse and man made such a pretty picture that Rio sat back in the saddle to enjoy it.

"Nice day for a ride," he said when Whitey reached his side.

"That it is." Whitey displayed a toothy grin. "And a nice day for picking flowers, too. I don't imagine you're taking them back to the bunkhouse."

"Nope. I thought Miss Gilhooley would like them."

Whitey's grin deepened. "I'm sure she will. She said to tell you hello if I saw you, and to say she hasn't forgotten the debt."

Rio tipped his hat to shield his eyes from Whitey's probing glance. He hadn't forgotten the debt, either. The last two months he'd been able to think of little else— and a man who worked with longhorns ought to have the good sense to keep his mind on the business at hand.

"Where are you headed?" he asked, thinking to change the subject.

"I plan to call on Miss Ella Mae." Whitey gestured at the brightly wrapped package protruding from one of his saddle bags. "I brought her a little something in honor of the season. She sure is a fine-looking woman."

"I won't argue with you there." So that was the lay of the land, Rio thought. Whitey had courting on his mind, too. Suddenly Rio didn't feel so foolish.

"*Hasta la vista*—and merry Christmas, too," he called out, spurring his horse to a canter.

Velvet was sitting in the parlor when she heard a loud knock at the door. Who could it be? she fretted, getting to her feet. She'd be damned if she'd open early for a randy cowboy, no matter how he begged.

Rio de Vargas stood on the stoop, wearing his Sunday best, holding a bouquet in one hand and a small package in the other.

"Are those for me?"

He nodded and thrust the package in her hand.

Who would have thought Rio de Vargas would show up calling bearing gifts, she thought as she opened the package to reveal a green satin ribbon.

"It's lovely," she murmured.

"It's for your hair." He continued to stand on the stoop, frozen in place *no doubt* by his own shy nature.

"Where in the world did you get such lovely flowers this time of year?"

"Under an oak," he replied with his customary brevity.

"I appreciate your stopping to pick them." Taking his arm, she lead the way into the parlor. "Just let me get a vase and some water."

Spinning around so quickly that she almost tripped, she hurried to the kitchen, not even noticing that a thorn had pricked her finger. Good Lord, you'd think a thirty-three—oh, hell, who was she kidding?—thirty-six-year-old whore would know better than to let the sight of a man—any man—set her heart racing.

But Rio certainly did look fine in his dark suit, with his hair slicked back and his mustache neatly trimmed.

She put the roses and the holly in a vase, filled it with water from a pitcher on the table, and carried it back into the parlor. "These certainly do look festive," she said, placing the vase on the upright piano. "I can hardly believe it's almost Christmas."

"Me, either."

"Do you have any special plans for the holiday?"

"No ma'am."

Damn. It sure was hard, carrying on a one-sided conversation. "You just missed Elke. We had lunch together. Unfortunately the bakery isn't the success it used to be. She's thinking of selling. Poor thing. It seems she has more than her share of troubles."

"I'm sorry to hear it," Rio replied, shifting from one boot-shod foot to another.

"I know you didn't stop by just to bring me flowers. Would you like to see one of the girls?"

He shook his head in vigorous denial. "No, ma'am."

"Then why are you here?"

He turned redder than the roses. "To collect the debt."

"I recall saying you could have your pick of the girls at no charge."

"You recall right."

"Which one do you want?"

"I wuh wuh-want you."

"I don't entertain customers anymore."

"I know."

"Me? Are you sure you want me?"

He took a handkerchief from his pocket and wiped the perspiration on his brow. "I'm sure. Dang sure. I haven't been able to think about anything else. I can't work and I can't sleep for thinking about you. Mr. Pride says I'm getting to be a menace."

Although Velvet felt as if her stomach had just been invaded by a rowdy bunch of hummingbirds, she managed a throaty chuckle. "Then I guess there isn't any point in standing here jawing. Follow me."

She took the vase from the piano, carried it into her bedroom and set it down on a dresser. She felt foolish doing it but she just didn't want to share Rio's flowers with her girls—not when he had already shared everything else.

Shutting the door on the rest of the world, she turned to face the man who had been in her thoughts so much lately. "It's a long time since I've done anything like this."

"How long?"

"Six years."

"You mean you haven't once—not in all that time? I'm honored you chose me to be the first," he replied with seeming sincerity. "I just hope I don't disappoint you."

She could have told him that from what she'd heard her girls saying about his performance and staying power, she wouldn't be disappointed. She could have told him she'd had so many men in her lifetime that nothing he said or did could possibly disappoint her.

She could have said all that—and more. But she found herself wishing this was her first time with a man. And from the way her hands shook as she started to undress, it might as well have been.

Rio's heart bucked in his chest like a startled colt as he watched Velvet peel off her clothes.

"Oh my God," he groaned, seeing her creamy white shoulders emerge from her lacy blouse.

"Is something wrong?"

"No, ma'am. Things couldn't be more right."

"Aren't you going to get undressed?"

"Not right away, if it's all the same to you." The more clothing she took off, the easier the words came. By the time she had stripped to her camisole, bloomers, and stays, they just tumbled from his mouth. "You are the most beautiful woman I've ever seen in my life! I'd be content to spend the rest of the afternoon just looking at you."

"That's the nicest thing any man has ever said to me."

"A pretty woman like you? You must have had lots of men sweet-talking you."

"My customers used to be so anxious to get me in bed, I don't think they even knew what I looked like, and they sure didn't waste time talking."

"Then they were fools!" *Dios mío,* he thought as her stays fell away and she lowered her camisole, he'd never seen such perfect breasts.

When she finally stood naked before him, he felt as if his every last dream had miraculously come true.

Her body gleamed like alabaster but for the coppery curls between her legs. And what legs they were—nice and full in the thigh like a good mare's and neatly tapered at the ankle. He could hardly wait to feel them wrapped around his back—but first he wanted to see every last inch of Velvet Gilhooley.

"Would you mind turning around? Real slow like."

A perplexed frown marred her smooth forehead. "I won't bite if you touch me."

"The touching will keep. Right now I'm in a mood to look. You surely are a work of art. Seeing you in the all together makes me believe there might be a God after all."

She laughed long and deep. The rich sound seemed sweeter than music. Seeing the way her breasts shimmied, he felt as if she'd just reached into his chest and grabbed his heart.

By the time she'd turned a half circle to reveal the full globes of her buttocks, he had fallen in love as well as in lust. Frantic with desire, he pulled off his best suit of clothes and dropped it in a heap.

As a girl, Velvet had been inordinately proud of her good looks—so proud that two or three times a day, her mother would look at her and say, "Pride goeth before a fall."

The prediction had proven right. Velvet had fallen longer and harder than her mother could possibly have imagined. As a woman who made a living peddling female flesh, she had seen her share of beautiful bodies and, in her opinion, hers no longer qualified. Undressing in front of Rio, she had been painfully aware of every unsightly bulge, and amazed that he didn't seem to see them, too.

She completed her slow pirouette to face him, and it was her turn to stare in awe. His erection poked at his long johns like a tent pole.

Men liked to think it wasn't the size of their penises that counted, but rather what they could do with them. But men were wrong. Skill couldn't compensate for a missing inch—or two.

Rio had no worries in that department, she thought with an indrawn breath as his long johns dropped to the floor. "Do you spend much time working with bulls?" she asked in a strangled voice.

"Yes, ma'am. Mr Pride can't trust them with just any old hand."

"I thought so."

"Why?"

"Because it must be catching. You sure are hung like one. And the rest of you isn't half bad, either." Reaching out, she ran her fingers over his shoulders and into the gray fur on his chest, relishing the whipcord strength of his muscles. Then she took his hand, sank onto the bed, and pulled him down with her.

Rio seemed unaware that whores didn't kiss their customers. But that couldn't be, considering his experience. Maybe he didn't think of her as a whore. He claimed her lips as if he'd owned them all his life, tasting and nibbling with a hunger she felt clear down to her toes.

He proved to be an inventive, exciting lover. The things he did with his tongue, teeth, and lips had her moaning with pleasure.

He gauged her desire perfectly so that when he finally entered her with one long masterful stroke, she thought she'd died and gone to heaven. To her surprise, her body spasmed at once.

She had faked many an orgasm to please a customer, moaning and groaning with such fervor that she had considered taking up the stage as a career. But this orgasm couldn't have been more real. It pounded at her navel and shivered down her thighs, curling her toes, too.

"I hope you don't mind if I take my time," he murmured in her ear.

"Be my guest. We've got all afternoon."

She figured they would need every minute.

Chapter Fourteen

"I still can't believe I'm doing this," Elke said to Carolyn Grobe as she wrapped a dish in newsprint. "When Otto and I built this place, we planned to live here forever. He would be so disappointed if he knew I'd sold the bakery."

Although she had given Otto's clothes to the poor, his scent—a not unpleasant blend of masculinity and yeast dough—still seemed to hang in the air.

"You're being too hard on yourself. Your Otto was a very sensible man," Carolyn replied. "He'd know you were doing the right thing."

"But the bakery was his life." Elke rolled her shoulders to ease the tension in her muscles, then brushed back a tendril of hair that had escaped from her chignon. She had been packing all day and weariness weighed her down—a weariness that seemed to come from her very soul.

She felt as if she'd been moving in slow motion for days, like a poor creature trapped in a bog. If Carolyn hadn't arrived a few hours ago to help with the packing,

Elke would never have finished in time. Herr Dietz was due at four in the afternoon to pick up the keys. By then, she wanted to be ready to leave.

"Otto did love the bakery, but you have to think about your own life now," the ever sensible Carolyn admonished. "Have you decided what you're going to do?"

"I'm still planning to take a room at the Nimitz Hotel, if that's what you mean."

Having made the decision to sell the bakery, Elke had been incapable of making any others. She knew she should have formulated some design for her future—and she awakened every morning determined to do just that. But she went to bed every night without reaching any conclusions.

She gazed around the parlor, thinking how she might not see it again, recalling all the hours of quiet companionship she and Otto had shared there. She had never loved him, but she would always miss him.

"It's too bad Herr Dietz didn't need you to stay on in the bake shop."

"Yes, it is," Elke replied, concealing her private relief.

Working for a stranger in the place she and Otto had built—knowing another woman had claimed her home—would have been terribly painful. At the age of twenty-eight, she felt as if she had already endured a whole lifetime of pain. She didn't need to go borrowing more.

She continued to pack, willing herself not to think—not to hurt.

"Have you heard about the party Patrick and his new wife are giving?" Carolyn asked a few minutes later.

"Yes." Elke couldn't bring herself to comment further, even though the party had been the talk of the town for days.

"I can hardly wait to meet the bride. I hear she's very pretty. But then, we all knew Patrick would want a beautiful wife. He has such elegant taste." Carolyn took the last plate from the dining table where Elke had stacked her china earlier that day. "Why don't you ride out to Pride's Passion with us?"

Color flared on Elke's cheeks. Although the fire burned low on the hearth, she felt hot all over. "Thank you, but I'm not going to the party."

"Why in the world not, may I ask?"

Elke could hardly tell Carolyn that she hadn't been invited, that her husband's best friend wanted nothing more to do with her. "For heaven's sake, I've only been widowed for two months. I'm not exactly in the mood for a party."

Carolyn reached across the table and touched Elke's arm in a gesture of sympathy. "No one would think less of you for going."

"They certainly thought less of me for convalescing in a whorehouse—even though they knew I was under doctor's orders to stay put."

Carolyn leaned over and put the last dish in a crate. "My dear Elke, they weren't judging you. They were just embarrassed."

"I don't plan to embarrass them again. So I'm going to stay home."

Home. All the security in the world seemed embodied in those four letters.

In a few more hours, she wouldn't have a home. Elke rubbed her brow. How strange the room looked now that the packing was done. Although she had sold the furniture along with the building, the things that gave a home character and life, the personal belongings, were crated and ready to go into storage.

"My goodness," Carolyn said, getting to her feet and wiping her hands on her skirt, "we're finally finished. I hate to leave you alone to wait for the drover, but I really must get back to my family."

Elke rose from her place at the table, and gave Carolyn a quick hug. "I don't know how to thank you."

"Thanks aren't necessary. You'd have done the same for me." She took her shawl and bonnet from a chair and put them on. "Don't forget, we're expecting you for Sunday supper."

Elke followed Carolyn to the door and opened it. "I may not be here by then."

Carolyn gave her a searching look. "What in the world do you mean?"

"I don't know if I want to stay in Fredericksburg— and I do have enough money from the sale to go back to Germany. Perhaps the good Lord has been trying to tell me something all these years. Perhaps that's where I belong."

Charlotte sat at the desk in the library at Pride's Passion, reviewing the lists she had written in preparation for the Twelfth Night party. Four more days and she would finally fulfill her destiny as the hostess of the most fabulous home in the Hill Country. She was determined to make her husband proud, to show him he'd married a gracious, clever, talented woman.

Their marriage had gotten off to such a bad start—and she had to admit she was partly to blame. Well, maybe just a teeny-weeny bit. She'd made up her mind to turn over a new leaf, to get on with her life. Her mother always said there was no stopping her once she'd made up her mind to do something. The party was just the first step.

She picked up a quill, dipped it in the inkwell, and scanned the first list, putting check marks next to the jobs that had been completed. Under the heading of housekeeping, she had written: Polish silver. Wash good china. Wash and press table and bed linens. Wax furniture. Beat rugs.

The first three tasks had already been completed. She had divided them between Conchita Alvarez, Conchita's fourteen-year-old daughter Maria, and Ella Mae. Maria was working out so well that Charlotte had decided to ask Patrick to give her a permanent job.

The house was far too big to keep in tiptop shape with only a staff of two. Even with the extra help, she would need a couple of strong men to take the bigger rugs outside and whack the dust out of them.

She put the housekeeping list aside and turned to the one labeled Menu. In view of Conchita's limited culinary abilities, she'd had to compromise her original plans. Thank goodness they still had the ham that the widow woman had left. It would taste just fine with the sweet potato pie Ella Mae was going to make. Roast chicken, roast beef, potatoes, squash, fried catfish, a fiery stew called *Posole,* and assorted condiments would complete the buffet supper.

She would have loved to serve her guests a French sorbet for dessert, but lacking a recipe to make it and ice to chill it, she had settled for cake. Patrick had assured her their guests would be pleased with what she considered to be a severely limited cuisine. Sooner or later, though, they were going to have to hire an accomplished cook.

The next list, the one that dealt with music, had started out with a big question mark. She'd been positively desperate until Patrick told her that one of the hands played a fine fiddle and that another did quite nicely on the accordion. She grinned, thinking how embarrassed the two cowboys had been the first time they played for her. They'd be back to practice some more tomorrow, and to cart the furniture out of the parlor so it could be used for dancing.

Closing her eyes, she conjured up a vision of elegantly clad couples swaying in a waltz, the dining room set up for the buffet, the fine china and silver glowing in the light of dozens of candles. She looked *divine* by candlelight.

The decorations had presented her with another dilemma. She would have loved a fresh floral centerpiece for the dining room, but the nearest hothouse was in New Orleans. Garlands made from the holly and juniper that grew on the ranch, would have to do.

Last but not least, she turned to the guest list. It ran two full pages and included every important personage within a hundred miles.

Having the redoubtable Sam Houston accept an invitation had been a major coup. She could hardly wait to meet him. Although Patrick revered Governor Houston as a soldier and a statesman, it was his reputation as a duelist, a rakehell, and a womanizer that intrigued her.

He would be the first divorced man she'd ever met. The very word *divorce* had such a deliciously decadent sound. Her parents would be scandalized if they knew a divorced man was going to be a guest in her home. A shiver of delight rippled down her spine. What her parents didn't know wouldn't hurt them. She was her own woman now.

She could hardly wait to show off the water closet. A man could relieve himself just any old place, but it was considerably more difficult for a woman—especially in a hoop skirt. How the ladies would envy her after seeing it. By the end of the evening, she'd be the undisputed queen of Hill Country society.

And this time next year, she vowed, she would be the leading hostess in the entire state.

She had decided to wear the emerald Worth that Patrick had so admired the night he proposed. The dress had brought her luck then. Not that she needed any this time. Thanks to her carefully drawn lists and her organizational ability, she couldn't imagine any unforeseen problems. A knock on the door interrupted her work. A second later Ella Mae walked in wearing her best dress—one of Charlotte's own cast-offs.

"My goodness, where do you think you're going all gussied up?" Charlotte asked.

"Don't you remember, I axed to have this afternoon off."

Charlotte did have a vague recollection of the girl's request. "Have you finished all the chores I wanted you to do today."

"Yes, ma'am. I got up at five this morning to do them."

Working on her party plans had put Charlotte in a benevolent frame of mind. She beamed at Ella Mae. "Well then, you're free to go. Just be sure to be back by suppertime. You need lots of practice waiting table before the party."

"Yes, ma'am," Ella Mae said, trying not to grimace as she curtsied the way Charlotte insisted these days.

Miss Charlotte had sure been putting on airs since everyone accepted those party invitations. Not that Ella Mae begrudged Miss Charlotte a little pleasure. Happiness made her a lot easier on the folks around her.

Ella Mae cracked the library door open, slipped through it before her mistress had a chance to change her mind, and tiptoed down the long, wide hall that ran from the front of the house to the back. She'd left her hat, coat, and gloves on a table by the front door in anticipation of her escape. She picked them up and went outside to put them on. Only then did she permit herself the luxury of looking forward to time off and a picnic with Whitey.

The air felt as crisp, cold, and clean as a plunge in a swimming hole. Breathing deeply, Ella Mae gazed down the long driveway. For the life of her, she didn't know how Whitey always managed to be on time when he had to travel thirty miles, but she could just make out a carriage in the distance.

"It sure is a good day for an outing," she called out as he drove up, making certain to pronounce all the words just right.

She didn't mind the gentle way Whitey corrected her English, any more than she minded Conchita correcting her Spanish. She chatted about the party while Whitey drove to a secluded spot on the river a few miles from the house.

The two of them gathered wood for a fire, ate the food in companionable silence, and then held hands while the fire burned down.

"I reckon I ought to be getting back," Ella Mae finally said, taking note of the darkening sky. "But I sure do thank you for the afternoon—and the food, too."

Whitey showed no sign of being ready to leave yet. "There's something on my mind," he said, holding her hand even tighter, "something I have to ask you."

For the life of her, Ella Mae couldn't imagine what it might be. She had already told him all about her life in Natchez.

Charlotte sat in the parlor, growing more impatient with every tick of the clock as she waited for Patrick to appear for supper—and Ella Mae to show up to serve it. The euphoria induced by working on her party plans had faded an hour earlier when she tried to change for supper without Ella Mae's help.

Although Patrick had told her she didn't need to put on a different outfit for him every evening, she refused to lower her standards. She preferred to think of herself as someone who was bringing the niceties of polite society to the frontier. And so she had struggled out of one outfit and into another all by herself, damning Ella Mae the entire time.

As if an evil genie had summoned the maid, Ella Mae chose that moment to come running into the room. With her wide eyes and tangled hair, she looked as if she'd taken a terrible shock. Suddenly fearing for her own safety, Charlotte looked past her into the hall.

"Is someone chasing you?" she asked.

"No. But Whitey is waiting in the hall to talk to Mr. Patrick."

"Whatever for?"

"Miss Charlotte, I have the most wonderful news," Ella Mae blurted in a highly agitated manner. "I'm getting married."

"You're what?"

"I'm getting married. Whitey done axed me this afternoon."

"My lands, I never heard anything so ridiculous!" Charlotte pressed her lips together in disapproval. "You can't marry without my permission, and I won't give it. I need you here with me."

Ella Mae took a step backward. "I don't need no permission. I'se free."

For the first time since Ella Mae burst into the room, Charlotte realized she was facing a serious—no, a *disastrous* situation. How could she give a party without her only trained servant. Who would make the sweet potato pie? Who would serve the guests? Who would do up her hair and help her dress?

Quite obviously, she couldn't let the girl go. The question was, how to keep her?

Ella Mae seemed unaware of Charlotte's consternation. "I still can't believe Whitey axed me, and him such a fine, handsome gentleman. He says he has his own little house not far from Miss Gilhooley's, and I can fix it up to suit myself. I can hardly wait to stand up before a preacher man with Whitey."

Charlotte jumped to her feet. "You can forget all about it. You are not going to walk out on me after everything I've done for you. I won't have it. Hear?"

The excitement faded from Ella Mae's eyes, to be replaced by a look of pure dislike. For a moment, Charlotte wondered if the girl had the nerve to raise a hand to her.

"You never done nothin' for me except run my feet off. Mr. Patrick is the one who helped me, and I knows how much I owes him, right down to the penny. That's why my Whitey is waiting to see him. He wants to give back the money Mr. Patrick spent on my freedom. So don't be talkin' to me that way no more."

Charlotte had been repressing her temper for months, absorbing one disappointment after another without once telling her husband—or anyone else for that matter—how she really felt. Her anger flared like a brush fire.

"All right then, have it your way Miss High and Mighty. I'm just glad my mother isn't here to see this day. It would break her heart." Charlotte couldn't bring herself to admit it was breaking hers, too. "Since you're so all fired determined to walk out on me, you can just pack your bags right now. I don't care if I ever lay eyes on you again."

"You don't mean that, Miss Charlotte," Ella Mae said in a more conciliatory tone. "What about the party? How you all gonna manage by yourself?"

Charlotte stamped her foot. "How I manage isn't any of your business—and neither is the party. Get out of my sight and out of my house before I take a stick to your sorry black skin."

She stood rooted in place long after Ella Mae left, so startled and hurt that she didn't know what to do or where to turn.

When she heard Ella Mae slam the front door shut an eternity later, she finally found the strength to move. Walking over to the sofa on wobbly knees, she threw herself across its unyielding surface, not even caring that someone might come in and see her hoop skirt sticking straight up in the air.

But what did it really matter if someone came in and saw her undergarments when her whole world had come crashing down? She pounded the stiff mohair upholstery with her fists and wept until her nose and eyes felt swollen and ugly. The weight of the huge, quiet house seemed to press down on her. How could things have come to such a sorry pass?

It was all Patrick's fault, she told herself. If he hadn't paid for Ella Mae's freedom, she wouldn't be wondering how to manage the party on her own.

Well, she decided, drawing a shuddering breath, Patrick Pride was just going to have to figure a way out of this mess.

Chapter Fifteen

Patrick didn't permit himself to look at the Sonn-schein bakery as he rode down Fredericksburg's main street. His lips were compressed, his rugged features set in a stoic mask that hid the churning deep in his gut. He couldn't deal with his feelings for Elke while he was still so furious with his wife.

When he'd returned home last night, after spending thirteen hours in a saddle rounding up strays, he was looking forward to a warm supper followed by a hot bath. Instead he'd found Ella Mae and Whitey waiting for him on the porch with the sorriest tale he'd heard in a long time.

He'd marched into the house afterward, determined to have it out with Charlotte. But he found her on the parlor sofa in a state of nervous collapse, and had spent the evening caring for her.

He'd managed to get a little tea past her chattering teeth before he undressed her and put her to bed. She had clung to his hand and begged him not to abandon her the way Ella Mae had. No matter what he said, she refused to admit she had driven Ella Mae away.

Would Charlotte ever grow up and take responsibility for her own actions?

How could he even think about letting her having children when she was such a child herself?

Charlotte had been right about one thing, though. He needed to find a qualified housekeeper—and quickly—because God knew Charlotte was incapable of running a house herself.

He scanned the steady stream of pedestrians on the wooden sidewalks that lined both sides of the street. The women were all accompanied by men, undoubtedly their husbands. No prospects there, he thought. Unattached females were at a premium in a town like Fredericksburg. How in the hell was he supposed to find a housekeeper when decent women married at sixteen—and indecent ones quickly found another way to earn their keep?

Recalling that he'd had no supper last night and had left so early there'd been no time for breakfast, he decided to have a late lunch at the Nimitz before beginning his quest. Perhaps Charles would know a likely candidate.

He reined up in front of the hotel and left his horse contentedly munching on the contents of a feed bag. Then, knocking his hat against his knee to rid it of trail dust, he opened the hotel door and strode into the lobby.

Charles Nimitz sat at his accustomed place behind the front desk. His brow elevated when he saw Patrick. "I wasn't expecting to see you until we came out to Pride's Passion for the party. What brings you to town today?"

"It's a long story. To cut it to the bone, I'm looking

for a housekeeper. You wouldn't happen to know any-one who would fill the bill?"

Charles's reply startled him. "I think I know just the right person. Elke Sonnschein is looking for a position."

Patrick wasn't sure he'd heard Charles right. "What did you say?"

"I said, Elke Sonnschein is looking for a job."

"But that's crazy. She has her hands full running the bakery."

"Not anymore she doesn't."

Patrick's heart leapt in his chest. "What's going on? Have the Detweilers come back?"

"It's nothing like that. She couldn't make a go of the bakery by herself, and a buyer came along at just the right time. You can talk to her in person if you like. She's staying here while she decides what she wants to do."

Patrick forgot all about his problems. He forgot all about Charlotte. Thinking about Elke crowded out everything else. She had needed him and, once again, he hadn't been there for her.

The fact that he didn't know about her latest problem didn't make him feel any less culpable. He should have known. He should have made it his business to know. But he had taken the coward's way out, not coming to town even once since seeing her at Velvet's, for fear he'd declare his love the minute he laid eyes on her.

"What do you mean about Elke deciding what she wants to do?"

"It isn't any secret that she's had her share of misfortune of late. She mentioned something about going back to Germany."

Patrick swayed on his feet like a man who has suffered a terrible blow to his vital organs. He couldn't let Elke go away. A part of him—the best part—would die if she did.

"Are you all right?" Charles asked, studying Patrick's face. "You look a little green around the gills."

"I'm fine. Where did you say I could find Elke?"

"I didn't—but she's in the dining room."

"That's convenient," Patrick replied, trying to inject a little bonhomie into his voice so Nimitz wouldn't see how shaken he felt. "I was planning a late lunch myself."

Without so much as another word or glance in Charles's direction, Patrick hurried across the lobby to the dining room, where a handful of customers still lingering over their meals.

He saw Elke at once, seated near a window. At a table by herself, she stared off into space, seemingly oblivious of the curious glances that came her way.

Patrick felt like throttling a man who kept on gazing at Elke as if he wanted her for dessert.

As Patrick made his way past the other diners, he saw that Elke was wearing the blue silk dress she had worn the night before he left for Natchez. Although he had never given much thought to women's clothing, he suddenly realized she probably didn't have many dresses that she considered appropriate for dining out in a restaurant.

He doubted that she felt deprived—and yet the thought of her doing without anything gave him such a pang. He wanted to give her the world. Instead, he planned to offer her a job—and he hated himself for it.

Elke would be better off if she never saw him again. She deserved the chance to rebuild her life—even to find a man who was free to love her. She deserved all that—and more. And yet, he couldn't let her go.

If she left, everything that was gentle and good in his character would go with her. He didn't want to think about the embittered man who would remain—and he sure as hell didn't want to grow old inside that man's skin.

He had made up his mind to do whatever it took—including taking advantage of Elke's innate loyalty, her concern for other people, her naturally sympathetic nature—to get her to agree to take the job as his housekeeper. Once he had her back at Pride's Passion where he could watch over her and keep her safe, he'd figure the rest out.

Shakespeare had written, "All's fair in love and war." Considering the disdain in Elke's eyes as she looked up and saw him, this encounter had the makings of both.

"Mind if I join you?" he asked, giving her the blandest smile he could conjure up.

Elke's hands tightened on the napkin in her lap. Patrick's good looks struck her all over again. How could so perfidious a soul be hidden inside so beautiful a man?

Despite the quivering deep in her abdomen, she forced her features into a semblance of normality. "Of course not. But I trust you won't be offended if I don't stay long. I'm almost finished. You don't seem surprised to see me here."

"Charles told me you were a guest in the hotel. He

also told me why. I'm truly sorry about the bakery. I just wish you'd come to me for help."

Elke couldn't meet his eyes. "That's hardly possible—under the circumstances."

"I'm even sorrier because I've given you reason to feel that way. Friends are supposed to help each other."

Elke stopped toying with her food. "What are you up to now?" she blurted out.

He abandoned all pretense of studying the menu. "I'm not 'up to' anything. But I do need your help. Please, just hear me out. It's what Otto would have wanted."

He had her there, she thought. Indeed, Otto would have wanted her to listen to what Patrick had to say— and even to help Patrick if she had it in her power. And deep down, she wanted it, too. "All right. I'll listen. But I'm not promising anything. What's the favor?"

"I came to town to hire a housekeeper—and you'd be perfect for the job. You get along with Conchita, you know your way around Pride's Passion, you're a wonderful cook, and—"

"That's completely out of the question!" she declared, not giving him a chance to finish. She pushed back from the table so abruptly that her water glass teetered. Was there no end to his presumption?

He shook his head as if he couldn't believe her response. "You agreed to hear me out. I'm not asking you to take the job for myself. In fact, I'm away from the house so much that you'll hardly see me. I'm asking for my wife. You haven't met her yet, and she'd be mortified if she knew I had confided in you, but she simply doesn't have the skills or the maturity to run a large home. The truth is, Charlotte hasn't adjusted to ranch life. She's terrified of being out there by herself. The poor thing cried herself to sleep last night."

"She's hardly alone."

"She feels as if she is. Her maid, Ella Mae, left yesterday to marry Whitey Burke. Frankly, I'm at my wit's end. Surely you remember how you felt, your first few years in Texas. I know you could help Charlotte get through a very difficult time. And you'd have a chance to decide what you want to do, too, without using up your capital while you did it. Charles mentioned that you're thinking about going back to Germany."

"Charles should mind his own business."

"I want you to know that I'll look after Otto's grave if you do. But Otto wouldn't want you to make so major a decision in haste."

Elke had been sitting rigidly upright, hiding her inner turmoil behind a poised facade. At the mention of Otto's grave, her shoulders drooped. She had avoided going out to visit the grave for fear of running into Patrick. Now she silently cursed her cowardice.

"I see I've upset you. It's the last thing I intended."

His sympathy failed to touch her. However, she couldn't ignore his logic. The trip to Germany would cost a small fortune, and she had no guarantee of finding happiness at its end.

Her parents had come to Texas in search of a better life—and she had made their dream her own. Could she live with herself if she abandoned it? "I just don't know," she said, thinking out loud.

True to form, Patrick wasted no time pressing his advantage. "I'm not asking you to make a lifetime commitment. If things don't work out, you'll certainly be free to leave. And you'd be making a lonely girl very happy."

How strange that he called his wife a girl. Could she really be that immature? "How soon would you want me to start?" she heard herself ask.

"As soon as possible. I could have someone from the livery stable drive you out to the ranch first thing tomorrow morning. I suppose you've heard about the party Charlotte is giving?"

Had she lost her mind in addition to everything else? Elke asked herself. What in the world could she be thinking? How could she go to work for Patrick?

How could she not? a voice in her head quickly replied.

"Now that Ella Mae's gone, Charlotte's at a complete loss. I'm afraid she's really bitten off more than she can chew with this party. She doesn't have any friends of her own, poor thing, and she's so anxious to make a good impression on mine."

Against her better judgment, Elke couldn't help imagining herself in Charlotte's place. A large party would be a daunting undertaking for the woman Patrick had described. "I suppose I could help—just until after the party."

The tight set of Patrick's features relaxed. "You've made me a very happy man. I'll have Conchita make up one of the guest rooms."

Elke took a deep, settling breath. Her voice sounded remarkably steady, considering how shaky she felt. "Your happiness is the least of my concerns. I'm not doing this for you. I'm doing it for your wife. However, there are a couple of things we need to get straight."

"Name your terms, Sunshine."

"If I'm to work for you, I think you had better call me Mrs. Sonnschein."

"Name your terms, Mrs. Sonnschein."

She grit her teeth, controlling her anger. "First, I will not live in the main house. The dogtrot will suit me."

"But it's a cabin," he objected, "and not a very comfortable one at that."

"Either we do this my way—or we don't do it at all."

"All right. What are your other terms?"

"I want your solemn promise that you'll never ask anything else of me, and that you won't object if I decide to leave next week." *And that you'll never touch me again, either,* she silently added. "This is a business arrangement, nothing more. I'll expect the going salary."

"Whatever you say." Patrick jumped to his feet, as if he knew he didn't dare linger long enough to give her the chance to change her mind. "If you don't object, I'll skip lunch and take my leave. I want to get back to the ranch and tell Charlotte her worries are over. She'll be so happy."

At least one of us is going to be happy, Elke thought as she watched him make his way out of the dining room. She had the feeling her worries had just begun.

Once again, she had allowed her heart to overrule her common sense. But she refused to compound her mistake by lying to herself. She hadn't accepted the job to help a woman she'd never met. She had done it for herself.

The thought of seeing Patrick every day, of seeing to it that he had nourishing meals and a clean home, had just been too great to resist.

Patrick cursed himself all the way back to Pride's Passion. Taking shameless advantage of Elke made him feel like a cad. Using up a good horse in the process made him feel even worse. His weary mount had given all a horse could give by the time they reached Pride's Passion late that night.

Rather than wake one of the hands, Patrick led the horse into the barn, unsaddled it and rubbed it down himself, then gave it an extra measure of feed. Only then did he head for the house where, despite the lateness of the hour, he saw a light glowing in the parlor.

To his surprise, he found Charlotte waiting up for him. "I'm so glad you're back," she cried, running across the room and throwing herself into his arms. "I didn't expect you until sometime tomorrow, and I just couldn't sleep. This big house seems to know when you aren't around. It creaks and groans as if it wants to scare me away."

"You're imagining things," he said, releasing himself from her embrace. "This is your home as much as it is mine."

"I know—I know. And I suppose one of these days I'll even feel that way. But never mind all that. Did you find a housekeeper?"

How like Charlotte it was to put her own interests and concerns first, without so much as asking if he needed anything to eat or drink. He'd just made a sixty-mile round trip at her behest, and exhaustion rode him as hard as he had ridden his horse.

And yet, he couldn't seem to get angry with Charlotte. She couldn't be faulted for the way she had been raised. Her parents had taught her to think she was the center of the universe.

"I was in luck. Elke Sonnschein just sold the bakery, and she agreed to help us out for a while."

Charlotte clapped her hands like a gleeful child and danced around the room. "Isn't she the one who left all that delicious food?"

"Yes," Patrick replied in a strangled voice.

Dear God, what had he done? He could hardly bear to hear Elke's name on Charlotte's lips. How would he handle it when Charlotte began bossing Elke around, as she inevitably would?

"You old sourpuss, I told you finding a housekeeper would be easy. To think how you lectured me about the way I treated Ella Mae, as if we'd never get any household help again. Shame on you!"

Patrick grabbed Charlotte's arm and brought her cavorting to a sudden stop.

"Ouch. You're hurting me," she wailed.

He wanted to do considerably more than squeeze her arm. He wanted to tell her how much he regretted marrying her. But he kept his own counsel. He didn't much fancy himself for what he'd already done this day. Abusing his wife would lower his self-esteem even further.

"We have to get something straight," he said through clenched teeth. "Elke Sonnschein is not to be treated like a servant. She's an old and dear friend. If I just once catch you talking to her the way you did to Ella Mae, I'll send you back to Natchez on the next stage."

Charlotte made a moue in response. "You don't mean that, darling."

"You're dead wrong, my dear. I mean every word. And now, if you'll excuse me, it's been a long day. I'm going to bed."

Charlotte watched in openmouthed astonishment as Patrick spun around with military precision and marched from the room. She didn't know whether to laugh, cry, or do a little bit of both. No one had ever talked to her that way.

What in the world had gotten into him? It couldn't be anything she had said or done, she thought, wrapping her arms around herself. Why was he so angry? Why was he defending the Sonnschein woman?

A new and troubling emotion caught Charlotte by surprise. It took her a moment to label it as jealousy. In all her born days, she'd never been more dumbfounded. Surely Patrick couldn't prefer a baker's widow to the girl who had been the toast of Natchez?

The sounds of merriment barely penetrated the walls of Velvet Gilhooley's bedroom as she sat talking with Elke over a glass of wine.

"Do you think I'm making a mistake?" Elke asked.

Mistake hardly covered it, Velvet thought. But she'd be damned if she'd add to Elke's formidable list of concerns. "Honey, I'm not one of those gypsies with a crystal ball who can look into the future. But face it. You're in love with the man."

"Is it that obvious?"

"I doubt anyone else will catch on. But I'm the one who delivered your baby when you were half out of your mind with pain. And you didn't call out for your husband. You called for Patrick."

"Why didn't you tell me before."

"In my trade, you hear a lot of secrets. I guess I didn't think it was any of my business."

"Did Rio hear, too?"

"I reckon he did. But you don't need to worry on his account. The man is as careful with words as a miser with his purse."

Elke managed a smile. "That he is."

"From a selfish standpoint, I'm happier than hell that you're not going back to Germany. It's been a long time since I had a woman friend. And even longer since I put any faith in a man. But Rio's one of a kind. I'll be able to visit you at Pride's Passion and see him at the same time. Now that's what I call drawing a full house."

"I hadn't thought about that."

Or a lot of other things, Velvet mused, pondering what she had to say and how she wanted to say it. Straight out, she decided. "I do have one reservation, though."

"If you're worrying about Patrick, I made it very clear that I don't want anything to do with him."

"He's not my concern. It's his wife. Whitey told me that Charlotte Pride is a bitch and a half."

Chapter Sixteen

Charlotte sat on the front porch, surrounded by branches of holly and evergreens, trying to twine them into garlands.

"Damn," she muttered as a thorn pricked her finger for what surely must have been the hundredth time.

Over the years, she had watched the maids at Windmere make holiday garlands by the yard. Their nimble fingers always made it look so easy. She had counted on being able to do what any slave could do— and failed miserably.

Considering her lack of progress, there'd be no decorations for the party. And only beans and tortillas to eat if the new housekeeper didn't get here soon.

Charlotte frowned at the greenery littering the porch, and then at her bleeding fingers. Thank heavens gloves would hide her hands at the party. She certainly didn't want her guests to know she'd been slaving away like a darkie!

She was about to return to her odious task and give it one last try, when a distant plume of dust captured her attention. She wondered who it could be. They were too far from what passed for civilization in the Hill Country to have company just drop in.

Anxiety sent her heart hammering as she imagined marauding Indians or murderous bandits hell bent on carnage. Dear God. She'd heard that Comancheros raped white women. She peered into the distance while hideous visions danced through her brain.

On the other hand, though, it might be the housekeeper. Squinting to shield her eyes from the brilliant January sunshine, she could just make out a distant horse and buggy. Surely Indians and bushwhackers didn't travel that way.

As the buggy came closer, she could see a male driver up front and a woman in the back. Thank heaven, Charlotte thought, releasing her pent up breath. It had to be Elke Sonnschein—and not a minute too soon.

Suddenly, Charlotte realized she wasn't at her best. Her uncorseted waist strained at her dress and her hair probably looked as if birds had been nesting in it. She had dressed by herself that morning and hadn't been able to lace her stays, let alone do anything with her hair.

She jumped to her feet, kicking holly branches and evergreens aside, wondering if she had time to go inside and freshen up—not that she'd be able to improve her appearance without Ella Mae to help.

The buggy was moving at such a fast clip that she decided to stay put. In any case, she could hardly wait to get a good look at Elke Sonnschein.

A few minutes later the driver reined the vehicle to a stop in front of the house. A very tall woman alighted

from the back seat. While the woman supervised the un-
loading of her belongings, Charlotte had the chance to
look her over from head to toe.

As she did, her incipient jealousy faded. Patrick
couldn't possibly be enamored of a woman who was
taller than most men—a woman who wore her hair
pulled back in a spinster's bun—a woman with freckles
splashed across her nose and cheeks—an unfashionable
woman who didn't even wear a hoop—and an older
woman to boot. Why, she wasn't anywhere near as
pretty as Charlotte's own self!

Just then, Elke Sonnschein looked up, saw Charlotte,
and their eyes met. At least she has nice blue eyes,
Charlotte thought. Determined to be as gracious to the
widow as Patrick required, she moved toward the steps.

"Welcome to Pride's Passion," she said, forgetting all
about the greenery littering the floor.

Her hoop caught on one of the larger branches. She
tripped on another. Arms flailing, she lost her balance
and all thought of playing the lady of the manor fled her
mind.

"Help!" she cried out.

Elke raced for the steps, caught her by the waist, and
set her on her feet. Patrick hadn't exaggerated. His wife
didn't even have the sense to look where she was going.

"Are you all right?"

Charlotte shook her head yes, and burst into laughter.
So this is the bitch on wheels, Elke thought.

"The only thing that's hurt is my dignity. My mother
used to accuse me of throwing myself at men. This is
the first time I've done it to a woman." Charlotte

laughed again, producing a surprisingly hearty sound for so small a creature.

No wonder Patrick had called his wife a child. She was as fragile looking and as pretty as a porcelain doll. With a pang, Elke saw why Patrick had found Charlotte so irresistible.

Holding out her hand, Elke said, I'm your new house-keeper, Elke Sonnschein."

"And I'm Charlotte Pride. But I hope you'll call me Charlotte. I need a friend even more than I need a housekeeper. Have the driver bring your bags in."

"I won't be staying in the house," Elke replied. "I told Patrick—Mr. Pride," she quickly amended, "that I wanted to move into the dogtrot."

"Oh, no! I was counting on you living in the house." The dismay on Charlotte's face was too real to be dismissed. "Please, won't you reconsider? I'm not used to being alone, and Patrick works such long hours. Besides, that broken-down cabin isn't fit for human habitation."

Apparently Charlotte didn't know Patrick had lived there for years before he built the big house. Elke looked toward the cabin, then down at Charlotte, and weighed her choices. Patrick had said his wife was afraid of being by herself. Her near fall testified to her helplessness. "Please," Charlotte wheedled.

Elke suspected that she'd live to regret it, but she couldn't ignore the naked plea on Charlotte's face. "All right, then. I'll move into the house for now. I can always change to the cabin later if we both want more privacy."

Charlotte gave her a dazzling smile and took her arm.

"I grew up in such a big family with so many friends and neighbors coming and going that I'm not a very private person." She heaved a sigh. "I've been dreadfully homesick and lonely. But I feel ever so much better now that you're here. I know we're going to get along famously. Let me show you the house. Patrick said to make sure you felt right at home."

Patrick gazed at the dogtrot as he rode by on his way to the main house, and wondered if Elke had moved in yet. He repressed the urge to dismount and see for himself. He had been thinking about her all day with the sort of breathless anticipation he should have experienced before his wedding—and hadn't.

No woman had ever made him feel the way Elke did—all hot and bothered, and yet tender and caring and wanting to cherish and protect her. No woman had ever made him as angry—or as happy. How could he ever have imagined he would be better off with a traditional southern belle? If only he were coming home to Elke as his wife rather than his housekeeper.

He shook his head, as if doing so would rid him of the unseemly wish. He couldn't permit himself to think like that. Hadn't he once told her not to get all tangled up in *if onlys?* He had better take his own advice.

Reining his mount to a stop by the barn, he handed the horse over to a waiting cowboy. "Have Rio check his left front hoof," he told the hand. "He seems to be favoring it."

"I'll do it myself, boss," the young man replied, giving Patrick a knowing grin. "Rio's on his way to town again. I don't know how a man his age does it."

"The same way you do, Son," Patrick replied.

Rio had been beating a regular path to Velvet Gilhooley's door lately. The foreman always had a special fondness for whores. Patrick couldn't help wondering which one had taken his fancy, and envied his freedom to act on it.

Elke's presence announced itself the minute he opened the front door. He paused there, waiting for his own heart to steady while he gazed around. For the first time, Pride's Passion looked and smelled like a real home.

The floor of the central hall gleamed with wax. Overhead, the glass globes of the kerosene chandelier shone bright and clean. The pungent odor of a juniper fire blended with the scent of appetizing food. And the happy sound of female chatter added to the aura of well-being.

He called out a greeting to his wife.

Charlotte bounded in from the dining room, her hoop skirt swaying wildly, a pixieish grin on her face. "Patrick, guess what we're having for supper?"

"Beans?" he teased, grateful to find her in a good mood for a change.

"You silly man. Does that smell like beans?" She wrinkled her nose. "Elke made chicken fricassee and dumplings. I've been drooling over it like one of my father's hounds. She is the most accomplished woman. She can cook and sew, she knows how to deal with Conchita and Maria, and she seems so well educated."

Elke? So they were already on a first-name basis? He

repressed an unworthy twinge of jealousy. At least he wouldn't have to call her Mrs. Sonnschein. "The house does look marvelous. Where is Elke?"

Charlotte took his arm. "She's waiting for us in the dining room. You said you didn't want me to treat her like a servant, and you were absolutely right. I've asked her to take her meals with us, and she's going to teach Maria how to serve." Charlotte stood on her tiptoes, aimed a kiss at his lips, couldn't reach high enough, and kissed his chin instead.

"Come on, you old slowpoke," she said, taking his arm and tugging him toward the dining room. "I know you're just dying to say hello."

In view of the situation, dying came close, he thought grimly. "Whoa," he commanded as if Charlotte were a recalcitrant horse. "I need to wash up before I eat."

He needed a chance to compose himself even more, he mused as he took the stairs two at a time. He washed quickly, then deciding he ought to change his shirt, too, headed for the master bedroom.

He felt as nervous as a tadpole in a pond full of cat-fish. He'd spent the last ten years riding sixty-mile round trips to see Elke once a month, and wishing he could see her every day. Never once in all those years had he imagined the circumstances he faced tonight.

How could he sit down to supper with his wife on one side of the table and the woman he loved on the other? How could he pretend a casual interest in Elke and a passionate one in Charlotte? He doubted even a renowned actor like Edwin Booth would be up to the task. But he had no choice. His pretense had to succeed—for all their sakes.

"Patrick, we're waiting!" Charlotte called from the foot of the stairs.

With a final despairing glance at his mirrored image, he turned on his heels and headed down the hall, feeling like a condemned man about to eat his last meal.

Elke was showing Maria how to offer serving platters from the right and clear plates from the left, when she heard Charlotte and Patrick walk into the dining room. She had been dreading this moment all afternoon and now she steeled herself to meet it head-on.

Gazing straight at Patrick, she said, "Good evening, Mr. Pride. You're just in time. Supper's ready."

He seemed tense. Under his tan, he looked drawn and pale. Were those new lines of worry she saw etched on his face. Was he uncomfortable, too?

"Good evening," he replied. His glance barely brushed over her before traveling around the room. "Charlotte and I are delighted to have you here. You've worked wonders already. The house never looked better, and supper smells superb."

He helped Charlotte to her place with a solicitude that riveted Elke in place. In her mind, she had accepted the marriage as a *fait accompli*. But she had never accepted it in her heart. Now, seeing the evidence of a loving relationship, she felt like such a fool.

Patrick walked to her side and pulled out her chair. "Charlotte tells me she's asked you to take your meals with us."

"I hope you don't mind."

"Of course he doesn't mind," Charlotte interjected. "We're going to be one big happy family."

Charlotte certainly had a genius for saying the wrong thing, Elke thought, hoping her face didn't reveal her consternation. She felt Patrick's hand on her elbow as he helped her into a chair, and made a determined effort to ignore the longing the casual touch engendered.

She had been crazy to think she could live under Patrick's roof. But she couldn't walk out, either, her conscience reminded her. She'd promised Patrick she would stay through the party, and stay she must—no matter what it cost her.

Chapter Seventeen

A nightmare jolted Elke awake in the predawn blackness. The dream faded so quickly that she couldn't remember what it had been about, and yet the emotions it aroused clung to her mind like the strands of a cobweb.

During her childhood she had awakened on birthdays and holidays with the expectation that the sunrise heralded something wonderful. This morning she experienced the opposite sensation. She felt certain something dreadful lay ahead.

The house had cooled overnight as well-banked fires burned down to coals. Abandoning the warm cocoon of her bed, she dressed hurriedly. Winter held Pride's Passion in an icy grip that reflected the chill she felt deep inside her soul. Living under Patrick's roof these last few days—knowing he and Charlotte slept together down the hall—had been pure hell.

Always an early riser, she made a point of getting up before the rest of the household. The hour before dawn—the one she had always loved best because it offered a new beginning—belonged to her. This morning she planned to spend it alone in the kitchen, having her first cup of coffee and girding herself to face another day in Patrick's home.

Holding her calico skirt off the floor with one hand and a kerosene lamp with the other, Elke made her way to the servants' stairs at the end of the long hall that ran the length of the upper floor. The bottom landing opened onto a smaller hall.

Turning toward the kitchen door, she was surprised to see a light seeping from underneath the sill. Perhaps Whitey and Ella Mae got up even earlier than she did. Although she had been looking forward to time alone, she wouldn't mind sharing a pot of coffee and having a chance to thank them again for all their help. They seemed so happy together, so perfectly suited, so fortunate to have found each other. Perhaps some of their good fortune would rub off on her.

If Velvet hadn't insisted on their coming out to the ranch yesterday, Elke didn't know if she could have finished the party preparations before the guests arrived this afternoon. The debt she owed Velvet—for that and so much more—could never be repaid.

She opened the kitchen door and her expectant smile froze. Whitey and Ella Mae were nowhere in sight. But Patrick was. All six feet two inches of him.

With a barely repressed gasp, she realized he was naked to the hips. He stood at the sink, his back toward her, splashing his face with water. The light from an overhead lamp cast his muscular torso in bold relief and gave his skin a coppery glow. His shoulders looked even broader bare than they did in civilized garb, and his waist slimmer. His leather chaps enclosed his muscular buttocks like a picture frame.

Mesmerized by his barbaric beauty, she stood stock-still, hardly daring to breathe. If she fled, Patrick would undoubtedly hear her. If she stayed, he would certainly see her. Nevertheless she couldn't bring herself to move. She had never seen him in so unguarded a moment. The boyish way he sluiced his face contrasted with the mature masculinity of his torso—and both accelerated her pulse.

Her husband had been generous to a fault—as kind and loving a man as any woman could ask for. And yet she had never enjoyed looking at his body. The female in her responded to Patrick's virile seminudity in the most primal way. Her nipples hardened; the tender tissue between her legs moistened.

On the previous morning she'd spent alone in the kitchen, she had permitted herself to daydream that this was her house, and that the man she loved would soon appear to share her quiet time. It had seemed like a harmless fancy. Now she indulged in a far more dangerous one.

She pictured herself giving in to the longing that swelled in her chest and clutched at her abdomen. She saw herself walking up to Patrick and embracing him from behind. She imagined running her hands over all that power and kissing that coppery skin.

Helpless in the face of her overwhelming desire, she took one step toward him—and then another. Her mind commanded her to stop. Heeding a far more urgent message, her body didn't listen.

At the sound of footsteps, Patrick spun around to see

Elke coming toward him. For one magical moment, he thought she was going to walk straight into his arms.

"You gave me a fright. I didn't know you were here," she said, halting a few feet away.

"I'm sorry. I didn't mean to startle you." He reached for the shirt he'd left draped over the back of a chair. "I usually wash up in the bunkhouse so as not to wake Charlotte, but I wanted to talk to you this morning."

She had been gazing at him wide-eyed, her mouth partly open. Now, she clamped her teeth shut and jutted her lower jaw in the stubborn expression he knew so well. "We have nothing to say to each other."

She walked past him to the huge cast-iron stove bulking against the far wall, opened one of its doors, bent over and began putting chunks of wood in its gaping maw.

"You may not have anything to say, Elke. However, I do." He walked up behind her, took a lucifer from a shelf over the stove, and scraped it on the stove's metal surface. "Let me light the fire for you."

Although he'd been careful not to touch her, she leapt back like a scalded cat. Her gaze roved his bare chest before coming to rest on the open buttons of his trousers. "All right then, we'll talk," she said in a strangled voice, "after you're properly dressed."

As he began buttoning his shirt, she turned away. But not before he saw the flush on her cheeks. She might not like him very much these days; hell, he didn't particularly like himself. But by God, she still wanted him, he realized with a surge of triumph. Fate had bound them to each other. No matter how she fought to be free, a part of her would always belong to him.

He tucked his shirt inside his trousers, fastened the buttons, and cinched his chaps low on his waist. "You can turn around now."

She had been busying herself putting a pot of coffee on to brew, bustling around like a perfect servant. Hands on hips, she spun to face him.

"You can say your piece. And then I'd appreciate it if you cleared out. I have too much to do to spend time in idle chitchat."

He grinned, thinking this was the Elke he remembered, the Elke he had fallen in love with all those years ago—a woman so filled with fire and determination, so bold of spirit, so utterly fearless that at times, she scared the hell out of him. "Whatever you say, Sunshine."

"I'd appreciate your not calling me that," she shot back.

"I wanted to see you this morning to thank you ... for everything. I know it couldn't have been easy—you coming here—but I sincerely hope you'll stay. It means more to me than I can possibly say."

He waited for her to respond. She just stared at him as if she'd like to scrape him off her shoes.

"Damn it, Elke, don't look at me that way. I know you don't trust me and I can't say I blame you. But I have your best interests at heart, whether you believe it or not. No one knows where the Detweilers are. At least you're safe here. Otto would want you to stay."

At the mention of Otto's name, Elke's eyes sheened. Longing to comfort her, he took a step forward. His arms reached for her of their own volition.

She gave a wordless cry, whirled around and fled the room. He stood there a moment, breathing in her scent, his senses still aflame from the brief encounter. He wanted Elke with a longing that transcended anything in his previous experience.

Despite her anger, he thought she felt something for him, too. He'd seen it in her eyes before she raised the shield of her virtue. What he'd seen gave him reason to hope. He had lost this particular battle, but he'd be damned if he'd lose the war.

One way or another, he'd find a way to keep Elke at Pride's Passion.

The sun hung directly overhead as Rio reined his horse to a stop in front of Velvet's house. He'd made the ride so often in the last few months that he swore both he and the horse could have done it in their sleep.

Knowing they had reached their destination, the paint gelding lowered its head before Rio dismounted and began cropping the grass that grew by the hitching post. The gelding, a wild mustang he'd broken himself, had served him well. It wasn't the biggest horse in his string, and the good Lord knew it weren't the purtiest, but it had staying power. In the long run, that's what counted most in a horse, a man, a woman ... and a marriage.

Now where the hell did that thought come from? Rio wondered, as he made his way to the front door. Velvet answered to his knock and the sight of her filled him with a liquid warmth that made his legs feel as shaky as if he'd walked a hundred miles.

"Well, you sure are a welcome visitor," she said, taking his arm and leading him to the parlor.

She left him in the middle of the floor, then moved from window to window, opening the drapes. Sunlight glanced off the evidence of the previous night's revelry, glinting from glasses and bottles and brass spittoons—and most especially from Velvet's red hair. She sure did look good.

"I apologize for the mess," she said, sounding for all the world like a fretful housewife, "but I don't usually entertain at this hour. Can I get you a drink, or a bite to eat?"

"I don't want you waiting on me. But I wouldn't mind a tad of that special brandy you keep behind the bar."

"Help yourself," Velvet replied, settling herself on one of the sofas with a sibilant swish of silk undergarments, "and pour one for me, too."

He crossed the floor to the music of his spurs, found the bottle with the fancy French label, poured for them both, and returned to stand in front of her. She reached for the glass he held out, their fingers touched, and the damnedest sensation ran up his arm. It tingled as though a whole herd of butterflies had landed on it.

Dry from the long ride, and in desperate need of liquid fortification, he drank the brandy down in one long burning draught.

Her eyes glinted with an emotion he couldn't read. She patted the sofa by her side, motioning him to join her. "My, you certainly were thirsty."

Although he had shared every conceivable intimacy in her bed—including a few he had never shared with any other woman—he felt awkward sitting down beside her. Seeing that his spurs were about to scratch the floor, he bent over and unbuckled them.

"I'm a little surprised to see you today." She took a sip of brandy, then licked her lips as daintily as a kitten at its bath.

Seeing the tip of her tongue, and thinking what it felt like on his skin, sure as hell heated his drawers. "I hope you don't mind my dropping in."

"Of course not. You're always welcome here. It's just that I thought you'd be at the Prides' party."

"Mrs. Pride did ask me to sing for her guests—but I'd lots rather sing to a bunch of cows." He felt himself blush, and hoped Velvet wouldn't notice. "Seeing as how you sent Whitey to help the Prides, I thought I'd take his place and make sure you didn't have any trouble with the customers."

"That's very kind of you."

"It ain't nothing of the sort," he objected vehemently. "You're the kind one, sending Whitey and Ella Mae to work at a party when you weren't even invited."

The indignation in Rio's voice brought unexpected tears to Velvet's eyes. She couldn't remember the last time a man had ridden to her defense. And this one had done so literally as well as figuratively.

He unknotted the cloth at his throat and handed it over. "Aw, hell, Velvet, I didn't mean to make you cry."

As she blotted her eyes with his neckerchief, his scent—a blend of soap, pipe tobacco, and male sweat—filled her nostrils. The aroma reminded her of the afternoon when he'd collected on the debt, and the pleasures they had shared.

He had shown up several times since, and never once

paid to spend an hour with one of her girls. Instead, he had seemed content to have a quiet drink or two, and watch her from across the room.

"I'm not crying," she declared in a quavering voice. "I never cry. I'm just upset because I can't figure you out. It's been a long time since I didn't know what was on a man's mind."

His expression hardened. "Maybe I'm talking out of turn, but the way I see it, Patrick should have invited you to the party. The two of you go a long way back, a lot further back than he goes with his wife."

She touched his arm. "You know Patrick couldn't do that."

"It don't seem right, the way folks treat you. I just wish they knew you the way Mrs. Sonnschein and I do. I don't care about your calling—not one dang bit. I never met a finer woman than you, Velvet."

It was damn peculiar, how he could be so tongue-tied most of the time and still manage to say the sweetest things. Tears rose in her eyes anew. "And I never met a finer man."

Looking as if he'd been struck by lightning, he bolted to his feet, hurried over to the bar, refilled his glass and emptied it even faster than he had the first time.

"Before you get too drunk to stand up, maybe you'd better tell me why you're really here," she said with a throaty chuckle.

He continued to stand at the bar with his back turned toward her. "I don't know what to tell you—except I'm not in control of my actions anymore. All I know is, I get such a strong hankering to see you that I can't think about anything else."

Velvet felt as if her heart had found a way to escape her chest and lodge in her throat. She got up, crossed the floor, and put her hands on his shoulders. He started at her touch, and she felt him shiver. "Does that hankering include going to bed?"

"Yes, ma'am. It sure as hell does."

So that's why he hadn't asked to see her girls. He wanted her, and hadn't known how to say so. A frisson of excitement ricocheted from her head to her toes, and back again.

Still holding him by the shoulders, she turned him around and looked into his eyes. "Rio, you darling man, all you had to do was ask."

The Prides' guests started arriving at noon. Some came in carriages, some on horseback. All of them were in high spirits. Lavish parties were as rare in the Hill Country as indoor plumbing. At the Pride mansion, folks could enjoy both.

Elke had worked since dawn getting ready for the big event. Now she stood at the dining table filling glasses with punch while the sound of laughter rang in her ears. She had a perfect view of the entry hall where Patrick and Charlotte stood at the foot of the stairs, greeting their guests. How good they looked together.

Patrick seemed so sophisticated in formal attire that she could hardly reconcile his appearance with the half-nude male who had tormented her just a few hours earlier. Charlotte's petite beauty was the perfect foil for his rugged masculinity, while his height made Charlotte seem even more delicately made.

Elke had never seen wealth displayed so casually on a woman's body. Charlotte's emerald gown and topaz jewels would have bought and paid for the Sonnschein bakery with money left over.

Charlotte seemed to glow with a special radiance. She looked every inch the happy bride. Every few minutes, she cut a loving glance at Patrick, leaned close and whispered something in his ear. He never failed to smile in response.

Charlotte might have been scatter-brained and even selfish, but she certainly knew how to turn on the charm. The approving smile on every new arrival's face told Elke that Charlotte was winning their hearts as easily as she had Patrick's.

"She sho do know how to put on the dog" came the sound of Ella Mae's voice from over Elke's shoulder. Ella Mae picked up the tray of punch glasses that Elke had been filling. "You mark my words. She'll be making fun of most of them folks tomorrow morning."

"I'm sure she doesn't mean any harm."

"I reckon you're right."

"Then you aren't angry at her anymore?"

"Heavens, no. Miss Charlotte and I grew up together. I knows her better than she knows herself. She ain't mean. She just likes to have her way. The things I could tell you about how she trapped Mr. Patrick . . ." Ella Mae's voice trailed off.

Although gossip had been served up in the bakery right along with the free coffee, Elke had never liked listening to it. She hadn't counted herself richer for knowing which farmer owed money to the freight company, or which rancher's daughter had gotten herself in trouble with one of the hands. Now, though, she wanted to know more. "What do you mean about Charlotte trapping Patrick?"

Ella Mae was about to reply when Charlotte suddenly left Patrick's side and came into the dining room, a frown on her face.

"Ella Mae, we have thirsty guests," Charlotte admonished.

Ella Mae gave a guilty start and, tray in hand, scurried off as if she'd been shot from a cannon.

"You really have to watch darkies," Charlotte confided under her breath, "or they will take the most terrible advantage. My mother always said they were lazy right down to their souls."

"It was my fault," Elke said. "I asked Ella Mae a question."

"Now you sound just like Patrick. He was always defending the girl, too." Charlotte's eyes traveled to her husband, and she sighed. "But how can I be angry with a man who looks like that?"

At that moment, an excited hubbub arose from the guests. Elke saw an imposingly tall, white-haired man walk up to Patrick.

"Who in the world is that?" Charlotte asked.

Although Elke had never met the stranger, she had seen his picture. Before she could finish saying, "Sam Houston," Charlotte left in a flash of emerald green.

While Elke watched, Patrick introduced Charlotte to Texas's current governor. She saw the appreciation in Houston's eyes as he gazed down at Charlotte. Then Charlotte must have said something amusing because Patrick and Sam Houston burst into laughter.

Stop gawking, Elke told herself, *and get back to work.* Turning her gaze from the trio, she headed for the kitchen to put the final touches on the buffet. For the next two hours, she had no time to think of anything but work.

The mountains of food that had taken two days to prepare disappeared quickly. Elke kept Ella Mae, Conchita, and Maria busy scurrying back and forth from the kitchen to the dining room, leaving with full platters and returning with empty ones.

When the sound of music announced that the dancing had begun, Elke finally ventured into the dining room to help clear the table. The room was empty but for a tall man gazing out the window toward the Guadalupe River.

Hearing her footsteps, he turned, then smiled. She was surprised to see Sam Houston coming toward her, his hand outstretched.

"Permit me to introduce myself," Houston said in a deep baritone.

Although Elke didn't have to look up at most men, she found herself looking up at this one. He stood even taller than Patrick. His careworn features gave mute evidence of the handsome man who had governed two states—and broken his share of hearts. His thick white mane hung to his shoulders. His piercing eyes gleamed from under bushy brows.

"You don't have to introduce yourself, sir. Everyone in Texas knows you on sight." She held her hand out and he took it in both of his.

"I've wanted to meet you for a long time, Mrs. Sonnschein."

"You flatter me, sir, when so many important people are here."

Houston's expression sobered. "But few of them have done as much in the cause of freedom as you have. I know how hard you campaigned in favor of abolition. And I know the price you paid for doing it. My condolences can never make up for your loss, but they couldn't be more heartfelt."

"You're very kind."

He took a deep breath and an expression of despair came over his face. "I just wish more Texans felt as you and I do. I fear our beloved state will follow the South into a war it cannot win." He turned his leonine head toward the sounds of merriment coming from the parlor. "History tells us that the emperor Nero played his fiddle while Rome burned. Alas, it would seem history is going to repeat itself."

"Then you don't think President Lincoln will be able to hold the Union together?"

"No man, elected by a minority of the people, can successfully rule the majority," Houston replied grimly. Then he shook his long frame like a spaniel shedding water. "You must excuse me, Mrs. Sonnschein. Our hostess has decreed that there is to be no talk of politics at this party."

Although Elke was thrilled to have finally met the man who was a living legend in Texas, she also felt incredibly awkward at having him single her out for attention.

"I really must excuse myself, sir. I have work to do."

"Surely your work can wait. A beautiful woman belongs on the dance floor. I'd be honored if you would join me."

Elke hesitated. As a servant, she had no right to monopolize Houston's time. And yet she could hardly refuse his invitation. "It would be my pleasure," she murmured, untying her apron.

Patrick had danced the first dance with Charlotte, then relinquished her to the first in a series of adoring partners. Parties were her natural element, he thought, watching her from the sidelines. She glowed with an almost otherworldly radiance. Her laughter, her high spirits, seemed to have infected all their guests.

"Your wife certainly knows how to throw a social gathering," Charles Nimitz said, joining Patrick. "People will be talking about this shindig for months."

"I'll tell Charlotte you said so," Patrick replied with a bitter smile.

The credit for the party's success rightly belonged to Elke. She had turned Charlotte's lists into reality. How he wished it had been Elke by his side, greeting guests. He hated seeing her work so hard, and yet he would have hated it even more if she had left for Germany. The question was, how to keep her here?"

"Well, what do you know?" The sound of Nimitz's voice intruded on Patrick's musings. "It looks like Elke has an admirer."

Patrick tracked Nimitz's gaze to see Elke walking into the parlor on Sam Houston's arm. Her cheeks were flushed from the long hours she'd spent at the stove and tendrils of golden hair had escaped the chignon at her nape. She wore the gray silk dress again. Its severity contrasted starkly with the frills and furbelows other ladies sported, and yet Elke seemed to outshine every one of them including his expensively gowned wife.

Certainly, from the expression on Houston's face, Houston thought so, too. While Patrick stared at the two of them, the music changed form a lively reel to a stately waltz. Houston gazed into Elke's eyes, put a hand to her waist, and drew her into the dance.

Her nimble feet followed his so easily that they looked as if they had spent a lifetime dancing together. One by one, the other couples withdrew to the sidelines, leaving the floor to Elke and Houston.

When the last sweet note faded away, the governor gave Elke a courtly bow, then raised her hands to his lips. "I have never enjoyed a dance more," he said in the deep voice that had filled so many halls of power. "You are a very lovely, very graceful, and very gallant lady, Mrs. Sonnschein."

At that moment, Patrick didn't know which he wanted more—to challenge Houston to a duel or to fall down on his knees and thank him. The guests who had been avoiding Elke, the old friends who hadn't known how to treat her in her new role, burst into spontaneous applause and hurried to share her triumph.

To Patrick's amazement, Charlotte led the charge, her voice rising above all the others. "Governor Houston, you aren't going to steal my friend away with your flattery."

Charlotte beckoned Patrick to her side. "You had better dance with Elke and tell her how much we need her or the next thing we know, she'll be off to the state capitol on the governor's arm."

Charlotte didn't know the half of it, Patrick thought grimly. He needed Elke so much that there were times when he thought he would die of it.

Turning back to Houston, and fluttering her sable lashes flirtatiously, Charlotte said, "La, sir. I believe the next dance is mine."

Patrick had expected her to be jealous at losing the limelight to Elke. Instead, Charlotte had turned the moment to her own advantage. How little he knew his wife, he thought, watching her glide away in Houston's arms.

Turning back to Elke, he said, "I know better than to gainsay my wife. If we don't dance, we'll never hear the end of it."

But for two spots of color on her cheeks, Elke was as pale as milk. She gazed at him gravely for a moment, then moved toward him. "I suppose you're right."

The impromptu band was playing "Old Folks at Home," Stephen Foster's hauntingly sad tribute to lost youth and crushed hope. The slow rhythm invited the dancing couples to move closer to one another.

Putting his left hand on Elke's pliant waist, Patrick drew her toward him. The warmth of her body seemed to rush up his arm from that single contact point, to pool in his chest. He drank her nearness in with all his senses, filling his eyes with her beauty, his nostrils with her scent, his ears with the sound of her breathing, his touch with her slender femininity.

He hadn't expected to share a moment like this with her again. As their eyes locked and held, his concentration was so intense that the sights and sounds of the party faded away. He knew nothing but the pleasure of holding her, moving with her as one while his love for her ravished his soul.

Long hours later, the memory of the dance she and Patrick shared foiled all Elke's attempts at sleep. She tossed and turned in her bed, churning the covers into a twisted mass, got up to straighten them, then began the process all over again.

Every time she closed her eyes, she envisioned Patrick gazing at her with a concentration that was frightening in its intensity. Had he been any other man, she would have interpreted that look as longing—perhaps even love. But Patrick had tormented her too many times for her to trust her intuition.

She had intended to stay on at Pride's Passion long enough to restore the house to order. However, thinking about the dance, she realized she had to escape before her emotions broke free. She might leave her heart behind, but she intended to depart with her dignity intact.

She got up a couple of hours before dawn and, moving as stealthily as a thief, began to pack. She hadn't decided where to go, but anywhere would be better than Pride's Passion. With any luck, she'd be gone before the rest of the household awoke.

The need for silence slowed her down. By the time she finished, the first faint rays of the rising sun bathed the eastern horizon in pale gold.

Dressed in her gray serge traveling suit and carrying a valise in each hand, she tiptoed along the hall and down the servants' stairs. Depositing her things at the back door, she took one last look around.

In the week she had spent at Pride's Passion, she had come to love the house. The realization that she would be able to picture Patrick here in the lonely years ahead, offered scant comfort.

Biting her lower lip to stay her tears, she opened the door to the back porch. A gust of cold air swirled her skirts. *Get it over with,* she told herself. *Get out of here.* She knelt to pick up her luggage.

The sound of footsteps thudding down the back stairs startled her. Powerful hands gripped her shoulders and spun her around.

"Where the hell do you think you're going?" Patrick demanded.

Black curls tumbled over his brow. The shadow of a beard covered his lower face. He was wearing a paisley silk robe, and nothing under it. And yet Elke wasn't as shocked by his deshabille as she was by the urgency in his voice.

"I thought it best that I leave this morning," she replied firmly.

She hadn't asked for this confrontation but she'd be damned if she would back down. Nothing Patrick could say or do would keep her here.

His grip on her shoulders tightened. "Right now I don't give a damn what you think best. Charlotte needs you. She's burning with fever."

Elke's heart lurched. She had attributed the unnatural brightness in Charlotte's eyes and the high color on her cheeks yesterday to the excitement of the party. She should have realized that Charlotte had attended far too many gala events to be thrilled over a rude country gathering.

"What's wrong with her?"

"Damn it, Elke, I'm not a doctor. I don't know. I'll never forgive myself if anything happens to her. She's such a child. I should never have . . ."

His voice trailed off. Without another word, he whirled around and headed back upstairs, taking the steps two at a time.

Was this just a ruse to keep her here? Elke had to know. Holding her skirts high so as not to trip, she sped up the stairs in Patrick's wake.

He flung open the door to the master bedroom and hurried to the bed with Elke at his heels. Charlotte lay against the pillows, her hair matted with sweat, her amber eyes burning so bright that they seemed to be lit from within.

Seeing Elke, she cried out, "Mama, I knew you'd come. I'm so sick. Please, don't let me die."

Chapter Eighteen

"Of course I won't let you die," Elke told Charlotte in a steady voice that belied Elke's burgeoning concern.

"I feel so sick, Mama," Charlotte moaned piteously. In her delirium, she continued to mistake Elke for Hortense Devereux. "My head hurts and my bones ache."

Pity welled in Elke's heart. It would take more than a mother's love to make Charlotte well. She would need the help of the angels. "Don't talk, sweetheart. You have to save your strength."

Elke put her hand on Charlotte's brow. The girl was burning up. Lowering her head to Charlotte's chest, Elke listened for congestion in Charlotte's lungs.

"What is it? What's wrong with her?" Patrick demanded.

Elke straightened and beckoned him to the far side of the room. "My first thought was that she had pneumonia. But her chest sounds clear."

All Patrick's hopes and fears seemed to be written on his face as his gaze locked on Elke. "That's a good sign, isn't it?"

"Yes, but your wife is still very sick. I'm afraid she has influenza, and that's almost as serious as pneumonia."

The news hit Patrick hard. He swayed, then squared his stance. "People die from influenza, don't they?"

"Yes, especially the very young or the very old. Fortunately you wife is in her prime."

"Will you help her?"

Elke had already surrendered too much of her heart to Patrick. If she stayed, she ran the risk of surrendering her body and soul as well. And yet she couldn't resist the naked appeal on his face. She couldn't abandon Charlotte either, she realized, with a rush of empathy for the helpless woman.

Charlotte would surely die without proper care—the kind of nursing neither Patrick nor Conchita could supply. "My mother did teach me a little about tending the sick. I'll do what I can. But I'm not a miracle worker."

"How can I help?"

"I'm going to try and break her fever. I'll need a large basin of cold water and a dozen rags. Conchita and Maria won't be here for another hour, so you'll have to get them for me. But first, send one of the hands for the nearest doctor—and tell him not to spare the horse."

Patrick raced from the room, leaving Elke alone with her patient. She knew she faced a long and desperate fight for Charlotte's life. And she had very few weapons in her arsenal. Fever presented the gravest danger. It could bring on convulsions, and ultimately, death.

While she waited for Patrick, she straightened the tumbled covers and smoothed Charlotte's hair back from her face. Then she pulled a chair up to the bed and settled into it.

How young Charlotte looked, how vulnerable. Although Elke herself was only nine years older, she had experienced so much of life, had shouldered so much responsibility and suffered such devastating loss that she truly felt old enough to be Charlotte's mother.

Charlotte had drifted into a restless sleep and was mumbling unintelligibly. Leaning closer, Elke could feel the heat pouring from her body. Could so delicate a creature survive such a fever?

A few minutes later, Patrick burst into the room so precipitously that water sloshed from the large basin in his hands. At a gesture from Elke, he set it down on a table by the bed and piled clean white rags beside it.

Elke set to work at once, soaking the rags and laying one on Charlotte's forehead. She kept at it for the next hour, removing each rag as soon as it lost its chill and replacing it with another. At last, Charlotte felt cooler and her slumber deepened.

Exhausted by her own lack of sleep, Elke slumped into the chair. She had been so intent on her labors that she had forgotten all about Patrick. The sound of his voice startled her.

"Is she better?"

"For now."

"Then the worst is over?"

Elke shook her head. "It hasn't even begun. Her fever hasn't broken. It's just down a little. When she wakes up, I've got to try and get her to swallow a little broth. She's going to need every last ounce of strength."

"Can I get the broth?" Patrick offered.

"Not unless you know how to make it." Elke got to her feet wearily, remembering her futile fight to save her parents. She would never forgive herself if she let Charlotte's life slip away, too.

Squaring her shoulders, she prepared for the fight of her life. First, she had to make a good strong beef broth to keep up Charlotte's strength. She'd be lucky to finish before Charlotte's fever spiked again.

"I feel so damn helpless," Patrick said, gazing down at his wife.

"Why don't you sit with her a while? If she gets restless or wakes up, call me."

Conchita and Maria were in the kitchen when Elke walked in. They had built a fire in the stove and put a pot of coffee on to brew.

"We saw your bags by the door when we got here," Maria burst out, her round face contorted with worry. "And then Señor Pride came down and told us about the Señora. He said she has *la gripa.*"

"Are you leaving because you fear to catch it, too?" Conchita asked anxiously, making the sign of the cross.

"No, I'm staying here to nurse her," Elke replied. "But you're right. *La gripa* is contagious. I don't want you or your daughter to go near Mrs. Pride until she's better." *If she ever is,* Elke silently added. "I'll take care of her. You and Maria will have to take care of everything else."

"Just tell us what to do," Conchita replied solemnly. "You have made this *casa* a home—not Señora Pride. Maria and I, we would do anything for you."

Elke sank into one of the chairs at the kitchen table and gave Conchita a grateful smile. She wouldn't have blamed Conchita if she had taken her daughter by the hand and run as fast and far from the dread disease as she could. "For starters, I could use a cup of coffee."

While Conchita went to the stove and filled a mug, Elke outlined the household tasks to be done that day. When she finished, Maria hurried outside to kill and pluck a chicken for supper. Following Elke's directions, Conchita took a joint of beef that had been left over from the buffet, put it in a kettle with some spices, covered it with water and set it to simmer on the stove.

"Don't worry about a thing, señora," Conchita said. "Maria and I will do whatever you wish."

"Muchas gracias. There is one thing I forgot to ask, though. You might pray, too."

Elke headed back upstairs a few minutes later with a steaming mug of black coffee for Patrick. "Is there any change?" she asked, joining him by the side of the bed.

He shook his head.

She held the mug out to him. "You look like you need this."

He swallowed long and deep, seemingly oblivious to the coffee's scalding heat.

"I know you have a ranch to run," Elke said. "You don't need to stay."

"If I won't be in the way, I'd like to stick around until Charlotte's better."

Knowing he wouldn't want her to shield him from the truth, she replied, "It could take days."

Patrick's shoulders slumped, the corners of his mouth turned down, and his gray eyes clouded over like a stormy sky. "I do need to talk to Rio. But I'll be back as soon as I can."

He gave his wife one last despairing look, then turned on his heels and left Elke to her vigil. Seeing the depth of his concern for his wife forced her to face the futility of her own emotions.

Patrick belonged to Charlotte. He loved her and cared for her with a devotion that couldn't fail to move Elke. She would do everything to save Charlotte for him— and then she would go.

Charlotte dozed fitfully until noon. She called for her mother from time to time, and for other people Elke didn't know. Strangely, though, she never once called out for Patrick. When she woke, she recognized Elke.

"I feel awful, Elke," she moaned. "Don't just sit there. Do something."

"I'll do everything I can. But you have to do your part, too."

"Are you out of your mind? I can hardly lift my head."

"I want you to listen to me and do as I say."

Charlotte gave Elke a sour look in response. "I need a nurse, not a nanny."

Charlotte seemed unaware of the seriousness of her condition. She adamantly refused Elke's offer of a chamber pot and insisted on getting up and using the water closet. She was fretful, peevish, and complained of being too hot and then too cold. She wanted Elke to do her hair, change her linens, and help her into a fresh nightgown.

It took all Elke's patience and tact to cajole her into drinking the liquids that she had to take in if she was to have any chance at recovering. But Elke rejoiced at every sign of bad temper and did her best to comply with all of Charlotte's demands. She much preferred an irritable patient to one who had fallen too ill to complain.

Patrick returned late in the afternoon. He took one look at Elke, told her she looked worse than Charlotte, and ordered her to bed, saying he would sit with his wife.

When Elke returned to the bedroom, she saw her comb. brush, and mirror on top of the dresser. Opening the drawers, she found her things had been unpacked and returned to their proper place. Bless Conchita, she thought, slipping out of her gray serge traveling suit and putting it away in the chiffonier.

Clad in her petticoat and camisole, she crawled under the covers and fell instantly asleep. She dreamed of marrying Patrick. They were in the Vereins Kirche, standing in front of a preacher and saying the solemn vows that would bind them forever.

A flower-decked coffin loomed behind the altar. Suddenly the coffin lid rose and Charlotte climbed from the satin-draped bier. She was wearing the magnificent emerald gown, only in the nightmare stains and mildew marred its perfection.

She pointed a finger at Elke, and in a sepulchral voice intoned, "You let me die."

Seeing an expression of ineffable horror appear on Patrick's face, Elke cried out, "I tried to save you. Truly I did."

Charlotte's accusatory finger never wavered. "You let me die because you wanted my husband for yourself."

"No," Elke wailed as Charlotte drew closer and grabbed her by the shoulders, "no, no, no."

Elke reached up and tried to free herself from those impossibly powerful hands.

"Wake up, Elke" came Patrick's urgent command.

Elke's eyes flew open and she saw him looming over her. It was his hands that held her so tightly, she realized, blinking away the remnants of the dream.

"Charlotte's fever is up again," he said.

Elke pushed the covers aside as if to rid herself of the nightmare, and bolted to her feet. While Charlotte's death would free Patrick as Otto's had freed her, she could never permit herself to benefit from it.

She would never know if there had been something more she could have done, something crucial that might have turned the tide in Charlotte's favor—or if she had committed an unforgivable sin of omission. She could never give herself to Patrick with questions like those gnawing at her conscience.

A jolt of pure desire roared through Patrick's blood at the sight of Elke's half-nude body—and he hated himself for it. How could he want Elke so much when his wife lay down the hall on what might prove to be her deathbed?

And yet he couldn't stop himself from ravishing Elke with his eyes, drinking in the vision of her sleep-tousled hair, her bare shoulders, and the creamy swell of her breasts rising above her camisole. Thank heaven she was too preoccupied to realize the effect she was having on him.

"Just give me a minute to dress," she said.

His heart flailing in his chest, he fled her presence as if the devil were at his heels. Hastening to Charlotte's side, he cursed himself for being the lowest sort of scoundrel. He had made the worst possible mess of his life, and the two women he cared for were paying the price.

Elke joined him a moment later. She leaned over to feel Charlotte's forehead. Just then, a spasm wracked Charlotte's body. She bucked and jolted like a mustang feeling a saddle for the first time.

"Get me something to keep her from swallowing her tongue," Elke cried out, throwing herself across Charlotte's body to keep her from falling off the bed.

Patrick raced to Charlotte's dressing table, grabbed a mother of pearl hairbrush with a long handle, and thrust it into Elke's hand. She forced it between Charlotte's lips.

When the convulsion passed, Charlotte lay so still and white that for one dread-filled moment Patrick thought she had died. To his shock, Elke began stripping the covers from Charlotte's supine form.

"What in God's name are you doing?" he demanded.

"We need to get her fever down before she convulses again." While she explained, Elke stripped off Charlotte's sweat-damp nightgown. "I'm going to immerse her in a tub of cold water."

At the stroke of midnight, the cowboy that Patrick had sent to fetch the doctor returned to Pride's Passion bringing word of an outbreak of influenza in Fredericksburg. Although the doctor promised to ride out to Pride's Passion at the first opportunity, Elke knew he might not show up for weeks. For all intents and purposes, they were on their own.

The next three days passed in a blur as she pitted her strength and skill against the fever that ravaged Charlotte's body. All too quickly, Charlotte's irritability was replaced by a somnolent stupor. Elke counted every ounce of fluid she got down the sick girl as a tiny victory.

Patrick slept on a pallet outside the bedroom door and spelled Elke when exhaustion demanded that she get a little rest. His devotion to his wife seemed boundless, his love and concern as deep as an ocean. No task seemed too distasteful for him to take on. He helped bathe Charlotte, feed her, and even helped steady her when she used the chamber pot.

By the fourth night, Elke felt certain their efforts were doomed to failure. She sat at Charlotte's side while Charlotte slept, watching the delicate rise and fall of Charlotte's chest and thinking each breath might be the young woman's last. Heartsick, she replaced the damp cloth on Charlotte's forehead.

To her surprise, Charlotte's skin felt cool. The fever's flush had faded. Suddenly, Charlotte's eyes opened.

"I'm thirsty," she rasped.

With shaking hands, Elke poured a drink of water, helped Charlotte sit up, then held the glass to Charlotte's lips.

Charlotte drank long and deep, then fell back against the pillows. "I've been sick, haven't I?"

"Don't worry. You're much better now."

"I dreamed my mama was taking care of me. But it was you, wasn't it?"

Elke's eyes brimmed and tears threatened to spill over. Unable to speak, she nodded.

Charlotte licked her cracked lips. "I must look awful."

How like Charlotte to be worried about her appearance when she had been at death's door. "You never looked better," Elke said sincerely.

Seemingly reassured, Charlotte closed her eyes, and was instantly and deeply asleep.

Elke drew a long, shuddering breath, then, too tired to exult, got to her feet. Leaden weights seemed to encumber her legs as she tiptoed from the room. She made her way into the dark hall, tripped over Patrick, and her legs gave way completely.

"What's wrong?" he asked anxiously, coming instantly awake. "Has something happened to Charlotte?"

This time Elke couldn't stave off her tears. The last remnants of her strength seemed to ooze out with them. "Charlotte's fever broke," she said between hiccuping sobs. "She's going to recover."

Patrick grabbed Elke and gave her a fierce hug. "Oh my God, I'd just about given up."

"Me, too."

"Are you sure she's better?"

"Yes, Patrick. She's better. She talked to me, drank a little water, and went to sleep."

"You did it—you saved her life!"

"I didn't do it. *We* did," she replied.

For a moment, she allowed herself to lean into his body. The stubble of his beard brushed her face. His arm went around her shoulders. The feel of him was a benediction.

"You're dead on your feet," he murmured against her hair. "Let me help you to bed."

"You don't need to," she said, struggling to rise. Her traitorous legs refused to obey. She felt as weak as a newborn calf.

The next thing she knew, Patrick gathered her into his arms with an easy strength that belied the long vigil they had shared. He carried her into her room, and laid her down on top of the covers.

"I don't know how to thank you for what you've done," he said with a catch in his voice.

The moonlight coming through the open curtains highlighted his face. He looked drawn, weary, and transcendentally happy.

"I'm glad I was here to help," Elke said. "I know how much you love your wife."

She heard him sigh. Then a long silence filled the room. "You don't know, do you?" he finally said.

"Know what?"

Was it weariness that finally freed Patrick's tongue—or gratitude—or being alone with Elke in her bedroom. He would never be certain. All he knew was he had to tell her the truth.

"I don't love Charlotte. I never have. I love you. May God forgive me for it because I can't forgive myself."

She lay utterly still, as if his confession had turned her to stone. "You don't mean that. You can't. I saw the way you cared for Charlotte."

"I hated seeing her suffer. But that isn't love. Love is what I feel for you. When you hurt, I hurt. When you're happy, I want to jump for joy." The long pent-up words tumbled out uncontrollably. "Sometimes when you walk into a room, I'm afraid I'll weep for joy at the sight of you. The day you said you were thinking about going back to Germany was the worst day of my life. I can't live without you. You're in my mind, in my blood. I feel your presence inside my soul."

"Please, don't say those things to me. You have no right."

A primal sound of despair rose up his throat. "You think I don't know that? I've spent a thousand lonely nights trying to cut you out of my heart. I loved you the first time I saw you, and I've fought the feeling ever since. I went back to Natchez hoping—no, *praying* that getting married would change things." He groaned again. "Dear God, if I had known about the accident, I would never have married Charlotte."

Patrick's confession rioted through Elke's mind. She yearned to pull him down beside her, to feel the full length of his body against hers, to love him with her hands and mouth the way she had always loved him with her heart.

And yet, despite the powerful desire that threatened to sweep her away, she couldn't commit that ultimate sin. No matter what he said, she couldn't let herself forget that he belonged to another woman.

Armoring herself against the longing in his voice, she reached up and pressed her fingers to his mouth. "You mustn't say anything more. You're overwrought. We've been through hell together. It made us close, but it's over now. I know you're grateful to me, but that's not love. You'll see things differently in the morning."

"You're dead wrong. The morning won't change anything. This has nothing to do with Charlotte's illness and everything to do with us. I love you. I always will."

"Even if it's true, there's no room for both love and

honor between the two of us. I can never be your wife and I won't be your mistress."

He grasped her wrist and pressed her palm against his mouth. His lips felt firm—hot—irresistible.

But somehow, she found the fortitude to resist. "If you say one more word, I'll leave Pride's Passion at the first light. And Charlotte still needs me."

Patrick wanted to say that he needed her, too. However, hearing the resolution in her voice, and recognizing the stubborn jut of her jaw, he knew he dare not push her any further. "If it makes you feel better to think you've heard the babblings of a madman, go right ahead. Just promise me you won't leave, because you are right about one thing. Charlotte does need you."

He got to his feet, unfolded the quilt at the foot of the bed, and draped it over Elke's body, taking care not to touch her. Then reluctantly, he left her to her thoughts.

Chapter Nineteen

Two weeks after Charlotte's fever broke, she sat dozing in a wing chair in the parlor under Elke's ever watchful gaze. She's changed, Elke thought as she studied the sleeping woman.

The influenza had stripped the last remnant of baby fat from Charlotte's features, to better display their sculptured perfection. Her body, now concealed by an afghan, appeared more delicate than ever. The seventeen-inch waist she longed for would be easier to attain in the future.

Charlotte's brush with death had wrought other less visible changes as well. The old Charlotte would have complained endlessly about being housebound during her recovery. The new Charlotte accepted her enforced idleness with good humor, and asked Elke to help pass the time by reading to her.

Although Elke's taste ran to more serious fare, Charlotte preferred love stories. Over the past few days, Elke had read Patrick's leather-bound volumes of *The Scarlet Letter* and *Great Expectations*.

She had been reading from *The Courtship of Miles Standish,* when Charlotte dozed off. The slender volume sat open on Elke's lap. Charlotte had sympathized with Miles Standish and his impossible love for Priscilla, and wept over their plight. Would she be so sympathetic if she knew of Elke's impossible love for Patrick? Or would she rise up in righteous wrath and order Elke from the house?

The clatter of horses' hooves put an end to Elke's introspection. They weren't expecting company. Could the doctor finally be putting in a belated appearance?

She got to her feet, walked to a window and looked out to see Velvet Gilhooley reining a buggy to a stop by the front porch. Elke couldn't help smiling at the frivolous feather-festooned bonnet on Velvet's head.

"Who's there?" Charlotte asked sleepily.

"Just a friend of mine from Fredericksburg," Elke replied, keeping her answer deliberately obtuse. She had no idea how Charlotte would react to having a notorious madam at her front door.

"Do ask her in," Charlotte said eagerly. "I'd love some company."

"You still need your rest. I can visit with her in the kitchen."

"Oh, pooh. I've done nothing but rest these last two weeks."

"I'm not sure Patrick would approve of you entertaining this particular guest."

"Why ever not, since she's your friend? You know he worships the ground you walk on."

Elke was startled by Charlotte's assertion. "He's just grateful because I stayed on to nurse you."

"I'm sure he'd say any friend of yours was more than welcome here," Charlotte insisted.

Elke took a last anxious look out the window to see Velvet heading for the front door. She didn't want to hurt Velvet's feelings, let alone embarrass her—but the circumstances didn't leave Elke any choice.

Turning to face Charlotte and taking a deep breath, she said, "My friend owns a house of ill repute."

Charlotte's pealing laughter took Elke by surprise. "How utterly delicious. Now I really *do* want to meet her. Please ask her to join us."

A firm knock prevented any further discussion. Elke hurried to answer the summons. She opened the door to see Velvet looking resplendent in a russet hacking jacket with a brown velvet collar and a matching skirt. The drive from Fredericksburg had tousled her red curls and brought a high color to her cheeks.

"Well, if you aren't a sight for sore eyes!" Velvet declared.

"So are you!" Elke replied, giving Velvet a heartfelt hug.

"I would have come out a lot sooner to see how you were getting along, but a couple of the girls came down with the influenza. It's all over town."

"I'm just glad you're here now."

"I heard Mrs. Pride was sick, too. How's she getting along?" Velvet leaned closer and added, "I don't suppose the bitch had the good grace to pass on. People like that never do."

With a warning glance toward the parlor, Elke whispered, "She not a bitch—and she is recovering quite nicely, thank you. In fact, she wants to meet you."

"Meet me?" Velvet's eyes widened with shock. "Are you sure she isn't out of her mind from the fever?"

With a finger held against her lips, Elke cautioned Velvet to lower her voice. "I assure you, she's in full possession of all her faculties."

"Does she know who I am and what I do for a living?"

"I told her."

Velvet's brows flew up in an expression of pure amazement. "Well, I'll be damned," she said, "what are we waiting for?"

Gathering her skirts, Velvet marched straight into the parlor like a clipper ship under full sail. Elke held her breath while Velvet and Charlotte took each other's measure as carefully as a couple of men deciding if they wanted to invest in a very expensive horse.

Apparently they both liked what they saw.

"Where in the world did you get that gorgeous outfit?" Charlotte exclaimed, her covetous gaze devouring Velvet's fashionable outfit.

"I have the most wonderful little seamstress in Fredericksburg," Velvet replied. "She can copy anything from Godey's Lady's Book."

"You must introduce me. I used to order all my clothes from Worth's, but it's so far away and so expensive."

"Oh my God, don't tell me you know Charles Worth."

Charlotte dimpled prettily. "I met him when my parents took me to London a couple of years ago."

"Speaking of introductions," Elke smiled as she interjected herself into the conversation, "you two should officially meet each other before you get too wrapped up in talking about fashion. Charlotte Pride, permit me to present my very dear friend, Velvet Gilhooley."

"It's a genuine pleasure to make your acquaintance," Velvet gushed like a would-be socialite at her first important tea. "I've heard so much about you."

"And most of it bad, I suppose. Why else would you call me a *bitch?*"

Velvet blushed a deeper red than her hair. "Good God, you overheard."

Charlotte let go another of her irresistible peals of golden laughter. "I sure did. But I'll tell you what. I won't hold it against you if promise to forget all the bad things Ella Mae has undoubtedly said about me." She held out her hand. "Is it a deal?"

"Done and done," Velvet replied, shaking on the agreement.

Elke let go a sign of relief. She had been expecting open warfare instead of a love fest. "Can I get you two some sherry?"

"Yes," the two women replied in unison.

The next hour passed in merry conversation as Velvet and Charlotte talked about the latest fashions with the same fervor that Elke exhibited discussing politics.

The two of them were polar opposites in terms of the lives they had led. Perhaps that accounted for their getting on so well. Their conversation flowed unchecked until the tolling of the grandfather clock in the entry hall interrupted the spirited colloquy.

"Oh my goodness, it's already three," Velvet said, jumping to her feet, "I completely lost track of time. I really must be getting back to—ah—to my house."

Charlotte grinned, winked at Elke, then said, "How is business these days?"

To her credit, Velvet didn't skip a beat. "I closed when a couple of the girls came down with the influenza," she said in a matter-of-fact tone, as if she discussed her affairs with respectable married women every day of the week. "I didn't want some cowboy complaining about how he got sick at my place. You know how men talk. The next thing you know, it wouldn't be the influenza that he caught but something much worse. I had planned to reopen The Velvet Touch tonight."

"The Velvet Touch? What a fabulous name for your establishment," Charlotte declared. "One of these days, you'll have to tell me all about it. When it comes to pleasing a man, I could use a few tips."

Elke felt herself pale at Charlotte's remark.

"I'm the one to ask," Velvet replied, her easy assertion soothing over what could have been an intensely awkward moment.

"I'll walk you to your buggy," Elke said, getting to her feet.

"So everything isn't perfect in the Prides' marriage," Velvet commented as soon as they were outside.

Elke avoided Velvet's probing gaze. "I don't know what you mean."

"You heard what Charlotte said. And you surely know what it implied?"

"I know you mean well, Velvet, but I can't talk about the Prides' private life. It's just too painful."

"Me and my big mouth." Velvet grasped Elke's hands in her own. "If you ever do need to talk—about anything—just remember that I'm available." Then Velvet's gaze swept the circular drive. "Is Rio around?"

Elke's tension evaporated. "I should have known you didn't drive all the way out here just to see me. How are you and Rio getting along?"

A smile lit Velvet's face. "Better than I have any right to expect. If I don't watch my step, I could fall head over heels in love with that man."

"Then I'm especially sorry that he's not here."

Velvet let go a sigh pregnant with disappointment. "Don't tell me he's out singing to a bunch of cows."

"Not today. He's with Patrick and a couple of the hands. They're hunting a mountain lion that's been preying on the calves. I don't expect them back until dark."

Rio de Vargas had been tracking the mountain lion since first light, using the skills he'd learned from his Comanche grandfather. At least it kept his mind off of Velvet Gilhooley, he thought, studying the ground for sign.

Lately, he'd been having all sorts of ideas a man his age had no right having—like how nice it would be to have a place of his own, and a woman of his own to take care of it. He had to be plumb crazy, imagining Velvet would want to be that woman. She already had more money than he'd make if he lived to be a hundred, and a flourishing business that required her personal attention. What would she want with a beat-up old cowhand?

His mind was so caught up in the dilemma that it

took him a moment to notice the hoofprints that had suddenly cut across the cougar's trail.

He gestured at the ground, then said, "Someone else is hunting our cat."

"We've been following the cat too long to have him spooked by some damn fool," Patrick replied grimly.

Rio kept his gaze on the ground, reading what had happened as easily as Patrick read all those books. The cat had been a hour ahead of the rider when the two trails overlapped. Over the next few miles, the distance between them narrowed.

"The rider is catching up," he said.

"Damn," came Patrick's succinct reply. I hoped we'd get to the cougar first."

Fifteen minutes later, Rio came to a place where the rider had reined his horse to a stop, dismounted, then squared his stance and held it. "It looks like he took a shot," Rio said.

"And from the look of those vultures," Patrick replied, pointing at the circling birds in the distance, "he hit something. I just hope to God it was the cougar and not one of my cows."

Rio kicked his horse to greater speed and Patrick followed suit, leaving the two hands who accompanied them to ride in their dust.

Rio spotted the carcass first. "Well, I'll be. The damn fool must have shot his horse by mistake."

"What the hell happened to the man who was riding it?" Patrick shouted back.

As if in response, they heard a male voice calling out. "Halloo. Is anyone there? I could use some help."

"Where are you?"

"Here." The voice seemed to be coming from behind the dead horse.

"We'll be right there. Hold your horses," Rio called out, then chuckled at his own gallows humor.

When he reined to a skidding stop near the dead animal and saw a man on the ground—or to be more specific, part of a man—he realized he'd been wrong to make light of the situation. The poor bastard wasn't holding the horse. The horse was holding him.

Rio vaulted from the saddle and hurried to the stranger's side. The man's complexion had a decidedly greenish cast. Pain clouded his eyes. But he spoke right up.

"I say, old chap, I'm frightfully glad you happened along just now. As you can see, I'm in a bit of a bother. Would you mind rendering some assistance?"

The man certainly had a talent for understatement, Rio thought, turning to exchange a troubled glance with Patrick.

"Poor devil," Patrick muttered under his breath, then added in a louder tone, "We'd better get on with it."

"Before you proceed, I should tell you that I think my right leg is broken."

"It's a wonder the rest of you isn't broken, too," Rio replied grimly, eyeing the man and horse carefully while trying to decide how best to proceed. They'd have to tie the carcass to their horses and pull like hell, he decided.

It took Rio, Patrick, and the hands several struggling, sweaty, curse-filled minutes to extricate the stranger from his "bit of bother." To the stranger's credit, he didn't scream with pain even once. He swore right along with them in his la-di-da accent. However, his lips were bone white by the time he was finally free.

Rio knelt down beside him and ran his hands down the stranger's right leg, not liking what he felt under the elegant riding breeches. "You were right. Your leg is all stove up," he said, taking his Bowie knife from the scabbard at his belt.

The stranger turned even whiter. "Good God, I hope you aren't planning to cut my leg off with that."

"I'm going to cut off your pant and boot so I can get a look-see at the damage."

"Bloody hell." The man managed a wry grimace. "That's almost as serious. The boots were custom made by Spencer's in London and I don't have another pair with me."

"I wouldn't get in a sweat over it. You aren't going to need boots for a long time." Rio slit the doeskin trousers with the same expertise he used when skinning a deer.

The stranger's eyes rolled back in his head when Rio began working on the boot. "What a bloody balls up," he moaned as the boot finally came free.

Patrick grimaced at the horror Rio had exposed. Bone protruded from the stranger's right thigh, and blood oozed from the wound. The man raised himself up on his elbows to take a look, too, then fell back to the ground. His pain-glazed eyes sought Patrick's.

"Are you the head man?" he asked.

"That's one way to put it. I own the land as far as you can see and then some. My name is Patrick Pride."

"And mine is Nigel Hawthorne," the stranger said, extending an understandably shaky hand. "I'm the Earl of Glenhaven. My identification is in my saddle bags. If I don't make it, I'd appreciate it if you'd notify my family."

So the man was an English lord, Patrick thought. That explained the accent. "You'll make it, all right," he replied with far more confidence than he felt. "My foreman, Rio de Vargas, has set more broken bones than most doctors."

Once again, the stranger held out his hand, this time to Rio. "I'm pleased to make your acquaintance, Mr. de Vargas."

"We don't stand on no ceremony in these parts. Just call me Rio and I'll call you Earl."

Patrick almost guffawed at Rio's mistaken use of Hawthorne's title. However, there was nothing funny about Hawthorne's injury.

Rio got to his feet, walked over to his horse, and returned with yet another canteen. "I reckon you could use some of this." He handed the canteen to the Englishman.

"What's in it?" Nigel Hawthorne asked.

"Some of Velvet Gilhooley's best French brandy. It's good for damn near anything that ails you. Just be sure to leave a few inches at the bottom for your leg."

While Hawthorne took a deep swallow, Patrick turned to the two wide-eyed young hands. "We'll need saplings for a stretcher and splints. I saw some trees not too far back that will do."

"Sure thing, Mr. Pride," one of them replied. They mounted up in unison, seemingly relieved to be away from the sight of the injured man.

If they lived long enough, they would see worse, Patrick thought grimly. He didn't think too much of Hawthorne's chances for recovery. The danger of infection, the shock of having the bones set, the trip back to the ranch, might combine to snuff out the Englishman's life.

Patrick would have played the good Samaritan under any circumstances. No man could, in good conscience, leave another to die. However, Hawthorne's survival would serve another purpose. Elke would never leave Pride's Passion while an injured human being needed her help.

"I am in your debt, sir," Hawthorne said, reclaiming Patrick's full attention. "I was on the trail of a wounded cougar a couple of hours earlier, riding flat out like a damn fool when my horse stepped in a hole and broke its leg. I put him out of his misery and was beginning to consider doing the same for myself when you and your men came along."

"Are you by yourself?"

"I had a guide. But he got sick a couple of weeks ago and I sent him to the nearest town." Hawthorne gestured over his shoulder. "However, I also employ a cook and a general factotum. My camp's a couple of miles in that direction. By the by, I got the cougar, although I'm embarrassed to say it wasn't a clean kill. I aimed for the heart and hit a lung instead. He can't have gotten far."

"Then I'm the one who owes the debt. My men and I have been after that cougar all day." Patrick couldn't help marveling at Hawthorne's aplomb. He had to be hurting like hell and yet he still managed to carry on a polite conversation as if they were at high tea.

A distant plume of dust alerted them to the imminent

arrival of the cowboys. "Looks like the boys are back," Patrick said.

Rio got up from his place at Hawthorne's side, walked over to his horse, and took a braided reata from the saddle.

"I assure you, there's no need to tie me," Hawthorne objected with considerable force. "I shall bear up under your ministrations without being bound hand and foot."

Rio knelt down and handed the reata to the Englishman. "I just thought you'd appreciate having something to bite on besides your tongue."

Patrick grinned despite the serious of the situation. He knew Rio had never met a man like the Earl of Glenhaven—and he doubted that Glenhaven had ever met Rio's match.

As the two cowboys reined to a stop and offloaded the saplings, Rio took another long look at Hawthorne's leg.

"Are you sure you know what you're doing?" Hawthorne asked.

"If I were smart, I'd just cut the damned thing off and have done with it."

"For the love of God, man, I'd rather be dead."

"I figured you'd feel that way. Besides, I fancy a challenge. Like my boss said, I'm a pretty fair hand at setting bones—and we got the purtiest nurse back to the ranch you ever did see. Between the two of us, I think we can fix you up."

"Just do your best," Hawthorne replied with admirable composure.

Rio beckoned the young cowboys closer. "When I give the word, you take a hold of his shoulders and hang on. Patrick, you latch on to his other leg. This is going to take a little bit of tugging."

Nigel listened to Rio's every word, taking a measure of comfort from the foreman's apparent know-how.

When Rio nodded at the other men and said, "Now," Nigel bit down on the reata. Surely no Englishman had ever suffered worse torture on the rack, Nigel agonized as Rio pulled on his injured leg while the other three men held his body in an iron grip.

It took every ounce of courage Nigel possessed not to scream as he felt the his leg bones grating against one another. But he hadn't screamed when he'd been mauled by a wounded tiger, or when an army surgeon had sewed those wounds up, and he'd be damned if he'd scream now.

Sweat poured off his body and bile rose up his throat when, with a final sucking sound, the shattered bones realigned. A white-hot blaze of pure agony coursed up his leg and lodged in his chest as Rio carefully cleansed the wound with the rest of the brandy.

"That's a damn waste of fine liquor," Nigel gasped before he felt himself being sucked into a dark whirlpool.

Pain brought him to some time later. He was strapped to some sort of stretcher. One end of it rose up in the air and he assumed it was hitched to a horse. The other end dragged on the ground, jolting over every hummock. The jolting had wakened him.

Looking up, he saw the foreman walking by his side. "We're almost there, old horse," de Vargas said.

"Almost where?"

"The ranch house."

"I can't impose on strangers. Take me back to my camp."

"I never did a better job of setting a leg, and I ain't about to take a chance on your dying and spoiling my reputation. Mr. Patrick sent one of the boys over to your camp to tell your men what happened, and to tell them where to find the cougar. He figured you'd want the skin as a souvenir of your last hunt. From here on, Earl, you're going to have one hell of a hitch in your git along."

Through a fog of pain, Nigel struggled to decipher what Rio had said. Two words echoed through Nigel's mind almost as cruelly as the pain reverberated through his body.

Last hunt. Last hunt.

Like many other Englishman of wealth and status, he'd devoted his life to the sport. He'd stalked stags in the highlands of Ireland, bagged bison in Poland, and shot tigers in India. He'd come to Texas in search of trophy deer, cougar, and buffalo.

He'd known he'd have to give up his avocation eventually—to settle down and beget an heir. But he hadn't expected it to happen so soon. Dear God, he was only twenty-seven. His father hadn't married until his thirty-fifth year.

"In case you're wondering," Rio's drawling voice intruded on his unhappy thoughts, "that thing you're strapped on is called a travois. The Comanches use them to move their household goods. It ain't exactly a coach and four, but it gets the job done."

Just then, the travois went over a particularly rough piece of ground. Pain spread from Nigel's broken leg and enveloped him in its cruel embrace. The black vortex rose up before him and this time he gratefully surrendered to it.

Chapter Twenty

It's been a long day," Elke said to Charlotte as Maria cleared their dinner plates. "Don't you think you ought to go to bed?"

Charlotte pushed her chair back from the table and got to her feet. "Can't I stay up a little longer? At least until Patrick gets back."

Elke glanced out the dining-room window. She had the prickling sensation that something was amiss. "I thought he'd be back in time for supper."

"Don't look so worried. Patrick is the most capable man. He won't have any trouble handling a little old cat."

Elke just shook her head. Charlotte had never seen a cougar, and had no idea what a formidable animal Patrick had set off after.

"Let's take our coffee in the parlor and wait for him," Charlotte said.

"I suppose it won't hurt." Charlotte did look better, Elke thought. Her eyes had regained their sparkle and her cheeks glowed.

"Would you like me to read a little more from *The Courtship of Miles Standish?*" Elke picked up their cups and followed Charlotte.

"Why don't we just visit for a while?" Charlotte settled herself in the wing chair and covered her legs with the afghan. "You know so much about me and I hardly know anything about you."

"I'm not a very interesting person," Elke replied, handing a cup to Charlotte.

"You underestimate yourself. For instance, why don't you tell me how you came to be friends with Velvet Gilhooley?"

"It's a long story." Avoiding Charlotte's curious gaze, Elke walked over to the hearth and added a few logs to the fire.

"And a fascinating one, I'm sure."

"Not really. She used to come in to the bakery."

"I can't believe that's all there is to it," Charlotte persisted. "The two of you seem so close."

Charlotte had the tenacity of a pit bull when she wanted something. It was both her most problematic and most admirable trait.

Reluctantly, Elke said, "If you must know, Velvet saved my life."

"I knew there had to be more to your friendship. How did it happen? I want to hear every last detail."

Elke returned to the chair she had occupied earlier that day and gazed into the fire while memory took her back in time. Speaking haltingly, she told Charlotte how Patrick's letter had unwittingly set a tragedy in motion—how she and Otto were stalked by the Detweiler twins on their way home from Pride's Passion, how she had regained consciousness in Velvet's bed to learn she had lost both her husband and her baby, and finally how Rio had buried Otto and their child right there on the ranch.

When she finished, she was surprised to see tears welling in Charlotte's eyes.

"If Patrick and I hadn't gotten married," Charlotte said with a catch in her voice, "you and Otto would never have come out to check on the ranch. I had no idea. Patrick told me you were a widow. But he never said when your husband died—or how. Now I know why you always seem so sad. It must have been terrible for you."

"It was," Elke said softly.

"You still miss your husband, don't you?"

Elke nodded. She missed being married, having someone to talk to, knowing what her life would hold from one day to the next. She ached for the home and the future she had lost. But more than anything else, she missed the baby she had never held in her arms. The knowledge that there would never be another to take its place ached through her.

"Your husband sounds like a wonderful man. As soon as I'm well enough, I'd like you to show me where he's buried. We can say a prayer for him together." Charlotte let go a long sigh. "I can't help wondering if Patrick would have grieved for me the way you grieve for Otto if I hadn't recovered."

"What a terrible thing to say. Patrick barely left your side before your fever broke."

"I'm not suggesting that Patrick isn't a fine man, and a dutiful spouse." Charlotte paused. Her fingers plucked the afghan, betraying her agitation. "But I don't think he really loves me—at least not the way you loved Otto. Has he ever told you how he happened to propose?"

The question took Elke by surprise. "Of course not. It's really none of my business." And it was the last story Elke wanted to hear from Charlotte's lips.

"Considering the part I played in what happened to your family, I think it is."

"But you didn't have anything to do with it. You weren't even here. Really Charlotte, I think you ought to go to bed."

Charlotte's fingers continued their nervous plucking. "Please, Elke, I need to tell someone. You see, I trapped Patrick—with my mother's help. His mother's, too, for that matter. All three of us wanted Patrick to marry me. We never thought about what *he* wanted. And now I can't help thinking we made a terrible mistake."

"Don't be ridiculous. You're going to make Patrick a wonderful wife as soon as you're back on your feet. You made a wonderful impression on his friends at the party."

"I did, didn't I? If ranch life consisted of one party after another the way our courtship did, Patrick and I might be happy yet. But living here isn't anything like I imagined it would be."

Before Elke could voice another objection, Charlotte launched into the story of how she had set her cap for the most exciting man she had ever met. Like Otto, Charlotte was a born storyteller. She painted such vivid images that Elke easily pictured her at that first dinner, wearing the magnificent emerald dress and flirting for all she was worth.

The boldness of Charlotte's scheme, the outrageous impudence with which she had carried it out, left Elke openmouthed—and filled with impotent anger. She fought down the desire to jump to her feet, rush over to Charlotte, grab her by the shoulders and shake her until her teeth rattled.

Charlotte had ruined three lives with her selfishness—Patrick's, Elke's, and, unwittingly, her own.

"Did you love Patrick?" Elke pushed the words past her choking anger.

"I was certainly smitten. I'd never met a more imposing man. And I got completely caught up in the thrill of the chase. I guess you could say I wanted him the way my father wants a prize horse or a valuable slave. But love? I don't think so. You see, it was all a game to me."

At least Charlotte had the good sense to look shamefaced. Not that it blunted Elke's consternation. She had been searching for someone to blame for her predicament, someone to bear the brunt of her anger, her desperation, her sense of having forfeited something more precious than life itself.

She loved Patrick too much to hold him accountable. And she refused to wallow in the martyrdom that would have been the natural consequence of blaming herself. Charlotte was the ideal candidate.

"So you see," Charlotte concluded, "Patrick never had a chance. I knew he'd do the right thing once my father found us in the maze. But that doesn't mean Patrick loves me. Sometimes I think the ranch is the only thing he's ever really cared about. No wonder everyone calls it Pride's Passion."

If you only knew, Elke thought as guilt replaced her anger. How could she sit and listen to Charlotte's confidences when by doing so, she betrayed Charlotte's trust? How dare she, of all people, judge Charlotte?

"I wouldn't blame you if you hated me, considering everything that has happened," Charlotte said.

Elke closed her eyes a moment, and took a deep, calming breath. She opened them again to see Charlotte staring at her anxiously.

"I don't hate you. I've done far worse things myself,"

"I'm so glad you feel that way. Your friendship means a great deal to me."

The thunder of hoofs put a merciful end to Charlotte's revelations. Grateful for the distraction, Elke got to her feet and gazed out the window to see who was there.

The moonlight revealed young Terrell Meeks hastening to the door. He opened it with a resounding thump and came barreling into the room, his spurs jingling, his hat still on his head.

"Well, I never!" Charlotte burst out. "Where are your manners, young man?"

Meeks ignored Charlotte, addressing himself to Elke instead. "There's been an accident, Mrs. Sonnschein!"

Elke's stomach spasmed. "What happened? Is Mr. Pride all right?"

"He weren't the one who got hurt. It's some Englishman named Earl. He's broke his leg something awful. Mr. Pride sent me on ahead to tell you to get a bed ready and have the laudanum handy."

* * *

Nigel returned to consciousness to find the most beautiful woman he'd ever seen staring at him with a pair of wide-set topaz-colored eyes. She was wearing an ethereal white gown trimmed in lace. Her dark hair framed a face whose otherworldly perfection could only belong to an angel.

"Is this heaven?" He forced the words past his parched lips.

The concern on her face dissolved into a smile. "I'll take that as a compliment. But it's not heaven, Lord Hawthorne. You're in a guest bedroom in the Pride mansion. My husband brought you here a couple of hours ago."

Nigel was in far too much agony to comprehend everything she said. He struggled to sit up, the better to survey his situation, and couldn't prevent a moan from escaping his lips as pain knifed through his broken leg.

"Oh, dear, you mustn't move," the angel said. "I had better get Elke."

Completely disoriented by pain and shock, Nigel couldn't help wondering why the angel thought an elk would want to help him.

He'd shot a prize specimen just last month. The magnificent rack of antlers had already been shipped to England along with the skins of buffalo and bear. Perhaps this wasn't heaven after all but a special sort of hell reserved for men who had killed so many of God's creatures—not out of hunger but for sport.

He closed his eyes, preparing to meet his fate as stoically as he could. The low murmur of female voices intruded on the effort.

"You should be in bed," the first voice admonished.

As far as Nigel could tell, he himself was in some sort of bed.

"Don't scold me, Elke. I got ready for bed, but curiosity got the best of me. I've never met an earl," the angel replied.

"This particular earl isn't going anywhere," the first voice declared with considerable authority. "You'll have lots of time to get to know him when you've got your strength back."

Consumed with curiosity, Nigel opened his eyes to see the angel with the topaz eyes talking to a comely blond woman. If the rest of the inhabitants of this place looked like these two, he wouldn't mind staying—whether it turned out to be heaven or hell.

Patrick and Rio de Vargas sat in the library, relaxing for the first time since they had set off after the cougar fourteen hours earlier.

"I didn't think the earl would survive the trip back to the ranch," Patrick said.

"Me either." Concern deepened the grooves around Rio's mouth. "Getting him up the stairs and in bed weren't no Sunday in the park either. It's a good thing Elke gave him that laudanum first. Earl's a brave man but he'd had all the pain a man can handle by then."

"Do you think he'll walk again?"

"One thing at a time, boss. I just hope the poor son of a bitch wakes up in the morning."

"How about a drink?" Patrick asked.

"I could use one." Rio removed his sweat-stained hat

and put it down on the nearest table. "It's been a hell of a day, hasn't it?"

"I'm sure the earl would agree." Patrick smiled at Rio, thinking Hawthorne would set Rio straight about his real name—if he survived.

"Did the boys find the cougar?" Patrick asked, filling two glasses to the brim.

"Sure did. Shot through the lungs, too, just like Earl said." Rio took the glass Patrick held out. "I reckon he never figured on being done in by a freak accident. He's lucky we found him when he did."

"Indeed he is," Elke said, walking into the room.

Patrick's heart did a hop, skip, and jump, the way it always did at the sight of her. She looked as breathtakingly lovely in calico as Charlotte did in silk.

"How are your patients?" he asked.

"Resting, I hope. I went to get another pillow to prop the earl's leg and Charlotte was in his room when I returned. She's been on her feet since Velvet's Gilhooley's visit. I just hope all the excitement doesn't set her recovery back."

That was the first Patrick had heard about Velvet coming out to the ranch. Before he could ask about it, though, Rio said, "Velvet was here?"

It wasn't like Rio to jump into the middle of a conversation, Patrick thought. There was something different about Elke, too, something he couldn't quite place. She didn't look or sound like the harried woman who had been living under his roof the last few weeks, either.

"Velvet was certainly sorry she missed you," Elke told Rio.

What the hell was going on? They should have been talking about the Englishman instead of Velvet Gilhooley's comings and goings. Could Velvet's visit be the cause of the change he saw in Elke?

"I sure wish I'd been here to see Velvet." Rio sounded as woebegone as a dogie bawling for its mother.

A grin, so full of mischief that it took Patrick's breath away, appeared on Elke's face like the sun breaking out after a storm. "She felt the same way."

"If you two can forget Velvet for a minute, how was Lord Hawthorne when you left him?" Patrick asked, motioning Elke to join him on the sofa.

To his pleasure, she did. "I gave him a little more laudanum, enough to knock him out for a while. When I left, he was mumbling something about meeting an angel."

"Does he have a fever?"

"Not yet. He's going to need a lot of care, though, and I don't think he'll like having his personal needs attended to by a woman. I thought you might ask one of the hands—"

Before Elke could finish, Rio marched over and looked down at her. "There isn't one of those men who knows a durn thing about caring for the sick, Mrs. Sonnschein."

Patrick had been about to point that out himself. But he felt certain Elke would take it better from Rio.

"I know you've been through a lot the last few months," Rio continued with unaccustomed loquacity, "and Velvet told me you were thinking about going back to Germany one of these days. But Earl needs your help the same way you needed Miss Velvet's when you got hurt."

Patrick couldn't have said it better himself. He'd known Rio for fifteen years and had never heard him string so many words together before. Fortunately from Patrick's point of view, they were just the right words.

Elke lifted her shoulders in an eloquent shrug. "I suppose you're right. You don't need to worry, Rio. I'll do my best for your Englishman."

To Patrick's amazement, Rio actually came over and patted Elke's shoulder in a gesture of affection. "I knew we could count on you, Mrs. Sonnschein. You're one in a million. If it's all the same to you, I'd like to check on Earl in the morning."

"I'd appreciate it. I can use all the help I can get."

Rio seemed to realize he'd been monopolizing the conversation. His ruddy complexion turned scarlet. He looked around for his hat, found it, and jammed it on his head.

"I'll be on my way," he muttered, then shot from the room like a scalded cat

Elke turned to Patrick. "If I didn't know better, I'd swear you arranged that entire scene."

"Why would you think that?"

"Because you knew I was going to leave soon."

Patrick got to his feet, and hurried to the bar so that Elke couldn't see his grin. He refilled his glass, and poured a sherry for her.

"Much as I want you to stay on, I'm not responsible for Nigel Hawthorne's accident—or for the fact that Rio wants the man to have the best possible care. Rio seems to have taken quite a liking to Hawthorne."

He crossed the floor and handed the sherry to Elke. She met his eyes for the first time since that night after Charlotte's fever broke.

The contact—as potent as a caress—raced through him like liquid fire. Elke had such beautiful eyes. For a moment, he happily surrendered to their fathomless blue depths. She looked no less lovely for having spent so much time indoors. Her winter-pale complexion accented the freckles on her cheekbones. He longed to kiss each one.

How he loved seeing her here in his home. The sound of her footsteps as she moved about her daily tasks was as soothing to him as sweetest music. He had built the house and peopled it with his dreams. Elke was the only person who had the power to make those dreams come true, he thought, rejoining her on the sofa

"I'm delighted that you've agreed to take on Hawthorne's care. He couldn't be in better hands."

"Rio didn't give me much choice. But you're right. I had planned to leave in a few more weeks. Considering what happened today, I was even more anxious to go."

"Surely you're not talking about poor Hawthorne."

She let go a sigh and shook her head.

"What are you talking about? Did Charlotte make a scene about Velvet's visit?"

"Charlotte couldn't have been nicer. The two of us had a long talk after supper."

Patrick took a firmer grip on his glass, preparing for the worst. "About what?"

"She talked about your courtship, and about what happened the night you asked for her hand in marriage."

A cold sweat chilled Patrick's skin. Had Charlotte told Elke a pack of lies? "Exactly what did she say?"

Elke finally lowered her gaze. "I'm sorry, but I can't betray her confidence."

With sudden insight, Patrick realized that his unpredictable wife must have told the truth. "I'm not asking you to. I can read what Charlotte said on your face. I just never thought Charlotte would admit to her little conspiracy."

"Then you know she and her mother planned the whole thing?"

"It wasn't hard to figure out. I imagine my mother played a part, too."

"How could you let them manipulate you like that?"

Patrick took a deep breath. He'd waited months for a chance to tell Elke the truth. Now, he chose his words carefully. "For lots of reasons. All of them seemed valid at the time. As a gentleman, I didn't have much choice. And I was flattered that Charlotte went to such lengths. She's a very beautiful woman and she can be amusing when she wants. I was foolish enough to think that was enough. You see, I thought you were happily married. I wanted the same sort of happiness for myself. I wanted a family."

He reached for Elke's hand, and to his intense relief, she allowed him to hold it. "I made a terrible mistake, one I've regretted ever since. I'm fond of Charlotte but I never loved her. If you never believe anything else, you must believe me now. I love you, Elke. I'll go to my grave loving you."

Elke sat utterly still while his words spread through her battered heart like balm. She had longed for this moment for years, never imagining how bittersweet the reality would be.

At last, she found herself uttering the words that had been on her lips since the long ago day when she saw him ride into Fredericksburg on the white stallion, looking like all her dreams come true. "I love you, too."

Happiness chased the shadows from Patrick's eyes. He reached for her and she allowed herself to be drawn into the shelter of his arms. Time seemed to slow, then stop altogether while she clung to him, letting his warmth and strength sustain her.

His scent filled her nostrils, his tender touch filled her heart. All her old doubts and fears were swept away by the sure and certain knowledge that he had spoken the truth—that he had always spoken the truth. He loved her just as she loved him.

But there were cruel realities to be faced, and putting it off would only make it more difficult. They had to face them now. The knowledge that they would do so together made it easier to bear.

"What we feel for each other doesn't change a thing," she said, her heart breaking as she saw his joy fade. For a moment, he looked so drawn and haggard that she could plainly see what he would look like in ten or twenty years.

"Don't say that. Don't ever say that. Don't condemn me to a life without you."

She longed to kiss away the wounded expression in his eyes. Instead, she freed herself from his embrace. "No matter how I wish things were different, you know as well as I do that we don't have a future together. Sooner or later, I'm going to have to leave."

His groan tore through her heart. "Before I'd let that happen, I'd ask Charlotte for a divorce."

"My love—my dearest love, she'd never agree. And even if she did, do you really think either of us could be happy knowing we had ruined her life? You aren't that sort of man. If you were, you would have told me how you felt while Otto was alive."

Patrick knew she was right. And yet he couldn't give up hope. "Promise me you'll stay until Hawthorne is back on his feet."

She sighed. "Of course I will. If I know you, you'll think of another excuse to keep me here."

He managed a feeble grin. "You do know me—better than anyone else. I need to get my cattle to market before war breaks out. Charlotte couldn't stand being alone here. I was going to ask you to stay until I get back."

"When will you leave?"

"Sometime this spring. Late March or early April."

"How long will the drive take?"

"Barring any unforeseen disaster, I'll be back in July." Patrick silently counted the months. Only seven, he thought. Not much time for a miracle. And it would take a miracle to keep Elke from leaving after he returned.

Chapter Twenty-One

Nigel Hawthorne awoke to sunshine, glorious golden sunshine that gilded the bedroom walls and filled the air with motes of glittering fairy dust. He took an almost primitive pleasure in the scent of lemon oil that permeated the furniture, and the aroma of fresh air and soap wafting from the bed linens.

He even took pleasure in the steady throbbing in his right leg. By jove, he felt alive for the first time since that horrendously stupid horse had fallen on him. Alive, and by the grace of God and Rio de Vargas, still in one piece.

He had vague memories of pain-filled hours when he floated in and out of consciousness—of quiet conversations taking place on the fringe of his awareness—of comings and goings as people floated in and out of his field of vision.

There had been a tall blond woman who fed and bathed him, and did other even more intimate tasks with the sure, gentle touch of a skilled nurse. Her name, if he recalled correctly, was something German.

Elke Sonnschein. Yes, that was it. With her ice-blond hair and fathomless blue eyes, she brought to mind images of a cool, still pond in a hidden glade. There was a deep quiet place inside Elke Sonnschein that had been more soothing to him in the long hours of the night than any medicine.

Two of the men who had rescued him—his host, Patrick Pride, and the foreman, Rio de Vargas—had come to the room, too. Stalwart chaps, both. He owed them his life. He recollected a doctor as well, a sour-faced individual who looked as if a lemon drop had permanently lodged in his throat. The doctor had poked and prodded and made solemn pronouncements until Nigel passed out from a combination of ennui and pain.

Last but not least had been the woman he would always think of as an angel: the startlingly lovely Charlotte Pride. He had never expected to come across a rare beauty like her in an out-of-the-way place like the Pride ranch. It seemed a waste. A woman who looked like that could be the toast of London society.

The bedroom door opened and he turned his head to see Elke walk in carrying a tray. With her starched white apron and the no-nonsense look in her eyes, she appeared every bit as capable as the legendary Crimean war nurse, Florence Nightingale.

"Good morning," she said, depositing the tray on a table at the side of his bed. "How are you feeling, Mr. Hawthorne? Or should I call you Lord Glenhaven?"

"Neither. Mr. Hawthorne is far too formal and I still think of my father as Lord Glenhaven. Call me Nigel. Thanks to your care, I'm feeling much better." He ran his hand across his face. Stubble covered his cheeks and chin. "How long have I been here?"

"A week."

"That long?" he gasped. It certainly explained the stubble.

"I'm not surprised that you don't remember much. You've slept most of the time," Elke replied as she plumped his pillows. "The doctor told me to give you laudanum four times a day to help you rest."

Rest? What an understatement. Until this morning, he'd been more dead than alive. "How is my leg?"

"How does it feel?"

"It hurts rather badly. And it's incredibly itchy."

She beamed down at him as if he'd just told her she'd won a hundred pounds in the Grand National Steeplechase. "That's wonderful news. It itches because it's beginning to heal. I'm going to take a look, and I give you fair warning, it's going to hurt."

No female had looked after him since the days when he toddled around Glenhaven Hall in drooping nappies, a bottle of warm milk clutched in one hand and the ear of a protesting spaniel held tight in the other. Bloody hell. Was she really going to take a look beneath the covers?

Although she pulled them down with infinite care, he winced—as much from his fractured dignity as from his fractured leg.

The cold air on his nether parts told him he was naked. Apparently Elke had no interest in his manhood, though. And small wonder considering the way pain had shriveled it up.

He choked down a groan as her gentle fingers

touched the dressings that covered the place where the bone had come through the skin. "I don't think I need to change them after all. There isn't any sign of infection. Rio did a marvelous job."

"Will I walk again?" Or make love, he almost added, in view of the fact that his third leg seemed in as pitiful a condition as the one he'd broken.

"There's every reason to hope so."

He couldn't help noticing that she hadn't given him an unequivocal answer. *Every reason to hope so.* What the hell did that mean?

Elke pulled up his covers, then sat in the chair at his bedside and put the tray on her lap. "I brought you some breakfast. You haven't eaten anything solid for a week. I hope this doesn't upset your stomach."

She offered a forkful of heavenly smelling omelette and he opened his mouth. Although being fed like a baby affronted his masculinity, he ate hungrily, savoring every bite.

His sense as of himself as a man was further affronted when he finished and she asked if he had to make water.

At his frown of consternation, she smiled, produced a bottle from under the bed, then said, "I've been caring for your needs—*all your needs*—all week."

"At least, let me hold the damn bottle," he mumbled.

She did as he asked, turning her back and walking over to the window to give him some privacy. The omelette had tasted wonderful. Emptying his bladder felt even better. He sighed with the simple pleasure of it as his urine drummed into the container.

"I'm finished."

She turned, her smile deepening. "I know."

Damn, she had heard it all—every last drop.

Elke didn't flicker an eyelid as she took the odorous bottle from his hands and carried it from the room.

Bloody hell. What sort of household did his benefactor, Patrick Pride, run, anyway? Couldn't he spare a manservant to care for an injured guest? And how had the chap managed to get two of the most beautiful women Nigel had ever laid eyes on to live in this wilderness?

Before Nigel could even begin to come up with an answer to that question, Elke returned with a brown vial in her hands. "I really think you ought to take a spoon of laudanum now. It will help you rest."

"I'd as soon take poison."

The look in her eyes told him she thought very little of his bravado. To her credit, though, she didn't pursue the matter. She picked up the tray, said, "I'll check on you again in an hour," and left him alone.

He gazed at the ceiling a while, studying the overlapping wooden boards, counting them as his boredom mounted. He felt too good to be flat on his back and too weak to get up. He tried to wiggle his toes and was rewarded by a jolt of pain that took his breath away. His leg hurt like the very devil.

His mental pain was even worse. An unpredictable accident in the middle of Texas had changed his life forever.

There'd be no more hunting in foreign lands, no more wild adventures in search of trophy animals. Unless he was very lucky, he suspected he'd be an invalid the rest of his life. He pictured himself in a wheelchair, a blanket draped across his shriveled right leg, a faithful dog by his side as the endless hours of his purposeless life drifted past.

His old friends would long since have stopped dropping by. The woman who had shared his bed would regard him as an object of pity. His penis would dry up from lack of use and fall off. He'd end up one of those doddering old idiots he had seen at Brighton, drooling a little as they dozed in the sun.

"I'd rather die," he muttered between clenched jaws.

"Oh, I do hope not" came a lilting voice whose languorous drawl evoked images of long, lazy afternoons in some steamy tropical port. It was a summer voice, full of sensuality—and utterly unlike the elongated nasal voices of his childhood. A man could drown in such a voice.

He turned his head sideways and saw the angel at his bedside. "Do you walk through walls?"

She cut an arch glance at him, then dazzled him with a smile that outdid the sunshine pouring through the window. "I knocked. When you didn't reply, I tiptoed in. Elke told me you were feeling better. I thought you might like some company."

"I *am* better." Much better now she was here. "And I would love some company."

"La, sir, you are a puzzle. If you feel better, why did you just say you want to die?"

"I was feeling sorry for myself."

"What in the world for? I'd give anything to be in your place." She blushed prettily, then let go the most musical laugh he'd ever heard. "You must think I'm completely simple-minded. I don't mean I want to be in your place right now. But my goodness. You're an earl. I imagine you've had the most wonderful life. My parents took me to London a couple of years ago and I was mad for it. I'd give anything to go back, to see the places you've seen."

Nigel tore his gaze from the perfection of her features to take in her clothes. Her peach moiré dress molded her upper body, accenting the curve of her breasts and hugging her waist before flaring out around her hips.

He'd seen dresses like it in the finest London salons. Such a dress could only have been created by a master like Worth. The rings on her fingers and the jewels in her ears had Tiffany written all over them. Together, they created an indelible impression of wealth and circumstance.

"Your husband is obviously a wealthy man, Mrs. Pride. I'm certain he can take you anywhere you wish."

"But he won't. He's devoted to his ranch."

"Really?"

"Utterly," she replied, looking all the more adorable for the pout on her lips.

"Any man who would let a woman like you take second place to a piece of dirt is misguided at best."

"You flatter me."

"It's not flattery at all, Mrs. Pride."

"Please, call me Charlotte."

"Only if you call me Nigel."

The flutter of her lashes created the most delightful shadows on her cheeks. He had never seen a more ravishing creature, he mused, forgetting all about his aches—both physical and mental.

"You looked so miserable when I walked in. Would

you like me to get the laudanum. It will take away your pain."

"And my mind, too. Laudanum is derived from opium. In India, I saw men who had lost their souls to the drug. I'd rather endure a little pain than become one of them."

Her magnificent jewellike eyes widened. "Have you really been to India?"

"India, yes, and lots of other exotic places that most people only get to read about," he said, casting modesty to the winds. Only a fool played at modesty in the presence of a goddess.

She sat forward, an expression of breathless anticipation on her face. "You must have some fascinating stories to tell. I can hardly wait until you're well enough to tell them."

He'd never had a woman hang on his every utterance the way this one did. "I shall look forward to it."

"Is there anything I can do to make you more comfortable now?"

"You could send your husband's man in to give me a shave. This beard makes me feel like an old man."

"My husband doesn't have a manservant. And you're hardly an old man. But I'll shave you if you like. As I recall, you have a very attractive face under all that ugly hair."

Charlotte was surprised to hear the words coming from her mouth. She hadn't indulged in idle flirtation in months. Since the good Lord had spared her life, she'd made up her mind to turn over a new leaf, to be more serious and thoughtful—more like Elke.

And yet, here she was, up to her old ways again. And

having the most wonderful time doing it. What possible harm could come from amusing herself with Nigel Hawthorne? She could hardly wait to write her mother all about the handsome young earl.

"Have you ever shaved a man before?" he asked, a doubtful expression in his hazel eyes.

"There are lots of things I've never done. But there's one thing you should know about me. I'll try anything once." She didn't realize how provocative she sounded until she saw his response.

Nigel broke into a broad grin at her boldness. A man could read all sorts of things into what she had said. He'd never met a more enchanting little minx—or one as audacious. "Perhaps I should wait and ask Elke."

"Oh, fiddle. Don't you trust me, Lord Hawthorne?"

"I have the feeling you could be a very dangerous woman."

"Tut, tut. And I thought you were a brave man. Are you afraid to take a chance?"

To his surprise, he realized he wanted to impress her, to make certain she knew he hadn't spent his life flat on his back, laid out like a corpse at a wake. "I've taken more risks than most men. If I hadn't, I wouldn't be here. I suppose one more won't make any difference."

"I'll get Patrick's razor and be right back."

Charlotte hurried from the room before he changed his mind. She paused in the hall to catch her breath. Her heart was pounding so hard that she feared it might just pop out of her chest and fall on the floor.

She hadn't felt like this since the night she'd met Patrick. No, she silently amended. She hadn't been that excited then. There was something deliciously naughty about the thought of shaving a man she hardly knew.

Patrick's razor, shaving mug, and brush were on a shelf in the water closet. Charlotte gathered them up and filled a white enamel basin with water. She was on her way out the door when she hurried back to the mirror over the sink.

Her color was so high that she really didn't need to pinch her cheeks. The pale-peach day dress she'd put on that morning set off her dark hair perfectly. She arched a brow, wet her lips, and practiced her dimpled smile. She had, she decided, never looked better.

She hurried back to Nigel's room, then stood in front of his door while she gathered her wits. For heaven's sake, she had no reason to feel as if she was about to embark on some clandestine adventure. She had only offered to make an injured man more comfortable.

She knocked once, then let herself in.

"Am I going to live to regret this?" he asked in his wonderfully accented English.

"I promise you'll live. Only you know about the regrets."

He chuckled deep in his chest. She loved having a man laugh at her sallies, she thought, draping a towel under Nigel's chin.

She plunged the shaving brush into the pan of water, then into the shaving soap, and stirred it vigorously. When it was covered with lather, she ran it over Nigel's cheeks and chin.

She had watched her father and her brothers being shaved by their servants and had never given it a thought. But they had been white men being shaved by black men. There was, she realized, something intrinsically intimate about shaving a man when you happened to be female and the man in question was good-looking, rich, and aristocratic as all get out.

Nigel's high forehead and aquiline nose spoke volumes about his aristocratic lineage, as did the delicacy of his bone structure and the fine ash-blond hair that swept straight back from his face.

Patrick had overwhelmed her with his masculinity. Nigel's appeal was infinitely more subtle. As she stroked the metal across the coarse whiskers covering Nigel's face, she had the strangest sensation, as though the very foundation of the house had shifted beneath her feet.

She felt a connection to Nigel that went beyond sexual attraction—although there was plenty of that— beyond the touch of her hot fingers on his cool skin. She felt as if she already knew him through and through—as though by the prosaic act of shaving him, she had branded him the way her father branded horses, cattle, and runaway slaves.

How peculiar that she—a happily married bride— should feel this way about someone other than her husband. It couldn't have been more unsettling.

She had shared her attraction to Patrick with her mother, with Ella Mae, and with any of her girlfriends who would take the time to listen. But she wouldn't share what she felt this morning with another living soul—unless she told Nigel himself. Perhaps they would laugh over it someday.

"Am I doing this right?"

"You have a natural skill."

"I shall take that as a compliment."

She finished with the right side of his face and leaned across Nigel's prone body to shave the left.

Nigel couldn't have been more taken aback as her upper torso moved in close proximity to his face. She was wearing an exotic scent that stirred his senses—and his manhood, too.

Good God, did she realize her breasts were so close that he had but to lift his head to kiss them? If she didn't finish with him soon, his penis would rise up like a tent pole to support the covers.

Rio de Vargas had done a masterful job of saving his leg. Patrick Pride had given him a safe haven. And the redoubtable Elke Sonnschein had nursed him. But Charlotte Pride, he acknowledged with a primal thrill, had brought his penis back to life.

If he lived to be a hundred, he knew he would never forget this moment. Was she teasing him—or merely playing the samaritan? Was she a temptress—or an angel? He could hardly wait to find out.

Chapter Twenty-Two

Elke finished buttoning her blue merino wool dress, the one she wore for traveling because it didn't show dirt, then took a hasty look in the mirror over the dresser. In the wavering light of the kerosene lamp, her features were overwhelmed by new hollows and dark shadows.

She felt as if she had faded away the last few months while Charlotte and Nigel grew more robust and lively every day. She had given them so much of her strength that there had been nothing left over to sustain her. She was long overdue for a day off, she mused, gathering her skirt and heading down the back stairs.

Conchita met her at the kitchen door, a cup of coffee in her hands. "The buggy is already out front, señora. Drink this down and be on your way."

Elke took a few hurried gulps, then set the cup aside. "Don't forget to give Lord Hawthorne tea with his breakfast and not coffee—and he likes his eggs shirred—and make sure Rio helps him with his personal needs. The leftover ham will do nicely for dinner and—"

"Aiyee. You told me all that yesterday. I won't forget anything," Conchita interrupted, her dark eyes filled with exasperation. "You worry too much." She gave Elke a gentle push toward the door. "I packed a lunch to eat on the way. It's in the buggy."

"Are you sure you can handle everything?"

"*Sí.* I' n sure. You haven't had a day off in—let me see . . ." Conchita counted on her fingers. "Three months. You deserve some time to yourself. We'll manage just fine while you're gone. *Vaya con Dios, señora.*" She took Elke's elbow, led her to the kitchen door, and shut it between them.

"*Adiós, y muchas gracias,*" Elke called out.

She made her way to the entry hall, put on her winter coat and second-best bonnet, and opened the door on the frosted cold of a February morning. A great vault of star-strewn sky arched overhead. A coyote sent its ululating cry through the empty landscape in uneasy harmony with a rooster whose crowing heralded the dawn. Although the sun had yet to rise, the promise of its coming tinged the east with strands of molten gold.

Stretching her arms wide as if to embrace all outdoors, Elke took a deep restorative breath. The air tasted more refreshing than champagne.

She had been house-bound far too long, she thought, looking toward the waiting buggy. Nursing Charlotte and then Nigel had been emotionally and physically exhausting. She was looking forward to the long ride into town, to spending time with Velvet and the girls before staying the night with the Grobes.

"I've been waiting for you."

Patrick's voice startled her. She had heard him leave

the house earlier and had thought he'd be far away by now, rounding up cattle for the drive. She whirled around to see him leaning against the house, his long legs crossed, his sheepskin jacket snugged around his broad shoulders.

"What are you doing here?" she demanded, her heart accelerating the way it always did in his presence. "There's really no need to see me off."

He settled his hat more firmly on his head. "I'm not. I'm going with you."

A flush heated her cheeks. "Whatever for?"

"Did you really think I'd let you make the drive to Fredericksburg by yourself?"

"I'm perfectly capable of taking care of myself."

"You're the most capable woman I've ever known— but these are dangerous times."

"I don't need you to remind me," she said more harshly than she intended.

"I'm sorry. I didn't mean to bring up unhappy memories. But I promised myself I wouldn't let anything happen to you while you lived under my roof. I aim to keep that promise." Abandoning his indolent pose, he strode past her and down the porch steps.

When he reached the buggy, he paused and waited for her to join him. "It's a long ride," he said, taking her elbow and helping her climb up into the front seat. "Try to enjoy it."

"Does Charlotte know you're going?" she asked as he settled himself beside her.

Patrick chuckled. "She seemed rather happy at the prospect of having the house to herself. She said something about Nigel teaching her how to play whist."

He gathered the reins and snapped them across the horse's back, urging the animal to an easy trot. The whirring of the wheels, the clip-clop of hooves, the jingle of the harness filled the uneasy silence between them.

Elke braced herself against the sway of the buggy. She was intensely aware of Patrick's proximity and determined to avoid an inadvertent touch. *Enjoy the ride,* he had said. But how could she under the circumstances?

Her heart and mind were so open to his love, so vulnerable, that sitting beside him was both torture and joy. She had successfully avoided being alone with him since Nigel's arrival. Running a large house and caring for a bedridden man had filled her days. Thoughts of Patrick had filled her nights.

Now those unbidden thoughts, those primal longings, swelled in her mind like spring-ripe buds. It was all she could do to keep her hands primly folded in her lap and her gaze fixed on the road ahead, when she asked nothing more from life than to touch and look at the man she loved.

The miles rolled by and the sun lifted above the horizon while Elke vainly sought a neutral topic of conversation. Every one she came up with—abolition, politics, Charlotte and Nigel's recovery, the cattle drive—came freighted with its own unruly load of memories.

Patrick seemed content to concentrate on driving. However, as the buggy finally passed through the limestone pillars that marked the boundary of Pride's Passion, he turned to her and said, "This is silly."

She bridled, sitting up even straighter. "If you think

it's too soon for me to leave Nigel, why don't you just say so and head on back to the house?"

He surprised her with a hearty guffaw. "Nothing could have been further from my mind. The man's been in bed for four weeks. I'm damn certain he'd long since have tried out the crutches Rio made for him if you hadn't been hovering like a mother hen."

Could it be jealousy she heard in Patrick's voice? "Is that what you think I've done?"

He turned his smoke-colored gaze on her, and the warmth in his eyes almost melted her reserve. "I think you're the most conscientious nurse in the world. Besides, I wasn't talking about Nigel. I was talking about you and me. I know I have no right to your love. Much as I hate the thought of giving you up, I'm trying to accept it. But we used to be friends. I can't abide the thought of driving the next twenty-five miles without exchanging a word."

"I don't know what to say to you these days."

He sighed heavily and his shoulders slumped. "That hurts me most of all. I hate knowing you're on pins and needles every time we're in the same room. I hate having you eat in the kitchen to avoid being with me. I'm going to be leaving on the drive in a few more weeks. That's all the time in the world we'll have together. Can't we spend it as friends?"

Charlotte had heard Patrick moving around the bedroom in the predawn. When he left without so much as a goodbye kiss, she pretended to be asleep. Not that she minded the growing coolness between them—not any-more.

If Patrick had been a loving husband, she would have felt guilty about spending so much time with Nigel. After all, she did have a conscience! She wouldn't have felt right making love to her husband—and imagining it was Nigel who held her in his arms.

The trouble was, imagination no longer sufficed.

She had learned to squeeze her legs together and take herself over the edge of desire and into the realm of pleasure. But what lonesome pleasure it was! She wanted something more between her legs than her own throbbing flesh. She wanted a man, a hot, hungry man, and as a married woman, she was damn well entitled to one.

She'd overheard her father and her brothers talking about their marital rights. No one ever seemed to think that a woman had rights, too. But she might as well have slept alone for all the notice Patrick took of her after the lights went out.

It wasn't the act of sex she missed so much as the things that led up to it—the knowing glances, the secret communication of gestures and touches. She missed what came afterward even more—the cuddling, the conversation, the sure and certain knowledge that she was the center of her man's life.

Patrick had never given her that, not even on their honeymoon. Nigel seemed to promise it all. He listened, really listened to her as if what she had to say mattered. He laughed at her jokes. And oh, how could she ignore the long, hot looks he gave her, or the way her skin was seared by his most casual touch?

Call her a sinner—call her a wayward woman, she no longer cared. She absolutely, positively, yearned for Nigel so much that it sent her stomach churning and her head spinning. Why, these last few days, she could hardly think about anything else.

She waited until she heard the front door shut, then got out of bed and walked to the window to see Patrick heading for the big stone barn. Goose bumps covered her skin and her nipples firmed to points by the time he drove a buggy out of the barn and parked it in front of the house.

She heard lighter footsteps heading down the hall and recognized them as Elke's. *Hurry, hurry,* her mind commanded—*be on your way.* Time seemed to stand still while she waited for the buggy to head down the drive with Elke and Patrick aboard. She continued watching until the vehicle disappeared into the dark.

Shivering with anticipation as much as with cold, she put on her most seductive nightgown and negligee. The fragile silk whispered across her skin like a lover's breath. She daubed perfume at her neck and wrists, and between her breasts, then fluffed her hair.

Barefoot, she opened the bedroom door, tiptoed down the hall to Nigel's room, and paused there to gather her nerve. Her pulse throbbed in her throat and her imagination ran wild as she pictured Nigel's response to her appearance in his room. If he was half the man she thought he was, he'd ravish her then and there.

She had been flirting with him since the morning when she shaved him—and he had been flirting back. What had begun out of sheer boredom had become the most meaningful relationship she had ever experienced in her entire life. Nigel meant more to her than her husband, her parents, her brothers and sisters.

Every time she thought what life would be like after he'd gone, she felt as if she were staring into a bottomless pit of misery. She lived for the few moments when she and Nigel were alone. And now they had two whole glorious days.

She felt sinful, wicked—and utterly fabulous. Her nipples hardened even more at the thought of what she had been planning since Elke first said she would be gone for the night.

This time Charlotte needed no accomplice, no scheming mother to help her carry out her plan. Besides, her mother would be scandalized if she knew. However, Charlotte gave no thought to her mother, and even less to Patrick. She listened only to the impetuous clamoring of her own heart.

Twisting the brass knob, she pushed the door open and shut it behind herself with the same stealth she had used on those occasions when she had crept from Windmere to meet a youthful beau. However, this morning she intended to part with more than a chaste kiss.

Her eyes, accustomed to the dark, easily made out Nigel's form under the covers. He lay on his back, breathing easily. His body was far more slender than Patrick's, and at five feet eight inches, shorter, too. She knew they would look marvelous dancing together once he got back on his feet.

She crossed the floor, laid a hand on his shoulder, and gave him a gentle shake.

His eyes flew open instantly. "What is it?" he asked.

"I heard you cry out. So I came to see if you were all right. You must have had a bad dream."

"Oh, I did," Nigel replied, "the most terrible dream. I dreamed that Rio had cut off my leg. I'm so glad you're here. Please, don't leave me alone." He reached up and touched Charlotte's hand. "You're cold as ice. I shall never forgive myself if you suffer a relapse on my account."

Far from dreaming, he had been wide awake when Charlotte sneaked into his room. Her arrival had startled, then thrilled him. He'd been wondering when and if she would make her move. *L'audace,* he thought. *Toujours l'audace.* The motto fit Charlotte like one of Worth's dresses.

In another place and time, a woman like Charlotte Pride would have ruled an empire with a kiss—or commanded an army with an imperious lift of her brow—or, like Helen of Troy, launched a thousand ships. Although no one had ever encouraged her to use it, she had a fine Machiavellian mind. An actress would have envied her sense of timing.

He liked a woman who used her Godgiven talents to get what she wanted. And, thank God, she wanted him.

Her arrival couldn't have been more impeccably calculated, he thought as the erection he awakened with every morning pressed against the covers. He couldn't have been more ready for a dalliance.

"Here. Climb in beside me before you catch your death," he whispered.

She made a fine display of virtue. "You presume too much, Nigel. Now that I see you're all right, I'll just go on back to my room."

The time had come to call her bluff. "Have it your way, but we may not have another chance."

"I don't know what you mean," she declared haughtily, a deep breath lifting her breasts.

He grinned into the dark. "You know exactly what I mean. If I read you right, my angel, you've been planning—or at least imagining a moment like this since the day you flaunted your breasts when you shaved me. The way you're flaunting them now, I might add. If you're trying to arouse me, my dear, you have succeeded admirably."

"How dare you talk to me that way?" she sputtered.

"I'd dare anything to get you in my bed."

"You're absolutely shameless, Lord Glenhaven."

"That makes us two of a kind."

To his infinite pleasure, Charlotte broke into the musical laughter that was her trademark. "My goodness. I can't lie to you. We are of like minds."

He lifted the covers higher. "I can hardly ravish you in my condition—at least not without your cooperation. Get in and together we'll decide what happens next."

She let her nightrobe drop from her shoulders, posing a moment in her sheer gown so that he had a tantalizing glimpse of breasts, belly, and thighs. Then she climbed into the big bed, cuddling up to his side like a puppy seeking its master's warmth.

She fit against him perfectly, as though she had been expressly designed to lie in his arms. Feeling her icy skin, he pulled her even closer. "That's better, isn't it, angel?"

"Oh, it is," she cooed. She turned so that the points

of her breasts pressed into his ribs. "But don't you feel the least little bit guilty?"

"I feel like the most fortunate man in the world. I've watched you and Patrick these last few weeks and never seen so much as an affectionate gesture between you, let alone any love. And you, my angel, were made for love. Let me give it to you now."

He'd bedded married women before, preferring pure lust to the complications of wooing girls who had yet to admit to those feelings. He'd always thought virginity to be a highly overrated commodity and didn't care a fig if another man had blazed the trail before him.

Feeling Charlotte's yielding body, he gave scant thought to Patrick. If adultery was good enough for kings, it was good enough for him. In any case, Patrick had set himself up to wear a cuckold's horns by ignoring his hot-blooded young wife.

Nigel ran his free hand across Charlotte's ripe curves, reveling in the fullness of her breasts, the dimpled indentation in the middle of her belly, the heat between her thighs. He lowered his head to one crested nipple and sucked as ravenously as a baby at its mother's teat.

She rewarded him with a throaty moan. "Harder. Do it harder."

He didn't have to be asked twice. His angelic Charlotte obviously liked her sex rough—and so did he. Biting firmly enough to cause a maximum of pleasure and a delicious *soupçon* of pain, he pulled up her gown and thrust two fingers inside her body.

She spasmed at the invasion, then arched her pelvis to welcome his probing digits. God! She was as wet and slick inside as a seal sporting in the sea.

She was his for the taking and he knew he could manage the act despite the splint that still bound his leg. However, to his amazement, he realized he wanted more than a casual tumble. He wanted this meteor shower of a woman—this temptress whose daring equalled his wildest adventure—he wanted her for his very own.

"Oh, I do want you," she declared as if to mirror his starling revelation. "I've wanted you since the first time I saw you. But I'm afraid of the consequences. What if I get pregnant?"

"Don't worry. I'll pull out in time," he said, making the empty promise a million other men had made at similar moments.

To his astonishment, though, the warmth radiating through his heart was even more overpowering than the heat surging through his loins. God knew, he wanted to make mad passionate love to Charlotte—but he wanted to protect her, too, even if it meant saving her from his own lustful impulses. But with a sudden, terrifying rush of self-knowledge, he realized he couldn't have sex with Charlotte tonight—or any other night. He couldn't participate in her ruination.

Damn and double damn. Could this—at long last—be love? he agonized, kissing her damp brow. And if it was, what in the hell could he do about it?

No matter how Elke tried to think of Patrick as the friend he had been, rather than the lover he could never be, she just couldn't talk to him easily. While the buggy carried them toward Fredericksburg, their conversation was as ragged as an urchin's clothes.

Lost in thought, she didn't realize they were approaching the place where Otto had died until it was upon them. Her hand flew to her mouth and tears pooled in her eyes as vivid images of another buggy ride rose up before her. A wordless cry burst from her throat and she instinctively buried her face in Patrick's shoulder.

"What is it?" he asked, taking the reins in one hand and pulling her into his body with the other.

"This is where Otto was murdered!" she cried out against the rough leather of his jacket.

"I'm so sorry. I would have taken a detour if I had known."

"Poor dear Otto. He called himself a coward but he was so brave that day. I didn't deserve him."

Patrick flicked the reins, urging the horse to leave the unmarked place in the road behind. "Don't say that. Don't even think that."

"I can't help it. I wasn't always nice to him. I used to chide him about the way he spoke and the way he dressed."

"I don't think he even noticed. You made him very happy. He was so proud of his *schoene Madchen.* I wish I could have seen his face when he found out he was going to be a father. I bet he just about danced for joy."

"We both did. That baby would have been the making of our marriage." She stopped fighting her tears. "I miss Otto so much."

Patrick reined the horse to a stop. "I do, too. I've never been able to talk to anyone else the way I did to him—except for you. If it's any consolation, I know that Otto died a happy man. I can picture him right now, somewhere in heaven with the baby in one arm and a tray of cookies in the other, asking Saint Peter if he wants a *Pfeffernussen.*"

Hearing Patrick's words, all the dark memories that had crowded her mind for months began to fade. "Oh, I hope you're right," she said.

"I know I am," he replied, handing her a handkerchief.

She wiped her eyes and assayed a tremulous smile. "Do you really think they have a bakery in heaven?"

"If they don't, Otto will have started one just the way he did when he arrived in Fredericksburg. I'm so glad he's buried on the ranch. Sometimes I go down to his grave and talk to him about books."

"So do I, except I talk about politics."

Patrick's smile warmed her through and through. "I'm not surprised. You probably lecture him, too."

Patrick made no move to hold her again. He flicked the reins and resumed the journey, chatting easily all the while. To her amazement, she was able to keep up her end of the conversation.

Dear Otto had brought her and Patrick together years ago—and he had reunited them in spirit now. Somehow, she had the feeling he would have been pleased.

Velvet poured a little brandy into their teacups and handed one of them to Elke. "You're looking better than the last time I saw you," she said, noting the bright flush on Elke's cheeks. "You've got a shine on you, girl."

"I'm feeling much better these days."

"I take it that nursing an English earl isn't all that hard. I'd sell my best French silk stockings to meet him. Rio says he's a genuine top hand."

"Why don't you come on out to the ranch and see for yourself? Charlotte has been asking for you, too."

Velvet couldn't meet Elke's eager gaze. It had been one thing to blunder into a tête-à-tête with Charlotte Pride. Charlotte was small potatoes compared to a nobleman who, according to Rio, was kissing kin to a king.

"Aw, sugar, I don't think it would be right."

"I do," Elke declared. "Charlotte's already told Nigel about you."

Velvet closed her eyes for a moment, enjoying the image of herself saying howdy to Lord Hawthorne.

When she opened them again, reality hit her smack in the face. Displeasure rode her features as she gazed at her bedroom's gaudy decor. No decent woman would choose to live in such a place. She was a whore and she'd die a whore. And whores didn't chitchat with bluebloods.

"We'll see," she said, adding another tipple of brandy to her tea. She'd been doing that far too much lately, filling the loneliness inside her with liquor.

"Now, tell me how you and Patrick are getting along. Have you found a way to work things out?"

"Yes—and no."

"I'm no mind reader, sugar. Why don't you spell it out for me."

"We're finally friends again. I can't tell you how much that means to me. But I'm definitely leaving when Patrick gets back from the cattle drive."

"I wish you'd stop singing that tune."

"We both know I don't have any choice."

Velvet sighed. "You aren't the only one who is thinking about leaving. A few of the girls have offered to buy me out and I just might take them up on it."

"But what about Rio? I thought the two of you were getting along so well."

"Oh, we are, that's for damn sure. In bed. The rest of the time, Rio acts like he's got a frog stuck in his craw. You know he isn't much of a conversationalist, but he's even quieter lately. He looks at me with the damnedest expression in his eyes, like he means to say something and can't bring himself to spit it out. I figure one of these days he's going to tell me how he intends to take his pleasure elsewhere. I couldn't stand having that happen. To tell you the truth, I think it would break my heart. And this time I'm not sure I'd be able to pick up the pieces. So I figured I'd make my move first."

Elke reached for her hand. "Oh, Velvet, I had no idea."

"I reckon you've had other things on your mind of late."

"I'm so sorry. I thought at least one of us was going to be happy."

"No such luck. To tell you the truth, I've been thinking about going out to California. Maybe you'd want to come along."

Elke managed a feeble grin. "I sure don't have anything better in mind. We could tell people we were cousins. Maybe we could even go into business together."

Velvet's brows flew up and her mouth dropped open.

This time, Elke's smile was genuine. "I don't mean *your* business. I've been thinking about opening a boardinghouse." Her expression brightened. "It could even be fun."

"No it couldn't," Velvet declared, giving her head a little shake. "I can't imagine anything sadder than the two of us growing old without the men we love. But they do say misery loves company. I'll think on it."

While Elke visited Velvet, Patrick checked into the Nimitz Hotel, then walked into the saloon.

"I hear the Army will pull out of Fort Martin Scott once the shooting starts," Charles Nimitz said from behind the bar where he was dispensing drinks.

"Who will defend us and enforce the law?" an anxious burgher asked.

"We're going to have to defend ourselves," Nimitz replied grimly. "I've been thinking about forming up an organization of Gillespie County rifles to do the job. We ought to be able to handle the local scum."

"Speaking of scum, has anyone heard anything about Jude and Eli Detweilers?" Patrick asked.

"Those boys hightailed it out of here after the set-to with the Sonnscheins," Nimitz replied. "They haven't been heard from since."

"Good. I hate leaving Elke and Charlotte at a time like this."

Nimitz put a bottle of whisky on the bar so his customers could help themselves and gave Patrick his complete attention. "Does that mean you've decided to return to Natchez to fight for the South?"

"Not at all. I did my fighting at the battle of San Jacinto." Patrick absentmindedly fingered the scar running down his right cheek. "I'm driving every steer I can get my hands on to market."

"By the time you get back, the war will be over," a southern sympathizer commented.

"I doubt it," Patrick replied dryly. "I won't be gone that long. A buyer has agreed to meet the herd in Nacodoches." He didn't add that the buyer was a southerner who would take the herd on to Mississippi and not to northern stockyards.

"How long will that take," a nattily dressed drummer asked.

"Three or four months," Patrick replied, "barring any unforeseen trouble."

"I wouldn't leave my womenfolk alone if I were you," the burgher said dourly.

"I don't plan to. We have a guest who is rather handy with a gun. I've been thinking about asking him to stay on."

"Back East, no one thinks the South will fight," the drummer said knowingly. "But I figure some hothead will get things going before the year is out. It's going to be hell on business."

It was going to be hell on all of them, Patrick thought unhappily. He finished his drink and left for the mercantile to buy the supplies he needed for the drive. He slept uneasily that night and was up at first light. Before leaving to pick Elke up at the Grobes', he rechecked the load in the revolver he wore holstered against his hip.

She was out in the front yard, playing with the

Grobes' children when he drove up in the buggy. She looked younger and happier than she had in months, he thought. If only he could find a way to keep that sweet smile on her face.

Elke had a natural way with children. When they had come into the bakery to spend their pennies, she had attended to their meager purchases as seriously as she did any of her adult customers, never hurrying them while they debated the merits of one sweet against another.

Seeing her now, he couldn't help thinking she would have been a wonderful mother. Regret pooled in his belly as he thought how much he wanted to have children with her instead of with Charlotte.

Well, she sure as hell didn't have to worry about getting pregnant, Charlotte thought, creeping from Nigel's bed and returning to her own room for the second time in as many mornings. For the life of her, she couldn't figure men out.

They wanted you like crazy until they declared their love. And then they put you up on a pedestal and insisted on doing the honorable thing.

She had told Nigel she didn't care a thing for honor, that he meant more to her than anything else. She had cajoled, caressed, and downright begged him to make love to her. And what had he said in return?

"You mean too much to me to indulge in a dangerous liaison."

What other kind of liaison did he think he could have with a married woman?

She slid into her icy bed, pulled the covers over her

head, and wept out of sheer frustration. Her nose felt as though it had been stuffed with cotton by the time her tears finally stopped.

She lay there, trying to figure a way to convince Nigel that she was right and he was wrong. Patrick would soon be leaving with his damn cows. If she could figure a way to get Nigel to stay on, she might have her way yet.

Chapter Twenty-Three

Rio de Vargas stropped his razor, lathered his face, and scraped away the week's accumulation of whiskers. He'd shaved more, taken more tub baths, and changed his underwear more in the four months and eight days that he and Velvet had been seeing each other than he had in the last few years put together.

Not that she wasn't worth it. He'd do damn near anything—including wearing some of that sweet-smelling 4711 cologne the boys had given him as a joke at Christmas—if it would help him find favor in her eyes. The trouble was, he seemed to be failing.

He'd been more tongue-tied around Velvet than ever. Every time he thought he'd screwed his courage to the point where he was ready to ask for her hand in marriage, his mouth dried like a water hole in a drought, his tongue swelled up as though it had been snake-bit, and his legs turned to corn-meal mush.

If that wasn't bad enough, from time to time he caught Velvet looking at him as if she wished he were someone else or some*place* else. For the life of him, he couldn't think what he'd done to displease her so. He had to be crazy, daring to dream that a fine woman like Miss Velvet would marry a run-down cowboy with a face full of wrinkles and an empty wallet.

And now there was this dang dinner party to contend with. Thinking about it made his hand shake so much that he damn near cut his throat. He staunched the wound with a corner of his towel and used the clean part to wipe the remaining soapsuds off his face.

"You look like you ran into an angry cat," Terrell Meeks called out from his bunk.

"Mind your own business. We're driving cattle day after tomorrow. The way you're lollygagging around, I guess your gear is ready."

Chastised, young Meeks made a great pretense of rooting through the belongings stored in the trunk at the foot of his bed. The dozen other men in the bunkhouse suddenly seemed to have lots to do as well.

Rio pulled a clean shirt over his head, knotted a fresh neckerchief around his throat so that it hid the cut, returned to his own bunk, sat down, and ran a cloth over his best boots.

Although foremen on other ranches dined with the owner, Rio preferred to take his meals with the men. It helped him to sense their mood, to know their concerns, to see who was up to making that extra effort and whose string had temporarily run out.

He could count the times he'd been invited to eat up at the big house on the fingers of both hands. There had been a number of Christmases when Patrick hadn't gone into town to dine with the Sonnscheins or other friends, and a couple of birthdays when Patrick had gotten drunk and wanted company.

But a dinner party?

Never.

Rio searched his mind, trying to conjure up the table manners his father had taught him. Eat with your fork and not your knife. Wipe your mustache from time to time to remove any food. And never belch or pass gas in a lady's company unless there was a dog handy to blame it on.

Somehow he doubted that would be enough to see him through a meal with Charlotte Pride and Earl Hawthorne. Those two were used to living high on the hog.

Earl would most likely ignore a mistake or two. But Mrs. Pride scared the hell out of Rio. He'd as soon tangle with her as gallop head-on into a lightning-spooked herd of longhorns.

Taking a surreptitious glance around to make sure none of the boys were looking, he took the cologne from the unpainted pine shelf over his bunk and splashed it on liberally. Then he smashed his hat on his head and strode out of the bunkhouse into a fine March evening, heedless of the cheerful catcalls that accompanied his departure.

The short winter days had given way to an early spring that boded well for the drive. Cottony clouds dotted the sky. The first wildflowers were poking their blossoms through the grass. A fine dust, churned up by the hundreds of head of cattle nearby, permeated the air.

It would be good to get back to the all-male world of a cattle drive, to doing the job he knew best, to living a life that fit him like a second skin. But he was going to miss Velvet like all get out. The way things had been going, he couldn't be sure she'd want to see him when he returned.

At the thought, his heart shriveled in his chest until it felt no bigger than a black-eyed pea. He should have known, at this stage in his life, he was too old and too set in his ways to get the man/woman thing right. If he'd had any sense, he would have stuck to cattle, he mused, being careful as he made his way to the big house not to kick any dust on his newly polished boots.

The sound of a carriage coming fast made him hasten to the side of the drive. He wondered who the hell was in such an all-fired hurry. He gazed back over his shoulder to see Velvet reining her buggy to a halt.

Her unexpected appearance wreathed his face in a wide grin of pure delight. "Howdy, Velvet," he called out, tipping his hat. "This sure is a pleasant surprise."

Was she just dropping in the way she'd done the day he'd missed her? If so, she had sure picked the wrong time. He could just imagine the way Charlotte Pride would react to an uninvited guest.

If Miss Charlotte didn't treat his beloved Velvet just right, he made up his mind to walk right on out of the dinner party.

"Charlotte and Patrick asked me to join them for a farewell supper," Velvet said, looking as happy as a pup who has finally found a teat. "Hop on up and I'll give you a ride to the house."

Well, if that didn't tie a knot in the cat's tail, Ric thought, climbing up and automatically taking the reins from Velvet's hands. Maybe Charlotte Pride had a heart under all those fancy duds. Who could figure her? Who could figure any woman?

"You sure are a sight for sore eyes," he told Velvet, wishing he could think of a more flowery compliment, one that would do justice to how truly beautiful she looked.

She was wearing a deep-blue dress made of a fabric so soft that it reminded him of a newborn calf's hide. A saucy bonnet that wouldn't even begin to protect her from the wind perched on the red curls she'd piled high atop her head.

She looked like something straight out of one of those Godey's magazines. She looked like a real lady and he hoped to hell that Earl and Charlotte treated her like one.

"How nice of you to say so," Velvet replied, giving him a long stare that seemed to convey a hidden message he couldn't even begin to decipher.

Damn, he wished she'd speak up—or even cuss him out if she had a mind to. The trouble with women was they never told you what was bothering them the way a man did. And something was sure as hell bothering Velvet.

Although they were now so close to the house that the horse could have found its way blindfolded in a blizzard, Rio concentrated on his driving. It was happening again, he thought unhappily as he felt his tongue thicken.

He wanted to tell Velvet how much he was going to miss her, to confess that she'd gotten so deep under his skin that he felt her presence with every beat of his heart.

Instead, he just clucked to the horse.

He's tired of me, Velvet thought as Rio reined the buggy to a stop in front of the Prides' broad veranda—*so tired that he can't think of a single thing to say.* Rio was no different from any other man she'd known, she realized with an icy consternation that seemed to turn her blood to slush.

He'd gotten what he wanted from her. They had done every conceivable thing a man could possibly want in bed—short of inviting a couple of the girls to join them in a flat-out orgy. Now they'd done them, Rio didn't want her anymore.

How in the world was she going to get through dinner when she felt as if Rio had squeezed her heart and hung it on a line to dry? If Elke hadn't been waiting at the door to greet them, Velvet might have burst into tears.

As Rio helped her down from the buggy, she pasted a bright smile on her face. "Hello there," she called out as if she hadn't a care in the world.

They certainly do make a handsome couple, Elke thought, watching Rio and Velvet come up the porch steps side by side. More than that, they looked right together, as if they'd been born and bred for each other.

Rio's lean, saturnine looks were the perfect foil for Velvet's ripe figure and roseate coloring. *Please God, let something wonderful happen for them,* Elke prayed as she stepped forward to greet them.

"It's so good to see you again," she said, giving Velvet a hug, and bussing Rio's cheek even though she knew it would embarrass him. "Charlotte and Nigel are waiting in the parlor and Patrick will be down any minute."

"How's Earl getting along these days," Rio asked in a peculiar croak.

"Very well, thanks to you. The crutches you made for him have been a godsend."

"Glad to hear it." Rio swallowed so hard that his Adam's apple almost disappeared.

He shuffled his feet nervously, while Velvet kept her gaze fixed straight ahead. The two of them didn't look any happier about the coming evening than Elke was.

Elke had anticipated Charlotte's party with mixed emotions. She looked forward to the gaiety and laughter that Velvet and Charlotte brought to every occasion. However, she felt sick at the thought of how little time she had left with Patrick.

Over the last six weeks, they had found their way back to the friendship she had always treasured. Instead of hiding in the kitchen, she had taken her meals in the dining room with Patrick, Charlotte, and Nigel. Afterward, while Charlotte and Nigel played cards or talked, Patrick and Elke had been free to reminisce.

They had even excused themselves a couple of times to walk to Otto's grave down by the Guadalupe River. Sharing her loss with someone who had loved Otto too had finally freed Elke of Otto's ghost. She would always be grateful to Patrick for that.

In turn, he had discussed his concerns about the ranch, explaining its daily operation until Elke felt fully conversant on the subject. It was, she had learned, a complex and fascinating business that required constant vigilance against the depredations of disease, marauding Indians, and wild animals.

Other Hill Country ranchers permitted their cattle to breed at will. Patrick kept his bulls apart from the cows, timing their mating so that Pride calves were all born in the fall, a tactic which increased their chance of surviving the infestations of insects and disease that came with summer's heat. Being able to brand and/or castrate all the calves at the same time provided an additional benefit in time saved.

How she had loved listening to Patrick speculate about ways to improve his herd, perhaps even acquiring some fine stock from Europe to cross-breed with his hardy Longhorns. He dreamed of buying more land, drilling more wells, growing feed so that his cattle could survive those months when the weather was their worst enemy.

If only she could help him make those dreams come true. Pride's Passion had become her passion, too. She loved the ranch as if it were her own. But the one thing she and Patrick had never discussed was the ever diminishing ration of days they had together.

She knew it weighed as heavily on his mind as it did on hers. She saw it in the increasing sadness in his eyes, in the ways his shoulders sagged every time they said good night at the foot of the stairs. Most of all, she knew it from hearing his weary footsteps as he prowled the house after she had gone to bed.

But for the distraction of Nigel's presence, Elke felt certain Charlotte would have realized something was amiss. Thank heaven Charlotte was so engrossed in the

Englishman that she paid little attention to anything or anyone else.

This evening proved no exception. Charlotte was laughing at something Nigel said as Elke ushered Velvet and Rio into the parlor. Nigel saw them first and levered himself to his feet with the help of his crutches.

Balancing precariously, he held out his hand to Rio. "It's good to see you, old chap."

"Howdy, Earl," Rio replied, pumping Nigel's hand so vigorously that Nigel almost lost his balance. "I've been aiming to stop by but Patrick has kept me busy rounding up cattle. How's the leg?"

Nigel gave Rio a wry grin. "You warned me that I'd have—how did you put it?—a hitch in my git along." He mimicked Rio's intonation perfectly. "I'm afraid my hunting days are over. However, I'm in your eternal debt for saving my leg."

Rio turned as red as a Hill Country sunset, jerked his hat from his head and stood holding it in both hands, staring down at the floor. "It weren't nothing."

"It was everything," Charlotte said, finally tearing her worshipful gaze from Nigel long enough to join the conversation. "Nigel may have a limp, but he's going to be able to walk." Remembering her manners, she added, "And now, Nigel, permit me to introduce the lady you've heard so much about. This is my new friend, Velvet Gilhooley."

When Nigel murmured, "It's a pleasure," and kissed Velvet's hand as if she were nobility, too, Elke let go her pent-up breath. She'd been anxious about this moment ever since Charlotte proposed the dinner party.

"The pleasure is all mine, Lord Glenhaven," Velvet

replied, dropping such a perfect curtsy that Elke knew she had to have practiced it.

"Please, do call me Nigel. I don't believe in standing on ceremony when I'm among friends. In fact, given my condition, I'd rather not stand at all."

He's so clever, Charlotte thought as Velvet responded to Nigel's remark with a throaty chuckle—so clever and so handsome in his brown tweed suit with its matching vest. The color suited his dark-blond hair and seemed to intensify the blue of his eyes.

Her father, brothers, and husband all dressed well when the occasion demanded. But their finest clothing couldn't compare to the elegant tailoring that Nigel wore with such casual grace. He was the only man she'd ever known who had any interest in his appearance—and it showed.

How naive she had been to allow Patrick to sweep her off her feet—how unsophisticated. Only a child would have thought him a man of the world. Her only excuse was that she had led a sheltered life. At the time, she hadn't known a man like Nigel even existed. Compared to Nigel—who had been everywhere, met everyone, and done everything—Patrick was a bumbling hick.

Taking a proprietary hold of Nigel's arm and helping him to the sofa, she said, "Do let's sit down. I can't imagine what's keeping my husband. In the meantime, would you be a dear, Elke, and serve sherry all around."

"Patrick said something about having a surprise—and making an announcement," Elke replied before fetching drinks from the sideboard.

"Whatever," Charlotte replied with disinterest. Per-

sonally, she didn't care if Patrick ever joined them. He'd
been so dour lately that his arrival would undoubtedly
put a damper on the party.

For the life of her, she couldn't imagine how Elke
managed to put up with Patrick's constant talk of cattle.
In Elke's place, she would long since have expired from
sheer boredom. By contrast, she found Nigel's talk of
the places he'd been, the adventures he'd had, endlessly
fascinating.

Considering the situation, it was all Charlotte could
do to keep her spirits up. She had hardly given a moment's thought to Patrick's imminent departure with the
herd. Her mind had been completely taken up with the
realization that Nigel intended to leave Pride's Passion
as soon as he was able to sit a horse.

How could she endure living on the ranch without
him? Would her plan to keep him there succeed? Time
was running out.

She almost wailed out loud. If only her mother was
around to help put her scheme in action. Patrick would
have paid attention to her mother. Would he pay attention
to her? She felt as if her life were hanging by a thread.

"Are you all right, Charlotte?" Velvet asked. "You
look a thousand miles away."

"Of course. What were you'all talking about?"

"I asked Nigel to tell me how he met Rio. But he said
you'd heard the story far too often to bore you with it
again."

"Nigel could never bore me," Charlotte drawled. Although she had heard the story often enough to tell it
herself, she riveted her attention on Nigel. She loved
hearing the way he spoke.

* * *

The merry sound of laughter greeted Patrick at the parlor door. Charlotte, Rio, and Velvet were so caught up in something Nigel had said that they were unaware of his presence. However, Elke looked up at once. She seemed to have a sixth sense that told her when he had walked into a room, a sense he had, too, where she was concerned.

For a long moment, their gazes caught and held. He read love, concern, and sympathy in her eyes. How could he leave her in just two days? How could he ever let her leave him? He'd spent the last six weeks wrestling with those questions, roaming the house at night as if the quiet rooms held the answer.

At least he wouldn't have to worry about her—or Charlotte, either—while he was gone. If only his other problems could be so easily solved.

"Ah, here's our host," Nigel said as Patrick joined them. "Elke has poured us all drinks. You're in time for a toast."

"I have something to say first," Patrick replied, taking a glass of sherry from the tray that Elke was passing around.

"Elke said something about a surprise," Charlotte interjected. "Don't keep us waiting."

Patrick finally turned his gaze on his wife. She was a stranger to him—an incredibly lovely stranger. "As Rio and Nigel know, I've been worried about leaving you and Elke alone on the ranch. I talked to Nigel about it again earlier today and he has agreed to stay on and watch over you and Elke until I return." Unbuckling the holster from around his hips, Patrick handed it to Nigel. "These matched Colts are a token of my gratitude. As the temporary guardian of all I hold dear, I know you will use them well."

Nigel took the holstered guns with a graceful inclination of his head, and examined them with a connoisseur's intense concentration. "I've never seen finer guns. But I can't accept them. They're the latest models. Surely you'll need them on the drive."

Any answer Patrick might have made was drowned in Charlotte's delighted squeal. "Does this mean you'll stay?" she asked Nigel.

Patrick knew she had been fearful of being left unprotected. Although half a dozen hands would stay behind to look after the breeding stock, Charlotte dwelled in moral dread of not having a man in the house. She had spoken of it often the past few weeks, shuddering and weeping over the danger, begging Patrick not to leave her when she knew he had no choice.

But Charlotte was given to exaggeration. She exuded melodrama the way Elke exuded serenity. He hadn't realized the scope of Charlotte's terror until this very moment, seeing the scope of her relief.

"Oh, Nigel, you've made me the happiest woman in the world," she exclaimed, throwing her arms around the Englishman.

"I could hardly refuse," Nigel said drily, disentangling himself from her embrace. "I owe my life to your husband. If I may finally propose that toast," he lifted his glass high, "to Patrick Pride and Pride's Passion. May they prosper long and well."

While the others raised their glasses, too, Patrick

sought Elke's gaze and lifted his glass to her in a silent salute.

Interesting, very interesting, Nigel thought, tracking Patrick's eyes. He'd often wondered how Patrick had managed to keep two such beautiful women on an out-of-the-way ranch.

Patrick had married one of them. And, unless Nigel's intuition was totally off base, Patrick was in love with the other. Now that certainly shed a different light on what had become an increasingly uncomfortable situation, Nigel mused, emptying his glass of sherry in a single swallow.

Chapter Twenty-Four

The day of Patrick's departure, Elke rose before dawn to see him off. The last morning belonged to the two of them. Charlotte and Nigel had said their goodbyes the night before.

They met in the kitchen to share one last meal . . . and couldn't eat. They sought for words to reveal their feelings . . . and couldn't speak. They longed to embrace . . . and didn't dare touch. Their hearts were heavy . . . but they managed to smile.

The drumming of horses' hoofs, the shouts of young men excited by the prospect of adventure, the lowing of hundreds of longhorns serenaded their final minute. A knock on the door interrupted their silent communion, and they rose together to answer it.

Rio stood there, dressed for the trail, wearing chaps, a battered hat, and a sheepskin jacket to ward off the morning chill. "Morning, Miss Elke," he said, then cast a weather eye at the swirling blackness overhead. "Looks like we're in for a blow, Patrick."

"Are the boys mounted up?"

"Sure thing, and raring to go."

"I'll be with you in a minute," Patrick replied. He waited until Rio was out of sight, then took Elke in his arms.

Don't cry, she commanded herself. *Don't do anything that will make leaving harder on him.* She held him tight for just a minute, then leaned back, looked up, and filled her eyes to overflowing with the sight of him, making a special effort to memorize the beloved lines of his face, the solid feel of his body, the masculine scent that rose from his trail clothes.

"God speed, my love," she said.

"I shall think about you every minute we're apart," he replied, his eyes shining, his voice thick with emotion.

Without another word, he turned on his heels and hurried away.

She shut the door and ran to the front of the house, hoping for one last glimpse of him. By the time she got there, though, he had mounted up and spurred his horse away. Just before the moonless night swallowed him up, he turned and lifted his hat in a final salute.

And then he was gone into the darkness and the unknown dangers of the drive.

"I'll think about you every minute, too, my love," she murmured, choking on tears.

Her legs felt so weak that they barely supported her as she made her way to the nearest chair. She couldn't endure his departure, and yet endure it she must. The goodbyes she had already said—to her husband, her baby, even to the bakery—added their unwanted burden to this most recent farewell.

Her shoulders bowed under the weight of it. She lowered her head into her arms and simply sat while the long minutes of the first day of Patrick's journey ticked away. She felt completely empty, as if her innards had been scooped out—as if her very bones might collapse inward.

She had found the one thing she had been seeking since her parents died—a love so strong and bright that it could support and warm her through eternity—and she had to give it up. But right now, she didn't have the strength.

Had she been alone in the house, she would have screamed her sorrow to the rafters, torn her clothes, and pulled out her hair like a Comanche widow. Instead, she suffered in a silence punctuated only by the sound of the grandfather clock. Its chiming announced that what felt like eternity had been a mere fifteen minutes.

"I know, señora, I know everything."

Conchita's voice broke the quiet. Elke had been so lost in misery that she hadn't heard the woman arrive.

"My heart breaks for you and the señor," Conchita said.

In the days to come, Elke relearned the lesson she had learned in Velvet's bedroom so many months earlier. Breaking hearts continue to beat. Hers did. Conchita's did. And she prayed Patrick's did, too.

She filled her days with work, launching into a spring cleaning that left her tired enough to sleep at night. The house responded to her efforts by smelling sweeter, glowing more brightly. It was reward enough.

Charlotte seemed no more aware of Elke's turmoil than she was of Elke's hard work. She spent her days with Nigel. The piano Charlotte's father had sent from Natchez as a wedding present arrived too late for Patrick to enjoy. But Charlotte and Nigel took a full measure of pleasure from playing it together.

Charlotte, who claimed to have studied piano for years, pounded away, making up in noise what she lacked in talent. However, Elke recognized a true master's touch when Nigel took his place at the keyboard. He played the emotionally charged music that Elke's mother had favored, by composers such as Chopin, Liszt, and Mozart.

One afternoon Nigel caught Elke listening, and motioned for her to join him on the piano bench. "You seem to have a deep appreciation of music," he said.

She nodded. "It seems to say more about love and life than any words I've ever read."

"Does it remind you of one special love?" Nigel's gaze searched her eyes, probing them as if he could read what was written there as easily as a book.

She quickly averted her gaze from his invasion. Dear heaven, had he guessed the truth? And if he had, would he tell Charlotte?

Determined to steer the conversation onto safer ground, she answered, "It reminds me of my mother. She was a fine pianist—but not as good as you. You have a true gift, one my mother would have envied. She taught music; however, you could have been a concert pianist."

To her dismay, a look of ineffable sadness came over

Nigel's face. "But for being the Earl of Glenhaven, I suppose I could have been and done lots of things."

It was, Elke mused, a strange remark coming from a man who had already seen and done so much. She had never before thought wealth and position could be an impediment to happiness. "It's not too late. You're still young."

His fingers caressed the ivory keys without producing a sound. "It was too late the day I was born."

She laid a sympathetic hand on his arm. "What will you do when you return to England?"

"That, my dear Elke, remains to be seen."

With a crash of sound, he launched into a lively Mazurka that broke their brief intimacy as cleanly as if he had cut it with a knife. A moment later, Charlotte danced into the room, her flying feet keeping time with the music, laughter bubbling up her throat.

"If only you could play and dance with me at the same time," she exclaimed.

Nigel looked up at her and smiled. "There's an old saying that goes, 'Beware of what you wish for lest your wishes come true.' "

"La, sir. You know what I wish for, and I promise you, it will happen. Sooner or later, my dear Nigel, it will happen. You can wager your life on it."

The lonely hours of Patrick's absence rolled into weeks, the weeks became months, and Elke marked them all on the calendar of her heart. She longed for Patrick's safe return almost as much as she dreaded her own departure from Pride's Passion.

The primroses and blue bonnets of spring gave way to fields of summer daisies and colorful wildflowers called Indian blankets. Elke had planted a huge vegetable garden before Patrick left. She spent June preserving its bounty in a frenzy of activity, propelled by her need to ensure that Patrick would continue to eat well long after she had gone.

She brushed all his clothes and hung them out to air, polished all his boots, washed all his personal linens and put them away with a sachet of dried lemon verbena so they would still smell fresh and sweet when he finally wore them again.

She did everything a loving wife would do for an absent husband, while Charlotte and Nigel played through the increasingly longer days. Except for feeling relieved that she wasn't responsible for keeping Charlotte entertained, Elke paid no more attention to what they did than they did to her.

Velvet's visits were the one bright spot in Elke's existence. Velvet seemed to have an uncanny way of showing up on the very days when Elke's spirits were at their lowest ebb. Her visits were a welcome distraction, and she often brought news of the wider world beyond the Hill Country.

Shortly after Patrick left, Velvet had driven out to the ranch to report that the union army had attacked Fort Sumpter in Charleston's harbor. A few weeks later, she had shown up again to tell of the war's first battles. And so Elke wasn't surprised to see Velvet drive up early in July on yet another unexpected visit.

Elke rose from the flower beds she had been tending

in front of the porch, brushed her dirty hands on her apron, and waved a greeting.

"Thank God, you're all right," Velvet called out, bounding from the buggy as soon as it came to a stop. "My heart was in my throat all the way here, thinking I might be too late."

"Too late for what?" Elke asked, noting that Velvet's horse was so lathered that it seemed about to drop in its traces. It wasn't like Velvet to abuse an animal. "What's wrong? Have you heard something about Patrick?"

"It's not Patrick I'm worried about," Velvet said, taking Elke's hands and tugging her up the porch steps. "It's you. Where's Nigel?"

"He's in the parlor with Charlotte," Elke replied, planting her feet so firmly that the smaller Velvet couldn't budge her an inch. "If you have bad news, I'd better hear it before we tell Charlotte. You know how she panics over the least little thing. Is there more news of the war?"

"The war?" Velvet looked totally nonplussed. "Elke, I wouldn't half kill my horse to give you news like that. I came to warn you that the Detweilers are back. They've been seen in Llano."

"But I thought they headed east to join the southern army."

"I never believed that story. Those two bullies aren't brave enough to fight in a real war. I don't know where they've been these last months and I don't care. They rode into Llano a couple of days ago and started shooting off their big mouths about how you'd spread a lot of lies about them—how you tried to set the law on them when what happened to Otto was an accident—and how they were going to pay you back one of these days." The words poured from Velvet's mouth like water from a pitcher.

Elke's hands fisted. "Who told you?"

"One of my girls. She turned some fast money with a drummer who passed through Llano on his way to Fredericksburg, and he asked if she knew you. I had to warn you, and tell Nigel he had better start wearing those guns Patrick gave him."

"You'll do no such thing. I don't want Nigel involved in my business. And I'll not have Charlotte scared out of her wits, either."

"But Patrick asked Nigel to look out for you," Velvet wailed, her rising voice betraying her agitation. "Besides, how will you explain my being here?"

Elke had never turned a friend away from her door before, let alone one she loved as dearly as a sister, but she had to get rid of Velvet. "I'm not going to explain anything, because you're going to get right back in that buggy and keep your poor horse at a walk all the way back to town."

Velvet reeled back as if she'd been slapped. "You don't mean that."

"I'm sorry—but I do. I can't let you upset Charlotte. And she will be terrified if she hears what you just told me. You know how she dramatizes everything. She'll be imagining assassins lurking in every dark corner."

"Can't I even have a glass of water?"

Elke steeled herself against the entreaty in Velvet's voice and the shock and misery in Velvet's eyes. "No, you can't. If I let you in the house, Charlotte will see that something is wrong."

"I can't believe you're treating me like this." Velvet leaned closer, peering into Elke's eyes, her own blue orbs widening with sudden knowledge. "Oh my God, you're going to do something crazy, aren't you?"

"I've never felt saner in my life," Elke replied, keeping her tone as flat and free of emotion as she could. She gave Velvet a none too gentle push toward the porch steps. "I appreciate you're coming out here to warn me, but—"

"But what?" Velvet interrupted. "You're not fooling me one minute, Elke Sonnschein. God, I wish I could hog-tie you for your own safety. I wish to hell I hadn't hightailed it out here. I wish the Detweilers had disappeared off the face of the earth."

"Please don't be angry with me. I don't mean to run you off, but I really don't have any choice."

"It's Patrick, isn't it? You know he'll go after the Detweilers as soon as he gets back, so you're going to do it yourself."

Elke should have known she couldn't fool Velvet. They had been through too much and knew each other too well. "They're my business and no one else's."

"What in the world are you going to do? For the love of God, you aren't any match for the two of them."

"I don't know yet. But I want your promise that you won't do anything to stand in my way."

A cry of pure despair burst from Velvet's mouth. Her taffeta dress rustled as a shudder shook her from head to toe. "Try and stop you? I imagine I'd have to kill you to do that. If you really are going after them, do one thing for me."

"If I can."

"I want your promise that you won't give those bastards any more chance than they gave you and Otto. Wait until it's dark, shoot them in the back, and then ride hell-bent for leather back to my place. The girls and I will swear you spent whatever time you were away from Pride's Passion with us."

Elke couldn't help smiling at Velvet's fierceness. "Remind me never to get you mad at me," she said.

"When it's over, you come straight to me, you hear?" Worry made Velvet look far older than her thirty-six years. "I won't sleep a minute until I know you're all right."

"I can look after myself," Elke replied, taking Velvet by the hand and leading her to the buggy as if she had lost her sight.

"So you keep on telling me." Velvet shook her head from side to side. The look of disbelief on her face told Elke she couldn't believe what was happening.

Elke helped her up into the driver's seat. "I meant what I said about walking that horse, too."

For a moment, Velvet sat as still as a sculpture. She seemed to be fighting an internal battle. Perhaps she was measuring her determination against Elke's. When she took the reins in her hands, Elke knew it was Velvet's way of conceding defeat.

"I love you, Elke Sonnschein," Velvet said, her voice trembling with emotion, "and I'm very proud to be your friend."

Velvet brushed the tears from her eyes with the back of her hand, and without another word, urged her weary horse to a fast walk. She had almost disappeared from sight when Charlotte opened the front door and came out.

"Who was that?" Charlotte asked, lifting a dainty hand to shield her eyes against the midday sun.

"Just someone asking for directions to Llano."

"Do you know the way?"

"I'd better," Elke replied grimly.

Elke had never known an afternoon to pass so slowly. She was in a fever of impatience by the dinner hour. Nigel and Charlotte retired to the parlor after supper for yet another of their interminable card games. Pretending to read, Elke listened to the sibilant shuffle of the deck in their hands.

Yawning and commenting on the lateness of the hour, she excused herself at nine and went to her room, hoping they would soon follow suit. She lit the kerosene lamp and searched her dresser drawers for the map she had used when she rode the countryside urging people to vote against secession.

She found the worn parchment under her night clothes, took it out, and studied it carefully. With the exception of Fredericksburg—which she intended to ride around—there were few habitations and even fewer landmarks on the way to Llano.

She had never undertaken so long a journey on her own, and had never traveled at night before. But she didn't dare wait for morning for fear Nigel would attempt to prevent her departure.

Years ago on the trip from Indianola, she had traveled in the company of a few daring men, content to follow where they led. One of them, a former ship's captain, had taught her the rudiments of navigation.

The North Star would guide her through the dark, the sun by day. With any luck, she should reach her destination early tomorrow afternoon.

She retrieved her father's clothes from the armoire where she had put them when she came to Pride's Passion, keeping them close out of sentiment rather than storing them with her other household goods. A sense of déjà vu swept over her as she laid them out on the bed.

She had been fourteen and newly orphaned the first time she put them on. She had grown a couple of inches since then. The moleskin breeches he used to wear for hunting fit her better now, she realized as she pulled them on. His scent still clung to the garment. It comforted her as she tucked his linen shirt into the pants, then settled his loden cloth hunting jacket over her shoulders.

She pinned her hair up, hid it under his narrow-brimmed hat, and gazed at herself in the mirror. A tall, slender man stared back at her, a man with a fierce glint of determination in his eyes.

Satisfied with her transformation, she retrieved her father's shotgun from its hiding place under the bed. He had taught her to shoot, never even dreaming the use she would one day have for her hard-won skill with firearms.

She couldn't put a noble name on her impending confrontation with the Detweilers, nor hide from her murderous intent by calling her quest a mission or the payment on a debt of honor.

Only men masked their cruel deeds with such pretty

words. When men spoke of war, they spoke of glory in the same breath. Elke knew there would be no glory in killing. But Velvet had been right. Elke couldn't take the chance that Patrick would feel duty bound to confront the Detweilers. She loved him far too much to let him risk his life while her own existence seemed of little consequence. In any case, the best part of her would die the day she left Pride's Passion.

No, she thought, she didn't fear death. It was living without Patrick that terrified her.

If something happened to her, Patrick would grieve for a while. But one day he and Charlotte would have the children he longed for. He might not love Charlotte, just as she hadn't loved Otto. But loving the children he shared with Charlotte would fill his life.

Elke wanted that for him—wanted it with every fiber of her being. She wanted him safe, wanted him to grow old, wanted him to pass Pride's Passion onto as yet unborn generations that came from his seed. The only way she could guarantee his future was to go after the Detweilers herself.

She waited until the sounds of Charlotte and Nigel's bedtime preparations faded away, until the grandfather clock tolled the change of the calendar day. It was the Fourth of July, she realized as she stole down the back stairs with her father's shotgun weighing heavily on her arm.

The drive had gone even better than Patrick had hoped. He'd told Elke he would be gone for four months. Thanks to good weather, an easy trail, and a ready and waiting buyer, the months had been cut to three. Two more days and he'd be home.

Rising from his bedroll, he glanced at the sleeping forms clustered near the fire. Rio de Vargas, always the first to awaken, was squatting in front of it, fanning the embers into flame with his hat.

After making camp yesterday, Patrick had given half the hands permission to ride into Llano to spend some of their hard-earned money on whiskey and whores. Now, a quick body count told him one hadn't returned.

The last remnants of sleep fled Patrick's brain and he hurried to Rio's side. "Who is missing?" he asked.

"Terrell Meeks," Rio replied, adding a couple of mesquite branches to the flames. "The boys said he stayed on to have one more drink. He was celebrating dipping his wick for the first time. Do you want me to ride into town and fetch him?"

Barely sixteen, Terrell was the youngest hand to make the trip. It had been his first drive. Patrick could only hope it wouldn't turn out to be his last.

Although Llano was a county seat complete with a hotel, a mercantile store, and several saloons, it had a reputation as a lawless town—a reputation due in part to its lack of a single church. A green kid could get into all kinds of trouble in such a place. If Terrell hadn't begged so much—and if the other hands hadn't teased him mercilessly about his virginity—Patrick would never have let him go last night.

He'd thought it a kindness to send the boy off in the company of more experienced men. He prayed that his kindness wouldn't end in tragedy.

"Meeks is my responsibility," Patrick said gruffly. "I'll go after him. We'll catch up with you on the trail."

"Whatever trouble Meeks is in can wait while you have a cup of coffee," Rio said, a nod of his head indicating the blue enamel pot just coming to a boil. "Besides, he's probably just sleeping off a wingding of a drunk."

"I'll have coffee when I get to town," Patrick replied.

Although Rio was undoubtedly right, Patrick felt an inexplicable sense of urgency. He returned to his bedroll, bundled his blanket, and tied it behind the saddle he'd used for a pillow. Hefting its considerable weight, he headed for the remuda grazing nearby under the watch of a lone cowboy.

Each hand had brought a half a dozen horses on the drive. Every animal had been chosen for a particular ability. Broad-chested horses were considered best for fording rivers, calm ones were preferred for riding night herd, and nimble-footed mounts were required to cut a single cow from the herd.

This morning Patrick chose the swiftest steed in his personal string, an Appaloosa that would make quick work of the ten-mile ride to Llano. He saddled it with economical movements born of years of practice, then launched himself onto its back without putting a foot in the stirrup.

As if it sensed his anxiety, the gelding danced under him. The sun blazed on the eastern horizon like a blood orange. It seemed an ill omen as Patrick spurred the horse to a ground-covering gallop.

He'd give Terrell Meeks one hell of a talking to when he found him, he mused angrily as he rode west along the bank of the Llano River. If Terrell had been older, he'd be looking for a new job when Patrick finished with him. But he'd performed well on the drive. Given a little seasoning, he had the makings of a top hand.

The river burbled in its rocky bed and newly awakened birds added their sweet song to the cheerful sound. But a gloomy miasma seemed to cling to Patrick. It wasn't so much caused by worry over young Meeks as it was by the realization that he and Elke would soon part for the last time.

He'd run out of reasons to keep her on the ranch. At best, they would have a few hours together. The thought keened through his mind like the cry of a lonely coyote, keeping him uneasy company all the way to Llano.

The town had just begun stirring as he rode along its main street, his gaze moving from right to left in the hope that he would see Meeks propped against a building, sleeping his way through the worst of a hangover.

Patrick dismounted, looping the reins around a handy cross tie in front of a saloon, and pushed through its swinging doors.

A barkeep was sweeping last night's debris from the floor. "We're not open yet," he said.

"That's fine with me," Patrick replied. "I'm looking for a young cowhand. You can't miss him. He has hair the color of a carrot."

"A fellow like that was in here last night," the man said grudgingly. "He sure couldn't hold his liquor. I sent him on his way before he fell down."

"You wouldn't happen to know where he went?"

"Not far, I imagine. He could hardly walk. You might check the saloon a few doors down."

Patrick blinked as he stepped from the bar's gloomy interior into the bright sunlight. As he strode down the roughly planked walk to the next saloon, he had the strangest sensation of being watched.

To his relief, he found Terrell Meeks slumped over a table. With his gaping mouth and peach-fuzz beard, he looked more like a boy than a man.

"If you're his boss, I'd appreciate your getting him out of here before he pukes again," a man said from behind the bar.

Chapter Twenty-Five

Riding through the dark proved more problematic than Elke had imagined. Time and again, she was forced to skirt impenetrable thickets of cedar and mesquite, only to find herself heading in the wrong direction afterward. She spent so much time checking the North Star that to her weary eyes it appeared to pulsate like a firefly.

The terrain that had seemed to roll so gently in the daylight felt prohibitively mountainous when traversed in the ghostly glimmer of a sickle moon. She longed for the sense of security the sun would bring.

When a hint of pink on the eastern horizon presaged the dawn, she spurred her mount forward to make up for lost time. Half an hour later with the sun fully risen, she realized she had ridden several miles into a box canyon. Damn fool, she swore silently, making her way back out and setting a new course.

She had heard tales of Texas Rangers who covered fifty miles on horseback in five hours. Rio had boasted that Comanches could cover even more ground in the

same amount of time. She found herself wishing she
had a little of his Indian blood.

She had measured on the map, the sixty miles to
Llano as the crow flies. It was turning out to be more
like a hundred on horseback—and each one took its toll
in aches and pains. The sun burned into her skin and she
found herself longing for its setting almost as much as
she had longed for its rising.

Her kidneys hurt from the constant jolting. Her arms
felt so weary it was all she could do to cling to the
reins. And her buttocks were so sore that if she ever got
off her horse, she wasn't sure she'd be able to force herself into the saddle again.

There were no real roads to follow, only a few game
trails or rutted wagon tracks that didn't go where she
wanted. When the sun sank behind a hill and the waning
day began its inexorable journey into night, she finally
gave up.

Rather than blundering around in the dark, she made
camp under an oak tree, unsaddling her horse and letting it graze. Leaning back against the tree, she forced
herself to eat an unappetizing meal of the jerky and
johnnycake she had stowed in her saddle bags, washing
it down with water from her canteen.

The dark was alive with sounds—the ever-present vi-
brato buzzing of cicadas, the rustling of smaller animals
going about the business of eking out a living, the more
ominous sounds made by the larger animals who hunted
them. She had gathered brush for a fire, but when its
small circle of light made the surrounding blackness appear even more intimidating, she let it burn out.

The stars offered cold comfort. With her father's

loaded gun by her side, she waited for the dawn. Her brain was so awhirl with plans for the coming confrontation with the Detweilers—with so many maybes and what ifs—that she felt certain she wouldn't sleep a wink.

She couldn't outgun two armed men, and yet she felt loath to shoot them in the back as Velvet had suggested. She wanted the Detweiler twins to see death coming the way Otto had—and to know it was her who gave it to them.

She hadn't used a shotgun since she last hunted in Germany with her father, and then she'd only used it on birds. Could she hit both Detweilers with one blast? And how close would she have to get? The questions danced through her brain as her eyelids drooped shut.

When she opened them again, she was surprised to see that the sun had risen well over the horizon. A sense of urgency drove her to her feet and she saddled her horse without eating. She had no idea how long the Detweilers would linger in Llano. She had to get there before they left.

At midday she came across what she hoped was Willow Creek. Its name didn't matter, she told herself. The stream came from the north, the direction she needed to go. She followed it to its source in a spring at the foot of a limestone-strewn hill. Urging her wearying mount across the rocky skree, she hoped against hope to see Llano from its top.

Sweat had soaked through her father's shirt, and her horse's sides were lathered by the time she reached the summit. Her heart lurched, her empty stomach knotted as she saw the unbroken ranks of hills that lay ahead.

Her horse stumbled on the way down the north face and for a horrible moment, she thought the two of them would tumble down the hillside together. Fortunately the animal regained its footing with a lurch and she let it pick its own path.

And so the day went, from one rocky hill and one brush-filled valley to another until she gave up hope of recognizing any of the landmarks she had seen on her map. All she could do was head north.

After fording innumerable streams, she finally came to a long, narrow basin that drifted in the right direction. By the time it ended in another hill, the sun was setting again.

Exhausted, discouraged, hot and hungry, she settled in for the night. The hoot of an owl, the mournful lament of coyotes, the strange stirrings in the surrounding brush sang her into an uneasy sleep filled with dreams of death and destruction.

She awoke at dawn, ate the last of her rations, drank the last of her water, saddled her horse and set off up the hill. From the crest, she could see the long silver ribbon of the Llano River sparkling in the distance.

Patrick shook Terrell's shoulder. The smell of stale whiskey and puke rose from the boy's clothing. "Wake up, Son. It's time to get back to your job."

Getting no response other than a groan, he shook the boy again.

Terrell's red-rimmed eyes flew open and he blinked owlishly.

"Ooooh," he moaned. "Where am I?"

"You're in a saloon in Llano," Patrick replied, repressing an amused grin. The boy smelled bad and undoubtedly felt even worse. Any lecture Patrick might give him would pale in the face of what must be a monumental hangover.

"Oh my God." Terrell finally seemed to realize his boss was standing in front of him. "Oh my God, I surely didn't mean to stay away all night, Mr. Pride."

Terrell's complexion turned an unappealing shade of green. He clapped a hand to his mouth, lurched to his feet, and ran for the door.

"I'm sure glad he didn't puke in here again," the bartender commented over the sound of Terrell's retching. The man's round face and the laugh lines surrounding his eyes belied the sour expression that rode his features. "Not that I imagine he's got anything left to bring up. He puked his guts out in a spittoon last night. Fair turned my customers' stomachs, too."

Although Patrick doubted that much could turn the stomachs of men who patronized such a place, he took a Mexican peso from his pants pocket and put it on the bar. "For your trouble," he said. "My name's Patrick Pride. I own a spread down on the Guadalupe."

The bartender's attitude changed instantly. "Pleased to make your acquaintance, Mr. Pride. I've heard of your place." He bit the silver coin to satisfy himself of its value, then pocketed it. "The boy weren't all that much bother. He didn't act no worse than any kid on his first big drunk."

The sounds of retching had stopped and Patrick was beginning to wonder what was keeping young Meeks.

"Just the same, I'm grateful you let him sleep it off at one of your tables."

Patrick was about to head outside to check on the youth when the saloon doors burst open and Terrell came back inside—or rather was dragged back in by Eli and Jude Detweiler.

What the hell were they doing here—other than terrorizing Meeks? The last Patrick had heard, they'd ridden east to fight for the Confederacy.

The twins looked even more disreputable than they had the last time Patrick laid eyes on them. Their clothes were shabbier, and he saw a deeper meanness in their eyes, as if their talent for cruelty had matured in the time they had been away.

"Does this piece of shit belong to you, Patrick?" Eli asked, giving Meeks a shove that sent the youth flying across the floor to sprawl in a heap at Patrick's feet.

"He works for me, if that's what you mean."

"You must be hard up, hiring a boy who still dirties his drawers," Jude drawled, then laughed at his own misbegotten humor.

Patrick was forced to divide his attention between the twins and Meeks, who was struggling to his feet, his wounded manhood evident in his aggrieved expression as he fumbled at the holster he wore around his hips.

Patrick kicked Terrell's hand away before the Detweilers could respond to the implied challenge. Then he put his foot on Terrell's chest and pressed him to the floor. "You stay out of it, boy. This isn't your fight."

"But they—"

Patrick pressed even harder. "I said, shut up. You've already caused me enough trouble."

"Better watch it, kid. Your boss is one mean son of a bitch," Eli said, his smile revealing crooked teeth.

Jude nudged Eli in the ribs and gave him a conspiratorial wink. "Oh, hell, he ain't that mean. Why, I hear he's a real ladies' man. He married some pretty little thing from down Natchez way, and then had Elke Sonnschein move out to the ranch before the honeymoon was over." Jude licked his lips, then gave Patrick a lewd grin. "It don't seem right, a man like you plugging *two* women when there's good-looking boys like us with nary a one. We'd be happy to pay you iffen you was to hand that Sonnschein woman over to us. It's time she knew what real men are all about."

Patrick had been struggling to keep the hot ember of his fury from blossoming into flame. He hadn't wanted to fight the twins, not when Terrell's life might be forfeit, too.

He would never have chosen this time or place to fulfill the promise he'd made to Elke all those months ago. But hearing the Detweilers sully her name, it suddenly seemed as good a time and place as any.

"Real men?" He spat the question at them. "Not by a long shot. Your peckers have never been as big as your mouths. But if you're looking for a fight, I'll be happy to oblige."

Jude's eyes narrowed. His hand sneaked down to the holster at his hip. His index finger flickered like the tongue of a snake.

"Hold it right there," the bartender called out. "I don't much cotton to two men going up against one."

Patrick slid his gaze sideways to see a carbine in the bartender's hand. The peso had bought him an ally.

"I'm obliged for your help. These two chicken-shit bastards are back shooting cowards."

"If you want to take them on, I'll be happy to make sure it's a fair fight," the bartender replied, still pointing the carbine at the Detweilers as he came out from behind the bar.

Meeks struggled up from his prone position. "I ain't afeared of them, Mr. Pride. And I can shoot straighter than most. Give me a chance to make things up to you and I'll show you what I'm made of."

Patrick's gaze returned to the Detweilers. Realizing they might face two armed men rather than one, while a third ensured a fair fight, they didn't look half as defiant. But Patrick couldn't let Meeks risk his life.

"If you really want to help, head on back to camp and tell Rio I ran into the Detweilers."

Meeks got to his feet, the night's debauchery clearly visible on his pale face. "But sir, you wouldn't be in this fix if it weren't for me."

"I'm not in a fix. It will be a turkey shoot," Patrick replied. "Where's your horse?"

"Tied out back, sir."

"That's a hell of a place to leave a horse overnight. I thought you knew better," Patrick said, playing the stern patriarch for all he was worth. "Get your ass out of here and head back to camp. You've already disobeyed my orders once. If I catch you disobeying my orders again, I'll shoot you myself."

Meeks wavered, his burgeoning masculinity at odds with the obedience he'd learned at his mother's knee. Obedience won. He let go a strangled sound, turned beet red, then headed for the back door.

Relief flooded through Patrick. Meeks would survive the affront to his manhood. He might not have survived a shoot-out with the twins.

Patrick waited until he heard Meeks's horse heading up the alley, then turned his full attention to Jude and Eli. "We have business outside," he said in the same cheerful tone other men use when greeting friends.

The twins' confidence had returned with Meeks's departure. Smirking, they eyed Patrick. "That Elke Sonnschein must be hell in bed for you to be willing to take on the two of us."

Patrick's answering smile was utterly devoid of mirth. "The only hell you need concern yourself with is the one you're headed for this morning."

A glimmer of indecision flashed across Eli's face. He had always been the lesser of two evils, following where his brother led rather than instigating trouble himself. Seeing through the thin veneer of Eli's bravado, Patrick decided to shoot Jude first. With any luck, Eli would cut and run after Patrick had gunned Jude down.

Patrick's stride was relaxed as he headed for the door, but he couldn't help wishing he hadn't given Hawthorne his Colts. Their fast trigger action would have given him an edge. The older five-cylinder revolver he'd taken on the drive didn't compare.

As he stepped outside, he saw people beginning to edge out of the surrounding buildings to cluster near doors and windows. God knew how they got wind of an impending gunfight. Hawthorne, with his fanciful imagination, would undoubtedly attribute it to voodoo drums.

Nothing seemed to stir a bystander's blood like the prospect of someone else shedding theirs, Patrick thought sourly. Ignoring the spectators, he lit a cheroot as if he hadn't a care in the world, and strolled to the center of the street.

The bartender urged the Detweilers toward Patrick with a sharp motion of his carbine. An excited murmur ran through the crowd when they realized it would be two men against one. The bartender seemed to be enjoying his role as Patrick's second and would undoubtedly sell many a drink while retelling the story of the gunfight.

"Here's how we're going to do this," he announced authoritatively. "You two, Eli and Jude, are going to stand back to back with Mr. Pride. When I say so, walk ten paces, turn and fire. If either of you draws your gun sooner, I'll shoot you where you stand."

The twins ambled to the center of the street with a loose, hip-forward gait that was halfway to a shuffle. "This will be as easy as picking ticks off a dog," Jude said, bolstering Eli's courage.

A surge of adrenaline poured through Patrick's body. The morning sun warmed his face. The air smelled sweet and pure as he inhaled it in measured breaths. His blood seemed to sing through his veins. He had never felt more alive.

He sucked in one last mouthful of smoke, reveling in the tobacco's pungent flavor and thinking how a cheroot was the only thing in the world that tasted exactly the way it smelled. He dropped it to the ground, put it out with a twist of his boot, and turned his back on his opponents.

The Detweilers followed suit, the rank smell of their unwashed bodies filling his nostrils. A deeper scent, the primal aroma of fear, rose from them. He suspected they hadn't faced a determined man in a fair fight before.

He had never taken pleasure in ending a man's life, but he took a fierce satisfaction from the thought of ending theirs. It was the last thing—the only thing—he could do for Elke.

Her face flashed across his mind. He felt her presence as clearly as if she stood by his side. *This is for you, my love,* he thought, flexing his gun hand.

"Ready?" The bartender's question echoed through the still morning.

"Ready," Patrick replied firmly.

"Ready," the Detweilers called out in unison. Jude's voice didn't break, but Eli's cracked in the middle of the word.

"Get to it then," the bartender called out.

Patrick moved off, silently counting each long stride. His boots kicked up puffs of dust. The raucous cry of a crow sounded overhead. His senses were so alert that he clearly heard the indrawn breath of the assembled spectators.

When his count reached ten, he spun on his heels, taking up the duelist's classic stance—feet firmly planted, shoulders turned to present a smaller target. His eyes fixed on Jude, he drew his gun and centered it on the young Detweiler's chest.

He felt a rush of air by his head, saw a puff of smoke emerge from Eli's pistol, and realized that Eli had hurried his shot.

Patrick's gun hand never wavered as he squeezed the

trigger. He saw Jude stagger, then felt something thud into his chest, as though he'd been punched by an invisible opponent.

Elke spurred her mount as Llano's outbuildings came into view. Her horse carried her onto the main street at a gallop. A block away, she saw three men standing fifty or sixty feet apart, pistols in hand. Although she had never seen a gunfight before, she knew one was about to take place.

There was something disturbingly familiar about the silhouette of the lone man facing the other two, she realized as she rode closer. Dread coiled in her stomach like a serpent about to strike. It was Patrick. She didn't dare call to him for fear of spoiling his aim.

A single shot rang out.

Two others followed in swift succession.

Two men fell.

"Patrick," Elke wailed. Racing to his side, she reined her horse to a brutal stop, hurled her right leg over the saddle, grabbed the shotgun from its case, and hit the ground running as though she had practiced doing it a thousand times.

Patrick was sitting up, bracing himself with one hand, his gun wavering as he tried to point it at his remaining assailant. He was so intent on his enemies that he seemed unaware she was there.

She didn't attempt to assess his wound, let alone to cradle him in her arms although her body ached with the need to do so. She had to protect him now that he couldn't protect himself.

A burst of pure fury flared in her chest as she lifted her gun and gazed at the murderous bastards who had shot Patrick.

Good God, she thought, *it's the Detweilers!* Jude had fallen, and from the way he lay, she knew he was dead. But Eli stood there, a revolver still in his hand.

Eli gazed down at his brother, wondering what sort of joke Jude was playing on him. Jude had such a weird sense of humor that Eli wouldn't put it past him to play dead just to see what Eli would do.

But good old Jude couldn't be dead, not for real, Eli thought, nudging his fallen twin with the toe of his boot. Surely the small hole in his chest couldn't have killed him. It was high and to the left, and hardly bleeding.

"Get up, Brother," he said in a cracked voice he didn't recognize as his own. "Come on, Jude. You're scaring me."

Jude stared up at the sky with sightless eyes. His mouth hung open in an expression of surprise. He was even holding his breath. Damn, he sure was putting on a show.

"Put your gun down or I'll blow a hole right through you."

The cold command finally captured Eli's attention. It sure didn't sound like Patrick Pride's voice. Besides, Jude had hit Patrick and Eli had seen him fall. Just the same, Eli looked toward Patrick.

He sat where Jude had dropped him with a perfectly aimed shot, looking more dead than alive. A tall, skinny fellow stood over him, a shotgun in his hands.

The fellow sure did look familiar. Oh, shit, Eli thought as fear loosened his bowels. It weren't no fellow. It were Elke Sonnschein and the shotgun was aimed straight at Eli's middle.

Terrell Meeks raced the wind back to where the Pride bunch had camped the night before, only to find the camp empty, the ashes of the morning fire as cold as the dread clutching his heart.

He galloped after them in hot pursuit, ignoring the bile that bathed his throat and the murderous headache that pounded behind his eyes. If something happened to Mr. Pride, it would be his fault.

He'd never met a finer man, and hoped to be just like him someday. He'd taken to walking like Mr. Pride, to sitting in the saddle with the same easy posture, to copying his manner of speech. He'd done everything he could think of during the drive to impress Mr. Pride. How could he have let all that slip away for a few minutes' pleasure in some whore's bed? it sure wasn't worth Mr. Pride's life.

He caught up with the Pride bunch a couple of miles farther on and near fainted with relief. Seeing Rio riding point, Terrell galloped past the other hands, ignoring their ribald sallies about his sexual exploits as they caught sight of him.

"Where the hell have you been?" Rio barked as he reached Rio's side.

"You can chew a strip off me later," Terrell replied, not even caring about the quaver in his voice or the tears flooding his eyes. "Mr. Pride is in trouble. He said to tell you he ran into the Detweilers in Llano. I think they're aiming to kill him."

To Terrell's immense relief, Rio didn't waste time asking him the wheres and whyfores. The grizzled foreman simply wheeled his horse around, dug in his spurs, and set off toward Llano at a gallop.

The startled hands came riding up, wanting to know what had happened.

"I ain't got time to tell you," Terrell replied, spurring his own horse and racing after Rio's dwindling silhouette.

Elke stared down the shotgun's lethal barrel, her index finger taut on the trigger, the power of life and death sitting hard on her shoulders. What was it Patrick had told her the last time she held this very gun on the Detweilers?

It's one thing to shoot birds and quite another to shoot a man, he had warned. Yet here she was, ready, willing, and able to gun Eli down.

"For the love of God, don't kill me!" Eli called out.

Loathing for him crawled its hot fingers across her skin. Her grip on the gun tightened. She closed one eye to perfect her aim.

Eli fell to his knees. He dropped his gun and held out his hands, assuming the attitude of a postulant in a church. "I never meant to harm you and yours. I swear it," he sobbed.

She'd never seen naked fear on a man's face before. It twisted Eli's features into a mask she barely recognized. A stain spread across his crotch and she realized his bladder had let go. Someone in the crowd tittered.

"You killed my husband." The steel in her voice startled her almost as much as Eli's abject terror.

"It were an accident," Eli quavered. "Me and Jude here, we only meant to put a scare into you and your husband. Tell her, Jude."

Dear God, he doesn't even know his brother is dead. She expelled her pent-up breath.

Eli was a broken man. Killing him would serve no purpose. She lowered the gun, knowing Eli would never hurt anyone again.

"Good girl," Patrick said in a pain-filled voice.

Tears flooded her eyes. He sounded so weak. She dropped down and held him in her arms.

A young man burst from the crowd, a black bag in his hand. "I'm a doctor," he said, kneeling at Patrick's side.

Chapter Twenty-Six

Elke sat by Patrick's bed, her silent vigil rewarded every time she saw his chest rise and fall under the broad strip of gauze bandage. He had always seemed larger than life to her. It was almost incomprehensible that someone as negligible as Jude Detweiler could have come so close to killing him.

"Mr. Pride was lucky," Dr. Wharton had said yesterday after he operated on Patrick.

"Lucky?" she had answered with a bitter laugh.

"Yes, very lucky. God must have been watching over him. If the bullet had been just a fraction of an inch lower, he would have died. A rib deflected it so it missed vital organs and lodged in the fleshy juncture of Mr. Pride's arm and shoulder."

But the true luck, the only luck involved in the nightmarish chain of events, had been in having a doctor like Wharton—a man trained in the sterile techniques advocated by Pasteur—in Llano. Although grievously injured, Patrick's wound wasn't likely to be a mortal one.

Elke reached out and touched his face, wishing he

were well enough to take in her arms—to hold him close and hard. Leaning over, she drank in his soft exhalations. The odor of medicine mingled with his personal scent as his breath caressed her cheek.

She had wrongly imagined that she couldn't possibly love him more. But in those terrible minutes when she thought she was going to lose him forever, her love had opened wide like a rose coming into full flower.

In that instant, her mind had accepted what her heart had always known. She loved Patrick Pride more than her own life. Nothing else mattered—not Charlotte, and certainly not society's notions about right and wrong.

When Patrick recovered she intended to love him fully and completely—with her body as well as her heart and soul.

Her attention was focused on the still figure on the bed so intently that she didn't hear Dr. Wharton enter the room.

"You really must get some rest, Mrs. Pride," he said softly.

The doctor had mistakenly assumed her identity, and she hadn't bothered to correct him. Being taken for Patrick's wife gave her the sort of access to his bedside that a friend—or a housekeeper—would have been denied. She refused to even consider how she would explain her masquerade if Charlotte showed up in Llano after Rio told Charlotte that Patrick had been wounded in a gunfight.

Dr. Wharton rested a gentle hand on Elke's shoulder. "You've gone far too long without sleep. You won't do your husband any good if you make yourself sick."

"I just want to be here when he wakes up," she said, turning in the chair to gaze up at Patrick's savior.

Henry Wharton appeared to be in his mid-twenties. He had a narrow ascetic face and the long slender hands and fingers of a born surgeon. How strange that with all her sickroom experience, she'd been unable to watch him operate on Patrick.

After the shooting, Dr. Wharton had asked a couple of men to carry Patrick to his office. He performed the operation in a surprisingly well-equipped examining room. Elke's gorge had risen at the first cut of the scalpel. She had been so light-headed that she barely made it into the waiting room before she fainted.

She had no idea how long she'd been unconscious. She came to in Rio's arms. He was fanning her face with his hat and calling her name urgently.

Fifteen minutes later, Terrell Meeks joined them. Elke had paced the floor, her agitation overcoming the residual weakness in her legs, while Meeks told them how and why Patrick had run into the Detweilers. He had blamed himself for the gunfight that ensued.

Elke had listened to his confession with half an ear. Meek's grief and guilt seemed to exist in a world apart from the terror that held her in its rapacious grip. She left it to Rio to grant Meeks the absolution of the truth—to tell the distraught young man that the bad blood between Patrick and the Detweilers had nothing to do with him.

Every time Elke had heard movement inside the examining room, iron bands seemed to tighten around her heart until she could barely breathe. Her apprehension was so great that when the door to the examining room finally opened, her legs gave way. She had always thought of herself as a strong woman—physically and emotionally—but she would have fallen in a heap if Rio hadn't been there to hold her up.

Dr. Wharton's wife, Mildred, a rosy-cheeked nurse who worked with her husband, had come out to report that the operation had gone well, and that Patrick would surely survive. Remembering that moment now, Elke couldn't help smiling. She didn't know who had wept more—herself or young Meeks.

Dr. Wharton's voice brought her back to the present. "Your husband's system has undergone a serious shock and he lost a great deal of blood. He may not wake up for hours yet. And you, my dear, look dead on your feet."

"Would you like me to make a pallet here by your husband's bed?" Mildred asked from over her husband's shoulder.

Emotion constricted Elke's throat. The kindness of these two strangers had restored her flagging faith in humanity.

"Yes, I would like that—very much."

Mildred nodded. A smile illuminated her features, transforming her from a plain woman into one blessed with a soul-deep beauty. "I don't blame you. I wouldn't leave my Henry if he were hurt, either."

Mildred left the room while her husband checked Patrick's pulse and listened to his heart. She returned a minute later with a thick pile of blankets and pillows clutched in her arms. Dr. Wharton left the two of them to make up the pallet.

"My husband told me how you rode to your husband's defense. It's so romantic." Mildred sighed. "I can't help wondering how you knew he was going to need you."

Elke refused to destroy Mildred's romantic illusions. "I guess where Patrick's concerned, I have an instinct about things like that."

Mildred nodded, as if what Elke said made perfect sense. "I do, too. One look at Henry and I know just how he's feeling and what he needs. Of course, I wouldn't tell anyone else something like that. But seeing how much you love your husband, I know you understand."

She gave Elke a shy hug, bade her good night, tiptoed from the room, and shut the door quietly.

Although the comfort of the pallet beckoned Elke's weary body, she continued to stare down at Patrick. Despite the mature breadth of his shoulders and the dark body hair curling against the white edge of the bandage, he looked so young—even younger than when she'd first seen him all those years ago.

The decisive man of action had retreated deep inside his slumbering brain. His unguarded expression exposed the tender nature he concealed so well. It was his vulnerability that she loved best about him.

She bent down, touched her lips to his forehead, then sank onto the pallet and quickly fell into the first true sleep she'd had since Velvet arrived at the ranch with news of the Detweilers.

Nightmares chased Patrick through the long hours of his slumber. He relived the gun fight over and over, seeing it in gruesome slow motion, feeling the bullet enter his chest inch by agonizing inch and watching his life's blood stain his shirt.

In the small hours of the morning he woke to numbing pain that spread across his chest and arm. The drawn curtains and the kerosene lamp burning on the nightstand gave no hint of the time.

His memories of what happened after he'd been shot were shrouded in fog. Where was he and how long had he been here? Then a vision appeared before his mind, an image of a golden-tressed avenging angel who had ridden to his defense—and it all came flooding back.

Elke, he owed his life to Elke. God, when he thought how she had stood up to Eli, how she could have been gunned down, too. He wanted to see her, needed to touch her to reassure himself she was unharmed, as much as he needed the breath that sustained him.

He tried to sit up and groaned with the effort. "Elke, are you there?"

As if in answer to his prayers, she came into view, seeming to float up out of nowhere. She was wearing a man's shirt and trousers, and her hair spilled around her shoulders in disarray, but she had never looked more beautiful.

"Is that really you, or is this the best dream I've ever had?"

The tenderness in her eyes flowed over him like a benediction. "I thought you'd never wake up."

He tried to reach for her with his right hand, only to find it securely bound to his chest. Seeming to read his intention, she came around the bed and took his left hand in both of hers. Her life and strength flowed into him as if by merely joining fingers, they had become one body.

"How do you feel?" she asked.

"Like I've been run over by a cavalry charge. Where are we?"

"In the Whartons' spare bedroom. Doctor Wharton didn't want to move you until you were better. I hope you don't mind—but they think I'm your wife."

"Mind? You *are* my wife in every way that matters."

Her grip on his hand tightened. "In my heart, you're my husband."

"Are we safe here? Where are the Detweilers?"

"Jude is probably in hell—and Eli left town with his tail between his legs. I don't think he'll ever bother anyone again." Her lips trembled and a small sob burst from her mouth. "Oh, Patrick, why did you take the two of them on? You could have been killed."

"Because I knew *you* would if I didn't."

Despite the sheen of tears in her eyes, a tiny smile tugged at the corners of her mouth. "You were right. Velvet heard they were in Llano and rode out to the ranch to warn me. That's why I came here."

"My brave girl."

Weariness tugged at him. He fought to keep his eyes open, to focus on Elke's face. He wanted to tell her how much he loved her—and fell back asleep with the words on his lips.

Elke spent every hour, waking or sleeping, at Patrick's bedside. His recovery loomed so large in her mind that nothing else mattered—not her own exhaustion, not the lies that piled one on top the other, and certainly not her lack of proper clothing. She would gladly spend the rest of her life in her stained masculine garb if she could spend that life with Patrick.

Two days after the operation, he felt well enough to sit up. The next morning, he tottered to a chair by the window and insisted on feeding himself.

On the fourth day, Mildred came to the door saying they had a visitor.

"Please, show her in," Elke said, feeling as if the floor had just dropped out from under her feet.

No one knew where they were except Rio and Charlotte. Rio wouldn't leave the ranch. The visitor had to be Charlotte.

"It's not a her. It's a him," Mildred replied, a puzzled look in her eyes.

Elke barely had time to get her breathe before Terrell Meeks burst into the bedroom, clutching a bundle in his arms. He broke into a broad grin as he saw Patrick sitting in an easy chair.

"You look a lot better than you did the last time, sir."

"And you look a lot worse. I don't imagine you've gotten much sleep. How are things at the ranch?"

"Just fine as far as I know. I didn't have much time to hang around. Rio told your wife what happened and she sent you a letter. I rode straight back here with it."

Thinking Patrick might want a private moment, Elke headed for the door.

"Please don't leave," Patrick said, halting her with his soft request.

Meeks thrust the bundle at her. "Conchita sent you some clothes, Mrs. Sonnschein."

"Give her my thanks." Elke held the bundle against her chest as if to ward off the bad news she felt certain the letter contained. Surely Charlotte had written to announce her imminent arrival.

Meeks pulled a folded paper from his shirt pocket and handed it to Patrick. "This here's the letter, sir."

Elke returned to the chair opposite Patrick and watched with apprehension while he scanned its contents. His expression gave no hint as to what Charlotte had written.

"Do you want me to wait for a reply?" Meeks asked when Patrick finished.

"That won't be necessary, Son." He reached in his trouser pocket, took out a coin, and handed it to the youth. "Have a meal on me before you head back."

"That's mighty generous of you. I hope you won't be angry—but Rio let me keep my job."

"I'd have been angry if he let you go."

Meeks blushed. "If that's all, sir, I'll go get some lunch."

"Not in a saloon, I hope."

Meek's blush deepened. "No, sir. I reckon I've learned my lesson."

Patrick waited until Meeks had gone, then said, "He's green as grass right now, but he's going to be a fine man. I'd love to have a son like him."

"You will—someday."

Patrick shook his head. "Not unless you're his mother."

Elke couldn't think of a reply. Although she tried not to dwell on the impossibility of their situation, it had a way of intruding on their present happiness. "What did Charlotte have to say?"

"Read it yourself."

"Are you sure you want me to?"

"I have no secrets from you." He passed the paper over.

"Dear Patrick," Charlotte had written in a bold scrawl, "I was deeply distressed to hear of your injuries, however Rio assured me that you are in the best possible hands. You have a superb nurse in Elke, and, I have been told, a well-trained physician in Doctor Wharton. Under the circumstances, my presence in Llano would serve no purpose.

Everyone here is praying for your speedy recovery. Conchita has lit so many candles at the altar she set up in the kitchen that the house reeks of wax.

Knowing that I leave you to far better care than I could possibly provide, I remain affectionately, Charlotte Pride."

Elke read the letter twice in disbelief. It seemed so cold. No, she thought, not cold exactly. More like disinterested. She had never understood Charlotte—but she had liked her. Now, she almost hated her. How could Charlotte have written such a letter?

She finally looked up to see Patrick returning her gaze as if he expected some comment from her. But what could she possibly say? *Don't be upset? You know how Charlotte is.* Empty platitudes would never do.

"Are you upset with Charlotte?"

His answering smile was so genuine that it took her by surprise. "Of course not. I've been living in mortal fear that she would feel duty bound to come stay with me. I can just hear her complaining about the rigors of the journey, the lack of amenities when she got here. Frankly, I'd rather face the Detweilers again."

"Then you really don't mind?"

"Mind? When I left on the drive, I thought I could count the hours I had left with you on the fingers of one hand. Thanks to Charlotte and the Detweilers, we have weeks. I intend to make the best of them." His gaze caught hers. The timbre of his voice grew husky. "Before the gunfight—when I knew I might die—I didn't think of Charlotte. I thought of you, and all the things we'd never had a chance to say to each other. I thought about loving you, being with you, making love to you. I've been thinking about it a lot ever since."

A frisson of anticipation danced along Elke's nerve paths. "I've been thinking about the same thing."

"Does that mean you've changed your mind about being with me?"

"Yes, when you're able."

"Sunshine, I *am* able. That's not where I got shot." He stood, took her hand, and pulled her into his embrace. "I can't wait. I don't want to wait."

Elke nuzzled his neck. His touch had ignited a fire that spread from the pit of her stomach straight to her brain. "I don't, either."

He guided her toward the bed. "You'll have to do most of the work."

"I've always been a very hard worker."

He laughed. "I'll take care of the hard part. All you have to do is undress me."

She untied the robe he wore over his trousers, eased

it off his shoulders, and lightly caressed his bandaged chest. "How am I doing so far?"

"Perfectly."

She kissed him while her fingers worked his trouser fastenings. "You meant what you said about taking care of the hard part," she murmured throatily, taking his manhood in her hands and stroking its length.

Although she had never done it before—never even imagined doing such a thing—instinct brought her to her knees and she took him in her mouth, licking a glistening pearl from the tip of his shaft. He tasted of salt—and pure maleness.

A spasm ran through Patrick's body and he groaned deep in his chest, making a sound that conveyed both torment—and bliss.

"Am I doing it wrong?"

"No. You're doing it just right. But you'd better stop. I want you so much, I may not be able to hold off." He tugged his trousers down with his good hand, then stepped out of them. He wore nothing underneath except his own magnificent skin.

She had known he would be beautiful, but her imagination hadn't been equal to flesh-and-blood reality. He was a perfect male animal.

He'd lost weight on the drive and his muscles were clearly defined. His neck and chest were deeply tanned. His legs and lower abdomen were the color of ivory. The startling contrast seemed to accentuate the area at his groin. He was superbly ready for lovemaking as he took a few backward steps and sprawled across the bed.

In a fever to join him, she tore off her own clothes,

not caring that she popped buttons on her father's shirt. She threw the shirt to the floor and quickly sent the trousers to join it. She had washed her underthings that morning, and, like Patrick, wore nothing beneath her clothes.

He let his breath go in an audible gasp. "You're so beautiful. Stand there a moment and let me look at you."

Elke had always been slightly ashamed of her own body. Seeing approval and desire in Patrick's eyes, she forgot all her previous inhibitions. She raised her hands and unpinned her hair, letting it fall free around her shoulders. Then with audacious sensuality, she turned her back, bent over and retrieved her clothes, knowing full well what she revealed and what seeing it would do to him.

Her payment came in a harsh, utterly masculine groan. "Come here before I die from wanting you."

She tossed her clothes on a chair, and, teasing him with the sensual sway of her hips, returned to the bed. She had waited half her life to be with him—but she couldn't wait anymore.

She covered his face with kisses, starting at his brow and exploring every feature before arriving at his lips. He returned her passion, then heightened it with his probing tongue. The other kisses they had shared were chaste compared to the ones they gave each other now.

"This is torture," he moaned, his breath coming in harsh rasps.

"I meant it to be pleasure."

"It is. Dear God, it is. But my wound keeps me from doing the things I want."

"And what might they be?"

"I want to feel your breasts in my mouth."

She feigned indignation. "Both at once?"

"One at a time will do."

Her skin tingled with anticipation as she raised her body over him and offered a nipple to his mouth. He sucked gently at first, then with increasing passion until she thought he might suck out her soul, too.

"Now, the other one," he said, shifting his head on the pillow.

He paid equally lavish attention to it with tongue and teeth.

It was too much.

It wasn't enough.

She ached to know all of him, every last velvety inch. Easing the tender bud from his mouth, she straddled him.

Patrick had never felt more ready for the act of love. Heat pooled at his groin. His penis throbbed. Seeing Elke poised above him, he gave a tiny thrust that parted her labia.

She was so moist that he could have easily completed the entry in one long glide to paradise. But he had waited too long to hurry.

"Slowly," he said. "Go slowly. I want to feel and see all of you taking all of me, one inch at a time."

She poised like a hummingbird in midflight, her thighs trembling with the effort, and let him look his fill. Her breasts were wet, her nipples crested to sensual peaks. His gaze trailed down her torso to the deep indentation at her navel before traveling lower.

Her pubic hair was a darker blond than the hair on

her head. It glistened with her juices. Her labia gaped wide where he speared into her. The inner lips were swollen with passion and slick with desire. He kept his gaze on their joining as her body swallowed him up.

He had never known that love and desire could blend so smoothly that it was impossible to know where one began and the other ended. He had never realized that souls and bodies could join at the same time. He had never known passion like this, and knowing it now made the act new, as if it were his first time with a woman.

She withdrew her body just as slowly and he rotated his hips to increase their mutual pleasure. Her head was thrown back, her eyes closed. She gave herself up to their lovemaking with a totality that stole his breath away.

He took almost as much delight from what he saw as he did from what he felt. Her juices pearled on his penis. The musky scent of her sex filled his nostrils. He felt her interior muscles clutch at him, then spasm repeatedly as she cried out his name.

He responded to her with a final thrust, spilling his seed deep in her body in a geyser of pleasure that sent him flying to the brink of heaven—and then gently deposited him back in his bed.

He almost cried out when she pulled away, not from pain but from loss. He could have stayed inside her forever.

Chapter Twenty-Seven

Patrick sat on the edge of the examining table, looking on with curiosity while Dr. Wharton cut away the swath of bandage that circled his chest.

"How am I doing?" he asked as the last layer of gauze came away to reveal an angry scar embroidered with black stitches, surrounded by a mustard-colored bruise.

Wharton's fingers probed the edges of the injury. A satisfied grin illuminated his ascetic features. "Very well. You had a damn good doctor. The stitches can come out today."

"How soon can I travel?"

Wharton took Patrick's right arm in his hand and gently rotated it. Patrick grimaced as the injured muscles in his chest protested.

"Does it hurt?" Wharton asked.

"A little."

"I'm not surprised. I had to dissect the muscle to get at the bullet. Frankly, I'd like to keep your arm in a sling for a couple of weeks. Of course, if you have to get back to your ranch—"

Patrick shrugged, pretending nonchalance. He could hardly tell the doctor how much he wanted more time with a woman who wasn't his wife. "My foreman is a very capable man. Two more weeks, you say?"

"That should do it."

Wharton turned his back to retrieve the instruments he needed from a glass-fronted cabinet.

A profound feeling of relief spread through Patrick as he contemplated fourteen days of heaven before he faced the hades of telling Charlotte he wanted a divorce. What was that quotation? Hell hath no fury like a woman scorned.

"Elke and I can move into the hotel for the duration."

Wharton used a delicate scissors to snip a stitch, then tugged it free of Patrick's flesh. "Mildred would skin me alive if I let you do that. She loves having Elke around to talk with, to say nothing of the fact that your wife is a terrific cook."

"If you're sure it's not too much of an imposition, I know Elke would love to stay on."

"That's settled then."

A few minutes later, his right arm in a sling, Patrick joined Elke in their bedroom.

"How did it go?" she asked.

"Henry took out the stitches. He said I can go back to the ranch soon."

"How soon?"

"Two more weeks."

He expected her to be happy. Instead, she burst into

tears. "Oh, no," she said, burying her face in her hands as if he'd given her the worst news.

"I can ride sooner if you're that anxious to get back."

"I'm not anxious at all. The truth is, I don't ever want to leave here."

"I know it won't be easy to face Charlotte. But it has to be done."

"What do you mean, *face* her?"

"I intend to ask her for a divorce." He reached for Elke with his good arm, but she evaded his grasp.

"If you touch me, I'll never be able to say this—and it has to be said. I'm going to pack and leave as soon as we get back."

Patrick felt as if he'd been sucker-punched. "But I thought—"

"I know what you thought, my darling, because I've thought the same things. But I can't stay on and have you come creeping into my room when Charlotte's sleeping. And we both know that's what will happen. Loving you, having you love me these last two weeks— they've been the most beautiful weeks of my life. This time has belonged to us. Your future life belongs to your wife."

He had expected her to say as much, and had carefully marshalled his arguments in advance. "We have to tell Charlotte the truth. She's much too proud to be married to a man who loves someone else."

Elke knuckled the tears from her eyes like an angry child. "You can't send her back to Natchez in disgrace. No man will want her after you've discarded her. And we both know she can't live without a man. Her life will be ruined."

"What about my life—and yours? Don't we deserve to be happy? If you don't want to stay at Pride's Passion we can go somewhere else and make a new start."

"Do you really think I could live with myself if I let you do that? I know how much the ranch means to you. The land is in your blood."

"You're in my blood. The ranch won't mean a damn thing if I can't share it with you."

"But you will share it with your children someday. It's what you've always wanted. It's your dream."

"Damn it, Elke, why do you have to be so stubborn. I'm not saying it will be easy to face Charlotte. But the way I see it, we don't have a choice. You can't walk out on me now, not after everything we've been through, Don't you know how much you mean to me? You're my dream even more than the land." Patrick would have fallen on his knees if he thought it would have helped. He was fighting for his life, and not doing a very good job. "Don't do this to us."

"There is no 'us,' my love. There never has been. We mustn't spoil the few days we have left."

Patrick didn't even try to hide his tears. With a hoarse cry, he reached for her again. This time, she came into his empty arms.

Charlotte watched her bath bubbles burst into nothingness, not caring that staying in the tub so long would prune her delicate skin. How she looked seemed of little importance.

Certainly Nigel didn't care how many hours she spent on her appearance for his benefit. He'd been increasngly distant since the news of Patrick's wounding in a gunfight reached Pride's Passion. Since that fateful day, Nigel had gone to great lengths to avoid being alone in a room with her. And the few times he was, he talked about Patrick's bravery and honor.

The bursting bubbles reminded Charlotte of her shattered hopes and dreams. She had run out of time—had used up all her chances. For once her scheming had failed to bear fruit. With Patrick returning to the ranch in a few more days, she had given up hope of luring Nigel into her bed.

A sour look rode her delicate features as she rose from the zinc tub like Venus rising from the waves. Her yearning for Nigel had increased in direct proportion to the distance he maintained between them. The long, cold baths she took every morning barely cooled the desire that pooled in her loins like molten metal whenever she saw him.

For the first time, fate had denied her something she wanted, and she didn't know how to cope. Sometimes when she watched Nigel at the piano, looking so preoccupied with his music that he didn't seem to know she was in the same room, she almost screamed out of sheer frustration.

Now, as she stepped from the tub, she unconsciously tamped one of her bare feet. It didn't relieve the tension coiled deep in her belly. She knew Nigel loved her. But he had told her he planned to leave her as soon as Patrick returned.

She stamped her foot again. Then, out of the corner of her eye, she saw something white and repulsive scuttle across the floor.

Charlotte didn't have time to think. She just reacted. A blood-curdling scream burst from her mouth as, mother naked, she leapt for the top of the toilet.

Nigel was in the library, composing a letter to a cousin advising that he would return to London by late autumn, when he heard a sound that lifted the hair on the back of his neck. It was a woman's scream.

Dear Lord, it was Charlotte's scream. She sounded in *extremis,* as if death or torture were imminent.

He bolted to his feet, heedless of the inkwell that tumbled to its side, spreading a black stain across the walnut desk. Charlotte needed him.

He'd worn the matched Colts holstered against his hips since hearing about the gunfight in Llano. They bounced on his thighs as he took the stairs two at a time, not knowing what he would face on the second story. Not caring, either. He'd happily take on a band of marauding Comanches to save Charlotte from harm.

She screamed again and he realized the sound came from the water closet. Lately, she had developed a passion for bathing.

"I'm coming," he called out, pulling the lethal Colts from their leather nests.

Thank heavens she hadn't locked the door. He shoved it open and burst into the room, guns in hand as he sought her assailant.

The room was empty. Charlotte perched on top of the toilet, naked but for the water dripping from her skin. And what magnificent skin—white and glistening with a thousand tiny droplets that caught the light like diamonds.

She made no effort to hide her feminine charms from

his hungry gaze. "Oh, Nigel," she cried out, "I've never been so terrified in my life. I just got out of the tub when a scorpion practically ran over my feet."

Her teeth chattered with fright.

His jaws clenched with barely repressed desire.

"Let me see if I can find it," he said, holstering the guns and oh so reluctantly tearing his gaze from the goddess on the toilet.

A cursory glance around the room failed to uncover the scorpion. "It appears to be gone now. I guess it was as afraid of you as you were of it."

Charlotte shook her head vigorously. Her breasts bobbled enticingly. "I suppose you think I made it up to get you in here."

"I'm sure you saw something that frightened you. But it's perfectly safe to get down now." To his horror, the words came out in a strangled croak.

"Not on your life. I'll just stay put, thank you very much."

A lesser woman might have made an attempt to cover her breasts or her lower parts from his predatory gaze. Not Charlotte. She just stood there, looking more beautiful and desirable by the minute.

"Do you want me to carry you to your room?"

"I thought you'd never ask."

She extended her arms and practically jumped into his. He hadn't had a chance to brace himself, and the two of them tumbled to the floor with her on top.

Nigel felt the hard points of Charlotte's breast through the thin line of his shirt.

Charlotte felt his rigid manhood throbbing against her stomach.

Nigel forgot all about honor.
Charlotte forgot all about the scorpions.
They concentrated on each other.

Elke stowed the last of her belongings in the saddle bags. Her legs felt leaden as she put a foot in the stirrup and swung up onto the horse.

"You must be so happy to be going home at last," Mildred said, "but Henry and I are going to miss you."

"I'm going to miss you, too," Elke replied. The Whartons had been the soul of kindness to her and Patrick. She had hated lying to Mildred, and now saying goodbye. All those lies threatened to obscure the happiness she had experienced under this sweet woman's roof.

"Come on, ladies, it's nothing to cry about," Henry Wharton said cheerfully. "It's not as if you won't see each other from time to time. The ranch is only sixty miles away, right, Patrick?"

"Right," Patrick replied, his smile so rigid that it seemed carved in stone.

"You've been good advertising for my practice," Wharton said, reaching up to shake Patrick's hand. "There's nothing like having a patient survive an operation to bring new ones flocking to a doctor's door. Take it easy on the way home. I wouldn't want you to get hurt and ruin my reputation."

"Ooh, I hate goodbyes," Mildred exclaimed. "I'm just going to go inside the house and clean up the breakfast dishes."

She fled with a whirl of her skirts, leaving Elke bereft. She had become genuinely fond of Mildred Wharton. If only they really were going to see each other again.

With a final wave, Henry Wharton followed his wife.

"Ready?" Patrick asked.

I'll never be ready, Elke thought, as in reply, she spurred her horse.

They rode back to the ranch in a silence pregnant with all the things they would never say to each other again—all the words of love and tenderness, all the soft sighs of pleasure.

The return trip proved far easier than Elke's journey in the opposite direction. She followed where Patrick led while her thoughts lingered on the precious days they had spent in Llano.

How she had loved waking up next to Patrick, seeing the joy in his sleepy eyes as she nestled by his side. Living as his wife, sharing their happiness with the Whartons—she had no words to describe how much it had meant to her. But Patrick had given her something far more important than a handful of sweet memories that were doomed to fade over the years.

The sun had yet to set on the long July day as they rode onto Pride land. When the roof of the house came into view, Patrick reined his horse to a stop and turned to Elke.

"Is there anything I can say or do to make you change your mind?" he asked, his voice so thick with emotion that Elke could barely make out the words.

"We've said and done it all. You've given me the

happiest days of my life. You gave me a part of yourself that I will take with me wherever I go."

He guided his horse up to hers and kissed her, closing the distance between them one last time.

Elke almost broke at the gentleness of his embrace— and the despair she saw in his eyes when he finally let her go.

Spurring his mount to a gallop, he opened the chasm between them for the last time. She watched him race away, thinking what a fine figure he cut on horseback, and how much he belonged to this land.

And then, she found the courage to race after him.

The hands were assembled on the bunkhouse porch as Patrick rode up. Although he felt as if he had aged a lifetime since leaving Llano, he did his best to return their cheerful shouts of greeting.

Rio emerged from the throng and walked over to Patrick. "It's high time you got back, old hoss."

"You know how cautious doctors are. Wharton didn't want me to ride with my arm in a sling." Patrick managed a grin. "Besides, I thought it was high time you earned your keep."

"Well, I'm glad you had yourself a rest. We're in for a rough go in the coming months. The union has blockaded the Texas coast. Thank God, we got the cattle out in time."

"Thank God for that," Patrick echoed. It was the only thing he imagined himself thanking God for in the foreseeable future. Life with Charlotte loomed ahead as bleakly as a dried-up water hole.

"You can fill me in on the ranch first thing in the morning. I'd better get up to the house."

Elke had been keeping herself apart while the hands greeted Patrick. She rode up to his side now, her face as white and drawn as it had been that day in Velvet's parlor. Knowing her pain equalled his only added to the misery of this homecoming.

He had written a letter telling Charlotte when he would be back. Considering her superb timing, and her penchant for melodrama, he half expected her to rush out and throw herself in his arms.

For once, though, her uncanny sense of timing had failed. He walked up the steps with Elke by his side, and opened the front door. Luggage crowded the entry hall—trunks, valises, gun cases, and even hat boxes.

Apparently Nigel couldn't wait to get away. Had Charlotte smothered him with her need for attention?

He called out to Charlotte that he was home.

The house felt strangely empty, as if the owner of the luggage had already decamped. Patrick looked over at Elke. Her lifted brows told him she was puzzled, too.

"Charlotte, where are you?" he called out again.

"I'll be right down" came a faint reply.

A moment later Charlotte appeared at the top of the stairs, dressed in the extravagant traveling suit she'd worn when they set out on their honeymoon. Nigel was at her side and he, too, had dressed for a journey.

Patrick's stomach muscles tightened involuntarily. Clearly something had happened during his long absence. But what?

"It's good to see you again," Charlotte said, joining

Patrick and giving him her hand as if they were nothing more than polite strangers.

What was she up to now? Did he even care?

"It's good to see you, too." He turned his attention to Nigel. "I must say, you're certainly getting around well. And I see you're going to be leaving us soon."

"Not soon, old chap. Straight away. The minute our business is concluded. I hope you'll be good enough to let us use the buggy."

What business? The mystery deepened. "You said *us*. Is someone going with you?"

Nigel cleared his throat. "I have spent the last four weeks trying to think of a good way to break the news. But there isn't any good way. I'm afraid you're in for a bit of a shock, old chap. Charlotte is going with me."

Patrick stared at his wife, trying to sort things out. "I know you miss your parents," he said to Charlotte, "however this isn't the time for a visit. The union has blockaded the entire coast."

"It *is* rather poor timing, but time and tide wait for no man." Nigel's comment merely added to Patrick's confusion.

"You poor man, you really don't understand, do you?" Charlotte gave Patrick a look of sympathy.

"Perhaps you'd care to make things clearer."

Nigel stepped forward, as if to shield Charlotte from Patrick. "I was hoping you'd figure it out for yourself when you saw our luggage."

So *that's* who the other pieces belonged to, Patrick thought. He should have recognized Charlotte's trunks and hat boxes. That he didn't was testimony to how little attention he had paid to her from the very beginning.

"Are you saying you have offered my wife your protection on her journey to Natchez?"

Nigel shook his head like a teacher with a particularly dim-witted student. "I'm trying to tell you that Charlotte and I are running off together. She's leaving you, man. I can't put it any plainer than that."

In her determination not to interfere with Patrick's homecoming, Elke had been standing to the side. The fact that no one had acknowledged her presence would have hurt under other circumstances. Hearing Nigel's words, she moved closer to Patrick to offer whatever support he needed.

From the almost joyful expression on his face, however, he didn't need any. "Would you mind repeating that?" he asked.

Nigel squared his shoulders and looked Patrick straight in the eye. "I said I'm running off with your wife."

Chapter Twenty-Eight

Patrick's guffaw thundered through the entry hall as explosively as rifle fire. *He's lost his mind,* Elke thought, putting a restraining hand on his arm. *Don't let him do anything he'll regret,* she prayed silently.

Between bursts of laughter, Patrick gasped, "Why the hell didn't you leave before I got back?"

Nigel drew himself up and squared his shoulders. To Elke's bemused eyes, he looked like a bantam rooster spoiling for a fight.

"It's one thing to fall in love with another man's wife—and quite another to steal her away in the middle of the night. I wanted to tell you man to man, and offer you whatever satisfaction your honor demands."

Patrick finally controlled his unseemly laughter. "Satisfaction? Do you mean a duel?"

"Exactly. Of course, as the injured party, the choice of weapons is yours."

"You have already given me more satisfaction than you can possibly know. Besides, I've been shot once this year. I don't have a hankering to risk it again."

"I take your point," Nigel replied, his poise and equanimity returning. The piercing gaze he had turned on Elke when they sat side by side at the piano searched Patrick's face now. "You're in love with Elke, aren't you?" he asked.

Before Patrick could reply, Charlotte stepped from his protective shadow and stamped her feet like a fretful child. "Why, I never! Don't tell me the two of you have been carrying on behind my back."

Nigel caught the hand she had raised to slap Patrick. "I love a fiery woman, don't you?" Not waiting for an answer, he turned to Charlotte and fixed his piercing gaze on her. "Don't pretend to be hurt, my beauty. I realize it's a shock to learn that Patrick wants someone else—and frankly, I can't help questioning his sanity. But if you give it a moment's thought, you'll see it's all for the best."

Charlotte's ferocity faded as quickly as heat lightning. She melted against Nigel's body like a kitten seeking its master's warmth—a very sensual kitten. "I do believe you're right," she said, bursting out in laughter. "Now that I think about the way things have turned out—you and me, Patrick and Elke—it's just too delicious."

Elke would hardly have chosen that word to describe their situation. It was shameless, scandalous. "The three of you have lost your minds."

"Ah, yes, but we've found our hearts," Nigel replied with a twinkle in his pale-blue eyes. "You love Patrick, don't you?"

"That's not the issue. What I feel isn't important. Think of the disgrace. You'll never again be able to hold up your head in polite society if you leave with Charlotte."

"My dear Elke, in view of the sheltered life you've led, you're hardly the best judge of what happens in society—and by that, I most certainly don't mean your Hill Country friends. There's nothing my countrymen love more than a scandal, especially when a title, a fortune, and a beautiful woman are involved. Charlotte will be the toast of London. I plan to petition the House of Lords for a bill of divorcement on her behalf. Considering my connections, I have no doubt it will be granted.

"Or I could divorce her here on grounds of desertion," Patrick chimed in helpfully, the corners of his mouth twitching as he fought not to laugh again. For a husband whose wife had just announced her intention to leave him for another man, Patrick looked bodaciously happy.

"You are mad," Elke declared.

"But it is the sweetest sort of madness," Charlotte replied in her most languorous drawl.

Velvet Gilhooley ignored the heat, the insects buzzing around her perfumed hair, the exhaustion that came from having spent a sleepless night. She was a woman with a mission, and minor discomforts couldn't deter her from its completion. One way or another, she intended to settle her future before the sun set.

Her horse knew the way to the Pride ranch so well that she barely needed to give it any guidance. Her mind was free to return to the previous evening, and the decision she had reached.

Recruits going off to war had thronged the house, using her girls up at a ferocious rate and begging Velvet for her favors as well.

Instead of putting them off with her normal good humor, she had been outraged at their presumption. Sometime during the course of the long night, she had realized she didn't want to be treated like a whore anymore.

Perhaps she didn't deserve to be treated like a lady, either, but there had to be some middle ground she could occupy.

She reined her buggy to a stop in front of the Pride bunkhouse, jumping from the seat so hastily that she almost fell, then marched up to the door and knocked.

"Is Rio de Vargas there?" she asked the half-dressed cowboy who answered her summons.

He stared at her as if she were an apparition rather than the madam whose house he visited every time he got paid. His mouth gaped open.

She reached up and closed it for him. "Please tell Rio I'm here to see him."

The cowboy left the door ajar as he went to fetch Rio, giving her a glimpse of men in various states of deshabille. He wouldn't have done that to another woman, she fretted. But she refused to let his boorishness deter her—not today. She'd seen plenty of unclothed men before, and she had more important things on her mind.

"What are you doing here, Velvet?" Rio asked, appearing from around the door. "Is something wrong?"

"You're damn right something's wrong," she said.

Rio stepped outside and closed the door on the curious men inside. He wasn't wearing anything except for trousers over his long underwear. A growth of beard shadowed his cheeks. He smelled of sweat—both human and horse—but it didn't offend her.

This is the real Rio, she realized. *And he's about to meet the real me.*

"If you'll just give me a minute to dress . . ." His voice trailed off. He gazed down at his stocking feet as if the way he looked was something to be ashamed of.

"There's no need. I came to tell you something, and having you all gussied up won't make it any easier. It's time we had things out."

Suddenly, he looked as if the cares of the world had descended on him. "You don't have to say another word. I've been expecting this."

"You're not getting off so easy, Rio de Vargas. I do have to say it. I know you have trouble speaking your mind. But I've never had trouble speaking mine—at least not until I met you." Velvet took a deep, invigorating breath. Nothing ventured, nothing gained, she told herself. "In case you haven't noticed, I'm in love with you."

His crestfallen expression began to change. "You —you. I—I—I," he stuttered.

"You what?"

"I didn't know. I figured, you being so independent and so well set up in life—" His voice grew fainter and fainter and finally gave out all together.

Obviously, he wasn't going to be any help, she thought, gazing at him fondly. Her Rio wasn't ever going to be good with words. "I came to ask you to marry me."

"You *what?*"

"I said I want to marry you. A couple of the girls have made an offer on the business and I—"

The rest of her carefully planned proposal was cut short as he grabbed her and held her so tight that she couldn't breathe, let alone speak.

Elke felt as if her world had turned upside down. She looked at Charlotte, seeing her as if for the first time. A woman of enormous determination, one who had the strength and courage to grasp what she wanted, had been hidden beneath Charlotte's southern belle exterior.

"Don't you see, Elke?" Charlotte said, "life has given the four of us a second chance. I for one intend to take it. Nigel and I are going to leave Pride's Passion to-night. Nothing you say or do can stop me. Won't you wish us well?"

The frozen knot of pain inside Elke slowly dissolved. Her parents had taught her to believe in happy endings, but she had long ago concluded they were only found in books.

For the first time, she dared to envision a happy ending for them all. "Of course I wish you well. You just took me by surprise."

"And you, Patrick?" Charlotte said, looking up at him. "Will you wish us well, too?"

"If you're asking for my blessings, you have them." His voice was tinged with unctuousness.

Conchita chose that inauspicious moment to appear at the far end of the hall. "I heard shouting. Is everything all right, Señor Patrick?"

"More than all right," Patrick replied. "Everything is absolutely wonderful."

Conchita made the sign of the cross against her breast. *"Dios mío,* I was afraid you and Señor Nigel were going to shoot each other before this night was over." Without another word, she vanished through a door as suddenly as she had appeared.

"About that buggy," Patrick turned to Nigel, "I'll harness the horse myself. You can leave it at the livery stable when you get to town."

"Let me help," Nigel replied. "I must say, you are a truly remarkable man."

He headed for the front door, hardly even using the cane in his right hand, with Patrick at his heels.

"Are you sure this is what you want?" Elke asked Charlotte as soon as they were alone, "because if you change your mind—"

Charlotte didn't let her finish. She closed the distance between them and gave Elke a hug of surprising strength. "It's what I want. It's everything I want. The only thing that bothered me about leaving was the thought of Patrick alone in this house. I never loved him—but I am fond of him. I want him to be happy and he will be with you. I should have seen it long ago. I guess I was too busy looking at Nigel to see anything else."

She let Elke go, opened her reticule and produced a small silver-backed mirror. "Do I look all right?"

"You never looked better," Elke replied, recalling the unhappy bride and the sick woman. This Charlotte was a radiant creature, a woman transfigured by love.

"Nigel and I are going to have the most wonderful

life. I can hardly wait to get started on it. We're going to visit Windmere so that my parents have a chance to know him the way I do—of course I know they'll love him, too—and then we're taking a clipper ship to England." Her small feet danced with impatience. "It's so exciting. Running the blockade will be such an adventure. And then there's London, and Nigel's crowd to meet, and seeing Glenhaven Hall. I'm going to have the life I've always wanted."

I am, too, Elke thought, feeling the wonder of it tingling through her blood.

The next half hour passed in a blur as Patrick and Nigel brought the buggy to the front of the house and loaded it so heavily that Elke couldn't help pitying the poor horse.

Never were goodbyes so happily said; never were two couples so eager to be alone. With a clatter of hooves and a final wave, Nigel and Charlotte headed down the drive into the gathering night, to the sound of Charlotte's joyous laughter.

A sweet silence descended on Patrick and Elke as, hand in hand, they made their way up the porch steps. Before they reached the top, they heard a buggy coming up the drive.

"Oh, God," Elke groaned, giving voice to their joint concern, "don't tell me they've changed their minds already."

In unison with Patrick, she turned to face the driveway. It was a different buggy, she realized, and different occupants. Velvet and Rio sat side by side on the front seat.

"Are you two all right?" Velvet asked anxiously as Rio helped her down.

"We're just fine," Patrick answered.

"But I thought I saw Charlotte leaving with Nigel," Velvet said.

Patrick grinned. "That's why we're all right. Look, it's a long story and we've had a long day. Why don't you spend the night. We'll tell you all about it in the morning."

"That's mighty kind of you, Patrick," Rio replied, "but Velvet and I are going to town tonight."

Elke shook her head as if to clear her ears. "It's a long drive. It will be midnight before you get there. Can't your business wait?"

She hadn't noticed how happy Velvet looked until the woman spoke up. "We planned to dawdle a little on the way, if you get my drift." She gave Elke a conspiratorial wink. "Besides, we're going to see a minister first thing in the morning. Rio and I are going to get married. I don't intend to give him a chance to change his mind."

"Congratulations," Patrick and Elke said together.

"I'm glad you feel that way, Patrick," Rio replied, his words flowing as smoothly as any Elke had ever heard him utter. "I plan on keeping my job if it's all right, and I was hoping you'd agree to my building a house for me and Velvet, here on the ranch."

Patrick gave Rio such a mighty thump on the back that the smaller man almost tumbled down the steps. "Agree, hell. Nothing could please me more. Just pick the site and I'll give you the land as a wedding present."

Patrick pumped Rio's hand while Elke, her heart overflowing with happiness, hugged Velvet. "It's going to be so wonderful to have you here," she whispered in Velvet's ear. "I haven't told Patrick yet, but I'm going to need a woman around."

Seeing Velvet's mouth starting to open, Elke whispered, "Now don't you say a word. Just get on to town and get married the way you planned. We have the rest of our lives to talk."

The second set of goodbyes were even more joyous than the first had been. Patrick and Elke stood side by side as yet another buggy disappeared from sight. Then, to her surprise, he picked her up in his arms.

"What do you think you're doing? You'll hurt your arm," she said, feeling a little foolish as he carried her up the steps.

"A man is supposed to carry his bride over the threshold."

"But I'm not your bride."

"Maybe not on paper, but you are in every other way." He nudged the door aside. "Welcome to Pride's Passion."

He gave Elke a gentle kiss before setting her down on her feet.

She gazed around while the realization that the man and the house were both hers made its way from her brain to her heart. "Do you have any idea how much I love you?"

"If it's half as much as I love you, it will last a couple of lifetimes at the very least," he said.

She sighed. "I never thought it would end like this."

"Neither did I."

"Charlotte is so brave, so honest about her emotions."

Patrick grinned wryly. "She's that—and a hell of a lot of other things."

Elke ignored his sarcasm. "I wish I was more like her. If I were, none of this would have happened."

"I don't understand."

"I used to think that committing adultery with you would be the ultimate sin. Now I know not being true to myself can be even worse. If only I'd had the courage to admit I loved you years ago—if I had listened to my heart instead of the laws others people lived by—Otto wouldn't have died, and I wouldn't have lost my first child."

Patrick tried to concentrate on what she was saying, but his heart kept on doing funny little leaps in his chest, and his feet felt like skipping the way they did when he was a boy. Two words finally managed to penetrate his euphoria.

"What's that you said about your first child? Does that mean you're planning a second one any time soon?"

"Very soon," she said, filling his very soul with the sweetness of her smile.

He took her arms and tugged her toward the stairs. "If you'd like to get to work on it right now, I'm not too tired to oblige."

Elke's already ravishing smile deepened. "We *are* working on it, with considerable success, I might add."

He felt himself go cold, then warm as a new heat scorched through his veins. "Does that mean what I think?"

"Yes, my love. We're going to have a baby."

"How soon? How long have you known?"

"I've known since the first time we made love. It may sound strange, but I felt something quicken inside me that night. However, I've only been sure for a few days. It's really very early. The baby isn't due for eight more months."

"I thought I was happy before, but this—I just can't take it in."

He felt as though he could climb mountains, conquer wildernesses. He felt more like a man than he ever had before. He was going to be a father. His son or daughter would soon ride the ranch by his side.

That night, dear heaven, that wonderful night when he first held Elke in his arms, he had prayed she would have his child someday. But he'd never thought his prayer would be answered. Still holding her hand, he led her to the stairs.

"Folks around here have been calling this place Pride's Passion for years. But they have it all wrong," he said huskily. "Come to bed with me, my love. Let me show you this Pride's real passion."

IF ROMANCE BE THE FRUIT OF LIFE —
READ ON —
BREATH-QUICKENING HISTORICALS FROM PINNACLE

WILDCAT (772, $4.99)
by Rochelle Wayne
No man alive could break Diana Preston's fiery spirit . . . until seductive Vince Gannon galloped onto Diana's sprawling family ranch. Vince, a man with dark secrets, would sweep her into his world of danger and desire. And Diana couldn't deny the powerful yearnings that branded her as his own, for all time!

THE HIGHWAY MAN (765, $4.50)
by Nadine Crenshaw
When a trumped-up murder charge forced beautiful Jane Fitzpatrick to flee her home, she was found and sheltered by the highwayman — a man as dark and dangerous as the secrets that haunted him. As their hiding place became a place of shared dreams — and soaring desires — Jane knew she'd found the love she'd been yearning for!

SILKEN SPURS (756, $4.99)
by Jane Archer
Beautiful Harmony Harper, leader of a notorious outlaw gang, rode the desert plains of New Mexico in search of justice and vengeance. Now she has captured powerful and privileged Thor Clarke-Jargon, who is everything Harmony has ever hated — and all she will ever want. And after Harmony has taken the handsome adventurer hostage, she herself has become a captive — of her own desires!

WYOMING ECSTASY (740, $4.50)
by Gina Robins
Feisty criminal investigator, July MacKenzie, solicits the partnership of the legendary half-breed gunslinger-detective Nacona Blue. After being turned down, July — never one to accept the meaning of the word no — finds a way to convince Nacona to be her partner . . first in business — then in passion. Across the wilds of Wyoming, and always one step ahead of trouble, July surrenders to passion's searing demands!

Available wherever paperbacks are sold, or order direct from the Publisher. Send cover price plus 50¢ per copy for mailing and handling to Penguin USA, P.O. Box 999, c/o Dept. 17109, Bergenfield, NJ 07621. Residents of New York and Tennessee must include sales tax. DO NOT SEND CASH.